Nightwalker

Rose Harvey

To the lovely ladies who were the inspiration for Tash…
this one's for you.

Also by Rose Harvey

The Ice Flame Trilogy
Heir to the Ice Flame
Heart of Ice
Fire on the Ice

The Order Series
Robin

Chapter One

Nightwalkers are creatures of the dark, unyielding places where all concepts of good and evil blur together. They are night prowlers who are rarely seen in daylight and gain sustenance from the blood of their victims. It is said that Nightwalkers are descended from a man who lost his heart to a faerie queen. When his love was rejected for another man, he lost control and murdered the queen's chosen consort. As punishment, he was banished and transformed, forced to live in shadowed exile. The queen, in her anger and grief, cursed him and his progeny to never know love again.

~ Extract from 'A Robin's Guide to Inter-world Monsters'

Tash gazed at the bathroom mirror, barely noticing her features as her thoughts spiralled through her mind, sending shards of anxiety into her stomach. She blinked and focussed on her reflection, the dark, pensive eyes and a long, black braid that had fallen down over her shoulder. Her mouth twisted sardonically, and her hands gripped the sink edges as she tried to think about what she was going to say when she left the bathroom.

She had arrived in this world three weeks ago and the time had come to move on. Even though the past weeks had been better than she could have imagined, it was not possible for her to remain here. No matter how much she may want to.

'Come on, Tash,' she murmured to herself, 'pull yourself together. It shouldn't be harder than any other time you needed to leave by the month's end.'

But this time was different, a tiny voice whispered in her mind, this time she had made the mistake of getting attached. She had tried to avoid that in previous world trips, yet on Earth she had been surprised by the unexpected.

Tash sighed and glared down at the porcelain sink, before turning the taps and watching the water spin down the drain. Really, there was no use in delaying the inevitable. She turned them off and left the bathroom, wishing that there would be an easier way. It was important to end things cleanly now, before stronger feelings could develop and make it harder to say goodbye. Her bare feet padded across the hallway and into the living room, leading her to the man who was sitting on the couch, a collection of students' art folios piled up next to him.

'Have a look at this Natachatet,' Fred said, and she hid a wince at his use of her full name, 'try and guess what it is.'

She moved closer, peering down at the drawing which seemed to be a mish-mash of colours across the page.

'I have no idea,' she replied.

Fred's brows drew together and he eyed the drawing thoughtfully. 'Neither have I. It was supposed to be a still life.' He fell into silence and continued to flick through the folio, unaware of the turbulent feelings that were fighting within her.

'Fred?' Tash's voice came out as a hoarse whisper, and when he didn't respond she swallowed and repeated, 'Fred? Can you stop for a minute?'

'Sure,' he said, glancing up. 'Is everything OK?'

'I…' Oh heavens, this was harder than she'd expected. 'I have to go.'

'Alright,' he said calmly, 'just remember to take the keys so you can let yourself in later. Remember I'm making carbonara tonight.'

Gods above, he hadn't understood. She swallowed and said, 'No, Fred. I mean– I need to leave. I've been on Earth for three weeks now. I need to return home.' Fred sat perfectly still for a moment as he absorbed the meaning of her words. Tash continued, filling the silence. 'I'm sorry, Fred. It's one of the rules of our Order– I'm not able to remain in a world longer than a month. If I do, I'll fade away and die.'

'Laura's been here for over six months now,' Fred said, his voice tight. 'How is that possible that she can be fine and you wouldn't be after a few weeks?'

Tash closed her eyes, forcing the tears that threatened to fall to remain hidden. 'Laura was born in this world, Fred. She is able to stay as long as she wishes, but for other Robins like Tim and I, we need to return to Venetica or move on.'

'And so, just like that, you're leaving?' He sounded angry and hurt, much like she was herself. 'We spend three weeks together and then you're done?'

'I'm sorry,' Tash said softly. 'I thought that you realised from the outset that anything we had would be temporary.'

'But you could come back?' he asked suddenly, 'You go to Venetica and then return here. It's like a form of medicine– each month you leave and then come back.'

She shook her head, 'It may not work like that. I can't guarantee where I will go or when I could come back.' She didn't have the heart to say that it was kinder for both of them to end things amicably and to move on with their lives, as it was uncertain whether she could return to Earth any time soon. From the way Fred looked at her, she could tell that he understood what she hadn't been able to say.

He rose and came around to her, taking her in his arms and she gripped him tightly. She squeezed her eyes shut, still unwilling to shed any tears. 'I'm sorry, Fred. I don't want to hurt you– please understand that.'

'I know,' he murmured, 'I'm sorry too.'

She let out a choking sob, unable to hold the emotions back anymore. Fred wiped the tears away, tilted her head upward and kissed her. It was the kind of kiss that said more than words could, full of bittersweet tenderness and regret. Tash knew deep down that it would be the last time.

When they drew apart, she raised a hand to his cheek and said, 'Thank you for everything you have done for me these past weeks. I'll never forget you. Goodbye Fred.'

'Goodbye Natachatet,' his voice shook slightly. 'Travel safely.'

She nodded, smiling painfully through the tears. And then, with a gut-wrenching sensation, she turned and walked to the bedroom, collecting her already packed bag and slipping into her boots. Fred watched from the lounge as she departed, shutting the front door behind her and stepping away towards the street, resolutely not looking back. He sighed and reached for his mobile phone, dialling his sister's number and calling it as Tash vanished from sight.

***

Tash scrubbed her cheeks, berating herself for succumbing to emotion. It was at times like these that she missed the Temple and her mentors, particularly Romulus, the elderly warden who watched over the initiates in the Order. He had always listened when she had troubles, and his calm, pragmatic approach to problems always helped her to see clearly. He had taught her to keep her emotions contained, to focus on the task at hand and for many years she had been primarily successful in that approach.

A car whizzed past, loud music blaring from the open windows, and Tash jumped, reaching into her bag for her dezmian. In this world it could be easily mistaken for just a stone, but back in her home in Venetica, dezmians were used as conduits for magic. Slowly she released it, recognising that magic didn't work here as the shock wore off. She still wasn't used to cars, finding them too noisy and fast for her to feel comfortable. There was nothing like them in Venetica or many of the other worlds she had visited, and she still found them alien.

'Tash!'

The voice shattered her reverie and she looked around, uncertain about how to react as she saw the girl hurrying towards her.

'Laura,' she said, 'I didn't expect to see you here.'

'Fred called me,' Laura replied, her hazel eyes flashing with a mixture of exasperation and worry. 'I thought you would at least give me a heads up that you were planning on leaving. We were all going to go together— Tim needs to cross the Barrier soon too.' Tash gripped her bag strap tighter, feeling suddenly self-conscious. Laura continued, 'I thought that you would perhaps want to come back. Seeing you and Fred together these past weeks…' Laura's voice drifted off, her gaze searching Tash's, looking for confirmation of her suspicions.

'You know that I couldn't stay,' Tash said softly. 'It's like with The Robin and your mother. I don't want to do that to your brother.'

Laura took a deep breath, perhaps to calm her rising anger. 'But you've hurt him all the same, Tash. You didn't need to spend as much time together or raise his hopes that something could happen.'

Tash flinched. 'It hurts me too, Laura.' As she spoke, her voice wobbled and she turned away, hating the temporary weakness.

Laura was her best friend and it cut deeply that in this, she seemed to be so judgemental, especially when her own family had known the loss of being torn apart. When Laura was twelve, her house had burned down and she was rescued from the flames by two Robins. They took her to Venetica, a world where magic and monsters thrived. She was taken to the Temple of the Nest, where The Robin, the leader of the Order of Song, had initiated her as his apprentice. It was there that she met Tash and they became like sisters.

When Laura was old enough, The Robin had given her a quest to reclaim the right to go back to her home world, and so she had set off with Tim, her long-time friend. Tash hadn't joined them, but knew that when Laura returned, she was alone, heartbroken and had departed immediately for Earth. Months later, The Robin had asked Tash to reunite Laura and Tim, and so she had set out, tracking down a despondent Tim and forcing him to come with her to Earth through the Barriers between worlds. Since their arrival, Tim and Laura had gotten engaged and Tash had been left alone. That was why she and Fred had gravitated towards each other, as she was eager to learn about her friend's home world and Fred had been all too happy to assist.

Was it so unrealistic that they had formed a connection? That she had allowed herself to explore more than she had anticipated in this new world? Was it any surprise then that she was feeling this overwhelming disappointment at leaving?

'Tash,' Laura stepped closer and hugged her, 'I'm sorry. I shouldn't have lost my temper. You're right– I do know what you mean.'

Indeed she did. It had been a shock to Tash when she reunited Laura and Tim and she learned that The Robin had in fact been Laura's father, separated from his family much like Laura had been. However, in his case, Laura's mother had remarried and raised her two children with her new husband, so that Laura had never been aware that the man who raised her was not her biological father. It was a story that made Tash feel a wave of sadness and she wondered if The Robin ever regretted leaving his wife and young children to return to Venetica.

'I don't know how long it will take to find a Barrier,' Tash said quietly and she returned Laura's hug. 'I didn't want to run the risk of… well…'

'I understand.' Laura said, 'but you need to let Tim and I come with you. We stand better chances of crossing the Barrier together.'

Tash didn't argue with her, but nodded. It was always useful to have another Robin when crossing Barriers, as you never knew what would be on the other side. Barriers were fickle things, regularly changing location and switching between worlds so that it was almost impossible to know where you would end up when you crossed one.

'I just want to get home as soon as possible,' Tash muttered, 'I don't want to linger any longer than necessary.'

She fell into step beside her friend as they made their way down the street, towards Laura's parents' house. Fred didn't live far from his parents, and she hovered awkwardly outside the house as Laura went in to find Tim. It seemed like an age had passed before Tim and Laura emerged, arms around each other and bags over their shoulders. From the doorway, Laura's parents appeared and gave them both tearful hugs, her mother clinging onto her daughter with a fierceness that made Tash's chest ache. There would be no one like that to bid her farewell. No mother to comfort her or beg her to stay. Tash's family was long gone and by the rules of the Order she would never see them again.

She turned away, waiting for Laura and Tim to join her and then froze, staring wide eyed at the shimmer in the air before her.

'I sent a request through to my Dad,' Laura smiled as she reached her. 'He's connecting us to a Barrier that will take us to the Temple.'

Tim faltered, brushing his dark hair out of his eyes with a suddenly shaky hand. 'Are you sure that will be alright? I *did* promise him that I would not return to the Temple if I came to find you.'

Laura laughed, 'I'll make sure that he will be fine with it. Come on.' With a toss of her long, coppery hair, a mischievous smile and wave to her parents, Laura stepped closer to the shimmering Barrier and began to sing. Tim and Tash joined her, their three voices melding together in the Ancient Tongue, urging a Doorway to appear for them to pass through. As she was about to leave, Tash sent out a final thought to Fred, wishing him well and feeling the bittersweet throb of having to say goodbye. She took a deep breath and disappeared through the Doorway, passing from one world into another.

Chapter Two

I understand the dangers of associating with such creatures but if it is the only way of seeing the ones I lost again, I will do anything. My master made the mistake of not taking the Dæmon's advice and he and our colleagues all died that day. I won't make the same mistake. Sometimes, one must work with those we usually avoid in order to achieve our goals. So when the Dæmon returns— and I know that he will— I will accept his offer.

> ~ An extract of a letter from The Robin, shortly after his instatement as leader of the Order of Song, to Romulus, his second-in-command

Tash's first thought on passing through the Doorway was that it was warm. Outside the window, night had fallen and the sky was black as pitch. A fire burned in the grate nearby and a man with shadowed features sat in a high-backed chair, calmly perusing a worn leather-bound book. As Laura, Tim and Tash emerged out of the shimmering air in the middle of his rooms, he looked up and gazed at them intently. Tash was grateful that his attention seemed to be focussed on Laura and Tim, although it was hard to tell with the permanent shadows that shrouded his features. For as long as she had been at the Temple, no one had seen The Robin's face. There had been rumours amongst the apprentices that he had engaged in dark magic years before which had hidden his face from view. No one had dared say such things in front of the teachers though, particularly Romulus, who held The Robin in the highest esteem.

'Laura,' The Robin said, his tone slightly guarded, as though he were unsure of the reception he would have now that his daughter knew the truth about his identity. Laura didn't hesitate, but disregarding all propriety hugged him tightly. The Robin's arms faltered for a moment, uncertain about how to respond, before they slowly came around his daughter and held her close. Tim hovered awkwardly on the sidelines, he had every reason to be uncomfortable. Before Tash had reunited the two lovers, The Robin had forbidden Tim from returning to the Temple of the Nest if he sought Laura out. Tim had accepted the proposal, although the Temple had been his home for many years. Tash, meanwhile, shifted her bag on her shoulder and moved quietly to the door, intending to leave the family reunion behind.

'Natachatet.' The Robin had noticed her movement and glanced up briefly, 'Thank you for finding her. Come and see me tomorrow morning, after the mid-morning bell tolls.'

Tash inclined her head respectfully, 'Yes sir.' She caught Laura's eye and added, 'I'll be in our room– perhaps I'll see you later? If not– until tomorrow.'

Laura nodded, hazel eyes bright with unshed tears from the reunion with her father. Tash smiled at Tim and gave a half wave, turned and left down the spiral staircase, heading for the female dormitories.

***

The Temple had originally been created as a refuge for those who could travel between worlds and over time had expanded from a single tower to a sprawling keep with various outbuildings. Tash had been at the Temple for most of her life and could barely remember what her life had been like before she arrived. Her parents had been the sort of people who couldn't handle money, with her mother liking to purchase trinkets and her father to gamble whatever few coins remained. Despite their flaws, her parents had loved each other madly, and this had resulted in far too many mouths to feed. When she was six years old, a Robin had been visiting her village and her parents had begged him to take her away to relieve their burden. The Robin had been a man called Romulus, and with one look at the malnourished, bedraggled child, had accepted her parents' pleas and promised to give her a better life. All Tash could remember of her parents now were faded memories, a faint rush of noise and crying, a gnawing sensation of hunger and daydreaming about escaping.

Romulus took her to the Temple and became her mentor. He taught her to read in the sprawling library that stretched down multiple levels into the mountainside, watched as she rode her first Willowing and gifted her a dezmian to channel magic when she turned nine. Now, all these years later, Tash couldn't imagine living anywhere other than the Temple, but deep down she knew that it would soon be time for her to leave. At nineteen, she was almost ready for her initiation and then she would need to set out on her own, travelling between worlds and doing whatever she could to maintain harmony.

Tash paused in the doorway at the foot of the tower stairs, gazing out at the distant forest through the open gates, trees rustling in the darkness. The torchlight wasn't strong enough to light their trunks up clearly, but the moonlight shimmered down, casting a pale glow over the leaves. As she watched, something moved in between the trees and her stomach clenched, anxiety rushing through her in a wave.

Romulus had always forbidden students from entering the forest, stating that it was dangerous. Although when Laura had arrived at the Temple, the two friends had snuck out at night, exploring the depths of the forest and finding new locations each time. For the most part, the forest hadn't been fearsome, until last year when they had encountered one of the creatures of the night for the first time. Since that experience, Tash hadn't dared to set foot under the leafy boughs, too afraid of having another encounter.

Tash shivered as she stepped closer to the trees, reaching into her bag and withdrawing her dezmian. With a skilful flick of the wrist, the small pebble flipped three times before she caught it and a small flame appeared in front of her, lighting up the shadows.

There was nothing there.

She breathed a sigh of relief, when, about to turn away, she noticed something shift out from behind a tree. A large, humanoid form came into view, emerging from the shrouded darkness. Tash froze, the memory of the creature returning vividly, before she took a fortifying breath and straightened her shoulders. From her childhood, she had learned that one should face problems head on and that to be strong she ought not show her fear. Resolutely, she drew closer to the Dæmon, wondering what it wanted this time.

As she approached, the light played across its features and she realised how much her memory had suppressed. Deep red eyes watched her intensely and the ridged tail swept out behind him, sharp edges cutting through the grass at the base of the trees. He was taller than she remembered, and the shadows seemed to envelop him in dark tendrils, as though they decided when to reveal his features. It reminded her of the darkness around The Robin, although with the Dæmon, she was able to glimpse him clearly from time to time.

'I was wondering if your curiosity would lead you back to the forest,' the Dæmon's voice was rough, like gravel. 'Just like last time you stand before me without fear. Impressive.'

Tash raised an eyebrow, privately grateful that her facade of calm indifference hid the pounding heart underneath. 'I only came over to make sure that there was nothing unto-ward. The creatures in the forest are dangerous to those of us in the Order.'

'It sounds as though you have changed your tune since we last met.' The Dæmon said wryly, mouth curved in a smile that revealed his pointed teeth.

'That was a long time ago.' Tash replied coolly.

'Almost a year, to be exact.' The Dæmon said and she felt a tremor pass down her spine. How did he remember that? Her breath caught as his clawed hand reached out, the long nails scratching slightly along her face. 'I have been waiting a long time to see how you will prove yourself as a Robin, little bird. I see much suffering and pain in my travels— perhaps you will be the one to ease it.'

Tash didn't blink, staring into his eyes which bored into hers. 'How much of that pain is caused by the deals you strike or the Mortals you kill?' Her voice was firm and hard, not revealing the tremble of fear she had felt as he lifted a hand to her face. The nails jerked at her words and cut into the skin, leaving a trail of blood behind as he drew them away. Tash didn't flinch, but watched him intently, noting the way his gaze lingered on the red droplets, a hungry desire in his eyes. It sickened her.

'You are quick to judge, little bird.'

'I have heard enough tales about your kind to know not to trust what you say too easily.' Tash replied. The Dæmon's mouth twisted.

'Perhaps. Still, I look forward to seeing your progress. Your friend demonstrated her ability in her recent quest– she helped to protect the innocent and restored the balance of a forest long tainted by a foul creature. Her work was impressive, but I am curious as to what you will do.'

Tash went cold. 'What did you say?' Had he been with Laura on her quest for The Robin? Why hadn't Laura mentioned it?

The Dæmon laughed brittlely again but didn't answer her question. 'Be safe, little bird. I will be watching.'

The light Tash had conjured flickered and died, casting the world around her back into shadow. It took her eyes a moment to adjust to the moonlight, so by the time she blinked at the space in front of her, the Dæmon had vanished into the night.

Now unable to hide her trembling, Tash stumbled back to the safety of the Temple, checking over her shoulder as she departed in case she saw him again in the trees. As she descended the stairs to the female dormitory, her shivers had become uncontrollable and so, once she had cast her bag down onto her bed, she moved straight to the bathing chamber.

The Temple had springs that came from deep within the mountain that it sat upon which were heated magically. Bathing in them always helped to relieve any tension or pain, and Tash wanted to wash off the memory of the Dæmon's touch.

The cuts on her face twinged as she stripped off and plunged into the waiting pool. The water was hot and bubbling, and she dove underneath the surface, shutting her eyes and allowing the heat to sink into her, warming her from the inside out and banishing the shock of seeing the Dæmon again.

When they had last met she had been consumed by thoughts of him for weeks afterward, wondering if he would reappear and make new cryptic statements. Finally, she had resolved that their meeting had been a one-off event, that he would never reappear in her life and that she could forget him and the prophecy that he had alluded to. Tash sighed, floating in the pool, her hair drifting around her as she gazed up at the stone ceiling, softly lit with torches flickering in their brackets. The prophecy had been another reason why she had lost sleep over the past months, especially since she understood from Laura that her own prophecy had come true. The two of them had been given their prophecies by a strange alchemist in the nearby town of Boolwra, and even though many months had passed since she had heard it spoken over a cauldron of shifting smoke, Tash could still remember it word for word. She had hoped that the supposed prophecy had just been a scam, a silly gimmick for a few extra coins, but now that Laura's had come true, she was not so sure.

She splashed her face and left the pool, pulling one of the nearby towels around her and ruthlessly drying herself. Even though it had only been mid-afternoon back on Earth, she felt exhausted. The pain from leaving Fred was still raw, and then seeing *him* again, just outside the Temple, was almost too much.

She pulled on a robe and made her way to her room, shutting the door and noting that Laura had not arrived yet.

Perhaps she and Tim would spend the night in one of the outbuildings, which had been refurbished into guest quarters several years ago. Or perhaps they had left for Boolwra, to stay in an inn overnight. Either way, Tash hoped that she would see her friend in the morning at least.

As she crawled under the covers of her bed, she gazed up at the ceiling, wondering what Fred was doing, if he missed her already, whether he felt as empty as she did. Now that she was completely alone, Tash allowed the tears to fall properly, wishing that she hadn't allowed herself to get so caught up in emotions during her time on Earth. Romulus had warned her many times that Robins couldn't afford to fall in love with people in the worlds they visited– it was heartache just waiting to happen. Up until now, she had re-mained aloof and kept herself apart, focussing on the tasks at hand and finding solace in the library's books.

'Gods dammit all,' she muttered, wiping the tears away and turning over into the pillow, punching it into a better position. 'It's over now, Tash. Get a grip.' All the same, it was a long time before she was able to fall asleep and then she was tormented by dreams.

***

Tash was stuck in her chair, unable to move away from the scarred woman who grinned at her from across the cauldron's bubbling surface. The walls around them were piled high with ingredients for potion-making and a murder of crows perched in the rafters, watching Tash with beady black eyes.

'You strike me as a brave girl, Natachatet,' the alchemist said. 'Let's hope that you will have the fortitude to overcome what the fates have in store for you.'

Tash shrank away from her, suddenly released from her invisible bonds, tumbling backwards over her chair, knocking jars and bunches of hanging dried herbs aside in her haste. Words filled Tash's mind, although the alchemist didn't speak them aloud, as she ran out of the shop, the crows swooping her in a rush of feathers and sharp claws.

Hearts wild,
Lovers flawed.
Contamination tamed,
Hope is wrought.
Help too far,
Leaving too soon.
He who awaits,
Each turning of moon.
Beware the night,
Be cautious of day.
When all strays,
You will stay.

As she beat away the pecking beaks, someone gripped her hand and pulled her onwards, leading her blindly through the onslaught. She tried to keep up, her free hand covering her face to protect it from the birds until the beating of wings had faded away and everything around them was silent.

'It's alright,' the voice was low, breathing hard from the mad escape. 'You're safe.' He sounded reassuring and kind, hands brushing against hers as arms came around her, enfolding her in a close embrace.

Tash struggled, not trusting the stranger and thrown by the converse feelings that rushed up inside her. 'Let me go.'

She was released abruptly and her eyes opened, realising that her saviour was not who she had expected. Instead of a golden-haired man with paint-speckled hands and a slightly distracted smile, Tash gazed into eyes the colour of cobalt, clubbed back dark hair and eyebrows drawn together in an irritated scowl. She paused, the surge of fear halting through her veins, opening her mouth in a gasp of surprise. He looked down at her, clearly waiting for her to break the silence that stretched out between them. A cloud covered the sun and the day was shrouded in darkness. She blinked and the man in front of her vanished. Now blood red eyes glared balefully into hers from a face that was the source of nightmares. The change was immediate, the momentary sense of curiosity and security vanished instantly as Tash opened her mouth and screamed.

Chapter Three

I have been in this hell for twenty days. No matter who I speak to, they all run away. Children cry out in terror whenever I pass them by. I don't understand what I did to deserve this. My old friends refuse to talk to me and the villagers chase me off with torches.

They call me a monster.

How can they say that when they have known me my entire life?

I am not a monster.

I pray to the Gods that I will not become one.

~ An extract from an old, tattered diary, located in a rundown shack on the Nordhaven Heath

Tash felt as though she hadn't slept a wink. The images from her dreams were still vivid in her mind and her chest felt heavy, as though something had been weighing her down during the night. She entered the dining hall early and made her way over to where the man she had been most wanting to see was sitting. Despite her fatigue, her smile wasn't forced as she hurried over and leapt into his waiting arms.

'Romulus!'

The old man's hug was stronger than one might have expected. Tash, though, was used to it and grinned into his shoulder.

'Natachatet.' Despite her regular protestations growing up, Romulus had continued to call her by her full name, saying that he saw no reason to shorten something so unique. 'I have missed you, my child. You must tell me about everything that happened– I noticed that The Robin, Laura and Tim spent time together last night. I'm sure that there is much to tell.' His eyebrows were slightly raised and he watched her shrewdly as they sat down.

'It is quite a story,' Tash admitted as she began to fill a bowl with steaming porridge. 'Earth was more than I expected. They have no magic there, but find ways to work around it. I found it… charming.' She bit her lip thoughtfully, pushing away the memory of her and Fred kissing beside the beach as the sun set over the waves. 'As you have probably gathered, I made sure that Tim and Laura had a chance to talk things out. They're engaged now.'

She fell silent. A treacherous feeling of envy rose up in her throat and she tried to suppress it, taking a large bite of porridge. She didn't like being envious of her best friend– it didn't seem right to feel resentment at Laura finding happiness. Soon she too would be achieving her dream of being a Robin and travelling between the worlds. That was what she had always wanted, wasn't it?

'And yet,' Romulus said quietly, 'you do not seem to be overly happy to be back. The shine that was in your eyes before you left has gone.' His words were like a kick in the gut. She forced herself to breathe calmly and didn't reply. Her mentor continued gently, 'Am I correct in assuming that you encountered someone special on this trip?'

She nodded tightly. 'I understand now what you warned me about. I wish I hadn't… but it happened before I realised it. It would be easier if I couldn't feel that way when I travelled.'

Before she had finished speaking, Romulus was shaking his head. 'Natachatet, you shouldn't think that way. Robins need to be able to connect emotionally with people when they travel– that is how you will develop positive relationships in-between worlds. But it is important to remember that one should keep these relationships professional. Moving on from this trip to Earth, you should focus on how you can grow from the experience and ensure that something like it does not happen again.'

Tash bowed her head. 'Yes, Romulus.'

She had known that he would say something like that. Deep down she knew that he cared about her and didn't want to see her hurting, but sometimes all she wanted was to be able to talk about her troubles without it turning into an exercise in self-development. That was why she hadn't mentioned the Dæmon to him all those months ago, but now, after the events of the night before, she felt like it might be a good distraction from her indiscretions on Earth.

'I saw something when I was leaving The Robin's tower last night,' she began, 'there was a creature on the edge of the forest.'

'You didn't go into the forest, I hope,' Romulus said, concerned. 'You know to stay inside the walls of the Temple.'

'No,' Tash replied, 'I went over to investigate. I mean,' she added quickly, 'I stayed in the Temple grounds, but I thought that with it being so close to the walls there might be something wrong.'

'And, of course, you didn't think about alerting any of the Robins?' Romulus enquired softly. Tash pretended not to hear him.

'It was a Dæmon,' she said, casting a quick glance around to ensure that they weren't overheard. Romulus' spoon paused halfway to his mouth and it seemed as though he was thinking very fast. 'A Nightwalker,' she clarified, using the other term to describe the creature, as she knew there were many types of Dæmons across the various worlds.

'I wouldn't worry about it, Natachatet,' he said finally, 'sometimes The Robin collaborates with creatures that are… outside of our usual associates. He has an unorthodox way of doing things, but his actions always yield results. Please put the encounter from your mind— I am sure that you will never have to deal with this creature again.'

Tash watched him steadily, but nothing in his expression gave anything away. She couldn't tell if the news had perturbed or surprised him, and she couldn't deny that she was curious about his reaction— or lack of one.

'Now, my dear,' Romulus said brightly, 'tell me about some of the things you learned about Earth. You say they have figured out a way to live without magic? Do explain it to me.'

Tash smiled and obliged him, regaling him with stories of things that Fred might have considered insignificant, but she had found fascinating. Romulus listened to her avidly, drinking in the tales of her first experience with a light switch, to sitting in a car, to watching food get heated in a microwave. She told him about computers and the Internet, about how she had been able to watch moving pictures, which had enthralled her. Even the music had been different, with people listening to it through devices that could communicate across vast distances in seconds.

When they had both finished eating, and the other apprentices and teachers had departed from the dining hall,

Tash and Romulus sat back in their chairs, sipping from their refilled cups of tea and falling into a lulled silence. The doors opened and Tash glanced up, before rising as Laura and Tim entered. With quick steps, she crossed the room and hugged them, smiling as she said,

'I was wondering if you both were alright. How did The Robin take to your news?' She directed her question at Laura, but it was Tim who answered,

'When he was finally able to get a word in, he took the news quite well,' he grinned as Laura shot him a glare. 'I'm still required to distance myself from the Temple, so Laura and I will be heading to Boolwra soon. I think we'll set ourselves up there for a few days until we figure out what we want to do next.' He and Laura shared a look that seemed full of unspoken meaning and Tash suddenly felt awkward. She shuffled her foot nervously and cleared her throat.

'Well, that's great. Make sure you let me know when you're planning to head off, though.'

'Of course,' Laura said quickly, 'I'll join Tim in Boolwra later. I've got to pack up my things,' she raised her shoulders in a light shrug and gave Tash a half smile, tinged with sadness. 'I'm sorry to be leaving you here.'

'Don't be,' Tash said, as she hugged her friend. 'I'm fine here, really. Besides— we've got to have our initiation soon, then I'll be able to leave too.'

Laura's smile turned even sadder, 'I won't be having one, Tash. My father has initiated me as a fully-fledged Robin already.' She continued on, unaware of the cold tremble that surged through Tash as she listened, trying to process the words. 'We completed the ritual last night, so technically, once I've collected my gear, I can leave. I'll be checking back though— there's still much to talk about with my father.'

'How exciting,' Tash's smile was now slightly forced and she gripped her hands tightly behind her back. 'But, speaking of The Robin, I should be going. He asked me to see him this morning.'

'Bye Tash,' Laura said, 'hopefully I'll still be here when you have your initiation. We'll try to make it if we can.'

Tash nodded and left as fast as she was able. When she'd left the dining hall and marched across the courtyard towards The Robin's tower, she paused just inside the doorway, leaning against the knotted wood. She didn't want to admit the hurt she felt at Laura having her initiation as a Robin before she did herself. They'd always said that they would be initiated together, that it would be something they would share– a fitting end to years on years of countless study and late nights. But now, yet again, Laura seemed to be entering the broader world ahead of her, finding a new purpose and life whereas Tash was left behind. She squeezed her eyes shut and let her breath out in a harsh sigh. There was no point in getting upset– it wasn't Laura's fault, yet all the same she felt the impending absence of her closest friend. It was not uncommon for Robins to leave the Temple and not see their fellow apprentices for years at a time. She just hoped that it wouldn't be so long before she saw Laura again.

There was a sound on the stairs and she jumped, startled out of her thoughts.

'Natachatet?' It was Romulus. Tash blinked, not having realised that he had left the dining hall earlier, or that he had also gone to visit The Robin. She wondered why. He patted her shoulder as he passed and said, 'go on up. He's waiting for you.'

'Of course.' She moved away, climbing the stairs to escape from his piercing gaze. The last thing she wanted was for Romulus to discern that something was wrong and try to figure out what it was. She didn't want to verbalise her emotions aloud, especially since her mentor was more prone to try and think of solutions which could be considered constructive and emotionless, instead of providing a sympathetic ear.

The door to The Robin's rooms was ajar, but she still knocked politely. She'd never had the same relationship that Laura had with him, even from the times before she found out that he was Laura's father. Tash had always viewed The Robin with a mixture of awe, respect and fear. He was the intimidating presence in the tallest tower, overseeing everything but rarely seen by the apprentices. She had seen him more than most, partially because of Laura being his apprentice and because Romulus was his right-hand man.

'Enter.' The voice was short, as though The Robin's patience had already been tested this morning. Tash felt a tremor of unease go through her as she pushed the door wider. The Robin was standing by the windows, she presumed that he was looking out over the forest, but with the shadows around his features it was hard to tell.

'Ah, Natachatet.' He didn't move from his position, but his tone warmed marginally. 'Please, sit.' He gestured to one of the chairs nearby and she obeyed, unable to suppress the feeling that she was about to be interrogated.

'You wished to see me this morning, sir?' she said with passable ease, sitting on the edge of the seat.

'I wanted to thank you for what you did for Laura,' The Robin said gravely. 'You helped her to find happiness and for that I am most grateful.'

Tash bit her tongue to resist saying that it was partially The Robin's fault that Laura and Tim had been separated in the first place. Instead, she gave a tight smile and said, 'She's my best friend. I want her to be happy.'

The Robin made a grunt of approval and Tash glanced down at the floor, privately hoping that the awkward meeting would be over soon. She didn't like being up here, not without Laura to distract his attention.

'You have proven yourself to be ready to undergo your initiation,' The Robin continued, and Tash felt her breath catch as she looked back up at him. 'There are several apprentices who will have their initiation together, so it will be held when they have all returned from their final trips.'

Tash's heart dropped again, this time with disappointment. The Robin must have seen the brief change in her expression before she schooled it into polite interest, for he said, 'I believe that they will not be too far away. A messenger sent word that Harrison would be returning within the next tenday.'

Tash nodded mutely. She hadn't seen Harrison in months, not since he had been sent away to settle some dispute in one of the outer worlds. She hoped that he had grown up during his time away, she didn't particularly relish the thought of suffering through his immature jokes when he got back.

'If that is all…?' Tash began hopefully, privately thinking that Romulus could just have simply given her this news.

'No, I'm afraid that it isn't,' The Robin had turned to look back out the windows again at the forest. 'I understand that you met one of my associates last night.'

'Oh,' she said, the memory coming to mind as though it had never left. 'Yes.'

'Tell me, Natachatet,' The Robin spoke as though she hadn't uttered a word. 'What do you know about Nightwalkers?'

She swallowed, mouth suddenly dry. 'I only know what some of the books in the library say about them. They are also known as Dæmons, live off blood and have a penchant for bringing death and destruction to those who cross their paths. The bestiary on monsters warns to stay away from them.'

'The books do not lie,' The Robin said slowly. 'Although I believe that there is much that is also left out. Nightwalkers are creatures that we know little about. For a time, I sought to understand them further, to try and access their magic during my studies.' Tash watched him avidly, too caught up with curiosity to wonder why he was sharing this so openly. 'I met one— back when I was an apprentice. The same one who you met last night. Over the years we have developed a partnership of sorts. He comes to me when there are disturbances in the worlds which we Robins should investigate.'

'Was that why he came last night?' Tash asked, remembering all those months ago how the Dæmon had come across herself and Laura in the forest and sent them to get The Robin. How many times had he visited the leader of their Order? Why would he seek to restore balance? From everything that she had read, such creatures seemed to prefer instilling chaos instead of peace. It didn't make sense.

'Yes.' The Robin said succinctly. 'I am currently trying to gather more information through other means before deciding on the course of action, but you will be the Robin responsible for this particular task.'

Tash bowed her head. 'Thank you. I will not let the Order down.'

'I am sure you will not,' The Robin said. 'Make sure that you are ready to depart after your initiation ceremony.'

Tash nodded and rose, 'Yes sir.' She left before he could say another word, and raced down the stairs, eager to share the news about her first official task as a Robin if not with Laura, then at least with Romulus.

***

Laura was sitting on the end of her bed when Tash entered their room, her bags spread across the ground, all packed and ready to depart. She stood as Tash paused in the doorway and said,

'I wanted to wait until you came back before heading off.'

'You're all ready to go, then?' Tash said and her friend nodded. 'I'll miss you,' Tash continued, 'but I know that you and Tim will be happy together.'

'Did you hear anything about your initiation?' Laura asked eagerly. 'Will it be soon?'

'The Robin said that it would happen when some other apprentices returned from their current trips,' Tash replied with a smile. 'He mentioned that it could happen in a tenday or so.'

Laura squealed in excitement and hugged her, bouncing up and down energetically. 'I was sure that it would happen soon. And I should be able to come and see it too!'

'I hope you can,' Tash grinned, 'because immediately afterwards I'll need to leave. The Robin told me that he had a task for me to complete once I was initiated.' She felt warm pride spread through her chest. 'It feels good to know that I'll be able to get started on my duties straight away.'

'I know,' Laura smiled, 'it's all you've wanted to do for years now. I'm glad it's finally happening.'

Tash nodded before a moment of doubt spread over her. She hadn't told Laura about the Dæmon– but then she didn't want her to worry either. Laura had been scared of him the last time they met, and with good reason. She didn't want to bring up those concerns– no, if she met that creature again, she would be able to deal with him herself.

'Come on,' Tash said, hefting two of Laura's bags over her shoulders. 'You'll want to reach Boolwra before sundown.'

Laura chuckled and grabbed her remaining bags, casting a quick look around the room they had shared for the past six odd years. 'I'll miss this place,' she said quietly, 'seeing you every day. But we all need to move on with our lives eventually, don't we?'

Tash nodded, realising that her friend might be feeling the same bittersweet sadness that she herself did. 'At least you've got Tim,' she said, 'you both can enjoy going between worlds for as long as you want. Just remember to let me know when you finally plan the wedding so that I can come.'

'Don't worry, I will,' Laura smiled. 'Who else would be my maid of honour?'

'True,' Tash said with feigned concern, 'and I wouldn't want to let you down.'

'You'd better not,' Laura said, chuckling as they exited the female dormitory building and crossed to the stables. As they entered, the familiar scent of musty hay filled Tash's nostrils and she felt a wave of sadness sweep over her. Laura noticed her friend's sudden change of demeanour and said, 'I forgot to ask– have you gotten a new Willowing since you lost Thiamon?'

Tash shook her head, remembering the Willowing that had originally been Romulus' before he gifted him to her.

'But that was months ago,' Laura said, shocked. 'Even before I left to find the bowl for my father. Have you really been borrowing Willowings all this time?'

Tash nodded again, resolutely not speaking as she approached the stall where Laura's own Willowing, Elaret, was munching on hay contentedly. She put down the bags she was carrying and moved to retrieve the saddle. Laura stopped her midway through lifting it onto the Willowing's back. 'Tash, you can't keep borrowing Willowings. You'll need one of your own– especially if you've got to leave after the initiation.'

'I know,' Tash replied, somehow speaking through the constriction in her throat. 'I just... I miss Thiamon. He was special.'

'Tash,' Laura shook her head, 'it's been months since he died. A Robin needs a Willowing to fly. You know that as well as I do. You don't want to be flightless and grounded.'

'No,' Tash said curtly, 'but you also know that Willowings are more than just pets, Laura. We form a bond with them— like you and Elaret. It is not so simple to bond with another creature.' Laura opened her mouth to argue, but Tash cut her off. 'Besides, I *have* got another Willowing in mind. But he's been too young to fly, so I've been borrowing others until he has grown up.'

'You have?' Laura's eyes brightened and she took the saddle from Tash's hands, placing it on the ground. 'Is he here? Let me meet him.'

Tash relaxed and gave half a nod, leaving the stall and moving down to the back of the stables, where the newborns and young Willowing foals were housed. Usually, Willowings took up to a year before they were old enough to be ridden. The one Tash had been keeping an eye on was almost at that age, and she had been visiting him regularly whenever she was at the Temple.

'His name's Lir,' she said as they halted in front of his stall. Laura smiled and held out a hand to the young Willowing, whose dark eyes flashed with anxiety as he saw the newcomer and shied away. Tash opened the stall and moved to his side, murmuring soft words to calm him, using the back of her hand to stroke his neck down to the wing joint, settling him.

'He's still quite skittish,' she said over her shoulder to Laura. 'Romulus said that I would be able to keep him if we could form a bond.'

'It seems pretty clear to me that you have,' Laura said, 'he's comfortable around you. Plus,' her eyes twinkled, 'he seems to calm you as well. You're gentler around him.'

Tash grinned, 'Is that supposed to be a compliment?'

Laura shrugged, 'You must admit, Tash, out of the two of us, I've always been the more emotional one. You… well…' Her voice trailed off but Tash understood what she wanted to say. It was true– she did prefer to keep her emotions hidden, to prioritise her actions and not be overwhelmed. That was what Romulus had taught her as she grew up, and– for the most part– she was pretty successful at it. Only recently had her usual efficient approach been shaken, thanks to Fred and then that Dæmon, but now that both of them were in the past, she could focus on what was important.

'Tash?' Laura sounded worried. 'I'm sorry– did I offend you? I didn't mean to.'

'No,' Tash replied, unsure how to define what she felt. 'No, I'm not offended. You're right.' She returned her attention to Lir, who nuzzled against her, snuffling contentedly.

From time to time his eyes still flicked to Laura with concern, but his initial fear had now subsided. 'Be calm, *liebeshem.*'

'What was that?' Laura asked curiously, 'I've not heard that language before.'

Tash smiled slightly. 'It's the language I grew up with, a lesser known Kinetian dialect. It's a term of endearment. Lir likes it when I call him that.'

'It's nice.' Laura said thoughtfully and then asked, 'How long will it be before he's ready to ride?'

'Fingers crossed, by the time I have to leave,' Tash replied. 'I'll need to check with Romulus though.' Laura nodded and then returned to Elaret's stall, taking over where Tash had left off and saddled the Willowing before attaching the bags. Tash gave Lir a final pat and left him, trying to avoid hearing his soft cry at being left alone.

'Are you ready?' she asked, leaning on the stall door and watching as Laura checked that the bags were secure.

'I think I've got everything,' Laura said thoughtfully, 'but it's easy enough to come back if I haven't. We're not leaving yet– as far as I know.'

'Fly safe,' Tash smiled, as she hugged her friend. 'I hope that you'll be able to come back for the initiation.'

'I'll do my best,' Laura promised, as she mounted Elaret and they moved into the courtyard. Elaret's wings extended and he lifted away from the ground, circling the Temple once, twice and then they were gone, headed out over the forest in the direction of Boolwra. Tash watched them disappear from view, feeling a familiar longing to also depart– to fly away and begin the next chapter of her life. But that would have to wait until after the initiation.

Her mind focussed on a memory from that morning and she turned resolutely away from the stables, The Robin's words echoing in her ears. *The books do not lie. Although I believe that there is much that is also left out.* The experience with the Dæmon the night before and The Robin's words this morning had piqued her curiosity. She headed for the library– her usual haunt whenever something troubled her.

***

The library in the Temple was vast. It spread down several levels into the mountain, and was filled with rickety shelves, laden with books and tightly furled scrolls. Over the years, Robins had tried to instil a classification system, but due to the vast number of tomes in the library, few had had the willpower to complete the task. Some had succeeded in placing books on the topic of different worlds in specific rooms, but apart from that there was no clear way to determine the various categories.

Tash didn't mind too much– she found some of the most interesting books that she had read had been those in her searches for something else entirely. She had learned Damas, one of the main World languages, partially through this means. When the master of the World Languages class had lost his temper with Harrison for playing some idiotic prank during their lesson, he had stormed out and the class had departed, overjoyed at the early dismissal. Tash, however, had snuck into the library, half annoyed at Harrison for disrupting the lesson, and half worried that Romulus might discover her and think she was skipping class.

She had found herself in one of the library's chambers, collecting a range of books at random from the shelves before settling down in an alcove, half hidden by a curtain. With a flick of her dezmian, she had created a glowing light above her head, and realised that the books she had chosen were written in Damas, which at that time she had only partly understood. From her bag she withdrew one of the dictionaries that the master had insisted they keep on hand in each lesson, and began to work on deciphering the extensive text. It had turned out to be an introduction to agriculture in the Damatian territories for a child of nine.

Tash smiled as she moved through the rooms, finally pausing in front of the one for the world of Kinet. It was rumoured that this was the world from which Dæmons, or Nightwalkers, originated. She pushed the door open and then closed it behind her, grateful that the room was empty. Even though there was no harm in her looking up the creatures, she still didn't particularly want Romulus finding out about it.

Tash moved around the room slowly, starting with the books at eye level before looking higher and lower, scanning the titles. Some she had read already, others she had merely glanced through but there were still some that were new to her. There was a musty smell in the air and dust motes danced before her eyes as she lifted some tomes down from the shelves, their yellowed pages rustling in the silence. After about twenty minutes, she had located several heavy books and quickly made her way to the female dormitory where she would not be disturbed.

Chapter Four

Tash,

I know that you will be worried about me, but rest assured that I will be fine. This is my chance to get back home and The Robin wouldn't be mistaken in his information. I know that you will spend most of the time that I'm away in the library and I hope that you won't be thinking about that night in the forest. I know that we haven't discussed it, but I've noticed how distracted you have become and how, whenever we are outside, you glance at the forest. At times I don't think that you're even aware of it.

Promise me you'll be careful, Tash. You know as well as I do what the books say about Dæmons and Nightwalkers. I don't want to return to a funeral– please stay alert and above all, don't go looking for that creature.

I'll be back before you know it– keep an eye on the skies for our return.

~ A letter from Laura to her best friend, Natachatet, before embarking on her quest

Tash leaned back in the chair by the fire, stretching out the kinks in her back from the hours spent bending over the pile of books beside her. It had been over a week since she had started trying to learn more about Nightwalkers, to see if she could find any evidence to support The Robin's theory. But instead, everything she had found had only reinforced the conception that they were untrustworthy creatures and were more often responsible for causing trouble than fixing it. She had also learned that they were considered one of the stronger types of Dæmon, with the power to bend people's minds to succumb to their will which concerned her.

She sighed and placed *A Robin's Guide to Inter-world Monsters* down on the pile beside *The Kinetian Bestiary*. The light was fading and she rose, realising belatedly that she had skipped lunch for the third day in a row. Her stomach was growling with hunger but it was still at least another hour before the dinner bell rang. She was just wondering if she could head to the kitchens early, to see if she could grab an apple to see her through until dinner when Blythe, one of the new apprentices, entered the dormitory and made a beeline for Tash's position by the fireplace.

'Natachatet, Romulus is looking for you.' The girl seemed a bit nervous, perhaps because Romulus at times had little patience with the new recruits. 'He said that you could find him in his study.'

'Thanks Blythe,' Tash replied, biting back the urge to remind the girl of how she preferred to be called Tash. Instead, she gave her a reassuring smile and left promptly, knowing that Romulus would disapprove of her tardiness. Romulus' study was not too far from the dormitories, in a wide set of chambers that looked out over the forest and distant mountains. They were on the first level of the main building and she found her mentor sitting on his balcony, a scroll in one hand and a glass of wine in the other.

'Ah, Natachatet,' he smiled and gestured for her to join him. 'Pour yourself a glass.'

'Are you celebrating something?' Tash asked as she tilted the decanter of wine over a goblet, watching the red liquid spill out in a steady stream.

'Technically, *we* are celebrating, my child.' He said smoothly, 'Tomorrow is your initiation.'

Tash lowered the decanter and replaced it on the small table, hand shaking slightly. 'I thought it wasn't until next week? Has—'

'Harrison returned just an hour ago from his recent task,' Romulus smiled. 'He was the last apprentice we were waiting for. I'm sure that he'll be happy to tell you about his travels over dinner.' He cast her a slightly shifty, conspiratorial look and Tash felt confused. 'You know,' Romulus continued, 'he really has matured since he arrived here. At first I wasn't sure if he would succeed, but his recent report is very pleasing indeed. Perhaps you might want some company on your task for The Robin.'

Tash's confusion vanished in an instant and she almost groaned. 'Romulus, please tell me you're not trying to become a matchmaker.' The slightly guilty expression on her mentor's face said it all. Tash sighed and rolled her eyes to the sky, 'I am *not* looking for anything romantic.'

It was the last thing she wanted right now. Only a few days ago she had left Fred and said goodbye for good. The painful ache from their parting was still there in her chest and she had– privately of course– shed a few more tears over it.

'Natachatet,' Romulus said patiently, 'I don't need to be the one to remind you that forming a relationship with a fellow Robin is far more preferable to someone in one of the worlds. It will save you a lot of challenges and—'

'Romulus,' Tash interrupted, 'you're right. You *don't* need to remind me. But I've never felt that way about Harrison. Please– don't try to make something happen that isn't there.'

Romulus huffed and took another sip of wine. 'I think you should give it a chance at least, Natachatet. I don't want you to be lonely when I'm gone.'

'Don't be so maudlin,' Tash replied, 'and don't think I don't know what you're doing. You only mention your age when you're upset that things aren't going your way.' Her mentor huffed again and she smiled. 'Besides, I know for a fact that you will be around here for many years to come. The Robin wouldn't be able to run the Temple without you.'

'I had hoped that one day you might take on my role,' Romulus mused, gazing out at the trees. 'You've always been very close to this place.'

Tash watched him for a moment, unsure how to respond. 'You never mentioned that before.'

'I didn't think it needed to be said,' her mentor said, 'I assumed that you knew.'

'Romulus,' Tash began but he cut her off.

'I know that you want to travel, Natachatet and I don't want to hold you back from your dreams. But sometimes when I look at you, I see the child you were and all I want is for you to be safe.'

'I'll take care of myself, Romulus,' Tash said gently, reaching over and pressing his wrinkled hand with hers. 'My years at the Temple have trained me for this. It's all I've ever wanted. Besides, I'll still need to come back to make sure that you're keeping the new apprentices in line.'

His mouth crooked in a smile and he squeezed her hand tightly. 'I will miss you, my child.'

'I hope I'm not interrupting.' The voice was cool and made both Romulus and Tash jump in their seats. They turned to see The Robin in the doorway, a pair of scrolls in his hands, familiar shadows shrouding his face.

'Of course not,' Romulus released Tash's hand and poured another goblet of wine. 'Join us, old friend. We were just having a quiet celebration of Natachatet's initiation tomorrow.'

'Indeed.' The Robin closed the door behind him and sank into the chair on Romulus' other side, crossing his long legs over each other and accepting with soft thanks the goblet handed to him. 'I was looking for you both. I have received correspondence to confirm the state of affairs in Kinet. It is as we were warned.'

Romulus glanced at him sharply, 'You didn't mention that the world in question was Kinet.'

The Robin shrugged. 'I didn't think it was necessary.'

Tash watched them both avidly, as The Robin handed Romulus the scrolls in his hands and the old man read through them carefully. She held her tongue, suppressing the rampant curiosity that was now racing through her. She drank more wine, both to distract herself and hide her impatience. She had originally come from Kinet, so now The Robin's choice in her to be the one in charge of this particular task made more sense— she would be able to stay longer than the usual month if there were any complications.

Finally, Romulus spoke, 'It's certainly strange.' He looked at Tash and handed her the scrolls, 'Have a read, Natachatet. What do you think?'

Tash opened the first scroll and scanned it, translating the words with ease.

Corvis,

The spring rains did not come. There is a blight in the fields and the crops are dying. We do not know what has caused this— it is unlike any disease we have seen before. Anyone who touches it is struck down in an uncanny slumber and after three days they are gone. We've seen instances of the fey returning. The villagers have begun leaving offerings by the Heath, but their prayers remain unanswered. Please, send someone to find the source of this scourge. We can't afford to lose all our crops before the winter snows.

Jervois

Tash opened the next scroll, searching her memory for various causes of blight and what could be done to fix it. The handwriting on this next scroll was sharp and jagged, an almost incomprehensible scrawl across the parchment, as though the writer had had immense difficulty with a quill.

Corvis,

They don't want to put it in their letter, so I'll spell it out plainly. The blight is only part of the issue. Their people are dying— some from the result of touching the fungus, but others are disappearing. Several bodies have been found on the Heath, and they didn't go quickly. Whatever or whoever killed them enjoyed the process.

I've already warned you about this once. Don't make the same mistake as your master.

These people need a Robin to help. They won't listen to me.

C.

Both notes were short. Tash rolled them back up slowly, using the moment to reflect and gather her thoughts. She had questions, oh so many questions.

'Well Natachatet?' The Robin asked.

'The blight could be an instance of improperly used magic reacting badly,' she said cautiously. 'Like the plague in the Damatian Plains was caused by a mage's apprentice trying to

perform a spell that he wasn't prepared for. The magic reacted and mutated into something else, in that case a swarm
of locusts. Perhaps someone in Kinet has been experimenting with spells they are not trained for– something to help
with the harvest or increasing crop yields perhaps?'

'You may be right,' Romulus said, 'it's a good theory, and
one you could easily remedy with your dezmian. Yet, I must
admit that the other information– the instances of deaths especially– has me concerned.' He glanced at The Robin, 'She
is still young. Perhaps another Robin– one with more experience– should be entrusted with this task.'

Tash forced herself to stay calm. Romulus' words cut
through her and she stared at The Robin, waiting to hear if
he would agree with her mentor and pass the mission on to
another. She hoped that he wouldn't– she wanted this, she
wanted to prove herself so much it hurt.

'I believe that I'm ready for this, sir,' she said. 'It's what
I've been training for. Please, let me try to help these people.'

The Robin considered her for a moment and then inclined his head. Romulus looked away, disappointed. Tash
felt warm relief flood through her as she bowed her head in
gratitude.

'The situation is worse than I anticipated,' The Robin said
gravely, 'I agree with Romulus' concerns about there being a
killer on the loose as well. Yet I understand that you are re-
sourceful, Natachatet. I have faith that you will be able to
resolve this for the people of Nordhaven.'

Nordhaven. The name wasn't familiar to Tash, but she
was determined to return to the library and find out about it.

'I'll be careful, sir,' she said, giving Romulus a reassuring
smile. 'I can take care of myself.'

'We will have the initiation at daybreak,' The Robin continued, 'from my understanding, the Barrier to Kinet recently moved from the Pelopesian Fields to the Defoe Cliffs.'

'It should be a fortnight before they change locations again,' Romulus added. 'You will need to take Lir.'

Tash nodded, the bubble of excitement threatening to overflow. In the distance, a bell began to toll and she remembered that it was the dinner hour. The Robin rose to his feet and said,

'Go and eat, Natachatet. You will need your strength tomorrow. Romulus will speak to the kitchen staff about preparing some rations for your trip.'

'Thank you,' she replied as she stood, bowed and departed, the scrolls still clutched in her hands. Her stomach had begun to rumble again, and she was determined to have a quick bite before slipping away to the library. She stowed the scrolls down her blouse, not wanting to have to answer any questions about them from the other apprentices.

The dining hall was loud with chatter by the time she arrived. Most of the tables were already filled with teachers and apprentices, but she spied a seat half in shadow at the far end of the room. It was the perfect spot to slip away from, where she would be on the peripheries of the room and not drawn into any conversations. Tash was halfway towards her desired seat when a loud voice called out,

'Oi! Tasha!'

She took a breath, held it and then released it slowly. Only one person called her Tasha and the last time he had done so, she had almost broken his nose. She turned to see the reason why her initiation had been delayed.

'Harrison, I thought I asked you not to call me that.'

He laughed and enfolded her in a bear hug. 'Come on, you love it really. Did you miss me?'

'No, *really*,' she snapped, giving him a sharp jab in the side to release her. He winced and let her go, wheezing slightly.

'No need for you to be like that, Tasha,' he grumbled, 'I was just happy to see you. It's been too long.'

In Tash's mind, it hadn't been long enough. As he joined her at her table and began to serve himself stew, she eyed him dispassionately. He was taller than she was, with brown hair that tended to get scraggly and grey eyes that were often alight with mischief. Now they were focussed on the food in his bowl, and she noted that he had grown a beard which had also started to get on the long side. It looked as though he had been living rough for months, and, judging by the way he was eating with such gusto, it had probably been a while since he had eaten properly too.

Even though she herself was starving, she'd be damned if he saw her gobble her food down like he was. With quiet dignity, she served herself and began to eat with a fork and spoon, taking care to not splatter the stew over the table. As they ate, she wondered how Romulus seemed to think that they would make a good match. She and Harrison were vastly different and, although their best friends were engaged, it didn't mean that they were particularly close. Instead, they got on each other's nerves far too often, almost as if he were an annoying older brother. She shuddered inwardly at the thought of them being anything closer, and then a memory of a different face filled her mind. One with sharp, angular features and cobalt blue eyes. Dark hair pulled back with a strap of rough leather. Her stomach flipped before she felt a sudden wave of guilt, Fred's image coming to the forefront of her thoughts, reminding her that they had only parted ways a week ago, and that she already felt *something* for a man she had never met.

'Penny for your thoughts?'

In an instant Tash was back in the present, realising that she had been staring at Harrison for far too long. He looked at her curiously as she hastily began to spoon more stew into her mouth.

'I thought you might want to hear about my trip,' he said when she didn't reply. Tash grasped onto the distraction and nodded, hoping that he would think that had been why she was staring.

'You had to settle a dispute, didn't you?'

'It turned out to be a bit more than that,' Harrison admitted. 'The king of the Damatian Plains had promised his daughter in marriage to a neighbouring kingdom— the Ice Fields, I believe. But his daughter was abducted by an ogre and all of the soldiers sent after them were killed. Their neighbour was threatening war because his bride had vanished and that was when the king of the Plains contacted The Robin. He sent me to try and ease the tensions between the two kingdoms. I convinced the two kings to agree on a trade agreement instead, since marriage was off the table. They both had things the other wanted, and with a bit of help, they were able to see that.' His chest puffed out with pride and he spoke impressively, clearly expecting her to applaud his approach.

'Did you just use your dezmian to enchant them?' Her question was blunt and rankled Harrison, as he glared at her defensively.

'They didn't give me much choice, Tasha. You should have seen them going at each other like two old idiots. It was the only way.'

She sighed, 'But what will happen when the enchantment wears off? Magic can't last forever, Harrison. They will remember the reason for their squabbling eventually.'

'Then I'll just go back and make them forget again,' Harrison said touchily. 'At least I got it done.'

'What about the princess?' Tash asked.

'Oh her,' Harrison said, 'she was a nasty piece of work. Turns out she'd planned on running away with this ogre for some time. So she won't be upset that her father can't remember her. Honestly, Tasha, I did her a favour. Now she can be happy with who she wants to be with. It's a win-win situation, in my opinion.'

'Just a slightly unethical one,' she murmured.

Harrison's cheeks reddened. 'You always like to find fault, don't you Tasha? Maybe, when you go out on your own, you won't be as picky about when magic can be used to achieve the necessary results.'

His words stung, and she placed her cutlery down, even though she had only half finished her stew. 'I don't want to use magic to enchant people, Harrison. I don't want to abuse that kind of power. Now, if you'll excuse me, I'm tired. Goodnight.'

With that she left, resolutely not turning back and headed for the library, determined to grab a few more books about Kinet's geography to go through before turning in for the night. Anger at Harrison's words still blazed through her, but she forced it down, refusing to give it the chance to erupt. Privately, she hoped that when her chance came, her convictions would not be compromised and she wouldn't succumb to the lure of magic as he had done.

Chapter Five

One hundred days of hell.

One hundred days in this new form.

I try to remain positive, to think of an escape, a means to break the curse.

The villagers sent out a hunting party to find me on the Heath today. Next time they'll bring dogs to track me and I won't be able to hide.

I have to remember who I am.

I am not a monster.

I am not—

~ An extract from an old, faded journal, found in a shack on the Nordhaven Heath

The morning air was chilly, grey light filtering through the clouds and the trees in the forest rustling in the background. The courtyard was filled with people but there was a stillness and silence that stretched across the cobbles. All eyes were on the man who stood over the brazier of burning coals, silver robes catching in the breeze. He was singing in a low, deep baritone in a language that had no words.

Tash was standing amongst the other initiates, her gown half hidden by the heavy cloak she had fastened around her shoulders. To her left, Harrison stood tall, avoiding her eye, solely focussed on The Robin by the brazier. In the crowd,

Tash saw Laura and Tim, standing hand in hand on the out-skirts, watching the ceremony unfold.

The Robin paused in his song and there was a hush, before the fiery coals turned a deep golden colour, bursting into flames reaching up hungrily to the sky. One by one, every initiate was called by Romulus to approach The Robin, who spoke to each one quietly, his words lost over the roaring flames. Each initiate responded to him, extending their hand over the fire. There was a flash of steel as The Robin drew a dagger across their palms, splattering blood on the coals. With every offering of blood, the flames flashed red before returning to gold.

'Natachatet.'

It was her turn. She stepped forwards and halted in front of The Robin and the brazier. Even with the bright flames dancing before them, the magical darkness still hid his face from view, but she thought she sensed him smiling.

'Natachatet, do you pledge to be the guardian of the old faith? To bring light to the darkness, music to the silence and justice to the wicked? Will you vow to protect the Barriers between worlds and the innocent? Do you commit yourself to ensuring that balance is maintained across each known universe?'

'I do,' she responded, 'until I breathe my last, it will be done.'

'May your song begin today, Robin,' he said, drawing the knife across her outstretched palm. She bit back a cry of pain and then turned her hand, squeezing the blood over the flames. For a moment, everything was red, and there was a humming in her ears. It was like the song The Robin had been singing before, except this one sounded older, like the song of the stars when the worlds were created. It was the musical language of the Gods of the old faith. The Ancient Tongue.

She stepped back in line as The Robin raised his arms up to the heavens and cried, 'May all here bear witness to the vows spoken by these Robins today. May the Gods, from before time began, watch over you and bless your holy vows. Remember to seek truth and justice and to aid the weak and helpless. From today, you are tasked with this duty.'

'We will not forget,' the initiates intoned as one.

'Let us congratulate our new Robins,' Romulus declared, as he and the audience began to clap. Tash felt herself grin— after all these years, she had finally achieved her goal of becoming a Robin. She looked up and saw Laura pushing her way through the crowd towards her. Now that the ceremony was concluded, the other apprentices and Robins were swarming around the initiates eagerly, clasping their shoulders and hugging them. Tash noticed that Harrison had moved over to Tim, the two of them laughing. When Laura reached her, she hugged her tightly, ignoring Tash's bloodied palm. The wound stung and Tash gently disengaged from her friend, finding the dezmian in her pocket and flipping it, focussing on the cut. Slowly the skin healed, leaving behind a pale scar.

'Here,' Laura pulled a clean handkerchief out and handed it to her to wipe away the blood. 'You don't want to get stains on your skirts.'

'Thanks,' Tash said, rubbing her hand until it was clean. She stowed the handkerchief in her pocket and hugged Laura again. 'I'm not going to be able to stay for long. The Robin wants me to go to Kinet.'

'You'll need to let me know when you get back,' Laura grinned, 'I can't wait to hear all about it. I'm sure everything will go well, Tash. If it's anything like the world trips we went on together, you'll be able to sort out whatever problems there are easily.'

Tash smiled, wondering if Laura would feel the same way if she knew about the strange murders or the blight that cursed its victims into a deathly slumber. She chose against revealing these points, knowing that if Laura found out, she might insist on coming along with Tim. And, despite the fact that she loved her friend dearly, Tash wasn't keen to be a third wheel again. No, this time, she wanted to travel alone.

Around them, the other initiates and apprentices began to head into the dining hall for a celebratory drink. Tash looked up as The Robin paused in front of her, straightening his robes.

'Natachatet,' he said, 'I've asked Romulus to prepare some supplies for you. He'll meet you in the stables shortly. Make sure to return to me with your report directly, once your business in Kinet is completed.'

'Yes sir,' Tash replied. The Robin turned to Laura and said,

'See me before you head out. I've got a job for you and Crow.'

'Yes Father,' she said softly as he departed for his tower.

'Sounds like we will both be exchanging stories when we next meet,' Tash said gaily as they headed for the stables.

'I wonder what he's found,' Laura mused, falling into step beside Tash and lifting one of the saddles from the wall. 'It must be something new; he didn't mention anything the last time I visited.' Tash shrugged, bending to pick up the bag that she had packed earlier, carrying it down towards Lir's stall.

He recognised her scent as she approached and came closer, making soft sounds of excitement. He moved restlessly, eager to leave the stall and spread his wings. Tash chuckled and lifted the latch of the door, leading him out with gentle words of encouragement, for when he saw Laura he began to shy away. Gradually, his confidence was restored and he followed Tash out, pausing as she began to attach the saddle and bags to his back. His liquid eyes watched her soulfully and she laughed again, patting his neck as she worked.

Laura leaned against the doors to the stable, but stood to attention when Romulus entered, a small bag of provisions in his gnarled hands. He dismissed her with a little wave and she stepped outside, giving them a moment of privacy.

'Natachatet,' he said, 'you can't go without this.' He handed her the bag of provisions, attaching it to her saddle, careful to ensure it wouldn't open mid-flight.

'I was hoping that you would come and say goodbye,' she grinned as she turned and hugged him.

'My dear child,' Romulus gripped her tightly, his beard tickling her forehead. 'I have some other little things for you that might be useful.' He pressed into her hand another small pouch and she opened it. Inside was a spare dezmian, a pair of woollen gloves and a carved, wooden ring. She lifted it up, noting the floral design in its surface.

'It's made of yew,' Romulus explained as she put it on her finger, 'a symbol of protection from evil spirits.' As she pushed it down to the knuckle on her right hand, a weight seemed to lift from her shoulders and she felt lighter, freer.

'Thank you, Romulus,' she said, 'I'll treasure it always. Did you carve it yourself?'

He smiled, 'I had some help. It's been a long time since I could whittle something like this.'

The ring stood out in pale contrast against her dark skin as she examined it closely. 'It's beautiful.'

'I'm glad you like it, my dear,' he said. 'Now, make sure to wear the gloves during the flight– it's getting colder and I don't want you to catch a chill.'

She chuckled and obeyed his request, pulling the gloves over her hands and stowing the spare dezmian in her bags. 'Take care, Romulus. I'll miss you.'

'And I you, my child.'

She hugged him again, sudden tears pricking her eyes. She wanted to thank him for the years of care, and tell him that she loved him like he was her own grandfather. But she said none of those things, knowing that he did not like to have open demonstrations of affection. Yet, he understood how she felt, she was sure. And, deep down, she knew that he felt the same for her, although he would not admit to it in public.

'Take care of Lir,' he was saying now as she drew away, lifting herself up into the saddle and winding her hands through Lir's mane.

'I promise,' Tash grinned, 'and he will take care of me too.'

With a soft nudge, Lir began to head out to the courtyard before he halted, unsettled by the sight of Laura, Tim and Harrison.

'Are you leaving already, Tasha?' Harrison asked, surprised.

'She's off to Kinet,' Laura said proudly, one arm around Tim's waist as she grinned at her friend. 'Fly safe, Tash.'

'Good luck, Tash,' Tim said, 'go and do what you do best.'

'Thanks,' Tash replied, guiding Lir to go around them. The Willowing froze when Harrison stepped closer, concerned.

'Tasha, you're sure you don't want some help? Kinet's not particularly safe at the moment…'

'I'll be fine, thanks Harrison,' Tash said, tone clipped. She was getting tired of people assuming that she needed help when she was perfectly capable of figuring this task out by herself. 'And my name is *Tash* in case you forgot.'

With that petty reminder, she felt a momentary sense of satisfaction and then leaned down to Lir's ears, which were flicking worriedly from her change in tone. Gently, she whispered in her native tongue, 'Fly, my angel. Let's get out of this place.' Ignoring Harrison's offended gaze, she smiled as Lir's wings spread and, with a powerful thrust, launched them into the air.

***

It took only a few minutes for Tash to adapt to riding Lir, settling her weight more evenly so that he wasn't put off balance mid-flight. She closed her eyes, feeling the wind tearing through her hair and letting out a loud whoop of delight as they soared higher. When she glanced down, the Temple was a mere speck behind them on its mountain peak. They had already passed several more mountain summits when she looked back, and then the Temple was lost in the clouds that descended from the heavens in thick drifts. Lir lifted higher still, passing through the clouds, making Tash's clothes damp with cold mist. But then they were breaking through the grey shroud and were up where the sun shone and skies were clear.

Tash leaned back in the saddle, gripping Lir tightly with her knees, and raised her arms and face to the sun, laughing in delight. Lir let out a whinny in agreement and spun through the air, forcing Tash to hold on even tighter. He plunged on, increasing their speed until she could barely keep her eyes open with the force of the wind. Her fingers twined through his mane and held firm, providing an anchor for her as they rode onwards. Gradually, Lir began to tire, not being used to flying with a rider, let alone having the additional weight of bags, and so they started to descend. Tash bid farewell to the sun as they returned to the world of Venetica, which was shrouded in gloomy clouds.

They had left the mountain ranges behind, passing over forests and rivers, heading for the Defoe Cliffs in the south. Below them the Whitewash, one of the largest rivers in Venetica, guided their way, moving from its source in the Temple's mountain range to the Southern Sea. It twisted like a vast serpent, cutting through towns and fields towards its destination.

There was a soft grunting sound and Tash noticed Lir's head drooping, his tongue partially hanging out. It was time to return to the ground and let him rest. She urged him downward and they dived, swooping towards the riverbank below. They landed with a jolt on the grass and Tash dismounted, skirts and cloak flicking around her ankles as she steadied herself.

The river was noisy, the water forming white foam as it beat against the bank with a mind of its own. Flying fish leapt out of the waves, tiny wings lifting them upwards before they dived back under the surface, unperturbed by the river's ferocity. Tash leaned against Lir's side, remembering all the stories she had heard in the Temple of children who ventured into the Whitewash for a swim and never returned. Looking at it now, she understood why.

Unaware of the topic of his rider's thoughts, Lir bent his head and began to drink greedily. Tash stroked his neck and lifted the bags off his back, before removing the saddle as well. As Lir was still young, he would need time to get used to being ridden and the last thing she wanted was to give him some lasting damage from carrying a heavy load for too long. Romulus had instilled in her many times the need to care for Willowings and to understand their limits, especially when they were young. Their bones didn't completely strengthen until they reached their third year, so until then, while they could be ridden, Robins had to take care to not over-exert them. Once they were old enough however, Willowings could carry remarkably heavy loads and fly for long distances at a time.

'You're alright, my *liebeshem*,' she murmured soothingly to him, her maternal tongue relaxing him. She had found over the years that Willowings responded better to her native language instead of Venetican, Damas or Erethian. The tones weren't as sharp, but mellower, like sweet honey. Yet in the Temple she had rarely spoken it, partly because no one else knew it and she didn't want to seem like an outsider.

Lir had stopped drinking and now was munching contentedly on the fragrant grass, tail flicking away the errant flies. She began to hum to herself, a tune that she remembered from her childhood but whose words had long faded from memory. Carefully, she opened the satchel of provisions, noting approvingly the small bag of rice, dried meat jerky and fresh apples. There was also a block of salt, tea and a bag of nuts which she stowed away. Reaching into her pocket for her dezmian, she flipped it and focussed hard on what she needed.

The magic coursed through her in a rush, the thrill dangerously addictive but the clenching pain in her stomach leaving her gasping. A small fire crackled by the riverside, a stool beside it with a kettle and pot waiting to be used. She filled both with water from the Whitewash and pulled out the rice, a tin cup and bowl from the satchel. As she waited for the water to boil, Tash stretched and laid her bedroll out beside the campfire.

It might have only been close to lunchtime, but she was exhausted. She had barely slept the night before, too caught up in perusing the books about Kinet to even contemplate sleep. Now though, after the invigorating flight, she could feel her body crashing, aching tiredness spreading through her. Lir sank down beside her, folding his wings, breathing heavily. She patted him gently, the sound of her song calming him and within moments he had closed his eyes and fallen asleep.

'I wish I could sleep so easily,' she whispered as she removed the gloves and stowed them in her pack. Sinking back, she watched the fire lazily, the smoke rising in spiralling tendrils towards the sky. She could use magic to make the water boil faster, but there was something peaceful about needing to wait, to just enjoy the moment of quiet and having to be patient. Besides, she had a fortnight to reach the Defoe Cliffs and was confident that they would get there well before then. They could afford to rest a while. Her eyelids flickered shut and she drifted off in a light doze.

She awoke to a high-pitched whistling from the kettle. Yawning, she opened her eyes and rubbed them, moving on to ease the stiffness in her neck and shoulders. It had been a while since she slept rough and her body was all too eager to remind her of its grievances.

'Tea?'

The voice made Tash's head whip up, realising for the first time that she wasn't alone. By her side, Lir was still sleeping, his chest slowly rising and falling peacefully, unaware of their unwanted guest. It took Tash a moment to calm her rapidly beating heart, that had almost shocked her into a scream when the voice startled her. Thankfully, she had controlled that response.

'What are you doing here?' The words sprang from her lips before she could stop them, but in the circumstances, she felt that the question was warranted. There was a soft, rough chuckle which did nothing to alleviate Tash's anxiety. Slowly, she sat up, one hand reaching behind her back to search for the knife that was in her saddlebag.

'I'm making sure that you stay on track, little bird,' the Dæmon replied.

'Have you been following me?' she demanded. His tail flicked in the grass, but nothing else in his expression gave his thoughts away. He watched her through half-slit eyes, and she paused in her movement, trapped in his gaze. Her fingers gripped the handle of the blade, still hidden behind her back.

'Of course,' he replied coolly, 'it was me who told The Robin about the Kinetian incident after all. I like to know that he follows through on his promises.' He poured the kettle over the mug she had left beside the fire, and reached over to hand it to her. She took it cautiously with her free hand, raising it to her mouth and sniffed. The scent of cloves, cinnamon and cardamon rose from the mug and she inhaled it, recognising it instantly. Chai was her favourite tea and always soothed her.

'Thanks,' she said grudgingly.

'You can let go of that knife as well,' he said lazily, 'unless you're intending on using it.'

She blinked, the tea sloshing in the mug as she jolted in surprise. 'Will I need to?' she asked carefully, and he laughed.

'That depends on whether you think I'm a threat or not, little bird.'

She didn't take her eyes off him, but gently prised her fingers off the dagger hilt and held the mug in both hands, sipping the chai. The Dæmon bared his fangs in what could have been a smile or a snarl, it was hard to tell.

'How did you follow me?' Tash asked, 'you can't fly.'

'Very perceptive of you,' he said, tone tinged with sarcasm. Tash felt her cheeks go hot for an instant as she bit back a retort. The Dæmon watched her closely, reading her thoughts all too easily as they flashed across her face before she schooled her features into an impassive mask.

'Is this going to be a regular occurrence with you?' she asked, 'Showing up at random by my campfire when I'm resting?'

'Would you like it to be?'

His question caught her off-guard and her eyes widened imperceptibly. 'I would like it if you answered my questions, actually.'

'Nothing comes for free, little bird,' the Dæmon replied casually. 'What makes you think I'll just give you your answers without receiving something in return?'

She held her tongue, remembering all too well the warnings written in the library books she had borrowed.

'You must think that I'm very naïve if you think I'll even consider making a deal with you.'

He laughed again, the sound waking Lir from his slumber this time. The Willowing reacted instantly to the Dæmon's presence, rising to his feet and shuffling away in distress, giving short snuffles of fear and tossing his mane at the intrusion.

'Control your animal,' the Dæmon said curtly, 'or I'll have to.' He lifted one of his hands, testing the sharpness of his claws. Tash's mouth tightened in an angry line. Putting down the mug, she rose and moved over to Lir. Her Willowing quietened slightly when he saw her approaching, but kept casting scared, wide-eyed looks at the Dæmon by the fireside.

'Be still, Lir,' Tash murmured, 'calm thoughts. Soft hay. Sweet grass. Endless sky.'

His head nudged into her shoulder, burrowing into her hair and whickering. Tash continued to murmur gentle words, hands caressing his neck and muzzle as he settled again. She glanced up from him to the Dæmon and said curtly,

'Don't you dare threaten Lir again.'

He raised his eyebrows, 'or what?'

Tash had reached for her dezmian before she could stop herself, reacting instinctively, tossing it into the air and summoning the vines to hold the Dæmon in their grasp. To her dismay, he moved just as quickly, slicing through the foliage with his claws and leaping over the fire in one bound. In an instant he had caught her arms, pinning them to her sides.

'Tut tut, little bird,' he chided, 'you forget that I have been using magic for far longer than you.' She stamped down on his foot and thrust her elbow into his stomach, twisting out of his grip but fell to the ground as he grunted and tackled her. Lir whinnied in fright and fled, leaving Tash to try and break out of the Dæmon's grip alone. She lashed out, the memories of her training fading away as she fought tooth and nail to gain the upper hand. The Dæmon had the audacity to laugh again, catching her wrists all too easily and trapping her underneath him.

'It's good to know that the little bird has talons,' he said as he caught his breath. She snarled and struggled even harder, forcing him to grip her tighter to maintain his balance. She could see the mocking glint in his smile, the twitch of the laugh that was barely suppressed and her blood boiled.

'I have a *name*,' she hissed. 'And I'm a *Robin*, not an apprentice anymore.'

'How intimidating,' he retorted and her eyes flashed furiously. She yanked her arm out from his clawed hand, cutting her forearm in the process but not caring. The ring of yew on her finger scraped against his hand and he grunted in pain as a dark welt appeared on his skin. Using the moment to her advantage, she flipped her dezmian and a wave of the Whitewash crashed over the riverbank, submerging them in icy water. The Dæmon was distracted by the sudden dousing and she took her chance, slithering out from underneath him and grabbing the knife from her pack.

The Dæmon looked up at her, dripping and shaking with laughter. She didn't flinch, holding the blade to his neck steadily, and snarled,

'As I said, don't threaten my Willowing again. And my name is Natachatet, not little bird.'

He didn't seem fazed by the knife, but inclined his head towards her.

'Very well, Natachatet. I will refrain from harming your beast.' She nodded, accepting his concession, sliding the knife into her belt and looking around at the now drenched campsite.

The Dæmon followed her gaze. 'You didn't think your decision through, did you?' He got to his feet, shaking the water out of his hair that had escaped from its bun, hanging to his shoulders. He bent and retrieved the leather cord from the ground, pulling it back up again.

'Not really,' she admitted, tearing her eyes away from him and moving to the remains of the fire. The ground was slick with water and before she knew it, her foot slid out from underneath her as she stepped on a wet stone. The momentary loss of balance had her reeling, until two clawed hands grasped her shoulders, steadying her.

'Careful,' the Dæmon said. She turned her head to thank him and realised that he was too close. She could feel his breath on her cheek and went still, unsure of how to escape. There was something in his gaze that scared her more than anything she'd encountered before and her stomach began to do strange flips. His mouth was inches away and desire rose in her chest, tightening up her throat and making her stomach twist even harder. Her eyes widened as she realised that for some crazy, unbeknownst reason, she wanted to kiss him. It was invigorating– and terrifying.

'Thanks,' she finally managed through numb lips, desperately trying to avoid looking at his. For once he didn't laugh, and she was struck with the feeling that he was able to interpret her emotions better than she herself could. With a slight cough she stepped away, breaking the moment of intimacy and forcing distance between them. Almost immediately her heart began to beat normally again, and she could temporarily push the strange desire she felt to the back of her mind.

There was a disturbance from the nearby trees and Lir re-emerged, swishing his tail pointedly and dancing around the wet earth. Coward, Tash thought resentfully. She began to collect her belongings, rolling up the bedroll and tossing the remnants of tea onto the grass. The Dæmon didn't offer to help and she didn't ask him to, saddling Lir with ease and attaching her bags to the back of the saddle. The Willowing was jumpy, eager to be gone now that he had had time to rest.

When she turned around, the Dæmon had made the remains of the campfire and pots vanish with a lazy flick of the hand. She blinked, returning the dezmian to her pocket and wondering how he could access magic without a conduit.

'Now, although that drowned rat look is very fetching,' he said, casting a thorough look up and down her body, 'unless you want to catch a chill, you'll need to dry off.'

She glanced down, noting for the first time how the dress and cloak clung to her and showed far more of her body than she was comfortable with. Before she could react, the Dæmon made another gesture with his hands and a warm breeze encircled her, drying her clothes and hair within moments. The wind felt strangely intimate, like a kiss, and she stilled, unable to look away from the Dæmon's lazy smile.

'Thank you,' she said awkwardly. 'Although I could have done that myself.' He moved closer, lifted her up onto Lir's back in one smooth motion, and then released her, being careful not to touch the hand with the ring. She glanced down at the mark on his own hand, the dark welt that had appeared when she fought him. The Dæmon noticed her gaze and said,

'Yew grants some protection from my kind. Make sure to never take it off, there are others out there with less scruples than I.'

'*You* have scruples?' Tash asked.

'I haven't feasted on your blood yet, have I?' he replied caustically, 'I try to avoid aggravating Robins. It doesn't normally end well when we reach an impasse.' Tash kept silent, unsure if he was teasing or not. 'Besides,' the Dæmon continued, 'you have an important task to accomplish in Kinet. I'd be loath to delay you further.' With that, he gave her a final smile before melting into the trees, vanishing from sight in a moment. Tash watched the space where he had been, trying to process where he had gone and then shook herself. Did it really matter? More importantly, she had to reach the Defoe Cliffs before the fortnight was over. Keeping this in mind, she turned Lir and urged him upwards, following the Whitewash as it meandered its way towards the Southern Sea.

Chapter Six

It's been five years since I last wrote. Five long years in this form.

I no longer have hope that the darkness will end.

The people want me to be a monster.

So I will be one.

~ The final entry in a discarded journal, found in an abandoned shack on the Nordhaven Heath

Tash did not sleep easy for the first few nights, paranoid that the Dæmon would return to her fireside. She and Lir had continued to follow the Whitewash by day, remaining on the riverbank to set up camp each evening. Tash made sure to pause every few hours so that Lir had enough time to rest and recover, for the Willowing was finding the journey diffi-cult. Each morning he would be eager to depart, full of energy, but after a couple of hours of flight he began to tire. Tash didn't mind overly much though, by her reckoning they were making good time. On the third night, she conjured her magical fire and waited for her rice to cook in the pot, stom-ach rumbling with hunger. She pulled the last remaining nuts out of her bag and began to chew on them, noting sadly that her supplies were almost completely depleted. It would be a meagre meal tonight, and she would need to find a town to resupply at soon.

Lir whickered softly and bumped her shoulder with his muzzle, searching for a treat. To his disappointment Tash had nothing left for him, having surrendered the last of the apples Romulus had packed the day before.

'We'll need to keep an eye out for somewhere to stock up tomorrow, Lir,' she murmured, 'otherwise we're not going to make it to the Defoe Cliffs. Romulus only gave us enough food to set us on our way.'

He nuzzled her again and she stroked his neck, humming a soothing melody. He quietened and settled down beside her, folding his wings and shutting his eyes. As usual within a few moments of listening to the lullaby, he fell asleep. Tash smiled to herself, before lifting the pot of rice and starting to spoon it hungrily into her mouth. As she ate, her mind wandered back to the Dæmon, who had never been far from her thoughts. She recalled what he had said and, particularly, her reaction to him that she had tamped down. It had also not escaped her that he had been able to walk in daylight, something that she had considered impossible for his kind. The books had been wrong on that front– they stated that Nightwalkers only lived in the shadows and couldn't be touched by the sun, otherwise they would be burned by the Sun God's holy fire.

Thinking back to that particular entry she had read, her mouth quirked in a smile. She wondered if the writer of *The Kinetian Bestiary* had ever actually met a Nightwalker before. They hadn't mentioned some of the Nightwalker's features, such as their uncanny speed, or strength. Or, she thought as she chewed another mouthful of rice, the way that they made one both want to strike and then kiss them simultaneously. No… it was highly unlikely that the author of the bestiary had ever felt *that* particular emotion.

And then there was the way the Nightwalkers could manipulate magic at will, without a dezmian or conduit of some kind. Now that was something she had never seen before, and she had visited several different worlds in her lifetime. The books also warned how Nightwalkers would charm their victims, luring them into a false sense of security but she didn't feel as though the Dæmon had been doing that. He'd seemed more amused with her than cajoling, more likely to mock her than try to win her over with flattery.

But still she thought about him. Even when she had used her dezmian to vanish the cooking pot, she was unable to shake him from her mind. The flames crackled and sparks flew into the cool night air as she threw another log onto the fire, the smoke rising in twisting spirals up towards the stars overhead. She closed her eyes for a moment, enjoying the quiet, the lapping of the river, the snapping of twigs in the flames, Lir's gentle breathing to her side. It was peaceful here, and while some people might have disliked the solitude, Tash found it relaxing. This was what she needed– time to herself, to regain that part of her that had been damaged when she left Earth. But then the Dæmon had reappeared in her life and that fragile part of herself had begun to hurt again, to feel again, and she didn't like it. She wanted, oh so much, to avoid the emotions that had resurfaced so suddenly.

She sensed the presence before he appeared. There was a shift in the light, the shadows turned darker, seeming to ripple in and out like the Whitewash, and then he was there. The firelight caught on his horns making them glimmer a deep umber. He leaned against one of the trees, looking for all the world as though he had always been there. Tash glared at him balefully, partially because of the way her pulse began to beat faster at his appearance. It was uncanny, almost as if her thoughts had summoned him back to her fireside. She didn't want to like the anticipation that rose in her.

'You've come a long way in just a few days, Natachatet,' he remarked and she bristled, all anticipation lost at his slightly patronising tone.

'Yes, I'm aware,' she replied pointedly, 'you don't need to state the obvious.' Now she was wishing that he would leave her be, the peaceful evening by the Whitewash was broken and she resented it. He smiled, as though he could read her mind.

'You didn't honestly expect me to not check in on your progress,' he said carelessly. 'Besides,' he cast a glance over her open, empty bag and the scant remaining provisions, 'I come with a warning.'

'Oh?' While her tone wasn't encouraging, his eyes twinkled at her from the shadows.

'Don't stop in the next town,' he said seriously, 'Pass straight through and continue on to the following one to re-supply.'

'Why?'

His expression hardened at the question, irritated perhaps at her curiosity, or her lack of trust in his warning.

'I cannot say. You have been warned, Natachatet. Don't visit the next town.'

'Now hold on,' Tash began angrily, 'why can't you—'

But he had vanished as quickly as he had arrived. She swore, glaring into the trees at the spot where he had been. Who would give a warning but no reason for it? Was it just some trick, some ploy to test if she would follow his orders? In the books it warned about Nightwalkers tricking victims into obeying their will, like mindless chattel, before they feasted on their blood. Was this one of those ploys?

Tash frowned. It went against her nature to not question

a demand that had no explanation. What was the reason behind it? The thought occurred to her that perhaps the Dæmon should be listened to, that perhaps she should concede in this instance. But, she countered, where was the evidence to prove that? Where was the *reason* for his warning?

Her enjoyment of the evening was lost, and as she lay down to sleep, Tash found herself silently cursing the Dæmon for intruding and leaving her with more questions than answers.

***

She dreamed of escaping from the alchemist's shop again. The words of the prophecy rang in her ears; the flapping of crows' wings beat against her head and their sharp beaks began to peck her mercilessly. Tash cried out, trying to get away, to block out the birds' onslaught and the words that kept repeating over and over. *Beware the night. Be cautious of day. When all strays, you will stay.*

'Shut up!' she screamed, striking out blindly, 'Leave me alone!'

'Stop yelling,' a harsh voice grunted, and suddenly she was beating her fists against a pair of arms that held her firm. She paused, opened her eyes tentatively and realised that the crows had vanished. But that didn't necessarily mean that she was safe.

It was the man she had seen before, his cobalt eyes watching her with a hint of caution, as though he was preparing for her to start screaming and fighting again. His cheeks were dark with stubble, the arms around her were strong, but their grip had lessened as she had regained her composure.

'Who are you?' Tash asked, torn between suspicion and intrigue, unwilling to look away from his impenetrable gaze. He looked like he was about to reply, but then something

67

caught his attention from behind her and his face paled. With a sharp tug, they were running down the streets, cobbles biting into her bare feet as they tried to avoid whatever– or whoever– was behind them. Tash wasn't able to look around to see it, the grip on her arm was too strong, forcing her to face ahead, to keep running until her chest was heaving and her sides ached with pain. Still, they plunged on, cutting up and down side streets, turning left and right through the shadowed laneways, until they reached a dead end and the man faltered for the first time.

He turned, his face a mask of sheer dread, sweat beading on his brow. Confused, Tash followed his gaze, searching the street they had just come down but seeing nothing at first.

'Can you hear it?' he whispered, voice shaking. 'The bells?'

And then she could. The faint, tinkling sound of bells jingling on a horse's bridle as it gradually drew closer. In an instant the sunlight was extinguished, just as a shrouded figure appeared at the end of the street. They wore a hooded cloak and the darkness surrounding them made it impossible to distinguish their features. Yet it seemed as though Tash's companion knew them.

'No,' he muttered, 'no, please.' He had crumpled to the ground, clutching his head in agony. Tash knelt beside him, trying and failing to help him. The figure approached closer and her companion's eyes opened, searching for her in the gloom. 'Find me. Help me. *Please.*'

'Where are you?' Tash asked desperately, 'How can I help you?'

There was loud crack of thunder and rain began to plummet from the sky in heavy torrents, drenching Tash in seconds. She covered her eyes to see through the raindrops only to discover that she was now alone.

Tash awoke, sweating and shaking. Her chest felt heavy and she was nauseous. It was barely dawn, the palest streaks of grey light spreading across the sky. She sat up and saw something slide into the grass, rolling off her skirts. It was the yew ring. Perhaps it had slipped off her finger in the night. Shrugging, she put it in her bag and then began to prepare to leave. She splashed her face with water from the Whitewash, shivering as the iciness assailed her senses, but grateful that it had helped settle the nausea and shakiness she'd felt on awakening.

Her stomach rumbled as she took a long draught from her water flask, reminding her that they needed to stop at a town today to resupply. The Dæmon's warning flicked through her memory but she shook it off. There weren't too many villages along the Whitewash– there was no guarantee that she would find two in one day, and her supplies were dangerously low.

'Lir, it's time to go, *liebeshem.*' Her Willowing rose to his feet and she began to attach his saddle, tying on the bags and mounting smoothly. Twisting around, she flicked her dezmian and the campsite vanished, leaving no trace that they had ever stayed there. She glanced for a final time at the trees where the Dæmon had appeared the night before, a faint wave of anxiety filling her as Lir spread his wings.

The air was frigid and cut through her thick cloak and gloves, chilling her to the core. She gritted her teeth and lowered her head against Lir's neck, trusting him to soar onward, the Whitewash fading into a thin stream beneath them. The scenes from her dream kept replaying over and over, the image of the cobalt-eyed man imprinted on the back of her eyelids. She wondered who he was, whether he was actually real– if there was some way that she could actually help him.

The clouds remained heavy overhead, looming over them in a sea of grey, and before too long it had begun to rain. It drizzled at first, then it grew heavier. Tash pushed Lir on as much as she could, getting drenched through, the hood of her cloak barely protecting her face. Within a half hour, her hair was plastered down her back, her eyelashes were thick with raindrops and she was shivering. Lir let out a hoarse whinny and began to descend abruptly, causing Tash to grip on tighter as the sudden motion made her slip in the saddle.

Lir's destination soon became obvious– a small village about a mile inland from the Whitewash, the lights in the windows twinkling through the gloom. Once again, the Dæmon's warning entered her mind but Tash pushed it away. She had to be practical– if they kept going through this weather, she ran the risk of catching a chill. She couldn't afford to get sick when it was imperative that she reached Kinet as soon as possible.

Lir circled downward, landing in the village square and slipping on the slick cobblestones. Tash steadied him, dismounted and led him towards a stable adjacent to a nearby inn. The sign hung over the doorway, creaking in the wind, a faded skull painted onto the wood. There was no one in the stable, but some horses and Willowings were in the stalls already. Tash focussed on rubbing Lir down, slinging the saddlebags over her shoulders and leaving him to munch on the hay in the stall.

The rain was almost impenetrable now, the water coming down in greyish sheets. There was a crack of thunder and the sky lit up with a flash of lighting coursing across the horizon. Tash shivered, grateful that they were no longer flying in this weather and relieved that they had found temporary shelter.

She hurried across to the inn door and pushed it open,

dripping onto the clean floor as she crossed the threshold. Inside a warm fire crackled and a couple of old men sat at the bar, chuckling over their tankards. When she entered, they turned and stared at her, clearly taken aback by her sudden arrival. The man who she assumed was the innkeeper stepped away from the group, eyeing her warily.

'Hello,' Tash said, slightly awkward in the silence. 'I was hoping to take shelter until the weather lets up. I got caught in the storm.'

'You're not from these parts,' one of the men at the bar said balefully before his friends shushed him.

'You got caught in the storm?' the innkeeper asked, eyebrows raised in slight confusion. Tash blinked, surprised. Couldn't he see that she was drenched through?

There was a commotion from the stairs and a small woman bustled down, a bundle of sheets in her arms. 'Jamison, I asked you to clear that room out hours ago. Don't tell me you've been down here giving out our ale for free.' She halted on the bottom step, taking in the scene and Tash's dishevelled figure.

'Linda,' the innkeeper said, 'we have—'

'Yes, I can see that we have a proper customer,' the woman snapped. 'Why don't you see about helping her, you idiotic man? Would you like to stay for a night, dear?' She turned a kindly smile on Tash, who immediately felt comforted and nodded. 'Get her bags, Jamison. Take them up to the free guest room for her. Why, you poor dear,' she dumped the sheets down on one of the tables and came to help Tash over to the fireside, 'you look like you've been through something terrible. Let me get you a towel and a cup of tea, and we'll have you warmed up and feeling better in no time.'

'Thank you,' Tash managed, her teeth chattering from the

cold outside. Jamison took her saddlebags and carried them upstairs as Tash settled down in one of the hard wooden chairs and held her hands out to the flames. Linda returned with a scratchy towel and wrapped it around Tash's shoulders, before she bustled away to get a steaming mug of tea, placing it on a small side table.

'What's your name, dear?' she asked kindly as Tash took a sip. It was hot and tasted sweet, almost like honey had been added to it.

'I'm Tash,' she said. 'Thank you for the tea.'

'Oh, it's nothing dear,' Linda said, 'I'll get Jamison to draw a bath for you and we'll look after you until the storm passes.'

'Thanks,' Tash repeated gratefully and then asked, 'what town is this?'

'You're in Lower Quilton,' Linda smiled. 'You must have passed Upper Quilton on your way here.'

Tash wasn't sure. She hadn't seen another town but when the weather changed so quickly, it had been hard to make anything out through the rain. Perhaps she *had* passed another town before landing here– if so, she didn't have to worry about that Dæmon's warning.

'I don't remember,' she admitted, 'is there a regular market or supply store where I could visit before I head off tomorrow? I need to reach the Defoe Cliffs.'

'The Defoe Cliffs?' Linda's eyebrows rose, 'those are quite a distance from here. Why on earth would you want to go there? The Cliffs have been overrun with Dragutash for several years now.'

'Really?' This was news to Tash. She'd thought that the scourge of Dragutash had been fought back into the Western Marshlands. Tim had told her many tales about those creatures; monstrous beings that lived to kill and maim anything and everything in sight. He had even been attacked by one as a child and still had the scars to prove it. When she'd found him in Boolwra to bring him to Earth, he had just returned from hunting one down and killing it. While Tash had never actually seen one, she had read about them and knew that it was best to stay far away.

'Surely you don't need to go to the Cliffs?' Linda said hopefully. 'It's not a safe place, especially for young women on their own. Where *is* your family, dear? Why are you travelling alone?' Her voice became tinged with concern and she eyed Tash worriedly, 'Don't tell me you got separated from your companions?'

Tash laughed, 'No, not at all. I'm used to travelling alone– I'm a Robin. You don't need to worry about me.'

'A Robin?' Linda's eyes widened and she ducked her head respectfully. 'It's been a long time since we've had a Robin pass through Lower Quilton. It's an honour to have you here, Tash.'

'I appreciate your hospitality,' Tash replied, a bit uncomfortable at Linda's reaction.

'Linda,' both women turned to see Jamison on the stairs, 'I've prepared the room and bath like you asked.'

'Wonderful,' Linda said breezily, 'come on, Tash. I'll show you to your room so you can recuperate from your journey. Dinner should be ready in a few hours.'

'That would be lovely, thank you,' Tash smiled. As she passed Jamison on the stairs, he pulled away slightly, watching her ascend the steps before returning to his group of friends by the bar. Shrugging off the strange interaction, Tash followed Linda, appreciating that at least one person in this inn was friendly towards her.

Tash's room was cosy, with a window facing out onto the square and a wide four poster bed. The fresh sheets gleamed white in the lamplight and a bath was steaming in front of a small fireplace.

'There's clean towels and soap just here,' Linda said, pointing to the items in a nearby cabinet. 'If you hang your clothes out, they should dry soon too.'

'Thanks Linda,' Tash said, removing her sodden cloak and lying it over a chair near the fireplace.

'It's no trouble,' Linda reinforced, 'like I said, we rarely get Robins passing through our town. It's a pleasure to have you stay with us. I'll call you in a few hours when dinner's ready.'

Tash nodded and Linda departed, shutting the door behind her. With a sigh, Tash removed her clothes, hanging them out in the hopes that they would dry, as well as the items in her saddlebags that were wet through. Then she climbed into the bath, sinking contentedly into the hot water and allowing herself to relax. It had been a few days since she washed properly, and she intended to enjoy it while she could. Outside the rain fell down harder and the wind picked up, rattling the windowpane and making the inn sign snap back and forth, creaking repeatedly. Tash lay back, grateful that she had found refuge from the storm and didn't need to press on through this weather. Come morning, she would be on her way again, after she restocked at the local shop with enough supplies to last the remainder of her journey.

Chapter Seven

> ~ An extract from a widely distributed pamphlet in the town of Nordhaven

Tash was lying on her bed, feeling a mixture of sluggish fatigue and concern. The storm had not abated overnight as she had hoped. Nor had it stopped raining the next day, or the next. Linda had tried to bolster her spirits, saying that the weather in this region was often temperamental and that storms could last for days at a time before blowing over. Yet with each day that passed, Tash was painfully aware of the need to reach the Defoe Cliffs and the Barrier to Kinet. She also hadn't been sleeping well, plagued by nightmares of the cobalt-eyed man and the hooded figure whenever she shut her eyes. She would awaken, chest tight and face sweaty, an aching tiredness filling her as though she had not slept at all. When the older woman had noticed Tash's shadowed eyes the first morning, she had insisted that Tash drink a honeyed tea before bed each night to assist with sleep. Despite that, Tash still awoke unsettled and short tempered, resenting being confined to the inn because of the bad weather.

It didn't make it easier that the other members of the town barely spoke to her, often eyeing her with wary suspicion each time they entered the inn. They seemed unsure of how to act in the presence of a Robin, sometimes feeling confident to exchange a few words before they would drift away mid-sentence, awkward and shy once more. Tonight, the fourth night of Tash's stay, another family of travellers had entered the inn, lodging in the room next to hers.

This had been a welcome surprise for Tash, and she chatted with them all evening, watching the children play marbles by the hearth, learning about how they were heading south to Palinor, one of the larger southern cities in Venetica. The parents, Ophelia and Rufus, were travelling bards, and for a time they provided the inn with free entertainment. Ophelia played the flute and Rufus the fiddle, and their children soon jumped up and began dancing, pulling Tash into the fray. She had laughed and enjoyed spinning around with them, clapping and swaying to the tunes, feeling lighter than she had for a while. The other townspeople had watched from the bar and tables, not joining in but also not openly disapproving of the music.

It had been almost disappointing to say goodnight when the entertainment ended. Now as Tash lay on her sheets, she watched the rain outside and wondered if it would stop anytime soon. Surely it would. There was still time to reach the Defoe Cliffs, she didn't really need to panic yet. On the table by her bed rested the cup of steaming tea, currently untouched. For a moment she pondered drinking it, before her eyes slid shut and she fell into a light doze.

For the first time, Tash didn't have her usual nightmare. Instead, she was rudely awoken by a sharp banging at her window. She blinked and sat up blearily, disorientated by the sudden noise. She glanced up and bit back a shriek of shock as familiar crimson eyes glared at her through the glass.

The Dæmon mouthed words that were lost in the howling wind, but Tash understood what he wanted. Tentatively, she approached the window and opened it, indicating for him to enter, before stepping quickly back to avoid colliding with him as he swung into the room. His tail swept back and forth angrily and his glare made her start to regret letting him inside.

'What—' she began but he cut her off in a furious whisper.

'Don't. Speak.' Tash bridled at his tone and was about to retort when he lifted a hand to silence her. 'Just *listen*,' he breathed, head turning to the side. She paused, listening hard. At first there was no sound other than the weather outside, but then she heard a strange thumping sound from next door. Low cries and gurgling moans reached her through the wall separating the bedrooms. A sudden, high-pitched scream rent the air, making Tash jump in surprise. She recognised the voice as that of the younger of the children, and moved instinctively to the door to assist them if she could. When she turned the door handle it refused to budge and she was confused. It hadn't been locked when she retired to bed.

'You have to get your things, Natachatet,' the Dæmon hissed. 'There's nothing you can do for them now. You have to leave.'

'But, the storm—'

'Blast the storm,' the Dæmon snapped. 'Get your things together *quickly.*'

She stood frozen to the spot, as another scream pierced the night, and then was cut off abruptly. 'The children—'

'You can't help them, Natachatet,' the Dæmon pressed, yet still she didn't move. He let out an exasperated sigh and began to collect her bags for her, stuffing her clothing and shoes into the satchel. Tash refused to believe that she couldn't do anything. Something was happening next door and, as a Robin, it was her duty to investigate. She couldn't flee when people were in potential danger. Grabbing her dezmian from her bedside table, she flipped it, unlocking the door and slipping into the hallway before the Dæmon could react.

'Rufus?' she called, 'Ophelia?' She knocked on their door and it swung inwards, revealing a grisly sight. Blood splattered the walls and floor, the bedsheets were stained red and the corpses lay on the ground, horrified eyes wide and staring. A creature was sprawled across them, bent low over their necks and glanced upwards to see Tash in the doorway. It let out an eldritch cry and Tash heard footsteps from downstairs. Someone grabbed her hand and yanked her away from the scene. Tash couldn't react, following blindly in numb shock, as she re-entered her own room.

'Come *on*, Natachatet,' the Dæmon muttered, pulling on her hand. He had lifted her bags and they were almost at the open window when something silver shot through the air and impaled his left shoulder. The Dæmon cried out, stumbling and Tash looked back to see Jamison approaching, a maniacal glint in his eye, crossbow in his hands. The creature from next door was behind him, with its large, black eyes, long red hair and pointed teeth. As it stepped closer, Tash realised that it was a woman, but like no human woman she had ever seen before.

'Naughty Tash,' the creature hissed, 'naughty girl.'

'How do you know my name?' Tash asked, fear mounting in her throat.

The creature laughed harshly. 'I know many things about you, Robin. But you were just a means to an end. Jamison,' it turned to the man with the crossbow, 'she's all yours. You and your friends can share in the spoils. I hear that a Robin's blood can give one power beyond belief.'

'Yes, Linda,' Jamison replied and he rushed at Tash, who barely had time to react before he had caught her in his arms, pinning her against his side. Her dezmian dropped to the floor and she twisted, terrified, glancing from him to the creature, trying to understand. It couldn't be Linda— there was no resemblance to the kind, motherly woman who had been her companion over the past few days. How was it possible?

'Get away from her,' the Dæmon snarled, staggering to his feet. Linda smirked, licking the blood away from her lips obscenely. Tash shuddered and tried not to retch, stilling for a moment as Linda moved closer.

'What a pleasure it is to see you again, Cai,' she said sweetly, 'I hoped that you would favour us with your presence.' She turned to Tash, 'thank you for letting him inside, dear. You've been such a help.'

'You bitch,' the Dæmon grunted, yanking the crossbow bolt out from his shoulder. Linda's smile widened.

'It appears that your manners have not improved, Cai,' she chided, 'I had hoped that you would have learned from the last time.'

'I don't answer to you, witch,' the Dæmon snarled.

'But you will,' Linda replied coolly, as she waved her hand and Jamison began to drag Tash towards the door. 'Go and have your fun, Jamison. Make sure she's still breathing when you're done– I want to have the last drop. The past few nights have only whetted my appetite.' She cackled as Jamison nodded, grinning.

'No,' Tash struggled harder, 'get off me. *Let me go!*' Her arm broke free and she punched upwards, smashing against Jamison's nose and hearing a satisfactory crack. He cried out, hands raising to his face, the blow making him step backwards. Tash took her opportunity and kneed him savagely in the groin, before stomping down on the inside of his foot and he tumbled to the floor, moaning.

'You idiotic girl,' Linda hissed, raising her hand and summoning a ball of flame. 'Why can't you just *submit* and accept that once you arrive here, you never leave?'

'Natachatet!'

She turned as the flames shot towards her, adrenaline giving her the strength to run through the pain and take the Dæmon's outstretched hand. There was a screech behind them as they leapt through the window, out into the pouring rain and falling down to the ground below.

The Dæmon waved his free hand and their fall slowed, so that they landed with a sharp thump on the cobbles and then he was leading her towards the stable. The Willowings and horses were agitated by the noises from the inn, and Lir was trembling and distressed, pawing the ground anxiously.

'Hurry,' the Dæmon said brusquely, dumping the bags beside the stall. 'Get out of here.'

'What about you?' Tash asked, fumbling with the saddle straps as she began to attach them.

The Dæmon was already halfway out of the stable, but on hearing her question he paused and said, 'I'll distract them.'

She could hear shouting from the inn and then the Dæmon was gone, streaking through the night towards the sounds. Tash forced her hands to work faster, slinging the bags up behind the saddle and tying them. Lir was skittish and whickered, terrified.

'*Liebeshem*, we have to go,' she muttered desperately, pulling herself into the saddle.

'You've not been given permission to leave yet, Tash.' The cold voice ricocheted off the stable walls, and Tash saw the short figure blocking their path. Linda bared her sharp teeth, black eyes glistening hungrily. 'You're not allowed to *ever* leave.'

'Fly *liebeshem*,' Tash's voice had gone raspy, the cold clenching around her chest as she watched Linda's hands rise and twist in a circle, a strange green cloud swirling in mid-air before her. Tash didn't know what it was, but by the Gods she didn't want to find out. There was a scream from the square and something large and horned crashed into Linda's side, knocking her down. It was a bull with a shaggy hide and curved horns, its head lowered as it charged the fallen woman again, stamping down on her body with its cloven hooves.

Tash urged Lir forwards but the Willowing faltered, shying away from the beast as it turned glowing red eyes their way, letting out an angry bellow. Something whizzed through the air and struck the bull, distracting it and it turned away to charge the group of men brandishing makeshift weapons. The fallen woman on the ground began to twitch, limbs contorting into different positions as she began to shift form again.

'Fly, *liebeshem!* Tash wailed, and this time Lir obeyed, spreading his wings and swooping out of the stables, narrowly evading a clawed hand that reached up to grab him as they passed. There was a high-pitched scream of fury as they sped away into the night, wings beating as the rain sliced against them, the raindrops sharp against the skin. Tash burrowed her head in Lir's neck and cried, partly from pain, partly from guilt at not being able to help the travelling minstrels and partly from anger because she had been so, so stupid. How had she trusted so easily? Why hadn't she noticed the odd signs that something was off in that town?

Thunder cracked and lightning shot across the sky, lancing towards them, as though the Gods themselves wanted to punish her for what had happened. Lir swerved, narrowly missing the rush of energy, eyes wide with fear, but he pushed on, dodging the tempest's best efforts to strike them down.

Time passed in a blur, yet all Tash was aware of was that one moment it was pelting down with rain, wind tearing through her hair and thunder booming around her ears, and then it was silent, the sky clear and stars twinkling high above. The change was sudden and she glanced backwards, noting that the lights of Lower Quilton were gone, along with the storm. She let out a choked cry of relief, the tears flowing freely as they flew on, back towards the Whitewash which glistened in the moonlight, providing a beacon for them to follow.

***

Tash and Lir descended after a couple of hours, once she was sure that enough distance had been put between themselves and Lower Quilton. Tash didn't want to run the risk

82

of being caught again by either Jamison or Linda– whatever she really was. When she dismounted, she realised that her dezmian was still in her room in the inn, lying where it had been dropped when Jamison caught her.

'Thank goodness Romulus packed a spare,' she muttered to Lir, reaching into the bag and withdrawing it. 'I won't let this one go so easily.'

'I'm glad to hear it,' an exhausted voice said and Tash spun around to see the Dæmon. He was covered in blood, eyes sunken and one arm hung limp at his side. He sat down on the riverbank, biting back a gasp of pain. 'Perhaps you could create a fire,' he finally got out through gritted teeth, 'it's freezing.'

Tash obeyed, spinning the dezmian and feeling the familiar tug in the pit of her stomach as she summoned the magic to do her bidding. Her arm and back stung, reminding her of her own injuries which she needed to tend to. The conjured fire burned low and she bit her lip, able to now see clearly the deep lacerations across the Dæmon's skin.

'You're awfully quiet for once,' he grunted, pulling his tattered shirt over his head and dropping it into the Whitewash. 'It's that bad, is it?'

Tash flicked the dezmian to summon bandages, a linen cloth and a jar of poultice and, on noticing the Dæmon's raised eyebrows, she said defensively, 'I've never tended wounds like these with magic. I don't trust myself to do it right.' She eyed the lacerations, 'what happened?' Her voice had become a mere whisper.

The Dæmon snorted roughly. 'It's probably better not to ask, Natachatet.' He bent down and lifted the tattered remains of his shirt from the water, wringing it out one-handed.

'Here, let me.'

Tash wasn't quite sure why she reached out and put a hand on his arm, but her touch stilled him immediately. Cautiously, she rinsed the cloth in the river and then began to wash the wounds, aware of how the Dæmon became tense, neither moving nor flinching as she tended to his injuries. It struck her as strange that she seemed to accept his appearance by her fireside now, whereas days before it had been shocking. Tonight he had helped her to escape, and she knew that if he hadn't, she would still be stuck in Lower Quilton.

'Tell me what happened.' She wanted to distract herself from the silence between them, to understand the events of the night now that she was far enough away to feel safe.

'You could say please,' he hissed as he caught his breath. She glared at him and he rolled his eyes in defeat. 'Fine.' Tash allowed herself a small smile of victory as he continued, 'The men in the town put up quite a fight. When the witch joined in, it was all I could do to get away.'

'You were the bull,' Tash clarified, 'how were you able to change your shape like that?'

He chuckled, but his voice sounded tired and heavy. 'It's one of the quirks of my condition. Surely you've read about how Nightwalkers shapeshift to lure in their victims.'

'Yes,' Tash replied softly. 'I have.'

'Then you shouldn't be surprised when it happens,' he said.

'What was that place?' She opened the jar of poultice and began to rub it over the wounds, ignoring his short gasp of pain.

'It was a place I warned you to avoid,' he growled. 'I *warned* you, Natachatet. What possessed you to go there?'

'I needed to resupply,' she retorted, anger and guilt at his words rising quickly. 'Plus, there was the storm.'

'That *storm*,' the Dæmon snapped, 'wouldn't have bothered you if you had been wearing your yew ring. I remember I *also* recommended that you keep it on.'

'It fell off when I was sleeping,' Tash said defensively, 'I had it in my bag.'

'But *not* on your finger,' he sighed. 'If it was in your bag then it wouldn't have made a difference. She was able to lure you into her trap and use you as a temporary chattel.'

'A *what?*' Tash paused in her ministrations, disgust rising at his words.

'That town wasn't normal, Natachatet,' the Dæmon said with forced patience. 'Just like the storm wasn't natural. It was all part of the witch's game, to lure travellers in and trap them.'

'But what do you mean by *chattel?*'

He gave a half shrug of his shoulders, then flinched in pain. 'She's a witch— a powerful one. She feeds on human flesh and blood, and her minions have been either enchanted or seduced by her power to follow in her ways.'

'I don't understand.' The words came out automatically, but they weren't entirely true. Tash was starting to see the truth and it was terrifying.

'I'd hazard a guess that she gave you something to sleep,' he said, 'each night I came to your window, trying to wake you up. And I'd see her crouched over you, feasting.'

His fists clenched, the claws digging into the skin all too easily and causing more blood to flow. Tash paused and held them, 'stop. You're hurting yourself.'

Slowly the claws withdrew from the flesh, leaving jagged marks and Tash began to tend to them too, the shock his words had caused taking time to absorb. 'How come I didn't have any injuries when I awoke?'

'She healed the superficial wounds,' the Dæmon said, voice shaking with suppressed anger. 'That way you wouldn't know. She enjoyed putting on a show– it was all part of her plan.'

'Why couldn't you stop her?' Tash was confused now, 'You said you were outside my window each night, why didn't you just come in and stop her?'

'It seems your studying didn't turn up that particular gem of information,' the Dæmon said sardonically. 'Nightwalkers can't enter a building unless invited by a Mortal. It's part of our curse.'

Tash had begun to wind the bandages around his wounds now, starting with his hands and then moving to his arms and chest. 'So that was why you were trying to wake me up,' she mused, trying to ignore the fact that she was far too close to him for comfort.

'Repeatedly,' he growled again.

'So, tonight, when I didn't drink the tea, and the other family had arrived…'

'She was distracted,' the Dæmon said curtly. 'There were children in that family. When she descended into dark magic, she went mad and took pleasure from preying on the inno-cent. She's always preferred children.'

Tash felt the bile rise again in her throat as she remem-bered the scene in the bards' room. The blood, the echoing screams in her ears, the terrified, sightless eyes…

She was jolted back when the Dæmon touched her hand, anchoring her once more in the present. 'I'm sorry you had to see what you did,' he said quietly.

'How do you know what I saw?' Tash's voice was tight, the tears burning in her eyes. She hadn't realised that he had been behind her in the hallway, too focussed she had been on the scene in the adjoining chamber.

'I've seen this witch before,' he said with surprising gentleness. 'I've seen what she has done.'

Tash looked away and tied the final bandage, hoping that he hadn't seen the watery glint in her eyes. She edged back and winced, her own injuries demanding to be tended to.

'Let me see,' the Dæmon said, correctly interpreting her reaction.

'No,' Tash said quickly, 'I mean, I… it's…'

He raised his eyes to the sky in exasperation. 'I think when you have been injured, you don't need to worry about modesty, Natachatet.'

She blushed. He sighed, 'Turn around. You won't be able to reach the burns on your back without help.'

'Close your eyes,' she said and he obeyed, but not after a soft chuckle. Cautiously, she pulled off her cloak, which had been scorched and torn, and then had to pull down the top of her nightdress which proved tricky. Her burned flesh had stuck to the fabric and the pain became excruciating. Tears were now well and truly rolling down her cheeks and she bit back a sob as the dress caught on one of the burns on her upper arm.

'Here.' His touch was surprisingly gentle as he took over, removing the fabric from the wounds with quick efficiency.

'I asked you to close your eyes,' she grumbled.

'I did,' he murmured, concentrating, 'but it's pretty difficult to tend to your injuries when I can't see.' She gave a humph in response, unwilling to admit that he had a point.

There was a smile in his voice as he continued, 'It's not as bad as I originally thought. It should heal pretty quickly.'

Tash was relieved to hear it. As he bent over her, she remembered what Linda had said at the inn and asked, 'How did you know Linda? What does she want with you?'

He was silent for a moment, then said, 'I've known her my whole life. That's all I'm able to say.'

'Why did she call you Cai?' Tash was curious now, as a prickling sensation spread across her back and shoulder.

'Perhaps because it is my name,' he replied wryly. Tash blinked, realising belatedly how stupid her question had been. Of course it made sense that he had a name– how could she have assumed that he didn't? 'You seem surprised,' Cai said sardonically. 'You didn't honestly think that I would respond to *Dæmon* or *Nightwalker*, did you?'

'Of course not,' she lied, cringing inside at the fact that she *had*. He laughed.

'You're a terrible liar, Natachatet.'

Oh Gods, could tonight get any worse? Cai pulled away from behind her and his absence made her feel strangely bereft.

'I'd recommend putting another dress on,' he said brusquely, 'that nightdress is ruined. And I'll close my eyes.'

Tash reached behind her and felt the spot where the burns had spread across her back, checking her shoulder and arm which were now as good as new. 'You used magic to heal me?' she asked, perplexed, as she reached into her bag and withdrew another gown which she pulled on. 'How come you didn't just heal your own injuries?'

He laughed again, 'I'll let you ponder that one, Natachatet.'

She glared at his turned back, but found that she couldn't keep it up for long. Despite herself, something had changed tonight between them and she couldn't ignore it.

'Cai,' she said tentatively and, on hearing his name, he turned slightly to look at her. 'Thank you for helping me tonight.'

He gave small inclination of the head; a minor acknowledgement of her words and she felt a weight lift from her chest. She moved back over to the fireside, rummaged in her bag and withdrew the yew ring, which she pushed back on her finger. He watched her do so without speaking, but she could sense his approval. Tash flipped her dezmian and conjured a bedroll, which she settled into, exhausted from the night's events. On the riverbank, Cai stretched out on the outskirts of the glow of firelight, his good arm under his head, gazing up at the stars.

'Cai,' she said quietly, 'wake me if any monsters come, won't you?'

He chuckled, 'You've already got one here, Natachatet. But rest assured, I'll alert you if any more come.'

She frowned as her eyes closed, thinking that, perhaps this time, he was mistaken.

Chapter Eight

In some cultures, Nightwalkers are harbingers of doom, whereas in others they are considered to be an omen of impending change. The question, therefore, amongst scholars is how and why such contrasting stories came into being. From my own experience, I find that these creatures will only step in and engage with Mortals when they have an investment in the affair. Usually, they will not interfere in man's quarrels but, on occasion, they have offered warnings.

It is my belief that they could be of use to us, that together the magic between a Robin and a Nightwalker could cause a previously unseen shift in the cosmos. Whether that would be for good or ill, I cannot be certain. But surely we should seek to collaborate with such creatures instead of reviling them.

~ An extract from a speech delivered by Corvis as an
apprentice to his teachers

The birdsong woke Tash from the first peaceful night slumber she had had in days. She yawned and stretched, sitting up to glance over at the riverbank only to find it empty. Cai had vanished with the night, leaving no trace behind and she felt slightly disappointed at his absence.

'It would have been nice if he'd said goodbye,' she muttered to Lir, who was munching contentedly on the nearby grass. She flicked her dezmian and the campsite disappeared as she mounted, urging him upwards. The morning air banished the remaining sleepiness away quickly, leaving her cheeks flushed and eyes bright. Perhaps Lir understood that they needed to catch up on missed time, for he pushed onwards for longer stretches than they had done previously. Today, the only time they paused was to resupply in a small town, whose bustling market provided them the opportunity to get fresh fruit and vegetables. Lir rested in the town's stables for an hour as Tash ate a pork pie and restocked not only on food but also on tea and clothing, since her cloak and nightdress had been damaged beyond repair the night before.

Arms laden with a heavy bag, she returned to Lir and spread the weight evenly among the saddlebags. Tash's new cloak was a vibrant red, interwoven with scarlet thread, and fell around her in heavy folds, the hood lined with dark fur. As they returned on their way, it flew out behind her, like a crimson flag waving across the sky.

The new weight on Lir's back tired him even faster and so they descended again in the mid-afternoon. This time, though, Tash dismounted and led him along the riverbank, and he followed meekly, although he eyed the lush grass greedily at times as they walked.

'Come on *liebeshem*,' Tash murmured, after she had pulled him away from the delicious treat for the third time. 'You'll have time to eat when we stop for the night.'

On foot, their progress was slow, yet Tash still felt better moving rather than remaining still. A part of her was scared that they would be followed, although perhaps she was growing paranoid after the experience in Lower Quilton. Lir snuffled grumpily, tugging away from Tash's arm, indicating a rather tasty patch of clover and she smiled despite herself.

'Come, Lir,' she repeated, halting his movement with a brush of the hand and leading him on. The Whitewash spread away before them, wide plains on either side of its banks as far as the eye could see. There was nowhere for them to hide for miles and that made Tash nervous. They were too exposed. If Linda or Jamison and his cronies tracked them, it would be all too easy to follow their trail once they reached the plains. Tash regretted telling the witch her destination, rebuking herself for the millionth time for being too trusting. Most of all, she resented how helpless she had felt– how she'd been unable to help the bards who had simply had the misfortune of being at the wrong place at the wrong time. If Cai hadn't come when he did, if she hadn't forgotten to drink the tea last night, it didn't bear imagining what her fate would have been. Tash shivered, despite the warm cloak and gentle sunlight, anxiety piercing her stomach with sharp talons. She took a deep breath, trying to remain calm, forcing the memories down, desperate to not lose control, to keep her composure and walk on without falling to pieces. Yet the images flicked through her mind, taunting her with each gory detail, and she eventually succumbed, retching into the high grass, shaking convulsively.

When she finished, she splashed her face and rinsed her mouth with water, spitting it out onto the ground. Her throat was scratchy and aching, her stomach tender and her eyes burned. She leaned against Lir's side, legs unsteady beneath her. Sensing her weakness, he knelt down, encouraging her to get into the saddle. She wrapped her fingers through his mane as he rose and lifted them into the air, skimming the surface of the Whitewash with his hooves. Tash lowered her head against his neck and allowed herself to rest in that state between sleep and waking as the sun began to descend across the sky.

Lir halted as the sun set, settling down on the bank in a spot that was bordered with high, waving grass. Even though they had not left the plains, Tash was sure that they would soon and that calmed her anxiety. She flipped her dezmian, conjuring the familiar campsite and set to work, cooking some of the supplies she had bought earlier that day. She was halfway through a rather watery soup of boiled vegetables with an extra lacing of salt, when Cai emerged from the grass.

The only warning she had to his presence was Lir's response, a second before he appeared. The Willowing snorted and pawed the ground, dislodging the blanket that was resting over his back in his distress. Cai eyed him dispassionately as he stalked closer, until he reached the riverbank and sat down, casting a glance around the plains for any strange movements.

'Good evening,' Tash said pointedly, recalling that he had left without a word that morning and he still hadn't spoken. She took another spoon of soup and then gestured to the pot by the fire, 'want some?'

He raised an eyebrow sardonically, 'Thanks but I've already eaten.'

In a flash she remembered what the books said about his diet and she felt sickened. 'You mean…'

'I caught a rabbit,' he said roughly. 'Despite what you've read, I try not to drink human blood. Not all monsters are like that witch.'

His defensiveness shocked her, partly because she hadn't even connected him and the witch together in her mind. Already they were different, while both creatures of the night, their similarities ended there.

'I didn't mean...'

'Just eat,' he said brusquely. 'You need your strength.'

She obeyed, albeit grudgingly. Now she felt a sense of shame that he believed she thought him to be a monster. Cai had turned away, gazing out over the Whitewash, the bandages partially hidden by his grimy, tattered shirt. She watched him as she ate, while he pointedly avoided her gaze.

'You didn't say goodbye this morning,' she finally said curtly, irritated now that he was refusing to look at her.

'I wasn't aware that you would want me to,' he said coolly. 'There were no disturbances for me to see the need to wake you.'

She bit her lip, uncertain why his words hurt and chose her response carefully, trying to ensure that her voice wouldn't reveal the turn of her thoughts. 'It was a surprise that you weren't there. I didn't know if something had happened.'

'Were you worried?' His voice had turned slightly mocking, and he looked at her, red eyes glinting.

'No.' She answered abruptly and his mouth twisted upward wryly. Tash was flustered now and frantically scanned her thoughts for something– anything– to say. 'How were you able to find me so easily?'

'Tonight, or just in general?' Cai asked drily. Tash shrugged at the question,

'In general, I guess. You seem to find me without much trouble. I don't want others to track me so easily.'

'They won't.' His voice was so certain that it brooked no argument. 'She seemed like the kind of witch who is content to remain in one spot. I doubt you'll see her again. She's spent too much time getting that town just the way she likes it to move on.'

His answer did little to calm Tash's nerves or appease her curiosity. 'But how can you be sure?'

He shrugged. 'I can't. But there's little point in worrying about things that haven't happened.'

She was silent for a while, pinning him with a suspicious look. 'Then tell me how *you* find me so easily. Nightwalkers are supposedly good trackers, but at times its unnatural how you seem to *know* where I will be.'

He chuckled. 'I travel through different means to yourself, Natachatet. As you have remarked before, I cannot fly. It is painful to be in open daylight, but not impossible. The shadows provide me with the best means of crossing distances. One simply needs to know where the doorways are and then follow the correct paths to avoid getting lost. Plus,' he smiled, turning back towards the Whitewash, 'the scent of you and the Willowing make it easy to track you.'

Tash blinked, then surreptitiously sniffed under her arm. Did she really smell *that* bad? It seemed no worse than usual after a day of travel. She frowned and as she looked up, realised that he was shaking with silent laughter.

'You could just have told me to take a bath,' she snapped grumpily, reaching into her bag for some soap and a washcloth.

He couldn't control his laughter now. 'It won't make a difference how much you wash, Natachatet. Besides, there's no way I would tell you such a thing. I don't want to go for a swim in the Whitewash again anytime soon.'

She spluttered in anger as she got to her feet and stomped away through the grass to the riverbank. 'Turn around and shut your eyes,' she snapped, feeling particularly self-conscious since he'd mentioned her *scent*.

He lifted his arms in defeat and obeyed, giving her the privacy she requested. Hurriedly, Tash stripped out of her dress, shoes and stockings, splashing herself with river water and shivering at the biting cold before lathering soap all over.

'It won't make any difference,' Cai said tauntingly, 'although washing will make it a nicer scent to follow.'

'You really know how to speak to women, don't you?' Tash snarled, rinsing the soap away and drying herself with the washcloth savagely. 'Where's some of that Nightwalker charm, I'd love to know.'

'Must have lost it overnight,' he replied.

'No doubt,' she retorted. 'What else did the books say about your kind that was a gross exaggeration?'

'Probably a great many things, no doubt,' he mused, lying back and gazing up at the night sky.

'*Shut your eyes!*' Tash shrieked and Lir let out a sharp cry at her raised voice.

'I can't see anything, Natachatet,' Cai said reasonably and she ground her teeth as she pulled her stockings and dress back on. Shooting Cai a baleful glare, she strode over to Lir and settled him with a gentle caress.

'*Liebeshem*, calm. Steady now.' Under her hand, the Willowing quietened and knelt down, preparing to sleep. She pulled his blanket over his back and then returned to the fireside, placing the shoes down by her bag. Cai had turned his head to watch her and she met his gaze, hoping that he would be able to sense her indignation. Instead, he chuckled again and looked back up at the stars that were starting to wink across the sky. Tash muttered several words under her breath as she lay back too, and if he heard them, he didn't respond.

'Ikaros is bright tonight,' he said finally, breaking the silence and Tash glanced upwards, seeing the star in question flickering high above them.

'It's said to bring good fortune,' she said. 'Let's hope that's true.'

'Perhaps.' She turned to face him, confused at how his mood had changed as swiftly as the tides. Noticing her attention, he grunted, 'What?'

'What's wrong?' she asked, 'You sound bitter about something.'

He snorted, 'Don't put too much faith in stars, that's all. Just like the Gods. You should look out for yourself if you want to have good fortune in life. It'll save a lot of time and disappointment.'

'*That* sounds like a healthy outlook,' Tash said sarcastically.

'You have no idea,' he snarled, eyes turning feral and she felt a momentary spike of fear. She sat up to face him, tamping down the reaction and crossed her arms. Darkness was swirling around his features now, half obscuring him from sight.

'Then explain it,' she demanded hotly. 'Tell me.'

Through the shadows, she saw the angry gleam in his eyes fade to a smouldering glow and his lips tightened. 'I don't answer to you, Robin.' His words were like acid, burning into her heart and she clenched her fists angrily.

'Fine,' she snapped, 'then *go*. I didn't ask for you to come here anyway. Leave me alone.' He got to his feet, swept a mocking bow and vanished into the night, leaving Tash to vent her frustration to the stars above alone.

Chapter Nine

For weeks now I've dreamed of her. The witch who cursed this form upon me. She laughs, taunting me of how this fate befell my father and his father.

Growing up, I always wondered about my father. My mother couldn't remember him. Knowing what I do now, perhaps he did that to her to relieve the pain of his absence, or to erase bad memories. I guess I'll never know.

Then the dream changes. The witch is replaced by a girl, one who— if I had a heart anymore— might make it pause a moment. Her skin's a rich brown, she's slender and riding a Willowing at breakneck speed. Her hair is darker than the deepest night, braided back and her eyes flash with joy as she laughs mid-flight. Is she an illusion? Another witch's trick? It's at that moment that I awaken, just as her gaze meets mine and she smiles.

~ An extract from a newer diary, well hidden in the deep recesses of the Shadow Realm

The ocean was crashing on the rocks far below her, glorious and vast. The Defoe Cliffs stretched out, chalky white and majestic, rising up from the churning waves. Since she had arrived, Tash had kept her eyes open for any sign of Dragutash, just in case Linda's warning had in fact been real. To her relief, there hadn't been any evidence of the foul creatures, no crushed earth or splintered trees. Tash sat up straight, hair catching in the blustery wind, shading her eyes as she searched for the faintest of glimmers in the air, the sign that a Barrier was nearby. By her calculation she still had time before the Barrier to Kinet moved, although she had cut it fine.

'Where is it, Lir?' she pondered aloud, casting her gaze back and forth. Her Willowing lifted up, following the edge of the cliff as she searched above and below, twisting in the saddle. Finally, she caught a glimpse of it– a haze rising through the air not half a mile away. With a whoop of celebration, she urged Lir on, her excitement and exhilaration filling her voice as she began to sing in the Ancient Tongue, calling on the Doorway to appear in the Barrier. By the time they had reached it, there was an opening for them to pass through and they didn't hesitate, sweeping onwards as the Doorway closed behind them.

The world around them fell away and in a moment they were no longer above grey waves, but a dry wasteland, half-dead shrubs and grasses spreading out below, populated with stunted, wizened trees. Tash gasped, recognising a familiar rocky outline on the horizon. A sense of foreboding filled her as they drew closer, memories flooding back that she had thought were long gone.

'Oh *liebeshem*,' she murmured, 'what's happened?'

They flew over a dried-up riverbed, the soil cracked and dusty. Ahead of them the mountain ranges came closer, jagged peaks reaching upwards to the sky. As a child, Tash had tried to climb them, eager to look out over the world and see what lay beyond. It had been one of the few escapes from her parents and siblings, but when food had become scarce, she hadn't been able to climb as far, too quickly fatigued by hunger.

Now, thirteen years had passed since she had set foot on this land and she had never intended to return. It seemed that the Gods had a sense of humour, opening the Doorway here, in the place she had long wanted to avoid. She glanced at the sky, noting the sunset sending out burnt tendrils of gold and orange, and knew that she would need to stop for the night.

'Let's see if they will recognise me, Lir,' she murmured, as the distant huts came into sight, a motley collection of shacks and lean-tos. 'I'll just make sure not to mention this to The Robin when I return to the Temple. If he doesn't know I've seen them again, it won't hurt him.' They had landed a way out from the village, and it struck Tash as odd that there was no sign of smoke from cooking fires. No sound came from the huts as they approached, not the crying or wailing that she remembered. Deep inside her, concern unfurled and she dismounted from Lir's back, her pace increasing.

'Hello?' she called, 'Is anyone there?'

There was no response from the town as she reached the first hut, peering around for any sign of life, but there was nothing. Something wasn't right.

'*Ama?*' she cried, '*Pare?*' In her desperation, she began to run, the cold chill knowledge of her people's fate starting to descend. She checked hut after hut, at first knocking then opening doors when there was no answer. No one re-sponded to her voice, and as she peered into each shack she passed, she saw dust and decay, remnants of a people who were now crumbling away.

'*Ama!*' she shouted, '*Pare!*' Her feet led her down a path that had once been as familiar as breathing. The small, ramshackle hut was squeezed into the mountainside, the eaves splintered and brittle, and the door hung off its hinges, revealing the shadowy interior. Tash's face drained as there was no response and her heart plummeted. Her hand shook slightly as she reached out and pushed the door further open.

She flipped her dezmian, summoning a light to hover in mid-air as she entered, taking in the devastation. It was like something had rampaged through the hut, overturning furniture and leaving deep lacerations in the walls. She stepped over the dust and debris, searching for anything that would give a clue about her family's fate. The light caught on a faded stain on the wall as she entered the communal bedroom, which once upon a time had been cramped with far too many bodies. There was a snapping sound under her foot and she looked down, before recoiling, a primal scream ripping out of her chest. She sank down in the doorway, unable to control the grief and tears that spilled out of her, racking her body back and forth with guttural sobs. The bones glowed white in the dust, jumbled together in strange piles, as though animals had scattered them at some point over the years.

'Natachatet?'

His voice pierced the darkness, full of concern. She wailed, covering her face as she wept, unable to form words through her pain. His footsteps drew closer, running to her side and then he was there, arms enfolding her in his warmth. She reached out blindly, gripping him like an anchor in the riptide of emotions. Tash didn't know how long Cai held her for, how long she cried out the anguish of discovering her family's demise. This wasn't the homecoming she could ever have foreseen.

The first words she was aware of speaking were, 'Get me out of here.'

He obeyed silently, helping her up and supporting her arm as they left the hut and its skeletal occupants behind. Tash wanted to get as far from her hometown as possible, which had become a graveyard many long years ago.

Lir followed them to the outskirts of town, where Cai paused and sat her down on a low rock, creating the familiar campfire with ease. Tash shook uncontrollably, the tears had finally stopped but her eyes were wide with shock, glazed and blankly staring. After a while, Cai knelt beside her, a mug of chai tea in his hands.

'Here, Natachatet,' he said gently. 'Drink.'

She took it mutely, like a young child, and drank. He withdrew some of her supplies and set to preparing a meal, glancing at her from time to time to ensure she was still drinking the tea. Tash started to come back to herself when he placed a steaming bowl in front of her and indicated for her to eat. Gradually, she did so, not because she was hungry but out of habit. Her rational side told her that she should have expected this— after years of drought and starvation, surely the fate of her village should not be so shocking. Yet there was something about coming back, about seeing the devastation herself, and her family's remains that was more confronting than she had thought possible.

'What is this place, Natachatet?' Cai asked quietly. 'Where are we?'

She took a while to reply, the ability to focus struggling in the aftermath of her discovery. When she did speak, her tone was bitter and cracked, much like the dry earth beneath them.

'This was my birthplace. My home before Romulus came and took me away to the Temple.' She cast a look at the ghostly huts, silent sentinels in the darkness. 'I grew up in that hut, with my brothers and sisters.'

'Ah.' There was a realm of understanding in the word and she felt something in her snap.

'I don't want your pity,' she said with forceful intensity.

He sat next to her, not too close for his presence to be intrusive, but close enough for her to feel ashamed at the expression in his eyes. 'I don't pity you, Natachatet.' He spoke softly, 'I know what it's like to lose one's family and friends.'

'I'm sorry,' she whispered, voice breaking. 'I just… I can't…'

'You don't have to explain,' he said calmly. 'You don't even need to talk if you don't want to.'

'Thanks,' she managed. Cai smiled and cleared up the bowl and cooking pot, vanishing them back into thin air.

'I'll watch over you tonight,' he said. 'Try to get some rest.'

She looked at him, noticing that the bandages had gone, leaving faint scars behind. 'You got better.' It distracted her from the grief for a moment, and he glanced down at the tattered shirt and healed arm before shrugging.

'Magic always speeds up the process,' he said lightly. 'Besides, Nightwalkers are difficult to kill, as the writers say.'

At the mention of killing, her face tautened as she remembered the scene in her family's hut. An hour after the discovery, she had had time to process what she had seen and her rational mind was starting to reassert control over her emotions. 'Unlike Mortals. We're too easily hurt.' He fell silent, watching her cautiously as she continued, 'Something was here, Cai. Something that shouldn't have been here. There were… marks on the wall. No human could have made them.'

'I didn't see any,' he said, frowning. Tash bowed her head, realising that when he had appeared, he had only been focussed on her. The knowledge spread warmth through her, along with something else that she couldn't describe. It made her nervous, a quickening of the pulse that beat even harder than before, and she was suddenly grateful that he couldn't read her thoughts.

'I'll have a look,' he said, abruptly rising to his feet and leaving her by the fire. Tash opened her mouth, about to ask him to stay, but bit her tongue, remaining silent as he strode away, back towards the village. Lir whickered and nudged her shoulder comfortingly, and Tash lifted her hand to stroke his muzzle absently, gazing after Cai.

He wasn't gone for long, but it was enough time for her to start to feel anxious. Tash didn't want to be alone tonight; she didn't want to relive entering her family home and hearing the snapping of bones under her shoe. It made her feel sick. She kept glancing at the spot where Cai had disappeared, keen for him to return. When he did, his expression was grim and he didn't speak.

'Do you know what caused it?' Tash asked immediately as he sank back down onto the ground and tossed a log onto the fire. His tail flicked in the dirt, a small wave of dust rising from where it traced the dry earth.

'It looks like the work of Dragutash,' he said, brow creased in thought.

'How is that possible?' Tash asked, voice catching in her throat. 'They're only in Venetica, aren't they?'

Slowly, Cai shook his head. 'No, they've spread across several worlds. They have a habit of slipping through Doorways which are left open for too long. It only looked like the work of one Dragutash, though. A herd would have left nothing standing.' He met her worried gaze, 'The other houses had similar markings inside. I think it's a safe bet to assume that the creature came through a Doorway, probably many years ago. There's no sign that the creature is still here.'

'Do you mean,' Tash could barely get the words out, 'that when Romulus took me away, he might've... a Dragutash may have...'

'Come through the Doorway?' Cai clarified and she nodded. 'Possibly. But remember that Barriers shift constantly, Natachatet. It's just as likely that the beast came through another Doorway, and began to lay waste to what it found in its path.'

Tash nodded, wanting to believe that what he said was true. It was too much to think that, by leaving this town, she had been part of the reason why a Dragutash got into Kinet and destroyed everything. Cai touched her arm, 'It's not your fault, Natachatet. You've got to remember that.' Tash wasn't so sure, the memories of her life before Romulus took her away returning to linger in her mind. She felt tainted by what had happened, her grasp on her emotions fragile and she thought that, with the slightest push, she would lose control again.

'Still,' she murmured, the words spilling out after being held back for so long, 'at times I wanted something to happen to them. My parents. I resented them for so many years, I never wanted to come back. Robins aren't supposed to see their families again once they join the Order anyway, but I thought that if I did, I would return successful, showing them what I could amount to under the care of someone who gave a damn.' Cai's grip tightened infinitesimally, as she continued, staring into the flames, 'At times I hated them. They were selfish and so absorbed in each other that they never saw, they never cared…' She broke off, the bitter resentment rising like bile. 'They should never have had children. Not in a town like this, not when the drought made times hard and it became more difficult to get through each day. Yet, after all these years, I never expected to find them like *this*.'

She fell silent, trying to process the mixture of grief, shock and anger that still lingered. Cai's hand remained on her arm, grounding her, and she appreciated it, sensing that in this moment, quiet compassion was all she could manage.

'How did you find me?' she asked finally, when her emotions were once more safely pushed down. 'After the other night, I thought I wouldn't see you anymore. I'm sorry about what I said.'

'I wasn't completely blameless either,' he said softly, 'but some things are challenging to talk about. You're one of the few people in many years who has wanted to know. It's not something I'm used to.' He removed his hand from her arm and hugged his knees to his chest, leaving her missing his absence. 'I never really left you,' he admitted, his voice low, 'I kept tabs, checking on your progress just in case…' He drifted off for a moment, the darkness descending over his features and blocking his expression from view. 'When I heard you cry out, I didn't care if you'd be angry about my intrusion. I needed to know that you were alright.'

'Why do I matter so much?' Tash probed, trying to make out his reaction through the darkness, but it had become impenetrable. When he responded, it was in a shuttered tone, and she knew that he would not tell her more, even if she asked.

'You need to help the people in Nordhaven. Their town is at risk of a similar fate,' he waved a hand at the remnants of her village, 'I'd prefer it if they didn't suffer like that.'

She absorbed his words and nodded, before moving to her bedroll, spreading it out beside the fire and settling down onto her side, facing him. 'Alright.' She was sure that they both knew she was conceding tonight, that she chose not to pursue the issue to find out the truth. But she would keep it in mind for a later time, perhaps when he would be more amenable to sharing his true motives.

The darkness around his features shifted briefly and she saw the faint glimpse of a smile before it was hidden again. 'And thank you,' she said, propping her cheek against her arm for a makeshift pillow, 'for being here. I don't want to be alone tonight.'

'I'll keep watch,' he said. 'Never fear.'

She smiled as she shut her eyes. 'Just don't forget to say goodbye in the morning,' she murmured, 'goodnight, Cai.'

'Goodnight, Natachatet.' Hearing him say her full name was starting to rankle, and as she drifted off to sleep, she wondered why she didn't ask him to call her Tash instead.

***

He was there when she woke, just as she had requested, but only briefly to wish her speed in her travels and then he disappeared, fading away into the shadows in the silent village. Tash didn't wait around to see where he went, hastening to prepare Lir to leave immediately. She was determined to put this town of ghosts behind her as soon as possible.

Yet, first some rites had to be performed. She had to respect the old faith– all Robins did. As part of their vows, she had committed to upholding it and so she drew the five-pointed star in the dirt, kneeling in the centre and bowing to each point, twisting around in the dust. She lifted her hands, palms raised as she intoned in the Ancient Tongue, calling on the Gods to guide the departed souls to the world beyond. She asked for respite for the rain-starved land, for the plants that had once been lush and bountiful. Finally, she asked for peace for the fallen, to allow them to rest easy at long last. When she was done, the sun had risen and Lir was pawing the ground, eager to leave. Tash rose to her feet, wiping her cheeks dry, and they soared high over the rocky crags she had once climbed so often, until her ruined hometown was lost from sight.

For three days she flew, only stopping in towns to resupply and ask for directions, learning that Nordhaven was in the northwest of Kinet. Rumours had reached villagers already of the blight and the strange fungus, and many made a sign of protection when talking about it, as if they feared a similar situation reaching their own towns. Tash didn't stay in anymore inns, preferring to sleep rough, although Cai did not return to the fireside. She began to wonder if she had offended him in some way, if perhaps he truly was only interested in her reaching Nordhaven safely and there was nothing else causing him to seek her out.

It didn't make it better that her nightmare had begun to return, so each night she was tormented by the terrified face of the cobalt-eyed man, begging her for help before she awoke. The dreams confused her, especially since she still had no idea who he was or how she could help him. Tash tried to push his face from her mind, resolving that if– on the off chance– she met him in her travels, she would help, but until then she had a task to complete. The Robin was relying on her to assist the people in Nordhaven, and Cai seemed particularly invested in the situation being resolved sooner rather than later.

She had reread the two missives The Robin had received, to remind herself what she should expect to find. Pensively, she had traced the writing of the second letter, realising that Cai had probably been the author. It would explain his investment in the situation, but she still wondered why he cared. She had so many unanswered questions and it seemed unlikely that he would be prepared to answer any of them.

Finally, after long days and short nights, Tash and Lir stood on the paved road just outside of Nordhaven. Beyond the town lay Nordhaven Heath, a wild mass of sprawling heather, rolling hills and clusters of trees spreading as far as she could see. On this side of the town, however, the signs of the blight were plain. The fields lay fallow, crops curled and dry, and Tash could see evidence of the fungus growing in abundance.

'Don't go near it, *liebeshem*,' she murmured into Lir's ear and he whinnied in agreement, as they made their way into Nordhaven. The houses were closely packed in the town, unlike the sprawling farmsteads that dotted the ruined fields. Villagers with hollowed cheeks and shadowed eyes watched from the doorways as she passed them by, some shutting the doors immediately, while others followed her with a desperate hope. A group of children who had been playing in the street paused at her approach and then clustered around Lir, reaching out with grubby hands to touch his wings and neck. Lir was unsettled by the attention and Tash calmed him with a few softly spoken words.

'Let Jervois know that the Robin has arrived,' one of the women following Tash called to one of the boys, who nodded and sped off.

'She's arrived, she's arrived,' the villagers repeated, some sounding excited, others desperate.

'You're going to make everything just like it was, aren't you?' one of the children asked eagerly.

'I'll do my best,' Tash replied. 'But I think I need to speak to your leader first– Jervois, I take it?'

'Jervois is the mayor,' one of the men said, pulling his cap over his eyes to shade himself from the sunlight. 'Been ranting on about getting one of your kind here for a while now.' He spat on the ground, 'Took you long enough to get here though. Robins have their own schedules.'

Tash was taken aback by his hostility, but one of the women intervened, 'hush, Klem. She's just arrived.'

'She didn't arrive in time to save my Lilith, did she?' Klem barked angrily, 'No, Robins come and go as they please. They don't care about us commonfolk.'

'That's not true,' Tash said, cutting off his tirade. 'I'm here to help.'

Klem snorted, turned away and stalked off, disgusted. 'Don't mind Klem, miss,' the woman who had intervened said, stepping forward cautiously. She was tall, with faded, stringy hair and weary eyes. 'He's not been himself since the blight took his Lilith. She was only five summers old. She was playing near the fields and… well, he hasn't been the same since.'

'I'm so sorry,' Tash whispered, horrified.

'You're here now,' the woman said, 'that's what matters. We don't want more of our own to fall sick– he'll see that your arrival is a blessing, in time.'

Tash wasn't so sure. There had been something in Klem's gaze that scared her, something that went beyond grief and fear.

'I'm Mellie,' the woman said, holding out a hand which Tash shook. 'I run the inn here. My husband, bless his soul, left it to me when he passed. Perhaps you'd like to come and settle in– I'm sure Jervois will be happy to find you there.'

Tash's smile froze, the memory of the last inn she had stayed in flooding back. But it wouldn't hurt to have a proper bath or meal, not if she remained on her guard. She nodded slowly and followed Mellie, settling Lir in the stable that the children had showed her on the way, before entering Mellie's inn, *The Lost Fiddle*.

***

The inside was cheery with pale pink curtains hanging in the windows and tables covered with white lacy cloths. On the walls, instead of mounted animal heads or an assortment of weapons, there were paintings of animals and milkmaids, shepherdesses with flocks of lambs and bright-eyed children in a farmyard. It was different to any other inn Tash had been in, and she wondered whether it had been this way before Mellie's husband died. Did the men in the town enjoy drinking their ale here? Glancing around, she noted the embroidered cushions on the seats, each one decorated with pink thread.

'Charming, isn't it?' Mellie said happily, heading across to the bar, 'Be careful not to track dirt on my rugs, mind. There's a scraper just outside to clean your shoes.'

Tash glanced down and dutifully cleaned her shoes, noting that none of the other townsfolk had followed her inside. She turned to see Mellie pouring hot water into a kettle and bustling around with a duster, wiping the surfaces clear of any stray dirt.

'I always like things to be nice and tidy,' she said primly, placing a cup and saucer on a tray and carrying it over to one of the tables. 'How long do you think you'll be staying, dear?'

'Probably at least a week,' Tash admitted, 'perhaps longer.'

'It'll cost twenty shar for a week,' Mellie said, pouring out a cup of tea and sipping it daintily. Tash opened her bag and found the money pouch, counting out the appropriate coins and handing them over. She privately sent out a silent thanks to Romulus, for foreseeing this and ensuring that she would have enough Kinetian money.

'Lovely,' Mellie smiled, the money disappearing into a pocket faster than Tash expected. 'I'll show you to your room.' She replaced the cup on the saucer and sailed towards the staircase, blue eyes piercing Tash with an assessing glance. 'You look like you've been travelling a while.'

'Indeed I have,' Tash replied, 'it wasn't easy getting here from Venetica.'

'We were getting worried that you wouldn't arrive, you know,' Mellie said, 'but I had hope. I told Jervois— I said, the letter didn't get lost, it just got delayed in the inter-world mail.' She laughed and Tash smiled awkwardly, suddenly realising that she had never asked The Robin exactly how he had received the letters. It wasn't like Robins acted as postmen between worlds. Mellie prattled on, oblivious to Tash's lack of attention. 'We were expecting you weeks ago.'

'Yes, well,' Tash said awkwardly, 'I got held up on the road.'

'Like I said, it doesn't matter, you're here now,' Mellie waved Tash's words away. 'Now, I'm sure that everyone in town will want to pop in to say hello before too long, mark my words, so I'll leave you alone for a few minutes to get ready for the onslaught.' She stopped in front of a small chamber near the end of the upstairs hall. She cast Tash a surreptitious look and added, 'We don't have many of your kind here. It's best if you're prepared in advance.' She gave her a small key and returned downstairs in a flurry of skirts, leaving Tash standing in the doorway to her chamber, feeling anxiety pool in her stomach.

Slowly she closed the door and turned the key in the lock, before sitting down on the bed, sinking into the mattress and gazing at her reflection in the mirror on the dressing table. Her bags dropped to the floor and she sighed. Tash had dealt with bigotry before in several worlds. She had never been ashamed of being a Robin, no matter what some of the idiots had said. On the world trips they had gone on as apprentices, she had found that others treated her differently, either because she was an educated woman with dreams beyond being a wife and mother or due to her being one of the magic-wielding wayfarers between worlds who would never settle down.

There was a loud noise downstairs, a clamouring of voices and Tash took a deep breath, steeling herself for whoever was below. She opened the door and descended the stairs, pausing when the voices halted on her entrance. Mellie was sitting in her chair, cup raised to her lips, sipping serenely, while a range of villagers had entered, their shoes lined up outside the inn door. A stocky man with a receding hair line, glasses and a goatee smiled broadly and hurried over to greet her.

'I take it that you are the Robin I sent for?' he asked, shaking Tash's hand vigorously. 'I'm Jervois, mayor of

Nordhaven. It's an honour to have you here, we've been needing your assistance for some time.'

'I'm Natachatet,' she replied, 'although most people call me Tash.'

'Do I detect a southern influence in your name?' Jervois asked, winking.

'I was born in a village in southern Kinet, yes,' Tash replied uncomfortably as she thought of her hometown now.

'Lovely,' Jervois said happily and then turned to the assembled villagers, 'she's one of our own, everyone. Not one of those outsiders.'

'Outsiders?' Tash queried.

'Someone from another world,' Jervois said dismissively, 'the Robins who come and go but cannot stick around if things get really difficult.'

'Ah,' she murmured awkwardly and then chose to change the subject. 'I was wondering if we would be able to go somewhere private, Jervois, to discuss what's been happening in Nordhaven.'

She didn't particularly want to discuss either the murders or the blight in front of the gathered townsfolk. Jervois nodded.

'Indeed, that is the best option. Will you come with me to the town hall? It's not far.' As he headed to the doorway to put his shoes back on, Tash was approached by some of the villagers, who now seemed to feel more comfortable speaking to her.

'I'm Florrick,' a tall, thin man with a nose like a hawk said, holding out his hand for Tash to shake. 'The blight was first seen on my farm, probably two months ago now. This is my wife Ines,' he indicated a petite woman with a bob of brown curls, who smiled. 'And this is Pyrrus and his daughter Klara. They work the mill just out of town.'

Pyrrus was an older man, with deep set wrinkles around his face but his eyes were sharp with intelligence as he also shook Tash's hand. Klara was blonde and had the appearance of someone who had lost a lot of weight in a short amount of time. She might have been shapely once, but now was scrawny and looked almost haggard.

'A pleasure,' she said, taking Tash's hand in a firm grip. 'Let's hope you can sort out what's going on and set things to rights.'

'I'll do my best,' Tash promised, and then noticed Jervois eyeing her impatiently, 'I'd best have my talk with the mayor.'

'Before he has an apoplexy,' Klara muttered, Ines shushing her, casting a worried glance at Jervois who luckily hadn't heard the exchange.

'Come and visit us at the farm,' Florrick said, 'I'll show you the place where the blight started.'

'Thank you,' Tash replied, 'I'll make that a priority. Perhaps tomorrow?'

Florrick nodded. 'That works.' He paused for a moment and then added, 'Just make sure that you don't go out after dark. There's… something that roams the Heath when the sun goes down.'

'Nightwalkers,' Klara spat, 'filthy creatures. Here,' she shoved a bulb of garlic into Tash's hand, 'keep this on you at all times. It helps keep them at bay.'

Tash eyed the garlic and then thanked Klara politely, before removing herself from the group and heading towards Jervois. Outside the air was brisk, and she fell into step beside him as he strode down the cobbled streets.

'We've still got an hour or so before the sun sets,' Jervois said hurriedly, 'I'll make sure that you get back to the inn before night falls.' His pace increased and soon they had reached a tall building with closed wooden shutters and colourful roof tiles in a hexagonal pattern. Jervois opened the door and went inside, leading Tash into a room with a crackling fireplace, cedar bookshelves and a wide desk of oak. Jervois closed the door behind her and then crossed the room to sit behind the desk, indicating for Tash to take the seat opposite. She complied, looking at him expectantly as he twisted his hands back and forth.

'What can you tell me about these occurrences, Jervois?' she finally asked, when it became apparent that he wasn't quite sure how to start.

'The blight started just over two months ago,' Jervois began, 'at first we thought it just a normal fungus, one that was easily killed off, caused perhaps by an imbalance in the soil or the change in the weather. But no matter what we tried, it continued to spread and those who touched it fell into a deep slumber. Nothing would awaken them, and then they would die. The fungus seems to spread quickly— it took a week to overtake one field and then move to the next. We tried cutting it out, wearing gloves of course,' he paused to pour himself a small glass of an amber liquor from a crystal bottle. Shakily, he raised the glass to his lips and took a fortifying sip. 'We tried to burn it away. Nothing worked. The fungus would disappear after our efforts and then return twice as strong, spreading even further than we expected.'

'So, trying to get rid of it only made the fungus grow faster?' Tash clarified and Jervois nodded.

'We've lost ten people to the blight— the most recent one being Klem's daughter. That was last week. The town's still mourning her loss. With winter coming on, we've needed to rely on our stockpiles and our supplies are starting to run low. Nearby towns won't trade with us– too afraid of the blight spreading, I suppose. It's taking a toll on the Nordhaven residents.'

As he spoke Tash watched him carefully, nodding at his words, but thinking privately that, out of all the townsfolk she had seen, Jervois seemed the healthiest. Unlike the others, he didn't have the pinched look of hunger in his eyes or the ragged figure of going without regular meals for days on end. Instead, his clothes were snug, particularly around his middle, and she wondered how much of the town's stockpile he had commandeered for his own personal use. It would explain some of the looks the townspeople had given him when his back was turned.

'And what about the murders?' Tash asked, 'When did they start?'

'How do you know about those?' Jervois demanded, turning pale. 'I didn't mention it in my letter to your leader.'

'We have other means of gathering intelligence,' Tash replied evasively. 'Now, if you please, answer my question.'

'It's Nightwalkers,' Jervois said, taking another shaky sip of his drink. 'Monsters. I don't know if it's one or a group of them, but they've been preying on those who go out alone after dark. They've taken their victims onto the Heath and… well, it's enough to turn anyone's stomach.'

'Who has been killed?'

Jervois swallowed painfully. 'Mostly young women, those who are nearly of an age to marry.' He gave Tash a look and then added, 'Around your age.'

'Has anyone seen the creatures?' Tash asked.

'No,' Jervois said, 'no, but I know that Vallus has taken several groups of hunters out onto the Heath to find them. Each time they've found nothing. He might know more—he's in charge of the village militia.'

'I'll have a word with him,' Tash promised. 'Is there a possibility that it could be anything other than a Nightwalker?'

'Nightwalkers have stalked our town for decades,' Jervois said bluntly. 'There's no doubt that these murders are committed by the monsters.' It was clear from his tone that he wouldn't be swayed in his opinion and Tash let the matter drop. Perhaps if she had arrived here immediately after leaving the Temple she would accept his accusations without question, but now, after her recent experiences with Cai, she wasn't sure if Jervois was correct.

'Thank you for sharing this with me,' she said graciously, rising to her feet. 'I appreciate it.'

'Yes, yes,' Jervois stood too and walked her to the door, casting a quick glance out at the street. 'If you have any more questions or make any discoveries, please come back. Don't forget to head straight to the inn, most of the villagers tend to lock their houses after dark.'

Tash inclined her head and left, her cloak flapping around her heels as she tried to retrace her steps. Something distracted her and she looked up, a crow was flitting from house to house and cawing repeatedly. It fluttered back and forth, leading a way down a side street. Intrigued, Tash followed, one hand gripping her dezmian just in case. Houses rose on either side, and the crow flew left and right, taking her down narrow alleyways until she reached a dead end. It gave a final caw and then vanished, disappearing into the shadows at the end of the alley.

Tash halted, summoning a flame with a flick of the dezmian, and gazed around, recognising the stonework, the cobbles, the chipped wall in front of her. She'd dreamed about this place for days now. Cautiously, she reached out to touch the wall, tracing the stones and wondering where the crow had gone. In the light there was no sign of the creature–perhaps it had flown up and over the wall. Tash glanced back, to the point where the shrouded figure on the horse appeared each time in the dream. Thankfully, today, there was nothing there. She let out the breath she hadn't been aware she was holding and headed back to the main street, the wheels in her mind turning. Did this mean that the man with cobalt eyes and dark hair lived here? Would she finally meet him and learn who he was? It made her heart pound and she increased her stride, excitement coursing through her veins.

It took some time to retrace her steps, she had been so focussed on following the bird that she hadn't noted the twists and turns she had taken. When she returned to the main street, the sun was setting and there was no one around. Each house's shutters had been latched tight and as Tash continued down the street towards *The Lost Fiddle* she heard the sounds of bars being placed on the doors. She increased her pace, the sun had only just dipped below the horizon, surely there was still time to get back to the inn before night fell.

The main street curved around and she froze mid-step, as she saw the figure at the far end of the village. It was bent over, its long fingers probing at the base of a doorway, seeking entrance. From a distance, it was hard to distinguish what it was, but it seemed vaguely humanoid in shape, although as it stood Tash realised that it was much taller than any normal human would be. As it turned in her direction, face turned upwards, a pair of hands reached out from behind one of the houses and dragged Tash into the darkness, covering her mouth to prevent her from screaming.

'Don't move.' A familiar voice whispered in her ear. 'When I take my hand away, don't make a sound.'

Tash gave the slightest nod, the shock and fear she had momentarily felt fading fast. The hand moved away, but the other one still gripped her tightly against his chest, keeping her out of sight of the main street.

'Come,' Cai breathed, 'hold onto me and don't let go.' He took her hand and turned, pulling her towards the cluster of shadows. She faltered, certain that they would hit the wall but he tugged her onwards and then they were falling through darkness.

Chapter Ten

I dreamed of her again tonight. Except this time, she was in front of me. Her eyes flash with distrust but she doesn't shy away like so many others. I don't see fear– some revulsion maybe but no fear. All the same, her reaction is painful. I don't want her to see the monster, but then, it's been so long since I was human that I can no longer distinguish the difference between the two.

Her hair is loose, flowing in dark, shiny tresses down her back. I long to run my hands through it, to see if it's as soft as it looks. I want to pull her closer, to bridge the distance between us. Gods, I want to taste her, to see what she looks like when she's been kissed, to explore every part of her– tracing from the planes of her face down to her core. I want her to cry out in pleasure at my touch.

But then she turns away, leaving me alone and aching. And when I wake, I need to take a cold plunge in one of the lakes.

I must find her, to stop being haunted by these dreams.

~ An extract from a blood-speckled diary, hidden in the Shadow Realm

Tash held onto Cai's hand, unable to see anything around them, yet hearing the distant cries of screams in the rushing wind. She didn't know how long they fell for, but then they were hitting hard ground and Cai began to run, not giving her a moment to get her bearings on landing. She followed him blindly, disorientated by the shadows around them and wondering how he knew where to go.

'Jump,' he barked and she obeyed automatically, leaping after him before slipping as her feet met earth again. Something held her steady, encircling her waist for a moment as she regained her balance. She felt the spiny ridges and realised that it was his tail, until it flicked away again.

'Where are we?' Tash asked, gasping.

'Don't stop for long,' Cai said, 'we need to keep moving.' He hurried on, turning down various pathways that only he seemed to be able to see.

'Cai,' Tash pressed, 'answer me. Where are we?'

'We're in the Shadow Realm,' he replied curtly, 'it's not a safe place for Mortals.'

'Then what are we doing here?' she asked, trying to keep up with his increased pace.

'Finding a place to hide you,' Cai snapped, 'Honestly, Natachatet, you were given *one* instruction by the townsfolk and you disregarded it. Do you have a death wish?'

'No,' she retorted defensively. 'I didn't realise that they locked their doors *before* it was actually nighttime.'

'Well, you're not going back there tonight,' he said angrily, 'They won't open their doors for anyone, even Robins. Not with that creature there.'

'What was it?' Tash asked, 'Have you seen it before?' He grunted but didn't reply. Tash frowned, 'The townsfolk say that the murders are the work of Nightwalkers. You don't know anything about that, do you?'

His grip on her hand became painful and she felt his claws dig into her flesh. She bit back a gasp of pain as he released her hand and, for a moment, she was alone in the darkness.

There was a second of anxiety before a flickering light appeared, a campfire that banished the shadows. Cai knelt beside it, urging the flames to life, mouth set in a tight line, and she realised that her question had hurt him.

'You'll be safe here,' he said, tone clipped. 'Or as safe as you can be in this place. Stay beside the fire. It's easy to get lost in the shadows if you don't know which paths to take. This place is protected– just don't stray too far.'

'Thank you,' she said tentatively, crouching down by the fireside. 'For helping me out of there.' He gave another monosyllabic grunt. 'I need you to talk to me, Cai,' Tash pressed, 'please. Tell me if that creature was one of your kind.'

'Did it *look* anything like me?' he demanded angrily, eyes flashing scarlet. 'It's no more a Nightwalker than you are, Natachatet.'

'I'm sorry,' she said, 'I didn't mean—'

'And before you ask, I'm not responsible for the deaths in the town either,' he snapped bitterly. The darkness descended over his features as it seemed to do whenever he was upset, obscuring his face from view.

'I'm sorry,' she repeated. Her hand ached and she glanced down, noting the blood that glistened on her palm from where his claws had dug into her.

'I hurt you,' he said tightly.

'You didn't intend to,' Tash said, 'I know you didn't.' He reached a hand over her own and she felt the same prickling sensation from the night they had escaped from Lower Quilton. Under her gaze, the skin healed, and she wiped the blood away. 'See?' She lifted her hands, 'All better.'

He grunted again, but the shadows around his features began to recede somewhat. She unfastened her cloak and

spread it on the ground, before sitting down on it and looking around, taking in their surroundings properly for the first
time. They appeared to be in a small cave of sorts, to her
right was a hollow in the rock which seemed to be a kind of
nest, with a range of items scattered in it, from string to tattered clothing to tarnished trinkets and a worn book. The
firelight cast a golden glow on the walls, highlighting the hollowed ridges and sharp indents in the rock. It reminded Tash
of some grottos she had visited with Fred, the red-tinged
stone and sand stretching away to where darkness lined the
edges of the cave.

'Where are we, Cai?' she asked.

He followed her gaze, sliding over the rocky walls and
dusty ground, a resigned look in his eyes. 'This is where I
live.'

'This is your home?' Tash was surprised, 'Its… well, it's
very…'

He chuckled. 'It's not much, but it's one of the few places
where I'm left alone. For my kind it's important to have
somewhere safe to escape to.'

'It sounds lonely,' Tash said softly.

Cai shrugged, 'The life of a monster *is* lonely, Natachatet.
It's the way things are.' He looked back around the cave dispassionately, 'This place might be where I live, but it's not
home.'

The firelight played across his features, the curved horns
and rough cheeks. His skin was tinged in a red glow similar
to his eyes, which, when they met hers, burned with a fiery
light. She wondered how she had once associated them with
the colour of blood, and how she had thought him a monster. It seemed like so long ago now.

'Cai,' she said curiously, 'tell me about where you came from. Where is your home?' He seemed surprised by her question and pondered it awhile.

'Would it surprise you if I said that I came from Nordhaven?'

'How is that possible?' Tash was confused, and he smiled wryly at her expression.

'I was raised in a shack on the Heath. I played with the village children, ate at their tables and attended the services at the temple each week.'

'But they're terrified of you,' she whispered, 'what happened to change their minds?'

His smile turned feral, 'Some say that I struck a deal with a devil or that my true nature finally revealed itself. Either way, my destiny to be the Monster of the Nordhaven Heath was achieved.' His voice became bitter and she moved closer, reaching out to catch his arm as he turned away. Just like the night when they escaped Lower Quilton, the light pressure of her hand stilled him, and both recognised that, once again, she had initiated touching him. The significance was not lost on either of them.

'Don't call yourself that,' she said gently. 'I don't believe it.'

He laughed brittlely. 'Natachatet, if you knew about what I have done, you'd be joining them with torches. I am no innocent.'

'I never said that you were,' she replied, 'but you're not a monster.' It seemed that she had struck him temporarily dumb, so she asked again, 'What changed their minds about you?'

His eyes turned sad, staring ahead but seeing things she couldn't. 'I didn't always look the way I do now. Many years ago, I was human. When I came of age, I changed.'

A memory came to Tash's mind, and she said slowly, 'the Faerie Queen's curse.'

'You've heard of it,' Cai said, 'I thought you might. You are one of the most well-read Robins that I've met.' His compliment caught her by surprise, almost startling her out of asking her next question.

'But can't curses be broken?'

He looked at her, noting the concern and desire to help play across her face. 'No, Natachatet,' he said sadly, 'It's a curse that will last forever. If I and my predecessors couldn't find a way to break it, I don't believe that it can be done.'

She huffed a sigh and settled down, lying beside him. 'Well, that's disappointing. I'll see if I can find something in the library at the Temple when I get back that could help. There must be a loophole somehow.' Her eyes closed and therefore she missed seeing the soft smile stretch across his face as he gazed down at her. 'Oh and Cai,' she mumbled as she rolled onto her side, 'I think, given recent events, you can call me Tash. Goodnight.' She settled down, adjusting her position until she was comfortable and relaxed into a doze so that she didn't hear his response.

'Goodnight, Tash,' he whispered, not moving from his position as sentinel while she slept.

***

Tash dreamed of the man again. She knelt beside him as the shadowy figure approached them, the jingling of bells ringing in her ears. The man screamed, flinging an arm out and knocking Tash backwards. She lost her balance and fell, tumbling against the wall and then sliding through it into darkness, plummeting away from where he cowered in the alleyway. She heard the sound of a crow cawing as she sank further into the endless void.

'Tash?' Someone was shaking her awake, 'Tash?'

She opened her eyes, disorientated and saw Cai above her, frowning in concern. She sat up abruptly, head pounding and feeling wetness on her cheeks. Gods dammit, she'd been crying.

'Are you alright?' he asked, 'You were calling out.'

Oh, Gods above. Had she said anything in her sleep? 'I'm fine,' she managed, rubbing her face with the back of her hand. 'Just a bad dream, that's all.'

Cai nodded, thankfully not pressing for more information. She felt as though she hadn't rested at all, and massaged her throbbing temples.

'Here,' he said, summoning a warm cup of chai to appear in front of her. She took it gratefully.

'Thank you.' The tea was fragrant, calming her pounding heart but her hands still trembled slightly.

'Do you want to talk about it?' Cai asked and she shook her head. The last thing she wanted was to describe the man she kept dreaming about, not knowing if he was real or a figment of her imagination. She particularly didn't want to talk about him with Cai.

'How long was I asleep?' she asked, hoping to distract him. Cai raised an eyebrow, seeing through her ploy, but answered her all the same.

'A couple of hours, maybe.' He shrugged, 'If you want to try sleeping again, you can.'

Although the thought of sleeping was tempting, Tash didn't want to relive the dream again. 'Maybe in a little while.'

'As you wish,' he said, settling back against the cave wall, one leg stretched out comfortably while the other was pulled up to his chest, held secure with his arm. He wrinkled his nose and then said, 'What's that goddamn smell?'

She sniffed and felt something dig into her side. Reaching into her pocket, she withdrew the bulb of garlic Klara had given her, which was now partially crushed.

'Gross,' Cai remarked, 'why do you have that on you?'

'Apparently it's supposed to keep Nightwalkers at bay,' Tash smiled, 'although I don't think it seems to be working.'

He chuckled. 'Sometimes Mortals like you are so gullible.' She flung it at him, which he dodged easily. The garlic hit the wall with a soft thump and fell to the ground. Cai looked at her with mocking incredulity. 'That could have *killed me.*'

'As if,' she retorted, taking another sip of chai. 'More likely it makes you break out in a rash or have indigestion.'

He laughed. 'You mean to say that you don't believe a bulb of garlic can strike down a Nightwalker?'

'No,' she said, 'I don't.' He moved so fast that she barely had time to react before there was garlic in her hair. She put the cup down with a shriek and pulled it out, tossing it into the fire. 'What did you do *that* for?'

'Thought you might want to appreciate what it's like to have someone throw garlic at you,' he shrugged, grinning. Tash laughed, shaking her head and picking up the tea again.

'Touché.'

'I thought so.' He sounded smug and she rolled her eyes, smiling. He examined his hands curiously, 'Strange, I was hoping that I'd at least have a reaction.'

Tash looked over, and sure enough his hands were spotless. 'So, how many of those charms actually have an effect on you? I know that you can't touch yew,' she raised the hand with the ring which he had avoided touching all evening. 'And that you need permission to enter houses.'

'How about you list what the charms are, and I'll let you know if they have an effect or not?' Cai leaned back, watching her with a lazy smile.

'Fine,' Tash said, thinking hard. 'A mixture of lamb's blood and sand on doorways?'

'Waste of a good lamb,' Cai replied, 'it'd be much easier to give me the lamb and I'd leave people alone.'

She wrinkled her nose in distaste. 'You don't have to sound so eager.'

'I've restrained my appetite for several days now,' he replied, 'I'm pretty sure that you would rather I drink a lamb's blood than a human's.'

Tash chose not to reply, but thought about what else the books had said. 'Burning sage?'

'I used to quite like sage when I was human,' he remarked.

'And now?'

'I mean, if it makes people feel safer, I can choose to avoid it.'

Tash rolled her eyes again and he chuckled. 'What about a silver dagger to the heart?'

'Who *wouldn't* that kill?'

'Spinning counterclockwise three times while hopping on one leg?'

'Are you *serious?* He was incredulous now and she laughed.

'Some scholars claim that doing that will distract the Nightwalker and hypnotise them so that they can be attacked.'

'Gods, these Mortals are ignorant.'

'I'll have you know,' Tash said with false severity, 'that Artemis Archaeus was a well-renowned Robin and scholar who spent years compiling entries in *A Robin's Guide to Interworld Monsters.*'

'I'll take your word for it,' Cai replied, 'but it seems like he was also delusional.'

'So,' Tash pressed, 'enlighten me. What can strike down the fearsome Nightwalker if the spinning and hopping doesn't do the trick?'

He shook his head, chuckling again. 'Should I be worried by this new curiosity of yours?'

'Come on, Cai,' Tash said, 'Tell me.'

'Let's see,' his forehead creased in thought, 'the silver dagger definitely has potential. As does any other form of weaponry, if we're not given time to heal. Magic, of course, but that goes without saying. And yew burns most monsters and creatures of the dark.'

'That's all?' Tash was slightly disappointed. 'I was hoping for at least something like a four-leaf clover or singing a particular note or—'

'That would just hurt my ears,' Cai replied, smiling. 'And a four-leaf clover? Really?'

They fell into silence, holding each other's gaze and Tash became aware of something else filling the space between them. It was barely noticeable at first, a pulsing, throbbing energy that ran from her hair to her toes, shooting sparks of almost painful sensation through her. She hadn't noticed it building throughout their laughing and joking, until everything was quiet and suddenly, she wondered why she hadn't felt it sooner. Each movement she made seemed slower, barely cutting through the rising tension like a dulled blade. Her eyes skated downward and then met his again, half discomfited, half intrigued to see if he felt the same thing she did.

The lazy smile had faded on his lips, and his eyes burned anew with the fiery light from earlier. Now though, she could read the desire there and felt the answering response from deep within herself. It scared her, the emotional pull tempting, urging her to succumb to these impulses.

The last time she'd done that, she'd been hurt. It had ended painfully, for both herself and Fred, separated and aching from saying farewell. But now, the emotions she had tamped down arose in force, begging, no, demanding that she bridge the distance between herself and Cai.

'Wouldn't you like to know what can strike down a Nightwalker, Tash?' Cai asked, his voice so quiet it was barely audible. He didn't leave his position by the wall and she realised that if she wanted to find out the answer to his question, she would have to make the first move.

Her blood pounded in her ears, pulse racing and hands sweaty as she sat, frozen. Slowly, she put the empty cup down and placed the yew ring next to it, her gaze not leaving his. He smiled slightly, inviting her to come closer and she responded automatically, moving next to him.

'So?' she murmured, 'tell me.'

His hand lifted to her neck, winding through her hair. 'Or,' he whispered, 'I could show you.'

All it took was for her to tilt her head against his hand and return his smile for him to bridge the gap between them and kiss her. She leaned into the kiss, allowing herself to give in to the feelings that had been building for weeks. His lips were insistent, driving her to breathless madness in all too short a time. She moaned, gravitating closer until she was pressed against him, arms reaching around to clasp his neck and shoulders. In response, he growled at the back of his throat, moving his lips from her mouth down her neck to her collarbone. She trembled, too caught up in desire to think about any ramifications. His hands traced down her body, catching on the fastenings of her dress and undoing them with ease. As her bare skin was revealed, his hands found new pathways to make her gasp and whimper, sending waves of sensation through her. She cried out blindly, gripping onto him as he moved lower, tormenting her with his lips and tongue. Her mind spiralled, unable to focus on any one thing save the rising ache, until it shattered into an agonising surge of pleasure.

His touch was overpowering. She longed to make him feel the same way she did, to see if she could have the same effect on him that he was having on her. Tash reached out, cupping the back of his neck, catching in his hair and pulling him up to kiss her again. He responded instinctively, tongue meeting hers as with her other hand she grasped the remains of his tattered shirt and tore them off. He broke away with a chuckle and she took advantage, rolling above him and pinning him beneath her.

Cai gazed up at her, as her hair fell down, like a midnight cloak around them. 'Gods, you're beautiful,' he whispered. The way he looked at her made her breath catch, for there was far more than just simple desire in his eyes. It scared her and so she avoided it, focussing instead on the addictive power she felt as she straddled him. She stretched her hands out across his chest, tracing the scars and ridges as she explored his body like he had hers. Tash lowered her gaze to the clear evidence of his arousal and smiled wickedly, reaching down to unbutton his breeches. Cai made a choked sound as she replaced her hands with her mouth, pressing kisses along his chest, down to his abdomen and then lower still. Tash felt a momentary rush of satisfaction, his groans making her feel more empowered than she had been in a while.

He allowed her only a short time to tease him, before he caught her arms, bringing her back to his lips and kissing her desperately. As her tongue met his, he lowered her down onto him, and Tash's eyes opened, breaking out of the kiss at the sudden sensation. They paused, breathless, unable to look away from the other's gaze, and then began to move, reigniting the fire that burned between them.

Tash wasn't aware of much else that night, save for the delicious, addictive pleasure that made her cry out again and again. Their bodies melded together, his tail encircling her as he shifted above her and she gripped him tighter, nails digging into his back as the pressure intensified to a climax. She gasped, clutching him as she felt the heat rush through her, calling out his name before he silenced her with a kiss, stifling his own groan as he shuddered with his own release.

When he had pulled away, they lay on the hard ground tangled in each other's arms, neither wanting to move. Tash's mind was a blur, and although she felt sated and content, a part of her was terrified of what had happened between them. She pushed it down, refusing to face the consequences of her actions just yet, and rested her cheek across his chest.

'You're awfully quiet,' Cai murmured against her hair, stroking it with the back of his hand.

'I'm just thinking,' she replied quietly. His hand stilled for a moment.

'Do you regret it?'

She shook her head and his hand recommenced its soothing motion as she whispered, 'But I don't normally do this.'

He chuckled. 'Well, neither do I.'

'Do *you* regret it?' she asked softly.

'No,' he replied. 'Far from it.'

His reply sent warmth through her and she smiled. 'I was worried for a moment there.' In response, his tail wrapped around her, anchoring her in place which was strangely comforting. She looked up at him, 'So is that how one can strike down a Nightwalker?'

His mouth crinkled in a smile and he said, 'perhaps not all of them. But definitely most.'

She laughed and propped herself up, before kissing him gently. 'And what about *this* one?' She pressed her hand against his chest, over the point where his heart would be.

He reached around her, bringing her back to his lips and kissed her hungrily. '*Most definitely* this one.'

'Seems like I have the upper hand then,' she teased, breaking away until she hovered above him. 'Just wait until the people in Nordhaven discover your weakness.'

'You wouldn't dare,' he said with mock severity, 'because I just happen to know *yours*.'

'And what would that be?' she grinned, the aching desire rising again inside her. He met her eyes and saw it, smiled dangerously and proceeded to remind her.

Chapter Eleven

Few scholars have written about the Shadow Realm, or as Cai once told me, the world between worlds. Us Robins cross through Doorways in the Barriers, but there is another way to journey between the dimensions— a back door approach, so-to-speak. It's a place filled with monstrous creatures and, after my one and only failed visit there, I never want to return. The Shadow Realm is a place where one's darkest impulses can be released with abandon, where it is altogether too easy to succumb to temptation and one's conscience is silenced. Cai warned me about going there, and now I have the constant reminder of what happened in those godforsaken lands with me until the end of my days.

~ An extract from The Robin's journal, written shortly
after his induction as leader of the Order of Song

Tash awoke with Cai's arms around her, and memories from the night before crashing through her mind. Carefully, she disentangled from him, not wanting to wake him from his slumber. They hadn't ended up getting much sleep, and her body ached from their exertions. It wasn't unpleasant but she wanted a proper bath, to wash the grime and sweat away and perhaps to help get her head together. She reached down and pulled her clothes back on, stepping over Cai and kneeling by the fireside, thinking about what had happened. Her hands shook slightly, and anxiety rose in her chest, making it hard to breathe as recriminations filled her mind. What had she done? How had she lost her head like that? How *could* she have done it? She'd been brazen and far more confident than past encounters and this scared her. She'd always preferred books and debates over other pleasures, until recently.

There was a movement behind her as Cai awoke, but she kept her gaze averted, suddenly shy despite her confidence the night before. She heard Cai pulling his clothes on, an unfamiliar awkwardness settling around her shoulders as neither of them spoke and she wondered what the right thing to say would be. Everything had shifted last night and now she wasn't sure where they stood.

'Are you ready to go?' Cai asked finally, when it became apparent that Tash wasn't going to speak first. He stood beside her, arms folded and watching her with an inscrutable expression. It was almost like they hadn't spent the night together, his eyes were shuttered, keeping any reaction to what they had done hidden. Perhaps it would be better to act similarly, as though nothing had happened– nothing that had meant anything, that was.

Following his lead, Tash stood and dusted her skirts off, 'Yes. I've got a lot to do in Nordhaven.' He grunted and offered his hand to her.

'Let's go then.' She took his hand and tried to ignore the warm tingle that spread through her, reminding her all too well of what his hands had done mere hours earlier. Tash nodded mutely, swallowing the lump that had risen in her throat. Unconsciously though, her fingers tightened around his as the campfire vanished and they were plunged into darkness. She wasn't able to see his penetrating gaze scan her face or his tentative smile before he led her down a path only he knew, navigating her through the Shadow Realm until she was no longer stepping forward blindly, but instead found herself on the wilds of the Nordhaven Heath. Cai's hand still gripped hers and she blinked, raising her free hand to cover her eyes from the sudden onslaught of morning light.

'How are you able to do that?' she asked, as she gradually lowered her hand. 'How do you know where to enter the Shadow Realm and how to return here?'

'Like I've said,' he replied, 'once you know the correct pathways it becomes quite simple.' He glanced down at her, suddenly serious, 'But don't go looking for those entrances, Tash. On your own, the Shadow Realm would be unsurpass-able without a guide.'

She nodded in silent acquiescence. Cai smiled, satisfied with her response and then he glanced up, expression chang-ing as sounds began to reach them from across the Heath.

'It seems that a search party has been sent out for you,' he murmured, entire body tense and alert.

'You should go,' Tash said, 'they'll blame you for the at-tacks.' His mouth twisted and he seemed on the verge of speaking when the calling voices became more distinct. 'Go,' Tash urged again, giving him a soft push. He gave her a slightly mocking look and then was gone, slipping away into the shadows behind one of the gnarled trees and vanishing from sight. Tash breathed a sigh of relief and began to make her way towards the search party through the heather and gorse, calling out to alert them to her presence.

***

'It's a miracle, it truly is,' Mellie was saying, as she fussed over Tash, pouring her yet another cup of tea and urging her to eat some rather bland porridge. 'Out alone overnight and re-turning in one piece the next day. It's something that's become unheard of in Nordhaven. You must be a strong Robin if you could keep the Nightwalker at bay.'

Tash's cheeks warmed as she pushed the memories of the previous night away, but didn't reply. On her other side, Klara and Vallus, the leader of the search party, eyed her shrewdly. They had been amongst the small group of armed villagers who had found her on the Heath and led her back to Nordhaven, trying and failing to get her to explain how she had survived the night. Tash kept her answers evasive, saying little beyond finding her way onto the Heath and doing her best to evade the monsters before the sun rose.

'You look tired, Tash,' Mellie continued, 'go up to your room and rest a while. It can't have been easy last night.'

'She needs to start investigating the blight,' Klara said forcefully, 'that's what she was sent here for.'

'She'll be of little use to anyone if she's exhausted,' Mellie replied reasonably, gripping Tash's arm and leading her with surprising strength towards the stairs. 'We've dealt with the blight for weeks now, we can manage a few more hours while our guest recovers.'

Vallus and Klara watched them leave, their irritation clear. Tash understood why, but she also appreciated Mellie standing up for her, allowing herself to be directed to her room.

'Thanks,' she said quietly and Mellie shook her head dismissively.

'You don't need to thank me, Tash. I was worried sick about you last night– but I'm just relieved that you're alright. All the same, you look half dead on your feet.' She gave her a swift smile and then returned downstairs, and Tash closed her bedroom door gratefully.

Mellie had prepared a bath for her, and she stripped off eagerly, desperate to feel clean and herself again. Sinking into the hot, scented water, Tash closed her eyes, allowing her aching muscles to relax. Parts of her still felt tender, and she registered places where her skin stung as she cleaned some of the scratches she'd sustained overnight. Memories kept filling her mind, replaying each touch and caress, the mad insanity that had overtaken her body, driving her to pursue different types of pleasure. She couldn't remember the last time she'd acted thus, and part of her felt the stirrings of shame, unsure how to process what had happened. Whereas another part of her had now been awakened, and this part wanted more. It longed to find out what other glorious secrets were waiting to be discovered.

Tash dunked her head under the water, trying to wipe the thoughts away, to deny the desire to call him to her, to invite him into her room and…

'Enough,' she spluttered, gasping as she reemerged, gripping her head in her hands. 'Enough, Tash. Get it together. You can't afford to fall to pieces like this.'

Gods forbid she lose her focus on her task, her mission, because of one night of passion. 'You haven't worked so hard, for so long, to lose sight of what's important now.' She reminded herself, scrubbing with the soap ruthlessly and rinsing it off with equal vigour. 'You need to remember the reason you're here.' She dried off and pulled on a clean dress, collapsing onto the bed and slipping into a light doze.

It felt like seconds passed, yet when Tash awoke, feeling refreshed, it was late morning. She got up and fastened her cloak, leaving the inn and following the main road towards the edge of the town, heading for Florrick's farmstead. Most of the villagers were out and about, some waved at her, others gave her a wide berth, perhaps unsure how she had survived the night unscathed. As she passed the fields, she saw the windmill up on the hill overlooking the town. She wondered if Pyrrus would be available later for a talk, and whether he would remember Cai from when he had been human.

Florrick's farmstead was looking particularly rundown, the thatched roof sagged slightly and the limestone walls were chipped and weathered. Some scrawny chickens were pecking around the front yard, and a rather tired donkey looked at her from one of the fields. Tash approached the door and knocked, before it was opened by Ines, whose grim expression changed to a bright smile as she realised who the visitor was.

'Tash, come in,' she urged, 'I thought you were Jervois. He normally comes around this time to collect the donations for the town stockpile.'

'Are the donations voluntary?' Tash asked as she entered the farmhouse. The ceiling was low and she had to duck through the doorway. Inside it was clear that Ines worked hard to make their home inviting. There were patched rugs on the floor, an empty fireplace and a polished wooden table with roughly carved chairs. The small kitchen was spotless, a vase of wildflowers sitting on the windowsill and open shutters looking out over the desolate fields.

'Jervois says that they are,' Ines muttered, 'but for those who refuse, he will send Vallus or his goons to ensure the donations are made. It's supposed to help the whole village, us pooling our resources together.' It was clear from her tone that she didn't agree with the concept, and, remembering the comparison between the ragged villagers and the well-fed Jervois, Tash didn't blame her.

'Is Florrick here?' she asked, 'I was hoping that he would show me where the fungus originated.'

'He's in the western field,' Ines replied, 'I'll show you the way. Just make sure to stay away from the fungus and keep your gloves on– you don't want to touch it with bare skin.'

'Thanks for the reminder,' Tash said, pulling the gloves on tighter as she followed Ines back outside. They crossed the yard, scattering the chickens in a flurry of feathers, Ines opening the gate onto a wide field. Perhaps it had been bountiful once, but the blight had tainted the earth and the plants growing in it, turning them a pale grey colour with wilted leaves, the fungus spreading across the ground unchecked. At the far end of the field, Tash could make out Florrick, his back to them as he worked with a hoe, churning up the hard earth.

'I'll leave you to it,' Ines said, 'I need to finish the laundry.'

'Thanks,' Tash said, as she closed the gate behind her and began to pick her way between the furrows towards Florrick. She paused midway, kneeling down to inspect the fungus more closely, but still keeping a safe distance from it. A cool wind brushed her cheek and a voice said,

'It doesn't look particularly dangerous.'

Tash jumped and looked around, seeing nothing but Florrick's distant figure, back still turned to her. 'Cai?' His soft chuckle made her look in the opposite direction, yet still she couldn't see him. 'Where are you?'

'I have ways of remaining unseen,' his voice was low and she frowned.

'You shouldn't sneak up on me like that.'

'Sorry.' He didn't sound particularly repentant and she glared in the direction of his voice.

'Why *are* you here?'

'Someone has to keep an eye on you, Tash,' he said simply, 'and this is the easiest way. I can't have the villagers setting hunting dogs on me all the time.'

She sniffed and began to walk on towards Florrick, muttering under her breath, 'I don't *need* you to be following me like this.'

'I beg to differ,' he retorted. 'If left alone, you might end up doing something incredibly stupid or foolish. It's a lot easier to assist you if I'm nearby.'

She gave a humph and strode on, trying to disregard the reaction his voice had caused, the tingling sensation that spread through her at his proximity. The last thing she wanted was for him to figure that out and so she didn't respond, ignoring another low chuckle from behind her.

'Florrick,' she called, waving and increasing her pace, as the distant figure turned on hearing her voice.

'Coward,' Cai whispered.

'Good morning Tash,' Florrick said when she had moved closer. He leaned the hoe against the stone wall that bordered the field, wiping a hand across his brow leaving a dirty smudge behind. She saw that he had been trying to dig the fungus out of the furrows at his feet.

'I thought that this only made it grow back worse,' she commented, kneeling back down to inspect one of the plant remnants. She reached out to pick it up, noting the ripples of grey and blue, a foul, acrid scent meeting her nostrils. She'd never seen anything like it before, but all the same, she withdrew a bag from her belt and placed the piece of fungus in it, determined to examine it later.

'It does,' Florrick's tone was resigned, 'but I can't stand idly by and not do anything. At least this way I feel like I'm making a difference.'

Tash heard a soft snort from behind her and coughed, muffling the sound so that Florrick wouldn't notice it. 'Where did you first see the fungus?'

'It was over here,' Florrick led her down along the length of the stone wall, to where it bordered the farm and Nordhaven Heath. 'It appeared along this side first, from the Heath. We'd just planted the new crops and were hoping that they would take to the soil. Usually, this field is more acidic than the other ones, so we're careful about what to plant here.'

Tash raised her eyebrows and glanced around the field, noting the slight incline of the ground and how the majority of the western field was at the base of the hill. 'When it rains, does the water build up along here?' She indicated the wall and Florrick nodded.

'We get heavy rains during autumn, and usually the water builds up along the boundary line.'

Tash nodded, mentally taking notes. 'And has there been a lot of rainfall lately?'

Florrick nodded.

'Before the fungus appeared?'

He nodded again. 'There was a bad storm– it rained for three days straight. At first we thought it was a godsend after the drought, but then it didn't stop raining. Afterwards, the crops were waterlogged so we were focussed on trying to drain the soil. In that time, the fungus appeared along here and didn't go away.'

'Hm,' Tash murmured, withdrawing her dezmian and inspecting the boundary wall. It was cracked and worn, with multiple places where the mortar had eroded away. Along the base, the fungus sprouted in thick quantities from a strange white webbing that clung to the point where the wall met the ground. From there lumps and fungi rose, reaching out across the ground towards the crops, whose leaves were speckled with dark grey splodges.

'What is this?' Tash asked, pointing at the white webbing. 'What happened when you tried to remove this?'

'I'm not quite sure what it is,' Florrick said unhappily, 'the fungus grew from it and it's quite strong. We tried cutting it out, but like the fungus, it just grew back. It seems to grow around the bottoms of walls and trees, you won't see it in the middle of the field.'

'Hm,' Tash mused, carefully reaching out and pulling a segment of the strange webbing away before stowing it in her bag as well. Unlike the fungus, the webbing didn't have a scent and she eyed it carefully, noting the delicate tendrils that clung to her gloved hands as she placed the segment in her bag.

'How quickly does it take to spread, Florrick?' she asked, rising again to her feet.

His brow crinkled in thought. 'Perhaps three to four days to cover a field. There's only one farmer left who hasn't had his crops decimated yet– Sian. His farm is on the top of the hill,' he pointed in the distance towards the other side of the village, 'the furthest one from Nordhaven Heath.' He added knowingly, 'lucky bastard.'

'So what do you think has caused the fungus to spread so quickly?' Tash asked, 'Has the weather remained consistent? Has it rained a lot? Strong winds?'

Florrick shook his head, eyeing the Heath distrustfully. 'If I was a betting man, I'd say that the Monster of the Heath was making its presence known.'

This time, Tash had to cough louder to cover up the snort from behind her. Florrick looked at her questioningly and she asked, 'What makes you think that?'

He shrugged. 'Along with the strange occurrences around here– the murders and such, and the blight, it seems as though we're being punished for something.'

Tash nodded slowly, then knelt back down to examine the root of the fungus, 'If it's alright with you, Florrick, I'll just inspect this a bit longer. Thank you for showing it to me.'

He nodded gruffly and walked off, boots stomping through the frosty ground. Tash waited until he had gone out of earshot before muttering, 'I wish you would keep quiet. It's hard to focus with you listening in.'

'I can't help it if they're ignorant,' Cai replied.

'Just because you didn't cause this blight doesn't mean that they're not wrong about it having an uncanny origin,' Tash murmured, flicking her dezmian in the air and focussing on the fungus.

'Am I to believe that you don't think the Monster of the Nordhaven Heath is responsible for this?' Cai asked but she couldn't interpret the emotion in his voice, too intent on her task. His question irritated her though, for she snapped,

'Oh, come on Cai. You probably have far more interesting things to do than cause a blight in this town. Besides,' she lifted her hand over the fungus, feeling the energy pulsing through the ground, 'this isn't the sort of magic I would think you would practise.'

'Oh really?' he asked sardonically, 'And how would you know what type of magic I practise?'

She snorted, 'Because I would hazard a guess that this magic is uncontrolled and rudimentary. You've had a lot longer to hone your skills.' She leaned back on her heels and pushed her hair out of her eyes. The pulsing sensation she had felt from the fungus was growing weaker now and she stood, brushing the remnants off of her skirts. 'I want to analyse the samples I've taken later. It might help me decipher the origin.'

'I assume you won't need help with that,' Cai replied, 'I imagine that the Temple had far more adept alchemy teachers than I had in the Shadow Realm.'

'I may need assistance though,' Tash murmured thoughtfully. 'It might help to have someone else there to isolate the source of magic.'

'You want me to help with that?' he clarified and she paused, realising his dilemma.

'I give you permission to come into my room, Cai,' she said quietly, wishing that her heart would stop pounding a sudden staccato beat in her chest. 'And this time, I'll make sure to be back at the inn before sundown.'

'Very well,' he replied softly. Tash straightened her shoulders and began to make her way back towards the farmhouse. As she passed through the yard towards the road, she noticed Jervois heading in her direction, a man behind him carrying a covered basket. When he saw her, Jervois waved and smiled.

'I was hoping that you would be here, Tash,' he said when they were closer. 'I understand there was an issue last night and that you were found on the Heath this morning.'

'I'm unhurt, Jervois,' she said calmly, 'but I'll make sure to heed your warning tonight.'

'Vallus wants to speak to you about what happened,' Jervois informed her, 'Surely you saw the Nightwalker that's been terrorising the town. With any luck, you might be able to let him know its movements. It'd be a boost for the town's morale if we could kill the beast.'

There was a low growl from behind Tash, and Jervois glanced at her, confused. Hurriedly she raised a hand to her stomach and said, 'My apologies, I'm hungry.'

Jervois' expression changed from confusion to one of concern and he ushered her back towards the inn, reminding her once again to be inside well before sunset. As Tash began to walk on, she noticed him entering the farmyard and knocking on the door.

Instead of heading back into the town, Tash changed direction and made her way towards the distant windmill.

'There I was thinking you were hungry,' Cai commented and she frowned, wishing that she could glare at him.

'And I thought I told *you* to be quiet,' she retorted, 'these people are scared of you, Cai. What do you expect from them?' He was silent to this and she took advantage, ruthlessly adding, 'Considering what they've been going through, you can't blame them for wanting to kill the monster that's been terrorising their town. Based on what they've told me, I'd assume that you've been visiting Nordhaven for years, so naturally they would consider you responsible for these events too.'

His silence had turned mutinous and she could feel the anger barely kept in check radiating off him. She sighed, starting to regret her bluntness, but not knowing how else to phrase it. Surely he could see that based on past experiences with the townspeople, he would become the scapegoat whenever things went wrong? Despite what he said about being a monster, it was apparent to her that the townspeople's accusations hurt him deeply.

'Cai, go and calm down,' she muttered under her breath, forcing a smile and a wave at some villagers who were hanging damp laundry out in their yards. 'I'll see you tonight.'

He grunted, clearly displeased with being sent away. 'Fine. I need to hunt anyway. Don't take any risks, Tash.' She frowned again, biting her tongue to avoid snapping back in response and then nearly leapt out of her skin when she felt an invisible hand brush her cheek. 'If anything happens,' he murmured, 'just call me and I'll come.'

She gave a minute nod, her breath seizing in her chest as her heartbeat slowly returned to normal. There was a low chuckle and then he was gone, fading away into nothingness as though he had never been there. Tash shook her head, glanced around to ensure that no one had seen her response to the interaction and continued on, placing one foot in front of the other as she ascended the steep hill towards the windmill.

Chapter Twelve

Nightwalkers have no soul. As they feast on the blood of innocent victims, they are considered spawn of the devils from the hells. These creatures are expert hunters, tracking prey over long distances and between the planes of existence. Their dark magic bewitches the unwary, luring innocents into a false sense of security before they strike. In this way, they are like the lamias in the old tales, creatures that were half women, half serpent who seduced their victims before killing them. Nightwalkers are just as deadly, perhaps more so because of their grasp of the dark arts.

~ An extract from 'The Kinetian Bestiary'

Klara was loading bags of flour into a wooden cart when Tash reached the windmill, muscles straining from their weight. She looked up, one bag hefted on her shoulder, and grinned.

'Well, if it isn't the resident Robin,' she said, 'what brings you here, Tash?'

Tash paused by the gate, leaning against the roughened wooden posts as she caught her breath. Gasping, she wiped the sweat and hair plastered to her brow away. 'I wanted to see you and your father.' She glanced down the hill at the town of Nordhaven and the Heath beyond, 'It really is a nice view from up here.'

Klara gave a short laugh. 'When I was growing up, Father would say that we could see the whole world from the mill. But now, when I look out there all I can see is a town that's dying.' Her tone became resigned as she dropped the final bag of flour into the cart and came over to join Tash. 'With this blight, I don't know how much longer some of the townsfolk will stay. Some families have already left. They think the town's cursed, and I don't blame them.'

'Do you think the murders and the blight are related then?' Tash asked and Klara snorted.

'It wouldn't surprise me if they were. That blight's not natural. Look at the people who have died from it already.'

'It's a punishment.' A tired voice reached them and both women turned to see Pyrrus stumping over towards them.

'Punishment?' Tash queried; eyebrows raised. 'What makes you say that?'

Klara rolled her eyes, 'Father, no one has done anything to merit a punishment here. Unless you think the Gods are angry with Jervois for hoarding all the food for himself.'

'You don't know what you speak of, Klara,' Pyrrus replied as his eyes met Tash's. 'It's a punishment for what happened years ago. Long before Klara and Florrick and Jervois were born.'

'It's just a story, Father,' Klara said dismissively. 'You *know* that.'

Pyrrus shook his head forcefully. 'No, Klara.'

'What is the story?' Tash asked curiously, her pulse increasing with excitement. Would she get the answers she sought about Cai's history? 'Is it anything to do with Night-walkers?'

Klara sighed and said, 'The tales say that a wild boy lived on the Nordhaven Heath. He tormented the villagers and then it was revealed that he was a monster. He pursued the townsfolk, preying on their flocks and beating on people's doors, calling for shelter. When a woman's body was found on the Heath, the men of the village finally took action. They hunted the monster and banished him to the shadows.' Her face darkened and she spat on the ground. 'The only good Nightwalker is a dead one.'

'The true horror though,' Pyrrus said quietly, 'was that the woman they found– Ryla– she had been his mother.'

Tash's breath caught in her throat. 'That's horrible.'

'It was,' Pyrrus nodded. 'Ryla was beloved in the village. Many people couldn't accept that she had birthed a monster, and once he showed his true form, she took refuge in the town.'

'So,' Tash asked eagerly, 'why then do you say that the events today are a punishment? What did the townsfolk do?'

Pyrrus swayed and lifted a hand to his head, suddenly weary. 'I... I can't remember...'

Klara hurried around and gripped his arms, holding him upright. 'Come inside, Father,' she said gently, 'you need to rest.' She cast Tash an apologetic look. 'Since these murders started, he's been having episodes like this. Excuse us.'

Tash watched as they went inside the mill, the father leaning heavily on his daughter's arm. After a while, Klara returned and said, 'He just needs some rest. The strain of the last months has started to take a toll on him.' She moved to the cart and jumped up into the seat. 'Want a lift back into town?'

Tash nodded gratefully, although slightly disappointed that her curiosity had been piqued and left unsatisfied. She clambered up next to Klara and together they began to descend the hill, the cartwheels rattling over the cobbled road.

'Will Pyrrus be alright?' Tash asked, 'I didn't mean to ask so many questions.'

'You didn't do anything wrong, don't worry,' Klara replied, 'he gets tired easily these days. The stories he tells start to get jumbled and confused so don't put too much weight in what he says.'

'OK,' Tash said slowly. 'That must make it hard on you, though. I imagine that you're operating the mill pretty much all by yourself?'

Klara nodded. 'When I was younger, I wanted to marry a man in another town, but when Father got ill, I couldn't leave. Now I couldn't imagine going away. Nordhaven is home, no matter what happens.'

'Do you know what your father meant when he said that what's happening is a punishment?' Tash asked hopefully.

Klara snorted and flicked the reins, urging the mule pulling the cart to increase its pace. 'Like I said, his memories are becoming confused. He seems to think that it's to do with the Nightwalker and something the townsfolk did to it all those years ago. Although,' she cast Tash a look that brooked no argument, 'it seems to me as though our menfolk were only protecting the town. No one in their right mind would sympathise with a monster.' Tash nodded, lost in thought, and Klara seemed to relax marginally. 'One of these days,' she continued, 'Vallus is going to catch that beast and give it the end it deserves.'

Tash didn't reply, yet Klara seemed to accept her silence as agreement. She hummed tonelessly as they descended into the village, pulling the cart to a halt in the main street, giving Tash the chance to get out.

'Thanks for the ride,' Tash smiled, 'I appreciate it.'

'No problem,' Klara replied, picking up one of the bags and balancing it on her shoulder. 'Don't forget to see Vallus. We're going to need all the information you can tell us about the Nightwalker if we're going to catch it.'

'I won't,' Tash stepped away, leaving Klara to deliver the bags of flour. She headed to the stable, eager to find Lir and have an hour or so to just get away. After being primarily alone for days, it was a bit unsettling to be back amidst people.

She found Lir happily munching on some hay in his stall, although when he saw her, he began to shuffle excitedly. Tash smiled and after a few minutes, they were soaring out of the stable and circling over the roofs of Nordhaven. The wind cut through her, sending a rush of sensation into her veins and she laughed in exhilaration as Lir beat his wings, cutting through the air with ease.

'Let's have another look at those fields, *liebeshem*,' she muttered, angling Lir to head towards the acres of farmland, particularly the area affected by the blight. From high above, the fields seemed to be speckled with a greyish tinge, which spread from Florrick's farm right around the town. As Florrick had explained, only one farm was not affected, the one that stretched across the hilltops on the other side of town. The fields there were lush and bountiful, plants growing tall and strong in drastic contrast with the neighbouring plots. Tash urged Lir to descend further, and caught a glimpse of several men in the field, tending to the crops. She raised a hand and saw a few wave back before they returned to their work. One didn't wave but watched her fly overhead, hat pulled low over his face so it was impossible to distinguish his features.

Lir landed outside the farm's boundary, out of sight of the farmers. Tash dismounted and knelt down by the stone wall, flipping her dezmian with one hand while the other one felt the earth beneath her. The dezmian spun in the air, allowing her to feel the magic rising from the ground. She closed her eyes and reached out with her mind, sensing the magical current and trying to follow it to its source. The pull was strong here, much as it had been in Florrick's field, although this magic felt more controlled, more stable in how it had been cast. Tash rose to her feet and glanced over the wall at the bounty of plants growing there, suspicions forming in her mind.

'Come on Lir,' she said grimly, 'we have at least an hour or two before I need to return to the inn. Let's explore the Heath.'

***

Tash arrived back at the inn an hour before sunset, cold, hungry and tired. The Nordhaven Heath spanned for miles, captivating her with its rough, harsh beauty. It was not a hospitable place, rocky crags and sharp bracken testing any potential visitor, but there was still something about it that made her pause. She remembered what Cai had told her and the story Klara had recalled, of the wild boy raised on the Heath. She was sure that Cai had been the monster in the tale, and as she had gazed around the land, she wondered what it had been like to grow up in such a desolate place.

By then it was late afternoon and Lir had nudged her shoulder, reminding her of the promise she had made to be indoors by sunset. They'd left the Heath behind, but Tash was determined to return. The Heath fascinated her— there was a feeling that something was there, waiting to be discovered, if she only looked hard enough.

The Lost Fiddle was bustling with people when Tash entered, carefully scraping the excess dirt and muck off her shoes before she walked through the door. She saw Mellie behind the bar, chatting happily with several people she hadn't met yet. At a table in the corner, she saw Vallus and some of the men who had been with him in the search party that morning. Not wanting to be noticed, Tash tried to make herself inconspicuous, slipping up the stairs to her room. Unfortunately, nothing could get past Mellie's sharp gaze, and she cried,

'Tash, dear, what a relief. Let me get you a cup of tea.'

On hearing her name, Tash paused, one foot on the stairs as Vallus' eyes jerked up, pinning her with an intense stare. He beckoned her over imperiously and Tash approached him reluctantly as Mellie bustled around the bar and placed a mug of tea at Vallus' table for her.

'Thanks, Mellie,' she said as she perched down in the vacant chair and took a sip. The tea scalded her tongue and she put it down hastily.

'Now Tash,' Vallus didn't waste time with pleasantries, but instead got straight to the point. 'This morning you didn't give us any solid details about what happened last night. It's unheard of for anyone to survive alone overnight in this town. All the previous young women who went out alone were found the following morning on the Heath like the beast's twisted trophies. We need to know how you accomplished it. Did you see the Nightwalker at all? How did you get so far out onto the Heath?'

'Well,' Tash began uncomfortably, 'I told you that I kept moving, I didn't stay in one spot for too long.'

'Did you see the monster?' he pressed impatiently and she gave a small nod, remembering the creature with the long, wiry fingers, trying to find a weak spot in the door to open.

'And?' Vallus urged, 'Where was it?'

'It was in the main street,' she said quietly, deciding that the best course of action was to stick to the truth as much as possible. 'It was trying to get inside one of the houses. I hid and got away, found my way out onto the Heath and, well, I told you the rest.'

'How did you protect yourself?' he demanded. 'It must have given chase when it sensed that you were there.'

'I…' Tash took another sip of tea, using the moment's respite to think quickly. 'I had garlic on me. Klara gave me some when I left the inn yesterday.'

Vallus' expression softened somewhat. 'Klara was right to do such a thing. She might very well have saved your life.'

Tash nodded again, trying to ignore the memory of the garlic bulb flying across a cave, slapping Cai in the face and the laughter that ensued.

'So,' Vallus continued, oblivious to the turn in Tash's thoughts, 'this emphasises what I've been fearing for weeks. The Nightwalker is entering the town and trying to infiltrate our homes.' He turned to the other men at the table, 'I vote that tonight we get our torches and patrol the streets. We need to keep the town safe.'

'We've tried that, Vallus,' one of the men said tiredly, 'it didn't work.'

'But the monster is blatantly provoking us,' Vallus snarled, hitting the table with a fist, causing Tash and his companions to jump. 'I won't have it coming into our town and trying to lure people into its grasp.' He looked at Tash.

'Perhaps one night you might join our party, Tash. I understand Robins can use magic– surely that would help to turn the tide in our favour.'

Going on a nighttime hunting trip was the last thing Tash wanted to do but she gave a noncommittal, 'perhaps.'

'Excellent,' Vallus said, pleased. 'I'll make sure to collect you so that you're not alone outside.'

She drained her cup and smiled briefly, before muttering a short excuse and escaping from the table, leaving the men to their plans and ascending the stairs to her chamber. With a satisfying click, she locked the door and unfastened her cloak which she draped over the chair. She bent down, untying her shoes and then poured some water into a bowl to rinse her face and hands. The bath from earlier had been removed from the room so she would have to make do with the simple washcloth to scrub the dirt away.

When she was clean again, Tash emptied the water out of the window, checking that no one was walking underneath the shutters just in case. She went back over to the dressing table, flipped her dezmian and conjured a mortar and pestle, a pair of scales, some glass vials and a lamp with a stand. Carefully, she lit the lamp and picked up her gloves, pulling them on before withdrawing the samples of fungus she had collected.

Part of the fungus she crushed with the mortar and pestle, wrinkling her nose at the acrid smell that filled the air. Gently, she lifted the remnants and deposited them in one of the vials, before placing some of the white webbing in another vial.

There was a knocking at the door, and she paused, 'Yes?'

'Tash,' it was Mellie's voice, 'I wanted to let you know that I'm serving dinner.'

'I'll be right down,' Tash called back, placing the vial with the ground fungus over the lamp and then removing her gloves, moving towards the door. She paused, brushing her skirts out and left, following the scent of cooked meat. The dining room was mostly empty, the majority of the inn's patrons having left already before the sun set to retreat to the safety of their own homes. Mellie had dished up bowls of stew to those who remained, a handful of men sipping tankards of ale and Tash, who Mellie joined at one of the tables.

'I'm afraid we don't have much,' Mellie said quietly, 'Jervois has been good about sharing the village's resources, but it's not enough to feed everyone.'

'It's delicious,' Tash lied with passable ease, spooning up the meat and vegetable stew hungrily. She tried to ignore the watery sauce and stringy gristle, focussing instead on the fact that it was hot and filling. Mellie smiled gratefully.

'Thank you, Tash.'

Tash took a long draught from her own mug of ale, hoping to remove the aftertaste of the stew. When Mellie offered her another bowl, she politely declined and finished the ale, watching the last patrons shuffling off to their own homes as Mellie slid several large bolts across the door and began locking the shutters.

'Remember to lock your window, Tash,' she reminded as she collected the empty bowl and mug. 'Don't open it until morning.'

'I won't forget,' Tash said dutifully, feeling almost like a child which rankled. 'Sleep well, Mellie. I'll see you in the morning.'

'Goodnight dear,' Mellie called as Tash returned to her room, locking the door once again. She closed her eyes and leaned back against the wood, until a sound from the window had her heart rise in her throat and she glanced up fearfully.

'I was wondering when you would be back,' Cai remarked from his position on the windowsill, balancing precariously on the edge.

'What do you think you're doing?' Tash hissed, rushing forwards to yank him inside and then closed the shutters and window. 'Are you wanting to be seen?'

'Don't worry,' he said breezily, 'no one saw me. They've already locked everything up. No one's looking out into the street at this time.' He pointed to the western sky with his thumb, 'the sun's setting. They know better than to tempt chance and give in to their curiosity.'

She glared at him, arms crossed. 'I can't believe that you would just sit there in broad daylight—'

'You know, it's nice that you're worried about my safety,' he said, sauntering over towards the dressing table.

'I am *not*,' she denied hotly, 'but I need these people to trust me. They're going to struggle with that if they see you here.'

'You gave me permission to be here,' he said smugly, bending down to observe the fungus in the vial. 'Interesting.'

'What is?' Tash snapped grumpily.

'Look at how this is reacting to the heat,' he murmured, moving to the side and indicating the vial. Curious, Tash approached and saw that the ground pieces of fungus in the glass were moving, reforming and growing in size. It seemed to pulse, like a heartbeat, its colour fluctuating from grey to steely blue to brown.

'It's almost as though the heat is causing it to rejuvenate,' she murmured. 'How strange.'

He sniffed the air, 'That smell is familiar.'

'You smelt it earlier today,' she remarked unhelpfully, 'in the field.'

'No,' Cai disagreed, 'I'm certain I've smelt it before.'

'Well, when you figure out when that was, let me know,' Tash said, peering closer at the fungus. She switched the vials on the stand and noted that, in contrast, the strange webbing seemed to shrink away from the heat, pulling upward to the top of the vial, sliding up the glass in an attempt to escape.

'Cover that thing,' Cai said sharply as Tash lifted the vial away from the lamp. She glanced around for something to place over the top, but when the heat source was removed, the webbing relaxed, sinking back down in the vial. She paused for a second and then poured some water into it. On impact with the liquid, the webbing swirled, absorbing the water and began to bubble, making soft popping noises. To their surprise, a small mushroom pushed through the webbing, standing firm in the mass of white.

'How bizarre,' Tash murmured, placing the vial back down on the dresser and reaching for her dezmian. 'Have you ever seen something like that?'

'No,' he replied. He eyed her dezmian, 'What are you going to do?'

She didn't answer, already flipping the round stone, and reaching out again with her mind towards the strange fungus, trying to discern the magic that it had been made from. She shut her eyes, sensing something dark and potent, an angry, bitter force that broke out of the plant in waves, knocking into her and making her grip the dressing table. There was a steadying hand on her arm and the sensation alleviated somewhat, allowing her to push deeper into the magical tide, to see a pair of bright, dark eyes in a pale face. She was overwhelmed with a desire for vengeance, to wreak havoc and lay waste to anything and everything.

Tash pulled back from the feeling, breaking out of the trance and fell against Cai, who held her securely at his side. His face was taut, and she realised that he too had felt the magical pull, that he had taken some of the burden, allowing her the chance to try to discern its origin.

'I've not encountered magic quite like that,' she whispered, trembling. 'It's not a spell gone wrong, like I suspected, but something darker. More… insidious.'

'It's from the Shadow Realm,' Cai replied with surprising calm. 'Someone has been experimenting with magic they shouldn't be using or made a deal with a creature from that place.'

'And I assume you're not going to make my job easier and say that you made a deal with a human?' Tash asked hopefully. 'It would be a lot more helpful if you did.'

'I'm afraid I cannot oblige you this time,' he said, mouth quirking in a wry smile.

'Damn,' she sighed, 'I guess we'll just need to figure this out the hard way then.'

'We?'

She rolled her eyes and continued as if he hadn't spoken, 'I want to go back to Sian's farm tomorrow. I sensed a different kind of magic there– something brighter, happier. Perhaps he will be able to shed light on how magic is being used to grow and protect his crops.' She thought for a moment and then added, 'And I want to find out who has died from touching the fungus. I saw someone and sensed this overwhelming anger. Perhaps the deaths are connected in some way.'

'You could be right,' Cai replied as she moved to sit down on the bed, propping herself up on the pillows and lifting a leather-bound book and quill from her bedside table. She dipped the quill in an inkpot and began to take notes on a new page, forehead creased in concentration. He watched her for a while, extinguishing the lamp on the dressing table so that the only remaining lights were from the candles at her bedside.

Tash felt his gaze but forced herself to note down what she had found and discovered that day, so that when she gave her final report to The Robin it would be a lot easier to write up.

'You can sit if you want,' she said distractedly, not looking up from her notes. He sat at the opposite end of the bed, legs crossed, watching the progress of her quill across the page. When she had finished, she replaced the quill and notebook on the table, purposefully avoiding his gaze as she tried to ignore the mounting tension she sensed between them, and as she tried to figure out how to best phrase her question.

'Cai,' she finally said, 'tell me about your mother. What happened to her?'

He flinched as if she'd struck him. 'Why do you want to know about that?' His tone was harsh and brutal, and she felt a momentary spark of fear.

'I heard a story today about her,' Tash said carefully, 'at least, I assumed it was her. You did say that you were raised on the Nordhaven Heath. The story I heard was slightly different to the one you told me.' She could sense his rising anger, the iciness spreading through the room from where he sat was chilling her. Yet she pushed on, needing to know the truth. 'They said that you were wild, that when you changed, you became a monster and killed your mother on the Heath.'

'I've told you before that I am not innocent,' Cai said coldly, voice brittle. 'I have killed many people over the years.'

'But Cai,' she leaned forward, catching one of his hands in hers and holding it firm, 'did you kill your mother?'

He hissed in sudden pain and yanked his hand away from her, the dark welt in his flesh forming after briefly touching her ring of yew. 'What do you want me to say, Tash?' he asked, healing the injury with his untarnished hand. His tone made her want to cry, it was distant and shuttered, vastly different from how he had been with her the night before when he had called her beautiful.

'I want to know the truth,' she pressed, removing her ring and capturing his hand in hers again. She edged closer, refusing to let him move away, ignoring the blazing anger that still simmered in his eyes. 'They say these things about you, Cai, and I don't know what's real and what's false. I don't think that you're a monster– but I want to know the truth.'

'The truth?' he snorted and glared at her. 'The truth is that the people in this town cast me out long before I changed. They turned my mother against me, keeping her separated from me when I became a Nightwalker. Back then I was scared: afraid of them, of myself and of what my senses were urging me to do. I don't remember that last night– they'd been hunting me with dogs on the Heath for weeks. I hadn't slept or fed for days. I just remember the sun rising and finding her, seeing her blood on my hands. I don't know if I did it or not. I don't *remember*.' His voice broke and he covered his face in his hands. Tash reacted instinctively, reaching out and holding him close, pulling him into her embrace. He stilled, and then continued, 'I ran. The villagers saw and chased me off. I fled into the Shadow Realm; I'd avoided it up until then but it allowed me to escape.'

'I'm sorry,' Tash whispered, 'I'm so sorry, Cai.' In her mind she saw him, terrified and confused, hunted by the villagers with their torches.

'I didn't come back for a few years,' Cai said. It seemed that he hadn't spoken about this before to anyone, but now that he had started to share it, he found it hard to stop the flow of memories. 'I allowed myself time to grow, to hone my powers and embrace the darker side of my nature. When I returned to Nordhaven it was with the intention of making the villagers pay, to hurt them as I had been hurt. But by then a new generation had been born and those who I had known were getting old. I enjoyed leaving them reminders of my presence over the years, reminding them that I was still out there, the Monster of the Heath.' He laughed harshly. 'But after a while I got tired of scaring them and moved away, exploring different worlds and places. Yet no matter where I went, I couldn't hide my nature and most who saw me fled.'

Tash remembered the first time she'd seen him, emerging from the shadows in the forest by the Temple, terrifying Laura and herself. She hadn't run away screaming though. Cai seemed to read her thoughts, for he said, 'You were one of the few to not immediately keel over. So was your leader.'

'The Robin?'

'When I first met him, he was an apprentice like you. Obsessed with the Shadow Realm and finding ways to making traversing between worlds easier. He was young, foolish… but he gained knowledge firsthand of the darkness and that changed his outlook. He's much wiser now.'

'Is that why no one can see his face?' Tash asked, 'Because he entered the Shadow Realm?'

Cai looked at her inscrutably. 'That's not my tale to tell. But, yes, he entered the Shadow Realm and lost his way. It was a miracle that he survived.'

'You speak about it as though you were there,' she remarked quietly and he shrugged, neither confirming nor denying it. Another thought occurred to her and she asked, 'Just how old *are* you, Cai?'

He chuckled, 'Nightwalkers take longer to age, Tash. It's been almost a century since I was born, I lose count of the exact number of years.'

She regarded him critically; he didn't seem older than his mid-twenties at best. 'How old were you when you changed?'

'Fifteen,' he shrugged. 'Or sixteen. I forget. It all blurs together after a long time.'

She nodded slowly. 'Did you ever find your father?'

Cai shook his head, 'No. I tried searching for him but never got anywhere. It seems I'm more successful at finding things for other people rather than myself.'

'Like The Robin?'

He nodded, dark eyes gazing into hers. She saw tenderness there now, the anger and hurt had faded away as they spoke softly to each other, leaving him calm by her side. She felt an answering pull in her chest, an ache that rose bright and fast within her, which was almost impossible to tamp down. Slowly, gently, he raised a hand and ran it through her hair, tracing around her cheek, his palm rough and calloused. She didn't look away, unwilling to cut the moment short, curious to see what he would do next, silently inviting him closer.

Cai smiled, guiding her face down to meet his with subtle pressure. The touch as his lips brushed hers was feather light, almost as though he hadn't kissed her at all, and he moved back, leaving an inch of space between them, teasing her. Tash bridged the distance this time, her hands tangling in his hair, circling his horns, refusing to let him move away. She felt him chuckle and silenced him, kissing him harder until he lifted her, pushing her down onto the mattress.

'Let's see how quiet a Robin can be,' he murmured, catching her in his hypnotic gaze again and she lay there, breathless and eager for more. With painful slowness, he unbuttoned her dress, hands tracing her skin. She shivered as he paused at her abdomen and moved down to her thighs, skimming over the part of her which ached the most. He began to kiss her neck, starting from the hollow by her ear and moving down, before he got distracted by her breasts. His hands rose, cupping and squeezing them and she let out a soft moan, whimpering as he lowered his mouth and began to tease her.

'Shh,' he whispered, pausing as she watched him through half-glazed eyes. 'You don't want to wake anyone.'

'Oh Gods,' she gasped as he lowered his head again, 'oh, please.'

He chuckled again and covered her mouth with his, effectively quietening her. She bit down on his lip, gripping him between her legs and locking him in tight. As he continued to kiss her, his hands resumed their slow, torturous perusal of her body, catching and teasing the desire between them into a flame. Tash moaned again, mindless with the hungry need that had taken over her. Nothing mattered, only the longing for this to continue on and on until there was nothing left. Her nails dug into his back, leaving red marks over the scars, and he gasped, breaking away as he removed his own tattered clothes.

The look in his eyes made her hold her breath, captivated by the glow she saw there. She reached out for him, silently urging him to return to the bed, to continue what he'd started. Although this time, she allowed her own hands to explore in kind, gradually learning how to make him catch his breath, how to drive him as mindless as she was herself. He groaned as she went lower, testing his self-control with a wicked smile, working her way down from his chest with her mouth, following the path her hands had taken.

Before Tash could get too far, he had pulled her up and away, whispering in her ear, 'Turn over.' She blinked, confused but obeyed, and then choked back a cry as he stroked down her spine, circling his hands around to squeeze her breasts. She arched her back, searching for release from this new form of torment. Cai pressed a kiss to her neck, and then she felt him inside of her and gasped. He took her hard and fast, driving her to the brink of insanity all too quickly. Tash gripped the sheets, biting down on the pillow to stifle her cries which only fuelled his desire more. She shattered as he came with a deep groan, and they collapsed together, damp and sweaty from their exertions.

Tash took a while to recover her thoughts, the warm languor refusing to subside quickly. She turned her head to look at Cai, wondering how she had lost her head once again in less than a day. What was wrong with her?

He was running a hand over her body, making it tingle with magic as the scratches and bruises faded, removing all traces of his uncontrolled passion. He didn't heal the scratches on his own body though, and she glanced at her hands, surprised that she had done such a thing. Cai followed her gaze and shrugged lightly, 'It's not that bad, Tash. You haven't hurt me.'

All the same, she thought that she'd need to trim her nails in case this happened again. She didn't like knowing that she had unthinkingly drawn blood with her bare hands. She paused, registering that already she was thinking about preparing for the next time. Was that wise? She should be focussing on her task in Nordhaven, not on what happened when Cai touched her. Tash frowned slightly, confused and conflicted at her own indecision.

'What's wrong?' Cai asked softly, one hand reaching out and grasping hers. It was intimate, the sort of thing a lover might do and her mind started racing with the implications of it. Her eyes clouded as she looked down at their entwined hands, half wanting to pull away, half wanting to stay put. A thought skittered across her mind, tempting her. He wasn't a Mortal, he could cross between worlds without repercussions, staying as long or as little a time as he wanted in each place. If– whatever this was between them– developed further, she wouldn't have to leave him behind.

She moistened her lips, took a breath and finally voiced the question that had begun forming since the night before. 'What are we?'

He was quiet for a while, scanning her eyes with his, reading her confusion and hesitancy all too easily. His thumb rubbed the back of her hand as he said, 'We can be whatever you want us to be, Tash.'

'But what do *you* want?' she pressed.

'I would've thought that would be obvious,' he smiled, and then on seeing her agitated expression, he relented and clarified, 'I want *you*. I've wanted you from the moment we met.' She stared at him and he blushed. 'I think the important question though, is what you want. I may not like the out-come, but if you want to stop this,' he indicated the space between them with a hand, 'you just need to say.'

She couldn't speak. She didn't know.

Cai watched her, noting the worries flicking across her open face, unable to hide from him the dilemma she faced. She couldn't afford to get distracted from her task, and Cai was definitely a distraction. Romulus had warned her about developing feelings for others, reminding her to not lose her head. But Cai wasn't human— he wasn't restricted to one particular world. Yet that was another problem. He *wasn't* human anymore— he was a Nightwalker, a creature distrusted and reviled by many, one of the cursed few who, if they had a child, would face a similar fate. He wouldn't age with her, but see her grow old alone. She would either have to see him secretly when the sun went down or live in forced exile, for few would accept her if they knew who she lay with.

And yet, there was the way he made her feel. He drove her crazy at times, she wanted to strangle him occasionally when he infuriated her, but he could comfort her when she succumbed to emotion and make her laugh. His touch awoke something dormant in her, he made her feel powerful and confident, secure in the knowledge that she could try new things and test boundaries. She wanted him nearby; she'd become accustomed to feeling safe when he was there and didn't want to be without that. She didn't want to be lonely anymore.

'You don't have to decide tonight,' Cai said gently, squeezing her hand. 'We can take things a day at a time until you are sure.'

'I think I'd like that,' she said, 'thank you.' She leaned forward and kissed him, feeling the warmth of his lips against hers.

The scratching at the window made both of them freeze. Tash felt the fear rise in her as the scratching continued, scraping up along the shutters and reaching around their edges, trying to find a way inside.

'You did lock the window, didn't you?' Cai whispered and she nodded, terrified. A strange, rattling noise came from outside, followed by a low, heavy panting as the creature pressed even closer to the shutters.

'Sweet, sweet mistress,' the voice was ragged and made one's blood turn icy cold. 'I know you're there. I can smell you. You can't escape me.'

Tash was holding Cai so tightly that her arms hurt, unable to stop trembling. On hearing the creature's voice, he had gone rigid, expression darkening.

'And what else do I smell, mistress?' the voice continued to rasp, 'Who else is… oh dear.' It began the rattling sound again and Tash realised that it was laughing, a horrible, choking sound. 'You *have* been naughty, mistress. You will suit me *very well*, I think. Darkness will soon consume your heart. Soon, very soon, you will be mine.'

Cai growled and leapt up from the bed, raising his hands and making a sweeping gesture. The window shutters quivered and the creature on the other side let out another rattling wheeze.

'Your blood will be worth the wait, mistress. My sweet Natachatet.' There was a cry as the creature lost its grip, a dark shadow forming around the window and vanishing almost as quickly as it had come. Tash shook uncontrollably on the bed, more scared than she had ever been.

'What was it?' she whispered, 'How did it know my name?'

Cai moved back over to her, wrapping his arms and tail around her, his touch gradually calming the tremors. 'I would hazard a guess it's a type of Dæmon. Some of them have the ability of speech, and this one seems to have fixated on your scent after last night.' His grip tightened. 'It'll be hunting you, Tash. Once a Dæmon has chosen its prey, it is nigh on impossible to keep it away.'

'How did you get rid of it?' she asked, eyes wide.

'I banished it back to the Shadow Realm,' he said, frowning, 'but that won't hold it for long. It is probably as familiar with that place as I am, it'll find its way back most likely by tomorrow night.'

His words didn't comfort her and she swallowed painfully. 'But how did it know my name?'

'I cannot say,' he admitted. 'It'll be necessary for you to remain inside though at night. I don't think that creature will be easily deterred. So long as it cannot enter the building, you should be safe.'

'Don't leave me tonight,' she said, 'I don't want to be alone.'

'If you want me to stay, I will,' he murmured, pressing a kiss to her forehead.

Tash nodded, and allowed him to guide her under the covers. After the candles had been extinguished, she gazed sightlessly into the darkness, her back resting against him. Gradually, his breathing deepened and she realised that he had fallen asleep. Tash closed her eyes, but the creature's voice kept replaying in her mind, making sleep seem impossible.

You have been naughty mistress. Soon you will be mine. Darkness will consume your heart. Your blood will be worth the wait, my sweet Natachatet.

Then the voice changed and the words no longer made her breath catch in fear, instead they reverberated around her brain with a strange, compelling force.

Hearts wild,
Lovers flawed.
Contamination tamed,
Hope is wrought.
Help too far,
Leaving too soon.
He who awaits,
Each turning of moon.
Beware the night,
Be cautious of day.
When all strays,
You will stay.

Tash shuddered at the voice, dreading what it meant and it was a long time before she succumbed to sleep.

Chapter Thirteen

I saw the witch tonight. She was on the Heath, in the spot where I used to go when I was human. Perhaps it was the place she met my ancestor before she cursed him and his future progeny. Even though I have never spoken to her, I know her name, whispered in my nightmares.

Melisande.

She wore a crown of thorns, her long, red hair catching in the wind and I could've sworn she saw me, hiding in the shadows. Even from afar I saw the cruel smile play across her features and felt my blood freeze. It was a look I recognise all too well from whenever I see my reflection, a hunter searching for prey. Gods I hope that she will not hunt me.

~ A hastily written entry in a blood speckled diary, hidden in the Shadow Realm

Tash awoke as dawn was breaking, unaware of when she had fallen asleep but feeling a sense of lingering dread from the night before. Cai had already risen, dressed into his tattered clothes and then unlocked the window. As she stirred, he turned away from opening the shutters, allowing the morning light to stream into the room.

'You're going already?' Tash mumbled, brain still fuzzy from the poor night's sleep and Cai nodded silently. She held out a hand and he moved back to the bed, taking it and squeezing it. 'When will I see you next?' she whispered.

'I need to return to the Shadow Realm,' he said gravely, 'I want to find out more about that Dæmon and it'll be easier to find answers there. Be safe while I'm gone.' He kissed her briefly and then drew away, swinging out of the window and vanishing into the break of dawn.

Tash got up, yawning as she dressed and braided her hair back. When she was presentable, she unlocked her door and descended to the dining room, where Mellie had already made up a batch of the tasteless porridge she'd eaten the day before. Tash was quiet while she had her breakfast, watching Mellie unbolt the door and open the shutters to reveal blue skies and cool sunshine. When she had finished eating, Tash cleared her bowl away, fetched her cloak and left the inn, striding through the brisk, cold morning air and heading for the farmhouse at the top of the hilltop.

She was determined to meet Sian to see if her suspicions were correct. The houses around her were quiet, it seemed as though the inhabitants of Nordhaven were slow risers to-day, unwilling to face another day of hardship. However, as she began to climb the hill towards Sian's farm, she noticed that in his fields people were already working, tilling the soil and tending to the crops. By the time she had reached the outer field, she managed to wave and get one farmhand's at-tention. He sauntered over, giving her a slow perusal which made her feel uncomfortable.

'Yes?' he asked casually, tipping his hat back. 'Can I help you?'

'I was hoping to speak to Sian,' Tash replied politely, 'is he here?'

'Sian's over there,' the worker pointed at a distant figure, who was hunched over in the dirt. 'I'll send him to you.'

'Thanks,' Tash said, grateful as the man walked off and she could relax. The farmhand approached Sian and called out, his words indecipherable, and Tash watched as Sian got to his feet and made his way over to her at the boundary wall. He was perhaps in his mid-forties and balding with a weatherbeaten, open face. His brown eyes crinkled into a smile as he reached her and extended a hand.

'You must be the Robin in town,' he said, 'nice to meet you. I'm Sian.'

'Tash,' she replied, shaking his hand with a smile. 'I hope you don't mind the intrusion.'

'Oh, not at all,' he said jovially. 'I thought it would be a matter of time before you stopped by.'

Tash inclined her head. 'It's an impressive farm you have here.'

'It's taken years to achieve it,' Sian replied proudly, gesturing around at the flourishing fields. 'It used to be that these fields were the worst plots around the town, but then luck turned in our favour. Now we're spared the worst of the weather and the blight has kept away.'

Tash's interest was piqued and she asked, 'How did you turn things around to improve the condition of the soil? It must have taken a lot of work.'

Sian nodded. 'My son, Atticus, developed a new type of fertiliser using plants from the Heath. It must have been three summers ago now, but since then we've been blessed with good harvests.' He smiled and waved at one of the other figures out on the farm, 'There he is. Atticus!' he called, 'Come over here!'

'What do you make of the blight?' Tash asked curiously, and Sian's face fell.

'It's horrible,' he said gravely, 'the deaths, the loss of crops– currently we're the only farm with fresh produce and it's taking its toll. I never built this farm with the intention of supporting the entire town. Some of those who died were the children of my neighbours or labourers who would do seasonal work for each of us. What happened to them… the way the blight just made them fall into some death-sleep, I wouldn't wish on anyone. The other farmers are my friends, but when I see them now, they… well,' he sighed. 'They don't understand how the blight has spared my fields and not theirs. I wish I knew that too. I'd love to help them get back on their feet.'

'You called, Father?' A reedy voice spoke from behind them and Tash jumped, having been too focussed on Sian's words to notice Atticus coming closer.

'Ah, my boy,' Sian clapped Atticus on the shoulder, grinning. 'I was just talking about you and how you created our new fertiliser. I want you to meet Tash, the Robin who's come to town. She's investigating the blight.'

Dark, flashing eyes met Tash's and she held out a hand, refusing to show that she recognised him. He had been the one she saw when she attempted to trace the magical source of the fungus. Atticus was pale, with sunken cheekbones and an angular, jutting chin. Distrustfully, he shook her hand, shooting glances from Tash to his father, assessing them.

'Well, we don't know anything about that,' he said bluntly, almost to the point of rudeness. 'There's nothing here for you, so it would be better for you to leave. We don't need Robins poking their noses in where they aren't wanted.'

'Atticus,' Sian said, shocked. 'Apologise this instant.' His son snorted and stormed off, casting a baleful glare back at

Tash. 'I'm very sorry,' Sian was embarrassed now, 'he didn't used to be like that.'

'What was he like?' Tash asked, watching Atticus disappear in the direction of the Heath.

'He knew how to treat visitors, for one thing,' Sian frowned, 'he laughed more, smiled more. In recent months, he's seemed different.'

Pieces were coming together in Tash's mind, slowly but surely fitting into the puzzle. 'Does anyone in Nordhaven practise magic?' she asked Sian and he shook his head, confused.

'Not as far as I know,' he replied, 'why?'

'There's magic in these fields,' she murmured, sensing the same force she had felt the previous day. 'That's why the blight hasn't affected them.'

'Witchcraft?' Sian's tone had turned aghast. 'But I never—'

'Don't worry yourself, Sian,' Tash said calmly, 'I mean to get to the bottom of it. If you'll excuse me?'

She began to track Atticus' progress, leaving Sian by the wall, forehead creased in confusion. Atticus had moved fast, crossing the field and already reaching the Heath on the other side. Tash circled the farmland, keeping an eye on his distant figure, walking steadily so as not to make it obvious that she was following him. By the time she had reached the Heath, he had almost vanished from view, and she increased her pace, determined not to lose sight of him.

He didn't glance back once, moving onwards with single-minded focus, cutting through the gorse and heather, ignoring it catching on his clothes. Tash tried to do the same, but her cloak and skirts got tangled more easily, burrs snagging in the fabric and mud sticking to her boots as if trying to hold her in place. The village disappeared behind them, and she began to wonder just where Atticus was going. Then she saw a structure rising up ahead, a weather-beaten shack whose roof was partially collapsed. Atticus ducked inside it, and as she approached, Tash withdrew her dezmian and held it tightly in her gloved fist, just in case. The door was ajar and inside was shrouded in darkness.

'Atticus?' She knocked on the door and it swung inwards. 'I just want to talk.'

'Go away,' his voice reached her from the darkest recesses of the shack. 'I don't want you here.'

'I need you to tell me how you made your father's crops flourish,' Tash said with forced calmness, halting in the doorway and remaining in the light. 'I need to know how the blight was created. I'd hazard a guess that you know the answers to both. I want to help.'

'You don't know anything,' he replied, voice turning resentful. 'You can't help me. No one can.'

She wanted to tell him to stop being dramatic and to answer her. Instead, she chose a more diplomatic approach and said, 'Tell me about the magic. I can feel it, the love and care that has gone into your father's farmland. How did you cast it?'

'I don't practise witchcraft,' he snarled and she smiled gently.

'I wouldn't call it that. The magic around your farm is good and generous, the sort of thing that I'm sure many farmers would love to have. Consistent good luck and fortune, bountiful harvests, no harm from extreme weather. How did you do it?'

There was a pause and then Atticus said, 'Father worked for years and years on that farm. Nothing he did worked. The other farmers mocked him, saying that he was an idiot for buying the farm on the hilltop. They never said it to his face, but their children would tell me about it, laughing at him. I wanted Father to succeed– he'd given up so much for that piece of land and it was causing problems between him and Mother.'

'You were angry?' Tash probed delicately. 'With the other farmers and their children?'

'Angry?' Atticus laughed, the sound reverberating around the walls. 'I suppose some people might have been angry. I just wanted them to suffer the same pain we did.'

'So you cast a spell?' Tash asked gently. 'To change your circumstances?'

'Not exactly,' he replied. 'I had help. Someone who understood what it's like to be reviled and excluded. Someone who knew how I felt and made me powerful again.'

'Who was it?' Tash held her breath, waiting eagerly for his answer.

'Would you like to meet them?' Atticus asked, 'I can introduce you if you'd like.'

A shiver of foreboding ran down the back of her neck, warning her to be on her guard. 'Tell me first about the blight,' she countered, and she sensed Atticus shifting in the dark room. 'How did it happen?'

'Why don't you come inside?' Atticus' voice had changed and she froze, realising that something else was now there too. Instinctively, she flipped her dezmian, summoning a torch that she gripped in her free hand, banishing the shadows from the shack and filling the room with a piercing, bright light.

Something let out an eldritch scream, pulling away and cringing into the wall, desperately trying to escape. Atticus lay in a heap on the ground, shaking uncontrollably, eyes rolling back into his head. Tash focussed on the shrieking figure on the other side of the hut, a skinny, malnourished creature whose features were warped and distorted. Perhaps once it had been human, but now it had become twisted, with fanged teeth and sharp claws. Its eyes were enormous in its face, wide black pupils glared at her venomously.

Tash began to whisper in the Ancient Tongue, moving closer to the creature, as streaks of light left her dezmian and wrapped around it in holy flames as she spoke, repeating the prayer of the old faith over and over. As the flames held the creature firm, Atticus yelled in agony, similar markings appearing on his own arms. Tash frowned in concentration, pushing closer to the monster as it weakened in its bonds, the words from her prayer echoing off the walls. Finally, it slumped down onto the ground and Tash went silent, inspecting the temporarily subdued creature.

'What are you?' she asked and the creature shifted, but it was Atticus who spoke, his voice broken.

'I am the harvester of souls and bane of the living, the last thing you will see when you sleep and the first when you wake. You will not escape me, Robin.'

'You're not the creature that's terrorising Nordhaven at night,' Tash replied thoughtfully, peering closer at its features. 'I'd say that you're a lesser variety of Dæmon.' She leaned in and sniffed, the acrid scent from the fungus rising off the creature's skin. 'But you are the one responsible for the blight.'

'A deal is a deal,' the Dæmon laughed, once more using Atticus' voice. 'This one was all too ready to accept the terms, all to give his father the life he always wanted. His anger and resentment made it all too easy. He was positively *begging* for otherworldly aid.'

Tash's stomach clenched. 'What did you offer him?'

The creature's malicious eyes bored into hers and she twisted her hand, tightening the flames around its body. It flinched and growled out, 'I don't owe you anything, Robin.'

She snarled, 'Tell me, Dæmon. I won't ask again.'

It whimpered, the flames biting deeper into its pale, sickly flesh. 'I offered him an ingredient from the Shadow Realm that would give him what he desired: the powdered bones of a Dæmon. He mixed it into fertiliser and his father's farm yielded better crops than ever before.'

'And in return?' Tash's voice was harsh.

'Souls,' the Dæmon whispered, its tone becoming hungry, 'I wanted to feed.' It laughed again. 'He thought I wanted to eat human food– the crops from the other farms. He didn't realise what I truly wanted. By the time he did, I had already begun to feast on his soul. He's been mine for months now, my eyes and ears in the town. No one noticed, and I was able to feast on those who reviled him, those who were stupid enough to touch the blight and succumb to my will.'

Tash had heard enough, yet still she forced herself to ask her last question, 'How can we stop the blight?'

It gazed at her unblinking, and seemed to ponder the answer. 'I think you know what would end it, Robin. But are you prepared to pay the price?'

Its words confused her. 'I don't understand.'

'Nothing is for free,' it whispered softly. 'The blood of a Dæmon will heal the land, and its bones will need to be returned to their resting place.'

Tash stared at it, still uncomprehending of what was required. 'What do you mean?'

'A life for a life, Robin. Until the bones are returned to the Shadow Realm, you will feel your force drain away.' It bared its teeth in a cruel smile. 'You don't want to get lost in the Shadow Realm, girl. It'll take more than your soul from you. You'll never come back. It'd be easier to leave things as they are. These people aren't worth the sacrifice.'

Tash considered its words, finally recognising the potential cost. Slowly she put the dezmian into her pocket and withdrew her knife from her belt, eyeing the blade critically.

'You're wrong,' she said before she plunged the weapon down, piercing the creature in its heart. The Dæmon writhed, scratching at her with its clawed hands, until it intercepted her ring of yew, which she pressed mercilessly into the side of its face, holding it down until it stopped struggling and breathed its last.

Dark blood was staining her hands, and she flicked the dezmian, drawing the creature's blood from the knife wound, lifting the liquid through the air into a nearby urn. When the Dæmon was drained empty, she cleaned the dagger's blade and sheathed it, before moving over to the faintly stirring Atticus. He gazed at her blearily, eyes slowly coming back into focus, darting around at the rundown shack in confusion.

'Where am I?' he asked, 'Who are you?'

'I am called Tash,' she replied gently, 'I'm a Robin.'

'A Robin?' Atticus asked, perplexed, 'But, why would a Robin be here?'

'I came to stop the blight,' she said, helping him to his feet and hefting the heavy urn in her arms. 'Let's head back to your father's farm now. Come on.'

He followed her meekly, giving the dead Dæmon's body a wide berth as they left the shack. 'What blight?' His eyes were clouded with confusion and she paused briefly, a new suspicion starting to form in her mind.

'What's the last thing you remember, Atticus?' Tash asked calmly as they began to navigate their way back towards Nordhaven, pushing their way through the tough bracken.

'There was the sound of bells,' he said, 'darkness and then something reached out and trapped me there.' He raised his hands and gripped his head. 'I was stuck. Then I saw a light– there was screaming and it was easier to get away. When I came to, you were there.'

'And before that?' Tash pressed, juggling the urn in her arms so that she wouldn't drop it as they climbed over a broken tree.

'Father was asking questions about the fertiliser,' he replied, forehead straining as he tried to remember. 'I didn't want to tell him. He hates witchcraft, and I was sure that if I told him the truth about what the special ingredient was, he'd throw me out. The other farmers were finally undergoing some of the hardships we had experienced– they had low yields from the drought and storms. But he wanted to share the fertiliser with them, to help them even after the way they treated him. I didn't agree with him and we argued. Then I went to the Heath and...' he paused thoughtfully, 'then I heard the bells and everything went dark.'

'We need to set things right, Atticus,' Tash said seriously. 'You're going to need to give me the rest of the powdered bones. The blight has already claimed several lives. It needs to stop.'

'People have died?' Atticus sounded shaken, confused. 'But how? What is this blight?'

As they crossed the Heath, Tash explained what had happened in Nordhaven, and as she spoke, Atticus became more distressed and guilt-ridden. Tash thought that he deserved to feel some responsibility– if he hadn't made a deal with a Dæmon, several villagers would still be alive. Yet, she understood how easily one could be tricked into making decisions with long-lasting consequences. She didn't want to think yet about what she had committed to when she thrust her dagger into the Dæmon's heart.

When they were outside Sian's farmstead, Atticus turned to her and requested, 'Please, let me tell my father, Tash. I've been stupid in thinking that magic like this would secure our happiness and make everything all right. And thank you, for saving me from that creature. If there's anything I can do to help make amends, just ask.'

She inclined her head, 'I'll be by tomorrow to collect the remaining powdered bones, Atticus. Keep safe in the meantime.' As he headed inside, Tash turned and made her way to the edge of the field, lowering the urn to the ground and stretching her aching arms. From a glance at the sky, she didn't have long before sunset, so she would need to work fast.

Her dezmian flicked into the air and she gave herself over to the sensation of magic, guiding it to obey her command as she began to sing in the Ancient Tongue. The sounds blurred together, urging the magical current to encompass her until she felt infinite and powerful, a herald for new life. Her fingers extended and the lid of the urn opened, the blood rising from it in a nebulous stream, spinning above her until her hands met and parted. The blood shifted into particles, rising up towards heavy clouds, before there was a clap of thunder and it fell back to earth, cleansing the fields and plants with a healing, red-tinged rain.

Tash's song came to an end and she felt the wave of fatigue assault her like a strong punch to the stomach. She swayed and gripped onto the wall for support, breath coming in quick gasps. Eventually, she felt strong enough to make her way back down the hill towards the inn. As she staggered onwards, she heard cries of shock and fear from the sudden rain, in particular when the villagers saw its colour.

'What have you done?' an angry voice yelled and she looked up to see Klem striding towards her furiously. 'You've angered the Gods; you're going to make everything worse. You've cursed us, witch.'

Tash stood her ground, although she couldn't help swaying slightly, considerably weakened by using so much magic that day. 'I don't expect you to understand,' she replied as he drew closer. 'I came here to help your town, not harm it. Perhaps you shouldn't make accusations before you see the results.'

He growled, reached out and gripped her arm painfully. 'Only a witch would survive on the Heath overnight without coming to any harm.'

'Let me go,' Tash tried to pull away but he held her firm. The light-headedness was returning and she felt ill, as if she would faint.

'For Gods' sakes, Klem,' another voice cried, 'let her go. It's nearly sunset. Settle your dispute in the morning if it means that much to you.' Another figure had joined them, roughly pulling Klem's arm away and leaving Tash to sway unsteadily. She realised it was Vallus who was standing between them, protecting her from Klem's murderous glare.

'I'll find you tomorrow, girl,' Klem snarled. 'We don't want witches in this town.'

'I'm not a witch,' Tash replied, a tinge of irritation colouring her tone. 'And perhaps by tomorrow you will be able to see that you're wrong in your assumptions about me.'

He stormed away and she felt herself sag, before Vallus caught her elbow, keeping her upright.

'You need to get inside,' he said, concerned, as he helped her down the street. 'I don't know what you've done with this,' he indicated the rain that was streaking blood across his face, 'but you can explain tomorrow. For now, it's more important that everyone gets off the streets.'

The inn was in sight, and Tash sped up, spurred on by thoughts of a hot bath and food. Vallus increased his pace as well, until he was half carrying her over the cobbles. He pushed the door open and deposited her on the threshold, before disappearing quickly in the direction of his own house. There was a soft cry and Mellie rushed over, helping Tash inside and sliding the bolts across the door behind her.

'What happened to you, dear?' She was so concerned that she didn't even comment on the bloody water that was dripping off Tash's clothing, or the mud-caked boots leaving dirty footprints on her pristine floor.

'I think I've found a way to cure the blight,' Tash murmured hazily, finding it harder to stay awake, 'by morning… see… a difference.' She stumbled and Mellie caught her, assisting her towards her room.

'I don't know what you've been up to, but you look like you need a hot bath, a strong cup of tea and something to eat. Come on, Tash, one step at a time.' Tash managed to focus just long enough to get up to her room, before Mellie deposited her on the bed. The woman cringed at the dirt staining the sheets but didn't say anything else as Tash's eyes closed briefly, sliding into unconsciousness.

She came to when Mellie was pouring steaming water into the bathtub, which she had clearly pulled into the room while Tash slept. She noticed Tash blinking at her and smiled.

'Give me a minute to fetch you some tea, then you can have a nice bath, dear. I'll have dinner ready downstairs when you're done.' She left and returned quickly, a tray with a teapot and cup balanced in her hands. She placed it on the dressing table, turned her back on Tash and then said, 'Give me your clothes, dear. I'll take care of them and clean them for you.'

Tash was too exhausted to argue. Mutely, she stripped off, pulled a towel around her body and handed Mellie the pile of sodden, bloody clothing. 'Thank you,' she said faintly.

'It's no trouble,' Mellie replied, 'have a long soak and drink your tea, and then come down for dinner.' She smiled again and shut the door, the sound of her footsteps on the wooden stairs echoing through the quiet inn. Tash sighed, released the towel and climbed into the bath. Her muscles ached and the scratches from the Dæmon's claws stung and burned. She gasped in pain, sinking into the hot water and closing her eyes, too weak to consider lifting up the bar of soap yet.

Her mind wandered, getting lost in a daydream where Cai appeared and held her, whispering sweet nothings in her ear until she felt whole again. Her eyes snapped open, glancing around the room with a mad desperation, but she was completely alone. Pushing down a dejectedness that she thought she oughtn't feel, Tash poured a cup of tea and sipped it, feeling a sense of calm descend. She lathered herself with soap, cleansing her body and hair from the grime and blood. There was another shock of pain and she glanced down at the inside of her forearm where some of the Dæmon's scratches spread from her wrist to the crook of her elbow. While the majority of her injuries were superficial, these wounds were black, with dark tendrils stretching out from the cuts, like miniature veins along her arm.

The Dæmon's words played through her mind and she murmured softly, 'A life for a life, until the bones are returned.' She turned her arm, noting that the contamination hadn't spread to the other side. So long as she wore long sleeves, it should be easy to hide. In the meantime, she would hope that Cai would return soon, so that he could take her back to the Shadow Realm.

Chapter Fourteen

The worst time is when there's a new moon. The tearing and pain, I feel the burning in my whole body and I cannot resist it. At first, I thought it was the blessing in the witch's curse, but then I realised that it was the harshest cruelty. When the sun rises, I am returned to my form, the monster they claim I am. I cannot return to my home, to the people I love, for they know what became of me. Other times I have tried going somewhere new, but always end the night on the outskirts of the town, too afraid to risk entering and losing myself again.

The new moon just makes the emptiness and loneliness worse. I wouldn't wish this fate on anyone.

~ An extract from a blood-stained journal in the Shadow
　Realm

Three days had passed since the blood-rain fell from the sky, summoned by the Robin who had come to help the town of Nordhaven. It had washed away the contamination in the fields, removing the fungus as though it had never existed, and already new plants were pushing through the earth, promising the farmers a reprieve from their hardships. The villagers were celebrating still, thanking the Gods and Tash for her aid in lifting the curse. Even Klem had approached her, hat in hand the morning after the storm, apologetic and remorseful, although his wife's beady glare might have been the reason for his apology. All the same, Tash accepted it, not wanting to cause more disruption and wishing to avoid any future disagreements.

Jervois was overjoyed, shaking her hand until her teeth rattled, and then announced to the entire village that they would have a proper celebration at the town hall. When several people voiced concerns, he waved their worries away.

'We haven't had an attack for almost a week,' he said, 'Vallus and our town guards will be on duty and will walk people to their homes once the festivities are done. Nordhaven hasn't had a reason to celebrate in a long time. We cannot allow the fear of Nightwalkers to ruin our good fortune.'

Gradually, the villagers had warmed to the idea and a sense of excitement spread throughout the town. It was going to be a big party, with dancing, free-flowing wine and Jervois had promised that a portion of the village's stockpile would allow for an enjoyable feast. Tash didn't have the heart to argue with his desire for extravagance, and he insisted that she would attend the celebration as guest of honour.

'For really, it's thanks to you that our farmers have a second chance,' he had said bluntly when he invited her.

Despite the contagious excitement that now spread through the village, Tash still felt uneasy. The creature that had roamed the streets when she arrived had not returned to Nordhaven, yet she waited each night in bed, expecting to hear its raspy voice and nails scratching at her window. More to her disappointment, Cai had also not returned and she missed him more than she cared to admit.

Tash looked across the room at the two heavy sacks of powdered bone that were new additions there. They had been delivered a day before by Atticus and Sian, who had thanked her quietly for helping his son. She hadn't seen them since, but had heard from Klara and Ines that they had been assisting Florrick on his farm, after harvesting their own crops. Tash thought privately that this had been a wise decision, for she thought it unlikely that Sian's farm would ever have the same good fortune after the natural balance was restored.

She stood, frowned and reached out to steady herself on the bed post. Since receiving the wound in her arm, Tash had noticed that she was regularly light-headed and magic drained her far too quickly. She had tried to heal the cuts and scratches, yet while most had faded, the jagged black cut along her forearm had only expanded in size. The black tendrils now stretched from her wrist to just beneath her armpit, like a parasitic tattoo. She hoped Cai would return soon, so that she could convince him to take her to the Shadow Realm to be cured.

'Tash?' Mellie's voice came through the door, 'Are you ready to go? Vallus and the others are downstairs.'

'I'll just be a minute,' Tash called, hastily pulling on her dress and fastening it, effectively hiding the wound in tight sleeves. She had bought her dress the day before, captivated by the vibrant scarlet fabric that clung to the figure and fell to the ground in elegant folds. It matched her cloak, which she fastened around her shoulders and then left, hurrying down the stairs to meet Mellie and Vallus.

A small group were waiting for her by the inn's door and Tash recognised the majority of the villagers, who it seemed had decided that there was safety in numbers. Klara grinned at her and waved, while Pyrrus stood at her side, seemingly much better than he had been when Tash last saw him. Everyone was dressed in their best clothes and she smiled, grateful that she wouldn't be overdressed. Vallus watched her keenly as she approached, as did one of the farmhands from Sian's farm, leaving Tash feeling awkward and uncomfortable. She joined Klara and Pyrrus in the group, trying to avoid the men's admiring glances.

The group made its way to the Town Hall, pausing at each house and gathering more Nordhaven residents, until they arrived just as the sun was setting. The doors were wide open and music came from the hall, lights flickered invitingly as Jervois stood on the threshold to welcome them.

As they entered, Tash gave a servant her cloak and glanced around, wide eyed. Last time she'd been here, she had only entered Jervois' office, but tonight the hall was decked out for the festivities. Chandeliers glimmered overhead as they crossed to the ballroom, tables were laden with platters of food and bottles of wine. To her side, Klara sniffed in disgust.

'I *knew* he was holding out on us all this time,' she hissed under her breath. 'While we've been struggling to put food on the table, he's had access to all this.'

'Hush Klara,' Pyrrus muttered, casting his daughter a reprimanding look. 'Now's not the time to make a scene.'

She snorted and dragged Tash over to the tables, snatching up a plate and filling it until it was almost overflowing. 'We might as well enjoy what he's been keeping from us,' she said curtly, shooting Jervois' back a dirty glare.

Tash restrained herself at the dining tables, but helped herself to a large goblet of red wine. The two women moved to sit on chairs around the edge of the dance floor, watching the other villagers cramming their own plates with barely suppressed glee. It seemed that everyone was pleased to have access to the town's food stocks, and Tash noticed Jervois casting a worried glance at the tables which were rapidly becoming empty. Behind him, Vallus and his men were bolting the doors, effectively shutting out the sunset.

The sound of voices reverberated off the walls, echoing around the room, melding with the musicians who played in the corner. Before too long, couples had taken to the floor, kicking their heels up in a fast-paced dance. Tash saw Florrick and Ines laughing and twirling, Vallus came to lead Klara out into the fray and she accepted with a vibrant smile. Draining her goblet, Tash began to make her way to refill it, preferring to remain on the sidelines, away from inquisitive eyes.

'Care to dance?' It was the farmhand who made her skin crawl. He was looking at her appreciatively, focussing on her breasts and thighs.

'No, thank you,' Tash replied, trying to sidestep him to escape. 'I'm not much of a dancer.'

'It's easy,' he pushed, edging closer and catching onto her arm. 'Come on.'

She tried to keep calm, although the temptation to slap his hand away was very strong. 'I'd rather not. Excuse me.' She pulled away and circled around him, but he caught up to her as she refilled her goblet.

'It's really not that hard,' he said and she shook her head, glancing away from him to try and see if she could escape. 'Or, if there's something else you'd rather do...' His voice trailed off with an invitation, and his hand had found its way to her waist, anchoring her at his side. 'We could find a room. Somewhere private.'

'Let me go,' she spoke through clenched teeth, forcing her expression to remain polite to passersby. 'Or you will regret it.'

'I wouldn't antagonise her,' a new voice interrupted, and it sounded strangely familiar. 'Better leave her be.' An arm reached out and plucked the farmhand's hand from Tash's waist, giving him a none-too-subtle push back towards the crowd.

'Thanks,' Tash said as the farmhand stalked off, looking around for a new conquest. 'But I had it under control.'

'I'm sure.' The voice was low, slightly amused and she turned, confused as to how she recognised it. She took in the man behind her, her mind going blank with shock. He wore a plain white shirt, dark breeches and leather boots. Cobalt blue eyes glittered in a tanned face, his black hair was pulled back with a scrap of leather, and he gazed at her with an odd expression. Tash blinked, remembering the man from her dreams, who now stood before her.

By the Gods he was real.

'Who are you?' she asked, taking a restorative gulp of wine to settle her nerves. His mouth twitched into a smile, and she felt her stomach dip in response. He didn't answer, still watching her inscrutably, as though trying to figure out a difficult puzzle. 'I'm Tash,' she said, extending a hand and freezing when he took it, fingers barely touching hers, yet the brush of his skin sent a jolt through her. Her breath caught and she realised that she was staring, looked away awkwardly and wondered what was happening.

'Do you want to dance?' he asked, tilting his head in the direction of the dance floor.

Tash wanted to say yes. She wanted to dance with him, but there were so many people in the room, so many who would watch her and see every misstep. She'd focussed on being in the library instead of dancing at the Temple, and while she didn't exactly have two left feet, she wasn't comfortable dancing in front of this many people. So, instead, with a mixture of disappointment and anxiety at his potential response, she shook her head mutely. She waited for him to move on, to find another willing partner and step out onto the floor.

'Perhaps a stroll then?' Tash glanced up, surprised, and saw that he was offering his arm for her to take. She accepted, putting down her goblet and falling into step beside him as they circled around the edge of the room. They didn't speak, the noise from the raucous laughter, stamping feet and loud chatter becoming deafening. His eyes met hers as he gestured to the doors and she nodded.

They left the ballroom behind them, her companion opening the door to Jervois' study, which was thankfully empty. She followed him in, grateful for the distance between themselves and the rest of the village, who were becoming rowdier. He closed the door partway, so that the strains of music and laughter from the ballroom could still be heard.

Tash moved next to the fireplace, scanning the spines of the books in the shelves, humming unconsciously to the tune. She stopped when she realised that he had come to join her, feeling awkward again.

'Don't stop,' he said quietly.

She looked at him, suspicion starting to form in her eyes. 'You still haven't told me who you are.'

In response he extended a hand, bowed and asked again, 'Will you dance with me?'

Tash was starting to get irritated now. It was just like in the dreams– he wouldn't explain anything. Yet, something drew her to him and reluctantly she placed her hand into his.

'Don't complain when I step on your feet,' she muttered and he chuckled. Startled, Tash looked at him searchingly, wondering, and then shook the idea away as wishful thinking.

He pulled her into his arms until they were chest to chest, in a far more intimate style than the residents of Nordhaven had been dancing in the ballroom. Slowly they began to move back and forth, swaying in time to the music, neither speaking but unable to look away from the other. Time seemed to fade away as they danced, until the final strains of the song reached their ears.

They halted, yet remained in the same position, both unwilling to be the first to move away. Tash eyed him thoughtfully, 'I've not seen you in the village.'

'You've been busy with other things,' he replied, and she frowned.

'You seem to know a lot about me.'

'It's not often we have a visitor in town— particularly a Robin,' he said, 'people talk.'

'Still,' Tash focussed on his expression which had, once again, become inscrutable. 'I've met the majority of people in town, but not you.'

'You're meeting me now,' he said simply and she frowned, the annoyance rising up in her again.

'Then tell me what you're called,' she said, a hint of curtness in her tone. His eyebrows raised and she stepped back, folding her arms and giving him an assessing look. Something wasn't right. 'How do you know me?' she asked, more forcefully this time. 'Are you in trouble? Do you need a Robin's help?'

'I don't know what you mean,' he sounded guarded now, and she sensed that she was right.

'I can't help you if you don't talk to me,' she said bluntly. When he didn't reply, she turned back to the fireplace, wondering if she had imagined it. Yet still the images from her dreams persisted and the feeling in her bones told her that she was right. Her head had started to ache and she closed her eyes, lifting a hand to her temples to massage them.

'Tash,' he began, 'please—'

'Stop.' Her eyes snapped open, the sneaking sense of familiarity becoming overwhelming. Not looking at him, she strode over to the door, checked that the hallway was empty and then shut it, turning the key in the lock. When she turned around, she noticed that he hadn't moved from the centre of the room, continuing to watch her steadily.

Deliberately, she stepped closer to him, refusing to back away from his gaze. 'Are you *quite* sure that we've never met?'

'Quite,' he replied, a touch too quickly for her liking. Her eyes narrowed, and then she let out a gasp as her ring slipped off her finger and fell to the ground, rolling away on the carpet to bounce off his shoe.

'How clumsy of me,' she said, 'would you mind terribly?' She indicated the ring on the floor, holding his cool gaze as he slowly reached down to pick it up. Her suspicions were confirmed when she saw the flicker of quickly masked pain in the cobalt eyes.

'Your ring,' he said softly, placing it back into her open palm. Immediately, she grabbed his hand with her free one, turning it over to reveal a round burn.

'I *knew* it,' she said with a mixture of pride and jubilation before questions filled her mind and she looked up at him. 'How is this possible? I thought that...'

He didn't reply, mouth pinched in a tight line as he removed the welt from his hand with a careful gesture.

'Cai?' Tash whispered, stepping closer and forcing him to look at her. 'Cai, tell me what's going on. Please.'

'That was a mean trick,' he said, waving his palm in her face, 'I should've figured out that you'd try something like that.'

'If we're talking about mean tricks,' she countered, 'how about you trying to convince me that we'd never met.'

'Correction,' he interrupted, 'you never *have* met me like this before.'

'I have,' she retorted and then froze, realising belatedly that she'd spoken aloud and now he was looking at her oddly.

'What do you mean?'

'But most of all,' she continued, ignoring him, 'how are you like *this?* Is it some illusion, some shapeshifting trick?'

He shook his head. 'What did you mean, Tash?'

She pulled away, sinking into the chair she had been in almost a week ago, the shock starting to make itself known. 'I don't understand how this is possible,' she whispered, casting surreptitious glances at him to make sure it was real. 'It's not a dream, is it?'

It would be the cruellest kind of dream if it was.

'Tash,' he knelt beside her, taking her ringless hand in his. 'Focus on me. I'm here.'

'*But how?*

He sighed. 'It's a new moon tonight.' She looked at him uncomprehendingly and he explained, 'Part of the curse on my kind was that we could resume our original form on the night of a new moon. We keep our powers, but look human until the sun rises again.'

'Why didn't you say anything?' she asked, still trying to absorb this new information. 'You let me think you were someone else. Why would you do that?'

'I might have wanted to indulge in a fantasy where a normal boy met a girl and asked her to dance at a party and she said yes,' he said quietly. 'I've had many years to come up with dreams of what I'd do but never found the courage to achieve them.'

Tash thought that she understood, although it was still a lot to take in. 'We're not normal, though, Cai,' she finally managed to say, 'we're both outsiders.' Another thought crossed her mind and her eyes widened with concern. 'What if they find out what you are? There are guards here– they'll hurt you. They might suspect—'

'They won't,' Cai interrupted. 'They won't remember that I was ever here.'

'How?'

'I can make them forget,' he smiled gently. 'Now, will you stop worrying and dance with me again?'

It was easier said than done. Tash allowed him to lift her up, back into the warm embrace of his arms, and she moved closer, resting her head on his shoulder as they began to slowly rock again to the distant music. Cai held her hand over his heart, and she shut her eyes, breathing in his scent, not wanting the night to end.

'Have I told you that you're beautiful tonight?' he asked quietly and she gave a soft laugh. 'I don't see what's so funny,' he murmured, twisting her out and back.

'It's nothing,' Tash replied. Deep down she was still finding it hard to register that the man she had been dreaming of and the Nightwalker she had slept with were one and the same. And, by the Gods, he was beautiful.

Her mouth went dry as he dipped her, his face inches from hers. He grinned, reading the invitation in her eyes, and then kissed her. Her arms came around his neck, twining in his hair, responding with enthusiasm. Cai chuckled when they broke apart, lifting her back up until she was standing without his support anymore.

'I missed you,' she breathed, 'more than I thought.'

'And I, you,' he said, tone low.

'There's been so much that I—' Tash began and then there were noises from outside the office, the sounds of many feet moving past. The music had ended, and so, it seemed, had the party.

'You need to go,' Cai said, breaking away from her.

'Come with me,' she urged, 'stay with me tonight.' In her mind she saw him running down the alleyway, hunched over in agony as the shadowy figure approached. She wouldn't let that happen. Not tonight, anyway.

He hesitated and she said, 'You said you could make them forget that you were there. Stay with me Cai, please.'

Her plea was enough for him to take her hand and lead her out of the office, unlocking the door and sliding into the group of villagers who were handing out cloaks, bulbs of garlic and preparing torches.

'Everyone, stay together,' Vallus barked, 'Nightwalkers will prey on anyone who leaves the group. Don't go into the shadows alone.'

Cai returned to Tash with her cloak, placing it around her shoulders and she bit back a laugh as a bulb of garlic was unceremoniously thrust into his hands. He eyed it assessingly and she whispered, 'Come on, Cai. You wouldn't want to give up guaranteed protection from the fearsome Nightwalkers, would you?'

His mouth tweaked in a smile and he chuckled. 'Of course not.'

'Let's move, people,' Vallus called from the head of the group, having opened the doors onto the cold, frosty night. Outside was nothing but darkness, there was no sound save for the stamping of cold feet and the villagers exchanging whispers. Everyone stayed huddled together, well within the torchlight, moving slowly, pausing at each house to ensure that each family returned safely to their homestead. As they walked, Tash could feel Cai's fingers teasing her, sliding to the curve of her back, the inside of her wrist, circling her palm. Several times she cast him reprimanding looks, but was unable to hide the flush that his touch brought to her cheeks. All she got in response was another chuckle and playful glint of the eye. When they reached the inn, Tash and Cai slipped inside, ahead of Mellie who was offering several families rooms for the night, seeing as they lived on the outskirts of town.

Tash gripped onto Cai's hand and led the way to her room, entering it and locking the door. The candles flickered to life with a click of his fingers and then he was pressing her against the wood, kissing her with a desperation that she reciprocated. Her body ached, reminding her that it had been days since she felt his touch, and that the past nights she had longed for it through the lonely hours.

His fingers made swift work of her cloak, sending it down to the ground, before he began to unfasten her dress. She pulled off her ring, dropping it on the discarded clothing. She moaned as his hands cupped her breasts, squeezing them through the fabric, and then heard footsteps on the stairs. Her breathing grew ragged as the footsteps moved past the door, yet his hands continued their teasing, unlacing the bodice and sliding it down so that her dress fell to her waist. The room was cold and she gasped, before he caught one breast in his mouth, making her whimper.

'Don't make too much noise, Tash,' he murmured, lifting his burning eyes to hers. She gave a jerky nod, unable to form coherent words in response. Cai smiled, returning to teasing her with his mouth until she was sure that she would crumple to the ground in a heap.

'Cai,' she finally managed, 'I can't… oh, please…'

He picked her up, the rest of her clothing falling down, and she wrapped her legs around him, clasping his neck with her arms. He kissed her hungrily, carrying her to the bed and laying her down. She was burning from the inside, mindless and eager, and she reached for him, tugging on his shirt in an attempt to remove it. He smiled, obliging her and kicked off his boots. She moaned, pulling him back down to kiss him, desperate with unrestrained need.

'Please Cai,' she whispered when they broke apart, breathless and panting. His eyes darkened slightly, and he obeyed, removing his breeches and entering her slowly. Tash gripped his back, wrapping her legs around him as he moved within her. His hands twined in hers, refusing to let them go, her name on his lips. The heat mounted, rising like the tide, as he kissed her sweetly, tenderly, until she was lost. With a cry she felt herself climax in a fiery rush, the waves of pleasure crashing through her veins and he was lost, the heat of his seed filling her until they were both spent.

In the aftermath, she lay in his arms, recognising that, tonight, what they shared had gone deeper than the times before. She didn't know how it had happened, but the possibility of cutting ties once she had finished in Nordhaven seemed even further away now. Again, she asked herself what she was doing and why she didn't want it to stop.

'I don't want the sun to rise,' Cai murmured against her hair. 'It's the first time in a long time that I don't want the night to end.'

'I can think of a few nights in recent times that I've wanted to last a lot longer than they did,' Tash replied silkily, running a hand over his chest to distract herself from her thoughts.

He chuckled, the low sound musical to her ears. 'That's a relief to hear.'

She smiled, stretching like a cat and biting back a yawn. 'Well—'

'Tash, what's that on your arm?' He'd sat up, tone changing to one of concern. A pool of dread began to form in the pit of her stomach and she said,

'Oh, it's nothing to worry about. I have it under control.'

He didn't listen, catching her arm and turning it towards the light so that he could see the twisting black veins stretching underneath the skin. He made a growl at the back of his throat. 'Tash, what have you *done?*'

'I—'

'I told you to stay *safe*,' he bit out furiously. 'What happened?'

'Well, if you'd let me *finish*,' she said, a tad snappishly, 'it's something that I can easily get rid of. I just need your help. To re-enter the Shadow Realm.' His eyes widened with horror and she hastened to fill him in on the entire story, from the moment she followed Atticus, to killing the Dæmon.

'By the Gods,' he whispered, 'how could you do such a stupid thing, Tash?'

'It was the only way to stop the blight,' she replied stubbornly. Didn't he realise that she had acted in the best interests of Nordhaven? Wasn't he grateful that she had helped to heal the town which he still cared about so much?

'Did you stop to consider any other options?' he asked, running a hand through his hair in desperation. 'Gods, Tash, I thought you were smarter than this. You know better than to make a deal with my kind.'

'You don't have to say that,' Tash said, annoyed. The sated bliss she had been feeling moments ago long gone, replaced with irritation and defensiveness. 'It wasn't a Nightwalker like you, it was a different type of Dæmon.'

'You don't get it,' he said angrily. 'Did it explain where specifically in the Shadow Realm you needed to go?'

She paused, thinking hard and then shook her head.

'Do you know how many different types of Dæmons there are in that place?' he asked, 'How many locations that might be where you need to go? It could take years of searching and you would still not find what you were looking for.'

Fear was now twisting in her stomach as she began to realise how she had fallen for the trick. Her eyes filled with tears as she looked back at him and said softly, 'I don't want to die.'

In a moment, he had taken her in his arms again, comforting her. 'We'll find it, Tash. Don't cry. We can start tomorrow.'

'Thank you,' she whispered, rubbing the wetness from her eyes and he kissed her forehead.

'Besides,' he murmured, 'if I'm with you, we'll be able to keep away from—'

He was interrupted by the scratching at the window and ragged breathing of the creature outside. Tash gripped Cai tighter, freezing, before the haunting voice asked,

'Have you missed me, my sweet Natachatet? Open the window and let me in, I will make it worth your while.'

'Has it come back any other nights?' Cai whispered and she shook her head, the scrabbling sound from the window shutters becoming harder to ignore.

'What made it return tonight?' she asked. From outside, the creature let out a rattling laugh and said,

'Don't be scared, Natachatet. I'll take care of you. Open the window, my sweet.'

Tash stood up, the fear she had initially felt when the creature returned now replaced with anger. She pulled on her nightgown and reached for her dezmian, stepping closer to the window.

'What are you doing, Tash?' Cai asked her from the bed warily.

'I refuse to be terrorised anymore,' she said, flipping the dezmian and feeling a sense of satisfaction as the shutters flew open, tossing the creature backwards into the night. There was a crash as it hit the ground, and she began to re-peat a prayer over and over, the Ancient Tongue filling her ears as outside the window, streaks of light filled the air, forming a protective barrier over the windowpane. Tash's eyes closed as she concentrated, the words coming as easily as breathing, filling her with a sense of security. Her magic strengthened, imbued with holy power, banishing the crea-ture back to the shadows from whence it had come.

'Tash,' Cai's voice sounded like it was reaching her from across a vast distance, 'Tash, stop.'

She turned to look at him and saw that he had collapsed on the bed, shaking uncontrollably, face contorted with pain. She paused, mid-prayer, unsure about what was wrong. His lips were pressed tightly together, perhaps to stop himself from crying out, hands clenched into fists. The tremors shook through him in spasms, contorting his body even as he tried to keep still.

'Cai,' she hurried to his side, 'what's wrong? What's happening?'

He gave another jerk, casting a bitter look at the window, to where the light she had summoned was now stretching across the sky as the herald of the dawn. She went to the pitcher and basin, poured out some water and wet a cloth, pressing it to his brow, which burned. Feeling weakened from her own use of magic, Tash murmured softly to him, much as she would with Lir when he was distressed, in the low, melodic tones of her mother tongue. She whispered calming words as he cried out, writhing in pain, reminding him that she was there and would not leave, that he was safe and she would watch over him until he came back to himself.

He screamed, as a ripping, cracking sound filled the air, and Tash watched, horrified, as his body began to change, legs extending and nails lengthening into the clawed hands she had become accustomed to. She felt tears prick her eyes again, the sound of his cries piercing her like sharpened arrows, striking one after another in a volley, straight to the heart.

'Cai,' she whispered faintly, '*liebeshem*, you'll be alright, I'm here.'

He didn't hear her, lost in the agony of his transformation, but she stayed at his side, narrowly avoiding being struck by his tail lashing out, cutting through the sheets. Tash felt the tears slide down her cheeks, as she held onto him, trying to stop him from potentially hurting himself. She continued to speak under her breath, knowing that he wouldn't understand the words but hoping that the tone would calm him, as it usually did with Lir. She told him the things she had pushed down into the deep recesses of her heart, of the way he made her feel, the loneliness she had felt while he was gone. She didn't stop when he flung his head back, eyes opening, the cobalt blue changing to scarlet red. His face became harder, more hollowed, the horns pushing through the skin, twisting up towards the ceiling. Two trails of blood slid down his temples from where the horns had emerged, and Tash wet the cloth again, cleaning it away.

He coughed, eyes slowly coming into focus as he gazed upwards and then down to where Tash knelt at his side, one hand holding the damp bloodied cloth, the other keeping his forearm pinned to the bed. She had frozen, unsure if he would start convulsing again, and when he continued to watch her steadily, she slowly relinquished her hold on his arm.

'I'm sorry you had to see that.' His voice was raspy and strained as he pulled himself up to sit cross legged on the bed. He looked exhausted and Tash was certain that she looked no better. 'Did I hurt you?' She shook her head mutely and he sighed with relief, resting his head in his hands.

'Do you have to go through that every month?' she asked, returning the cloth to the basin and rinsing her face, removing the evidence of the tears before he noticed them. He grunted in assent, giving a brief nod. 'Is it always so painful?' Tash moved back to the bed, perching at his side.

'It never gets easier,' he muttered as she reached out, lifting his face so that she could look into his eyes.

'I'm sorry,' her voice quavered slightly and she felt the pain from earlier rise up again. 'I'm so sorry.'

'Don't pity me.' He sounded angry, red eyes flashing and she recoiled instinctively.

'I don't,' she said quickly. 'But I wouldn't be human if I didn't empathise with what you went through tonight.'

He didn't speak for a moment, his expression changing to one of remorse, and she knew that he regretted what he had said. Sensing that he was about to apologise, she closed the distance between them and held him to her, pressing kisses down his temple, across his cheek to his lips, silencing the words in his throat. His arms surrounded her, keeping her locked in the embrace until they broke apart, and she saw that he had regained control of his emotions.

'I wasn't sure if you'd want the Monster back,' he finally whispered, 'I've always kept hidden at the new moon. If people saw—'

'It's not your fault that your ancestor was cursed,' Tash interrupted, 'and, for the record, I had no idea that you could return to your human form before tonight.' She cast a look at the window and amended, '*Last* night.'

In a way, she was relieved to finally know the truth. Now she wouldn't feel a conflict when she dreamed of the cobalt-eyed man before waking next to Cai. It had been him, all along, haunting her dreams. Another thought occurred to her and she frowned, suddenly anxious.

'Last night, you were screaming. What will Mellie and the others say?' In fact, she was surprised that no one had knocked on the door. She had been too focussed on Cai to consider how odd that was. His mouth twitched into a smile and shrugged.

'I might have encouraged the other people in the inn to sleep more soundly than usual, in case they heard anything. Although,' he added, 'I was intending to slip away before dawn to spare you seeing this.' He gestured to himself and then pierced her with a look. 'That was until *someone* decided to use magic to accelerate the sunrise.'

'I didn't realise that I was doing it,' Tash replied defensively, 'I was trying to get rid of that creature.'

'The magic you used,' he leaned back onto the pillows, pulling her down to join him, 'I felt it in here.' He touched the spot on his chest over his heart. 'It burned, hotter than hellfire. I know it wasn't directed at me,' he hastily continued as she drew in a shocked breath. 'But I still felt its remnants. What was it?'

'Robins are believers in the old faith,' she said simply. 'Sometimes, when in need, we call on the power of the Gods to assist us when casting magic. It strengthens us, helps us to perform more complex incantations.'

'I don't remember that friend of yours using such magic,' Cai said pensively. Tash looked at him, surprised by his change in thought.

'Laura has always had a deeper affinity with magic than I have,' she explained. 'Which I first found amusing considering she came from a world devoid of it. She's able to tap into that force without calling on the Gods' aid, but for the rest of us, we need their help to perform more serious feats of magic.' She bit back a yawn, 'it takes a lot of energy though.' The weakness she had felt earlier came back in force and she sank against his side, exhausted.

'Tash?' Cai sounded worried. She waved his concerns away with her hand, registering briefly that the inky tendrils had now spread to her palm.

'Shh,' she murmured, 'we can talk later. Let's just rest for a while.' Sleepily, she nestled closer to him, drifting off to the sound of his steady breathing to dream of a place where they could be together, without the threats from the darkness or the prejudice of the outside world.

Chapter Fifteen

For months now, I've scoured the Shadow Realm for what Corvis requested. Finally, I think I know where to go. He will want to come with me, I am sure, seeing as he's desired this map for so many years. But tonight, I almost forgot what I had come to tell him about.

She was there. Just like in my dreams, except this time I could hear her voice, breathe in her scent, reach out and touch her to check that she was real. There was another Robin with her, a girl who faded into insignificance as soon as I set eyes on the one I had looked for. Just like I had dreamed, she was fearless before me, and then she was gone.

I will find her again. And when I do, I won't let her go so easily.

~ An extract from a blood-splattered journal in the Shadow Realm

Tash was in a foul mood. She had awoken alone to find a scrawled note from Cai, telling her to meet him at the abandoned shack on the Heath with the powdered Dæmon's bone. She felt tired, hungry and ill, unsettled by the dark veins that now were stretching down her side which she noticed as she changed. No one else was awake yet, and she descended the inn stairs, the bags of powdered bone on her shoulder, struggling with the weight.

There was no chance of her carrying them to the Heath alone, so she made her way to the stable to get Lir. He snuffled excitedly when he saw her approaching, and didn't seem to mind as she heaved the bags over his back, attaching them to the saddle.

'Let's go, *liebeshem*,' she said, mounting and guiding him out of the stable. The momentary rush of leaping into the air helped to alleviate her bad mood, leaving her mind clear for a short while. She turned Lir in the direction she had gone with Atticus earlier in the week, soaring over the fields and houses, until the Heath stretched out before them. Spurring the Willowing on, Tash bent low over his neck as they flew, scanning the Heath for the remains of the shack.

They found it after a half hour, its crumbled roof blending into the heather and gorse. Moss clung to the shack's walls and grass grew amongst the broken roof tiles, small purple flowers speckling it in dabs of colour. Lir hit the ground with a soft jolt, and Tash slid out of the saddle, heading towards the slightly ajar door.

'Cai?' she called as she pushed it open further, 'Are you here?'

There was no reply, and she opened the shutters, forcing the daylight to illuminate the interior. She stepped over the Dæmon's body on the ground, looking around the space and noticing a turned over table and chair, a cracked bedframe pressed against the far wall, and a small, blackened stove. Something creaked as she crossed the room and Tash glanced down curiously, then knelt, lifting the loose floorboard to reveal a faded journal underneath. She reached through the cobwebs and withdrew it carefully, brushing the decades of dust from its cover.

The book fell open, the pages yellowed with age, the ink faded and slanted in a scrawl she recognised. Eagerly, she left the shack and settled down against its wall in the sunshine, now able to clearly decipher the entries. The first one was short, as though the writer had been in a rush.

Mother gave me a journal for my birthday. I wanted new hooks for my fishing line, and instead I get this. She says it'll be useful, that anyone who wants to achieve their dreams is able to put their thoughts down onto paper. I think she's starting to go mad. She was looking out at the Heath again today, not saying anything, just looking. Guess it'll be up to me to catch dinner again. It would've been easier if I had new hooks.

Tash traced the words, imagining the boy who had written them, a boy with dark hair and bright eyes. She shut the journal, holding it to her chest, wondering if she should tell Cai about her discovery but deciding against it. He might not appreciate what a gift this was. Any discussion about his human life only caused him to become angry and bitter, perhaps it would be best if she kept this to herself. She rose and slid the journal into her saddle bag, determined to read more when she was next alone.

There was movement from the shack and she turned to see Cai emerging from the shadows, covering his eyes from the morning sun. 'Did you call me?' he asked blearily. 'I thought I heard you.'

'I did,' she replied, crossing over to kiss him. He seemed surprised by it and when she pulled away, she said, 'We're in the middle of nowhere, Cai. Everyone in town is still half asleep after last night. Who's going to be out here to see us?'

He smiled wickedly. 'Well, when you put it like that, we probably shouldn't waste any time.' He held her to him, kissing her with far more energy than she had expected for someone who had barely slept. She responded in kind, and before either of them realised it, they were lying on the ground, entwined.

There was a snort of displeasure and Lir gave Tash a nudge with his muzzle, pushing her off Cai and rolling her into the heather. She laughed, partly from Lir's reproachful gaze and partly from Cai's stunned expression.

'I didn't realise we had a chaperone,' he muttered, getting to his feet and shooting Lir a sardonic look. The Willowing snorted again, moving to stand between him and Tash, which she found quite endearing, considering his usual timidity.

'I think he likes you,' she said, chuckling, 'he doesn't seem to be as scared of you as he used to be.'

'He can probably smell you on me,' Cai replied grumpily, giving up on trying to sidestep the Willowing and instead returning into the shack. 'Come on. Bring him with you.'

'I think he's sulking,' Tash whispered in Lir's ear and he snuffled contentedly.

'I can *hear* you,' Cai called from the interior and Lir flicked his mane in response.

'I think that you are jealous, *liebeshem*,' Tash smiled, stroking Lir's neck. 'But you don't need to be.' A snort came from the shack and she ignored it. 'You're my special *liebeshem*.'

'Don't let him find out that you called me that last night,' Cai said as she and Lir entered the shack, the Willowing snorting in discomfort. Tash glared at Cai, who was crouched over the corpse on the ground, inspecting it intently.

'I thought you couldn't hear what I said,' she mused, hoping that he hadn't understood the other words she had spoken.

'I heard fragments,' he replied quietly, ripping a piece of the Dæmon's ragged clothing and stowing it in his belt, before examining the corpse. 'This looks like a Jiefer, a less common variety of Dæmon.'

'What does it do?' Tash asked, hoping to distract him from what he remembered from the night before.

'Its kind particularly like to trick Mortals,' he said absent-mindedly. 'They were underlings of an older breed of Dæmon, which had the power to both bring destruction and prosperity. I'd say that explains how the blight was the reverse effect of the abundance on Sian's farm.' He passed his hands over the corpse, mumbled something incoherent and the body shrank until it was the size of a doll, which he also attached to his belt. He stood abruptly, not bothering to explain why he had done what he had, and held out a hand. 'Let's go.'

Tash held onto Lir with one hand, twining her fingers in his mane, and took Cai's in the other. He moved to the corner of the shack where it was darkest and vanished, leading her after him. Lir faltered, shying away, but Tash held firm, forcing him to follow her into the shadows.

This time, there was no sensation of falling, as the world around them became an impenetrable gloom. She'd forgotten how disconcerting it was, and Lir's snort of fear summarised effectively how she had first felt when she came here. Cai's hand became her lifeline, guiding her through the darkness.

'Where are we going?' she asked, hating her blindness. His fingers squeezed hers reassuringly, and he replied,

'I'm trying to locate where that Dæmon went. It was the one to collect the bones of its victim and bring them to Nordhaven for that farmer's boy. If I can just follow its scent, then we can narrow down where to go. Now, try to keep quiet, you never know what's listening here.'

Tash didn't speak again, leaving him to pause from time to time, sensing him look around and change their direction. After a while, he halted and she walked into him with a soft cry. In response, he lifted her into the saddle, and moved onwards, Lir following him obediently. His fingers slipped from hers and he increased the pace. She felt Lir spread his wings and take off, skimming over the ground after Cai, whose footsteps began to draw further away. Tash clung to Lir's neck, wondering how he could see through the shadows to follow their guide.

She didn't ask though, making a mental note to raise the question later, when they were somewhere safer. For now, she would wait patiently, praying to the Gods that no other creatures would intrude on their path. The sinister voice from the night before filled her mind, making her glance around with increasing paranoia, unable to discern anything in the darkness. It taunted her, replaying its words over and over until she was certain that the creature was there with them, lurking just out of Cai's sight. Her arm was aching, the places where the black tendrils crisscrossed her skin sending pain shooting through her. The feeling intensified, spreading down her side to her thighs, across her back, as though being in the Shadow Realm was speeding up its progress.

Tash clenched her jaw, determined not to make a sound, to not distract Cai from the hunt. She had to persevere. Her breath was becoming shorter, it was harder to get the air into her lungs and her head spun. Nausea roiled in her stomach, churning in response to the pain. Her hands gripped Lir's mane, trying to steady herself. She could feel herself slipping away, sliding sideways and she cried out as she fell into black nothingness and she knew no more.

***

Tash came back to herself slowly, as though she were trudging up a steep hill with heavy weights tied to her feet. It took an enormous amount of effort to open her eyes, to see the faint glow of the campfire flickering off the walls of the cave. Cai lay beside her, breathing slowly and deeply. It looked as though he had fallen asleep while watching over her. She looked up and saw Lir standing at the back of the cave, wings folded and eyes huge. He whickered as Tash sat up, wincing, and pawed the ground. The sound roused Cai, who jumped awake, searching out the noise before realising that it had been Lir.

'This is a different cave to the one you brought me to last time,' Tash said, the lights moving in and out of focus as she turned her head, taking in the space around them.

'Tash,' Cai's hands held her firm as the cave spun, 'stay still. You're not well.'

'I'm… fine,' she gasped, trying and failing to push his hand away. To her dismay, her strength was gone, and the hand she lifted up was blackened, as though frost-bitten. Her skin looked dead, burnt and on the verge of decay. She retched at the sight of it, and Cai held her as the tremors racked through her body.

'I should've foreseen this,' he muttered as she coughed. 'It's stronger here. It's feeding off the darkness.'

'Not your fault,' Tash managed to gasp out, 'Mine. Did you find… trail?'

Cai nodded and she smiled, hope returning with a vengeance. 'I don't know if it's wise to take you there, Tash,' he
said, 'it's at the bottom of Trencher's Pit.'

'What's that?'

'It's one of the deepest parts of this place,' he replied.
'The Pit is the place where the oldest Dæmons were created.
I don't know—'

She rolled her eyes and forced herself to stand, legs shaking as she swayed. 'Come *on*, Cai. We need to go.'

He bit his lip, before complying with her wish, lifting her
into his arms and glancing at Lir, who moved closer expectantly. Cai put Tash into the saddle then swung up behind her,
keeping her firm against him. Lir, unfamiliar with the extra
weight, snorted and bucked, before a sharp growl from Cai
made him stop immediately. He took off, and Cai reached
forward, guiding the Willowing through the shadows and
leaving the campfire to die behind them.

Tash was aware of wind cutting her cheek, distant cries
and moans in the darkness reaching them as they flew fast,
Cai urging Lir on. The Willowing dived, spiralling downwards, into a mass of shadow that seemed– if possible–
darker than the rest. Time became a blur, all that she was
aware of was Cai's arms around her, Lir's wings beating and
the pressure mounting in her ears as they descended further
into the bowels of the earth. Cai was whispering things into
the shadows in a language she didn't know, and even without
flipping her dezmian she could feel the magic encircling
them, although she wasn't sure what it was for.

She could feel the darkness in her blood spreading across
her legs now, encasing her in a shroud of pain. Her feet were
numb and it seemed that the further down they went, the
faster it spread. Tash was grateful that she couldn't see it,

knowing that if she did, it would probably make her sick again. For the thousandth time she wondered how she could've made such a stupid decision. Cai had asked if there had been another way to stop the blight, but she hadn't even considered it. Wasn't she supposed to be the smart one? That was what Laura always said, and here she was on her first mission as a fully-fledged Robin and there was a possibility that she wouldn't be returning to the Temple to give her report.

'Hang on, Tash,' Cai said in her ear, 'we're nearly there.'

She wanted to reply that she was not fine, but not dead yet either. To her horror though, she couldn't open her mouth to speak. It felt like her lips had been stitched together, and when she tried to talk only faint, terrified sounds could come out. She lifted her hand, the one with the yew ring, and pressed it to her mouth, trying to feel what was wrong. There was a sudden heat and she gasped, her lips free of their invisible bonds, but stinging horribly.

'Please say that it isn't far now,' she whispered faintly, 'I can't feel my legs.'

If she had had the energy, she would've cried, yet her chest seized, making it take all her focus on just breathing. Tash was so preoccupied that it took a moment before she recognised the smell, the acrid scent that had come off the fungus, filling the air until it was so overpowering she thought that she'd gag again.

Lir hit the ground and she shuddered, needing Cai to lift her down when her legs didn't respond. He placed her carefully onto something sharp before leaving her alone. She could hear Lir snorting and stamping his hooves, but couldn't muster the strength to calm him. Her eyes widened when a pale blue light began to flicker around them, illuminating the jutted, rocky walls that stretched up into blackness. Around them, the fungus grew in abundance, covering the ground, its white webbing spreading up the walls, radiating with the strange light. Tash was perched against something large, faded and cracked, and when she tried to shuffle her weight, it splintered apart. She collapsed amongst the mushrooms, crushing them under her, and moaned in terror. The last thing she wanted was to fall into the death slumber that had affected the people of Nordhaven.

To her surprise, she had no reaction to the fungus except to gag at the smell as the broken mushrooms smeared across her body. She rolled over, using the one arm that wasn't paralysed yet to push herself and saw what she had been sitting on with horror. The skull had been probably the size of an ox, with long, curved horns and tusks, sharpened teeth and gaping sockets where eyes had once been. Tash had broken it down the centre, splitting the skull into pieces which now lay haphazardly amongst the fungus.

Cai approached her, one of the sacks of powdered bone on his shoulder. 'Here,' he deposited it beside her, 'I'll empty the other one.' He moved away again to Lir's side, and began to tip the second sack over the glowing fungus, which brightened in intensity as the dust fell over it. Tash reached into the sack beside her, withdrawing a handful of powder and sprinkling it around her, watching as it was absorbed into the mushrooms like water after a drought. The blue light grew stronger and stronger, and with it, Tash felt her own strength returning, the pain that had infiltrated her veins relinquishing its hold on her. Tentatively, she turned the sack upside down, the powder spilling over her, and she coughed, brushing it off onto the ground. She lifted her hands and saw that the inky tendrils had faded, a sensation of pins and needles restoring movement to her limbs. Tash got unsteadily to her feet, shook out her skirts and cloak, sending another wave of powdered bone onto the fungus, which devoured it hungrily.

'We should also leave this here,' Cai said, pulling the shrunken Dæmon corpse from his belt, and he placed it down by the broken skull. 'This creature originated from this place too, based on its scent. Whereas this,' he touched the skull briefly, 'is much older. One of the original Markeesh Dæmons, I expect. They were created to be harbingers of plague on the Mortal realms. I'd like to know what managed to kill it though.' He removed the scrap of fabric he had torn from its clothing and discarded that too, nose wrinkling before looking at Tash critically. 'How are you feeling?'

'Better,' she said, bending her fingers and wiggling her toes experimentally. She eyed the fungus around them, 'Why do you think we haven't been affected like the people in Nordhaven? I thought touching the fungus would have an effect.' She rubbed her skirts and the smeared remnants of the mushrooms that had clung to her clothing.

Cai shrugged, 'Plants from the Shadow Realm don't belong in the outside worlds, and their magic can be warped easily when removed from their natural environment.'

She stared at him, annoyed. 'You knew that all this time? Why didn't you tell me earlier when I was investigating the blight?'

'I didn't think it was necessary,' he replied bluntly. 'It wouldn't have helped you figure out how to stop it.' Tash bit her lip, acknowledging privately that he was right. But all the same, she didn't appreciate him keeping information like this from her.

'We should leave,' Cai said abruptly, glancing up at the quivering darkness. From high above there was a rustling sound and Tash followed his gaze, concerned as he added, 'Whenever there's light, it attracts monsters. We don't want to still be here when they arrive. And, whatever you do, don't use any magic– if anything happens, let me deal with it.'

Tash didn't need to be told twice, and hurried to mount Lir, Cai pulling himself up behind her. Lir whinnied and soared upwards, leaving the glowing blue fungus far below as they plunged into the darkness. Cai recommenced muttering the incoherent words like he had on their descent, and Tash felt the magic once more, although this time she realised that it must be helping to reduce the pressure as they climbed higher out of the bowels of the earth. She gripped Lir's mane, the noise of rustling movement getting louder and closer, and she wondered how they could avoid meeting the monsters head-on.

Lir was straining to maintain his pace now, tiring quickly after having carried extra weight for too long. The pressure in her ears was lessening, the air felt fresher and smelt less musty although Tash doubted that the smell of the fungus would leave her clothes for a while yet. Cai let out a growl and swiped out, as something reached from the shadows, trying to catch onto them. Tash felt claws snag on her cloak, ripping it as she yanked it away, unable to see where the attackers were coming from. She clung onto Lir, squeezing her face into his neck as she heard snarls and the snapping of jaws on their tail. Something wet splattered her cheek as a pained cry came from behind her. She wanted to help, but if she used her dezmian, there was a possibility that she would lose it in the darkness.

'Tash,' Cai's voice was ragged in her ear and she jumped. 'Keep heading upward. Lir will find the portal for you.'

'But what about you?' she asked uneasily.

'Don't worry about me,' he said curtly, 'just get out of here. Go!' He slapped Lir's flank and let go of her, tumbling backwards into the endless night. Lir sped forwards, buoyed with a new surge of energy as Cai's weight vanished. Tash called out after him but had to grip tightly to Lir's mane so that she wouldn't fall either as they escaped. The sound of tearing flesh, ripping and snarling followed them, and no response came to Tash's cry. She felt dampness prick her eyes and blinked it back, forcing herself to remain strong. Cai would be fine. He would appear later, perhaps a bit bruised and bloodied, but in one piece. Wouldn't he?

Chapter Sixteen

Trencher's Pit is often considered by inter-world scholars to be one of the most dangerous sites in the Shadow Realm. Tales say that the oldest Dæmons were created there, born out of the bowels of the earth and climbed their way up the pit to the land of shadows. As I have discovered, creatures born from darkness will attune with it, succumbing easily to the crueller and often vicious desires in their hearts. If, on the off chance, someone was stupid enough to go there, they would need to traverse the miles under the ground to its lowest depths. The pressure at that point should be enough to crush a man alive, if the calculations are accurate. But the return journey is worse. The stories tell that the cursed souls of those lost in the Shadow Realm hang off the walls of Trencher's Pit, constantly seeking new members for their ranks. This is why, my apprentice Robins, you should avoid venturing into that realm between worlds at any cost.

> ~ An extract from 'A Robin's Guide to Inter-world Monsters'

'You need to eat, Tash,' Mellie said kindly, dolloping another ladle of soup into her bowl. Tash smiled vaguely, stirring the soup with her spoon, watching the vegetables float around in the broth but not eating.

It had been five days since she returned from the Shadow Realm. As Cai had told her, Lir had known the way, navigating through the darkness until he reached one of the mysterious entrances back to Kinet. They reappeared on the Heath, mid-afternoon on the day they had left. Tash had held fast to the Willowing throughout their escape, the screams and sounds of fighting constantly replaying in her ears. She wanted to go back and find Cai, to summon the Gods' light once more to help him, but she felt weak and scared, afraid of what other monsters would be drawn towards the beacon in the darkness. In the end she had fled, as he had wanted. It didn't sit well with her though, particularly because it felt wrong to run away when he was in danger.

The townspeople of Nordhaven were still in a state of joy, the fields now looking back to normal and, with some help from Tash and her dezmian, the renewed plant growth had accelerated. The magic had drained her, requiring her to rest for the better part of a day and a half, although she wondered how much of that fatigue was also due to her visit to the Shadow Realm, nearly losing herself in the process and then Cai's disappearance. The only physical reminder of her time in that cursed place was a new mark on her right forearm: a twisting black tendril, spreading from her wrist to elbow. She still glanced at it from time to time, but it hadn't changed form or shape, and she had begun to accept that it would remain with her forever.

'Tash,' Mellie was standing over her again, looking disappointed. 'Eat. Otherwise I'll start to think that you don't like my cooking.'

Tash began to spoon the soup into her mouth, barely tasting it, but making an effort to look impressed. Mellie gave her a smug, satisfied smile and left again to wipe down the bar to keep it gleaming. Tash rested her head in her palm, gazing out of the window with glazed eyes, not seeing the people walking past. The soup did little to settle her anxiety, which had only increased over the past days and nights, as she had waited, at first impatiently and then with growing concern, for Cai to return. She missed him and his delayed absence made her mind come up with new and disturbing explanations for it, such as him being killed and torn apart by the monsters in Trencher's Pit. Each time that particular thought occurred to her, she pushed it away, unable to accept that possibility.

'Tash?' She felt a faint trace of annoyance at being interrupted again in her silent reflection, and looked up to see Vallus. 'We're going out on a hunt tonight,' he said, 'I hoped that you would come along. The Nightwalker should be scared of a Robin.'

'Where will you go?' she asked, struggling to find any enthusiasm.

'The Heath,' he replied, 'it always strikes from there. With you at our side, we should be able to track it to its lair.'

If she accompanied them, she would have a distraction from her thoughts, from waiting and calling out to Cai under her breath until the other monster came to tap at her window. Its voice insinuated itself into her dreams, infiltrated her nightmares and she often awoke crying out in fear only to hear its rattling laughter from outside. Although, if she went onto the Heath with the hunting party, there was also the possibility that the monster would find them. She still hadn't seen it up close and so didn't know what to look out for. But at least then she could fight it and she wouldn't be alone. Surely that was better than the purgatory she had been in since Cai disappeared.

'Will you accompany us, Tash?' Vallus asked and she nodded. He grinned and made his way towards the inn door. 'I'll come back later to get you. Make sure you have a weapon on you, just in case.'

Tash nodded again and then rose, moving back to her room where she lay on the bed, trying to muster some energy. As had become her habit over the past days, she reached over to the bedside table and picked up the faded journal, opening it to the next entry. Cai's handwriting scrawled over the pages, and her eyes devoured it, feeling a fleeting moment of connection to him before it faded away. The first entries had all been short, yet over time, perhaps at his mother's urging or because he found that he enjoyed it, Cai had begun to make them lengthier until they spanned several pages. Tash's gaze fell on the next entry, which was close to the end of the journal.

Mother got lost again today. It's been two years now and she still wanders the Heath when she has these episodes, not remembering much afterwards. I had to remind her that it would be my fifteenth birthday next week and she seemed confused, repeating that I was turning fourteen instead. I miss how she used to be, when she would laugh and the shack was a home I wanted to come back to. She loses track of conversations and cannot absorb any news that I bring her from the village. I know that my friends and their parents think that she's gone mad. Derrick approached me about moving into town yesterday, suggesting that it would be better for both of us, for Mother to have better care and so that I could get a job. I told him that I would consider the offer, but I don't know. Of course I want her to get well again, but I don't want to leave the Heath. I don't think I would cope well in town, not with all those people around us all day, every day.

Tash turned the page, scanning the next entry eagerly.

I think I might be going mad. Not like Mother, at least— not yet. I've been hearing things— seeing things on the Heath. Figures in a sort of procession who appear in the morning mist and then vanish as though they were never there. At night I hear bells, like they've been attached to a horse's bridle, jingling across the Heath. Then there are voices whispering in the darkness, calling to me, saying that I need to go home. I couldn't tell Mother about it— she's barely able to remember my name at times these days. I mentioned the voices and figures to Derrick though and he said he'd put together a hunting party just in case there were witches or monsters about. It made me feel slightly better, although even now, as I write I can hear them again, just beyond the walls of the shack in the darkness. And what's worse is that, despite everything, I want to go to them.

The next entry was short, the writing even more jagged than usual with faint traces of blood colouring the page.

She's run to the village. She can't look at me. Everything hurts and I'm always hungry. I tried to eat normal food but it was tasteless, doing nothing to fill my stomach. What have I done wrong? Why have I been cursed into this form? Why won't Mother tell me what's going on? Why won't anyone listen?

Tash read it and then the remaining entries in quick succession, as Cai descended into despair, rejected by his friends, mother and village. Her heart ached as she read one of the last pages which, like so many others, was stained red.

She's gone. I don't know how. My fault. Her blood everywhere. All my fault.

She turned to the last entry and read the final words over again. A bloody handprint spread across the page, making it hard to decipher the faded handwriting.

The people want me to be a monster. So, I will be one.

'Oh Cai,' she whispered, tracing the words, tears rising unbidden to her eyes. She understood now why he had hidden the journal, why it had never been retrieved from the shack where he had grown up. The final entries spewed hurt and pain, resentment and anger at the world and Nordhaven for casting him out, for cursing him when he had done nothing to warrant it. She longed to hold the boy he had been, to tell him that things would be alright. No one had shown him compassion in those days, and her heart bled with the injustice of it.

There was a sudden banging at her door and Tash jumped, hastily hiding the journal under a pillow.

'Tasha?' a familiar voice called through the door, 'Tasha, open up.'

There was only one person who called her that and, once the shock had settled somewhat, she was clenching her jaw in annoyance. What, by the Gods, was he *doing* here?

She opened the door with a jerk. 'Harrison.'

'I was starting to think that you weren't here,' he remarked, grinning down at her and ignoring the responding glower.

'Why are *you* here?' she asked as he entered without permission, looking around the room with interest.

'Oh, I was just passing through, Tasha,' he said carelessly but she wasn't fooled.

'Don't lie to me, Harrison,' she said tartly. 'And I thought I told you to stop calling me Tasha.'

'Did you?' he asked lightly, peering at the items on her dressing table and then moving to the window, which had been bolted shut. 'I don't remember.'

'Why are you here?' she repeated, 'And *why* are you going through my things?'

'I heard that there was a problem with Nightwalkers in this town,' he said, twisting his dezmian around his fingers. 'Thought you might want some help.'

'I don't need any help,' she spoke through gritted teeth. 'It's a problem that I've been working on.'

'Well, now we can work on it together,' he said breezily, reclining on her bed as though it was his own. She glared at him and pointedly held the door open for him to leave. Harrison ignored the hint and continued to look around the room from his position on the bed. 'Besides, based on what some of the people said downstairs, you've not quite been yourself lately. It seems to me that you might need a hand.'

She blushed, her annoyance developing into anger now. 'I don't—'

'Also,' he pierced her with an assessing look, 'there's been some rumours about you, Tasha. Getting lost on the Heath, disappearing with a stranger at the village party, a figure leaving your room by the window. Just what have you been getting up to? This isn't like you.'

As he spoke her fists clenched, the ever-present anxiety that had already been churning because of Cai, rising again with a vengeance. What did he know? What did he suspect?

'I didn't give you permission to spy on me,' she snapped, 'and who I spend time with is *none* of your business, Harrison.'

'Isn't it?' His eyes narrowed and he watched her with an intensity that left her feeling shaken and confused.

'*No*,' she asserted forcefully, folding her arms. 'It isn't.'

'Alright then, Tasha,' he said smoothly, rising and pausing as he brushed against her on his way out. 'But I'm not leaving. You shouldn't face a Nightwalker alone.'

She watched him move down the hallway to the adjoining room, give her a small, sardonic wave and then enter it. She shut the door, trying to avoid slamming it and making it plain how he had gotten to her. There were some things that just could not be borne and his insinuations had left her shaking with anger, barely holding it together.

Tash shut her eyes, counting in and out, forcing herself to calm her breathing and reign in her emotions. Harrison had always gotten on her nerves; she couldn't let him get to her like this. Perhaps if they found the monster that had committed the murders and killed it, then, just maybe, he might leave her alone. Until that time came, it might be wiser to keep him nearby, to make sure that he didn't discover anything she would rather keep hidden. It would seem strange to the Nordhaven residents if the two Robins were consistently at loggerheads and the last thing she wanted to deal with was curious questions. Her eyes snapped open and she moved to get her things, strapping her knife to her belt, tying the cloak around her shoulders and stowing her dezmian in her pocket.

Resolutely, she strode into the hallway to bang on his door, which he opened with a smug grin. Tash forced herself to not return his expression with a glare, and instead asked, 'Are you ready to go monster hunting?'

Chapter Seventeen

At first I thought that the Shadow Realm was a cursed place. All the tales mentioned how it was the home for monsters and Dæmons. Perhaps that's why I feel safe here. The darkness doesn't scare me like it once did, and the beasts that dwell here have learned what happens when they cross me. I feel more powerful than ever before, the possibilities are endless. Sometimes I still hear a voice whispering in the night, urging me to succumb to my desires, to rip and tear and feast without abandon. Sometimes I deny its pull, but sometimes I listen.

> ~ An extract from a journal, hidden in the Shadow Realm

The torches didn't provide much light in the gloom, barely protecting the group of hunters in a pale, flickering glow. Clouds covered the moon and fog hung over the Nordhaven Heath, making it difficult to navigate through the undergrowth. They had been searching for several hours, although by now the numbing cold was starting to make Tash wish that they could return to the town. Vallus walked at the head of the group, a torch in one hand, club in the other, and Tash recognised some of the others from the village, like Klem, Florrick and Klara, each one gripping tightly to makeshift weapons. Harrison stayed by her side, helping her over fallen trees or prickly gorse. She didn't particularly need his help, but accepted it, nonetheless, focussing on scanning the darkness, searching for any signs of movement.

So far, apart from the odd bat flying overhead or the rustling of a scrawny fox as it sprinted away from the group, there had been nothing out of the ordinary. Yet Tash felt uneasy. Something was different tonight, as though there was a presence just out of sight in the fog, watching them and waiting until it was ready to strike.

'It's alright, Tasha,' Harrison said, patting her shoulder, 'you don't have to be afraid.'

She shot him an astonished look. Did he really think she was going to wilt over in a faint at any moment with fear? Didn't he know her at all?

'I'm not,' she replied coolly, and noticed Klara hide a knowing smile. Tash pulled away from Harrison, forcing some distance between them as she moved to the head of the group to join Vallus. He acknowledged her with a nod and lifted the torch higher, peering ahead into the darkness. Tash was about to speak when he held a hand up, pausing everyone mid-step.

'Can you hear that?' he asked, listening intently. A tremor ran down Tash's spine, dread starting to unfurl through her veins as the distant sound of jingling bells reached her ears.

'What is that?' Klara muttered, glancing around for the source of the noise. The others began to shift nervously, eyeing the darkness with a mixture of fear and intrigue. There was a soft, rattling laugh from just beyond their line of sight, a sound that froze one's blood and could terrify the bravest of hearts. The undergrowth rustled as something began to circle around the group, who huddled together automatically.

'Well, well,' the voice sounded hungry, 'what have we got here?'

'Stand together,' Vallus lifted his torch higher and bran-
dished his club. 'Nightwalkers are fast and deadly.'

The creature laughed again and Tash gripped her dagger,
sensing it move closer as she prepared to strike. Before she
could, Harrison had pulled her backwards and she staggered,
tripping on the heather and dropping the blade.

She glared at him, 'What was that for?'

'I'm keeping you safe, Tasha,' he retorted, flipping his
dezmian and sending a ball of flame towards the sound of
the voice. The fire flew out over the Heath, scorching the
earth and catching on the grass. The creature let out another
snort of laughter.

'You're going to make this far too easy, Mortal.'

Harrison responded with hurling another fireball into the
night, and then another, and another until Tash gripped his
arm.

'Harrison, stop,' she cried desperately, 'you're setting the
Heath on fire.'

'It doesn't matter, Tash,' Vallus called, 'if we need to burn
the Heath to kill the Nightwalker, we will.'

'What a foolproof plan,' the creature snickered and the
hunters' heads turned, searching for it. 'I can see why you
were put in charge.'

'The fire's lighting up the fog,' Klara muttered, 'look
there.' She pointed and Tash realised that she was right, the
red glow from the growing fire was banishing the shadows
in the fog, revealing a tall, thin figure.

'Strike together!' Vallus shouted and he charged at the
creature, brandishing his torch and swinging his club in a
wide arc. He was followed by the others, who were quickly
swallowed up in the thick mist. There were flashes and cries,

as the creature's shape distorted, reforming into multiple figures, who encircled the group, laughing.

'Don't lose heart!' Vallus' voice reached her through the night, but it sounded as though he was already far away.

'I can't see it,' Klara's voice rang out, 'I can't… Vallus? Florrick? Where are you?' There was a loud scream and silence.

'Klara?' Tash called, 'Klara are you alright?'

'Stay here, Tasha,' Harrison said, 'I'll take care of it.' He ran in the direction of the voices, flipping his dezmian to conjure a sword in his free hand.

'Harrison, *no!*' Tash cried, bending to retrieve her dagger and made to follow him but the fog became impenetrable and she lost all sight of her companions. She could still hear them in the distance, struggling to fight an opponent who was too fast for them, evading their attacks with ease. Tash glanced around, the smoke from the fire making her eyes water and she coughed, spasms racking her chest. The clouds darkened and she heard a hiss of satisfaction.

'My sweet Natachatet, we're finally alone.'

She turned, dagger raised and dezmian prepared to fly, heart pounding with fear. 'Only cowards hide in the shadows,' she said forcefully, hoping that her voice wouldn't crack and reveal how she really felt. 'Come out and show yourself.'

It laughed. 'Your Nightwalker isn't here to help you escape this time, Natachatet. Such a shame that he won't be able to see me spill your blood though. He's in a place from which he'll never escape.'

'What are you talking about?' Tash demanded, as tall shapes appeared in the fog, surrounding her. 'What have you done to him?'

'I didn't hurt a hair on his head,' the creature replied slyly, 'he brought it on himself.'

Tash sensed something reaching out behind her and spun, striking out with the dagger as the spindly fingers whipped back into the fog. 'Stop hiding, coward.' Tash snarled, 'Tell me what you've done to Cai.'

'Oh, he's Cai to you, is he?' the voice whispered silkily. 'Don't you know what that Nightwalker of yours is capable of, Natachatet? Don't you know what he's done? He's hardly an appropriate companion for someone like you.'

Tash glared in the direction of the voice, losing patience with its baiting and flipped her dezmian, determined to bring the creature out of the darkness once and for all. The song burned in her throat, the smoke making it hard to catch her breath. Her vision shimmered as the dezmian became a whip of light swinging out into the fog, stretching towards the creature that had stalked her since her arrival in Nordhaven. There was a shriek as the tendril wrapped around a pale arm, twisting around the long, narrow fingers and dragging it closer. The creature fought back, trying to slip out of the whip's grasp but Tash held firm, her song rising in a crescendo as she urged the light to pull the monster in. It took all of her energy to maintain control over keeping it contained as it thrashed against being drawn closer.

'I thought you would want to find out more about your Nightwalker,' it hissed, 'I can tell you where to find him. How to save him. I can take you there.' Tash's eyes narrowed and the creature shrieked again as the whip burned. The pain seemed to temporarily weaken it and she took her advantage, savagely yanking backwards and succeeding in drawing the creature out of the inky smoke.

The first thing to emerge was the arm and fingers, whose nails were filed to sharp points. Its skin was the colour of off-milk, pasty and sallow, the bones prominent and angular. It was tall and hairless, with a gaping mouth filled with gnashing fangs, wide nostrils and what might once have been its eyes, except they had been sewn shut. Tash felt a wave of disgust and urged the whip of light to wrap around the creature's limbs, cocooning it from shoulders down to its bare narrow feet.

It breathed in, nostrils flaring, and bared its fangs in a grin. 'My dearest Natachatet,' it stopped moving, lying scarily still. 'Don't you want to come closer and inspect your trophy? Don't you want to slide your dagger through my heart?'

She did want to. This was the creature responsible for killing innocent women, leaving them on the Heath to terrify the townsfolk and Cai had been blamed for it. It deserved to suffer what its victims had and she wanted to exact justice. Yet she held back, not trusting the silky voice.

'Don't you want to hear about what happened to your Nightwalker?' Its tone became feral, bordering on madness. 'His screams were so sweet as we tore his flesh from his bones. He needed to be reminded who he serves, you see. One cannot visit Trencher's Pit without paying a price, as he should have known.' Tash was listening, frozen in place as the monster continued, its voice rising maniacally, 'And now your Nightwalker is gone, gone, *gone*. He's never coming back.'

'No,' Tash whispered numbly. 'You're lying.'

'Why would I lie?' it cackled, 'I was one of the lucky few to feast on his corpse. I felt his lifeblood drain away.'

Tash cried out, a tearing sensation in her chest crippling her momentarily. She blinked and the whip of light vanished as she lost concentration, falling to the ground, her dezmian sliding out of her icy fingers. There was a slithering sound and something now held her firm, in skinny arms that were far stronger than they appeared. Sharp nails traced her cheek, smearing the damp tears across her skin, and she smelt its rancid breath inches away from hers.

'Would you like to know what he said before he died, my sweet?' Its voice was honeyed as she felt the breath being crushed out of her. It was getting harder to focus, the dark fog sinking around them, enshrouding them again in a realm of shadow and smoke. Tash struggled against its grip weakly, determined to not succumb to the temptation of just giving up.

Her resistance seemed to excite the creature and its tone pulsed with it, as it relinquished its hold marginally on her, allowing her to take a breath of air. 'I do so like it when they fight,' it hissed, pulling in close to her ear. 'It means we can play. I know you have a weakness for creatures from the Shadow Realm, Natachatet.'

Tash made a sound that could have been interpreted as a whimper as she twisted back from the creature's body. It laughed cruelly, snagging one hand in her hair, nails biting into her skull and forcing her head back, revealing her neck. There was a second's warning and then its teeth were digging in, piercing her skin with practised ease. Tash screamed, almost fainting with the pain of it, the sound of her cries inciting the monster further. Her hand lifted to push it away, the yew ring grazing its face.

The creature pulled back with a snarl, releasing her and leaving her neck in agony, blood soaking down into her dress and cloak. 'You can scream all you want for your Nightwalker, my dear. He's not going to come to save you. He's dead, remember?' She fell back onto the ground, sobbing and tried to drag herself away. The monster snickered, circling her. 'You can't escape, Natachatet. Just like Cai couldn't escape from his fate.'

'Cai,' she whispered, her tears mingling with the blood, fingers catching on something small and round which thrummed with energy.

'He was such a disappointment,' the creature mused. 'He had such potential and threw it away. He just needs the right push to accept it. It only seems right that I do him that favour.'

It took a while for its words to absorb in Tash's brain, but by then she had already flipped the dezmian upwards as the creature pounced onto her, nails scratching in deep. There was a moment of agony as she called out, and then the creature's screams were joining hers as it registered the conjured yew stake that it had been impaled on. Tash pushed harder, her brain going fuzzy as the monster bit into her again, its lifeblood mixing with hers in the soil. It thrashed and struck out, making her head reel backwards. Its screams lessened to low growls and moans of pain as it stretched out on the ground, convulsing before it finally lay still.

Tash struggled to move, folding part of her cloak and pressing it to the wound on her neck as the world spun in and out. The smoke from the fire was becoming overwhelming now and she coughed, tossing her dezmian again and thinking of rain as the familiar tug pulled on her stomach. She wavered, sinking backwards as raindrops began to fall from the sky. There was a distant sound of bells and hooves coming closer, and then she knew no more.

***

She came to slowly, realising that she was lying in a soft bed, bandages wrapped around her injuries. Her head felt heavy and fuzzy, and the light burned as she opened her eyes to see that she was in her room at the inn. Harrison was sitting beside the bed, forehead wrinkled in concern, as he watched her.

'What happened?' Tash asked. Her throat felt like it was on fire and she reached over for her water flask, taking a shaky sip.

'I'm so sorry, Tasha,' he said. 'The Nightwalker separated us, played tricks on our minds, making us see and hear things that weren't there. Some of the men lost their heads and it took all our efforts to regroup and try to find you. By the time we got to you…' He took an unsteady breath, 'I thought you weren't going to make it. I did what I could to patch you up.'

'Thanks Harrison,' she said weakly. 'What did you do with the monster?'

'The Nightwalker?' He looked at her strangely. 'There was nothing there with you, Tasha. It got away.' His expression hardened, 'And we'll make sure that it will not escape again.'

Tash didn't understand. 'But I stabbed it,' she murmured and Harrison's eyebrows rose.

'If that's the case then we should find it easier to hunt the beast. You're not well, though, Tasha. I've asked Mellie to look after you when we go out again tonight. The Nightwalker will pay for what it's done to you.'

'It's not a Nightwalker, Harrison,' Tash said urgently, 'it's something different. Nightwalkers aren't responsible for the murders here. They're not as bad as people say they are.'

'You're not yourself, Tasha,' Harrison said. 'You've been through a terrible ordeal and are still needing time to recover. Stay here and rest, I'll come and check on you tomorrow.'

'No, Harrison, wait—' Tash began but he had already left the room, shutting the door firmly behind him. She frowned, not understanding what had happened after she passed out and where the monster had gone. With a groan of pain, she leaned back into the pillows, reaching again for the water flask. As she looked down at her hand, Tash realised that her yew ring had disappeared, leaving her feeling strangely bare and unprotected. She cast a glance over her bedside table, onto the floor and amongst the bedsheets, but it wasn't there. It must have fallen off on the Heath. A sense of loss filled her and she felt a tightness in her chest at the thought of it. Romulus had gifted it to her to protect her, and Cai had insisted that she always wear it when he wasn't around.

Thinking about Cai made the pain in her chest intensify, as she remembered what the monster had said the night before. In particular, its final words replayed in her mind, making her question how much of what it had said was true or false. She had no doubt that the creature would lie without conscience if it thought that its words would cause extra pain. Tash had been foolish to give away her emotions when it mentioned Cai, she had given it a glimpse into how much she cared and it had enjoyed using that against her.

Yet if it had spoken truthfully then Cai was dead, a possibility that had tormented her over the past week. Tash didn't want to face that prospect, to deal with the fallout that that would have on her heart.

'He can't be dead,' she whispered to herself over and over like a mantra, 'he's strong. He'll survive.'

'Tash?' She jumped, realising that she hadn't heard Mellie open the door. The woman was laden with a tray of stew and a cup of tea. She moved closer and deposited the tray on Tash's lap, which made her wince from its weight. 'Are you alright, dear?'

'I'm feeling a bit better, yes,' Tash lied, reaching for the spoon and beginning to help herself to the stew. Mellie eyed her worriedly, misinterpreting her expression.

'It'll be alright, Tash,' she said kindly, 'that lovely young man of yours will be safe with the other hunters. They'll find the Nightwalker and get rid of it for good.'

Tash choked slightly on the stew. 'Harrison is not my young man.'

Mellie chuckled and shook her head. 'Don't be silly, Tash. You both make a fine pair, I'm surprised he didn't come with you when you arrived.' She smiled and Tash stared back, overwhelmed with how she was being misinterpreted. 'I think he's a much nicer young man than that one you met at the dance. You shouldn't be dallying with people of his calibre.'

'What do you mean?' Tash asked sharply, 'People of his *calibre*?' She was starting to get angry, outraged at how first Harrison and now Mellie seemed to think that they had the right to tell her how to live her life.

Mellie rolled her eyes. 'Rogues, my dear. The men who only want a night of fun and then move on to the next town. You deserve to be with a Robin like you. And the way you and Harrison act when you're together leaves little to the imagination. He cares about you, Tash, it's obvious.'

Tash's mouth dropped open in shock. What had Mellie seen to make her think *that*? 'But I don't like—'

'Well,' Mellie said breezily, 'I should go back downstairs. I'll be back soon to collect your tray. Just think about what I said, dear. I'd hate for you to miss out on an opportunity for happiness when it comes so rarely.' With that, she departed, leaving Tash staring at the bowl of stew in a heightened state of indignation, trying to fathom just what had happened.

Chapter Eighteen

Since I sent her away, the blackouts are getting worse. I hear the witch's voice in my head, telling me to succumb, to give in to her. I try to fight it, but it's getting harder. When I regain control, I find myself caked in blood, feeling sated and then sickened. What can I do? The monster in me wants to obey her and earn her praise. It craves it. I don't know if I'm strong enough to withstand it much longer.

> ~ An extract from a journal in the depths of the Shadow Realm

Tash was awoken by shouting from the street. It was the early hours of the morning and the moon was still halfway across the sky. She walked to the window and pushed open the shutters to see what the source of the commotion was, rubbing her eyes blearily. Something was sprinting down the street, glancing back and laughing at its pursuers. She saw Harrison and Vallus leading the chase, their torches held high and weapons in hands, shouting at the creature who evaded them with ease, laughing with exhilaration and dodging as some of the men threw spears.

Tash gripped the windowpane, mesmerised, a painful mixture of elation and terror rising in her as the creature jumped through a patch of moonlight. She saw a flash of claws, the sweep of a tail and the familiar mouth twisted in a wicked grin as he called out something over his shoulder, taunting the hunters. However, he didn't see the group approaching from the other end of the street towards him, faces set with vicious hatred, whereas Tash could.

'*Cai!*' she screamed, as one of the villagers loaded a crossbow and fired. He reacted instinctively, leaping backwards and turning to see her, leaning out of her window. She couldn't see his expression, the strange darkness that was wont to hover around him was back, masking his face from view. A cloud covered the moon and he chose that moment to change his direction; with a running leap he was scaling the inn wall.

'Tasha!' Harrison's voice rang out from up the street, 'It's going into the inn. Get it!'

Tash stepped back several paces as Cai swung through the window with a crash. She was so relieved to see him that she acted without thinking. With a hoarse cry, she flung herself into his arms, holding on as though she would never let go. She didn't initially register him freezing at her touch, or that he didn't respond to her embrace.

'Oh Cai,' she sobbed, 'you're here. You're alive. I—' She choked as a hand encircled her neck, squeezing intently. Her wound throbbed and she gasped, scrabbling at his hand as he lifted her against the wall.

'So naïve,' he whispered, his voice low. 'So innocent.'

'Cai,' she coughed, trying to look into his eyes but seeing only shadows. 'Cai, it's me. It's Tash. Don't do this.'

He laughed brittlely. 'I've always wondered what a Robin would taste like.' He noticed the bandage around her neck and removed it, dropping her and she slumped down the wall, gasping as he knelt, scraping a finger over the wound. 'But it seems someone has beaten me to it.'

Tash cried out, sharp pain spiking through her at his touch. 'Cai, what's wrong with you?' From outside she heard shouting and banging on the inn door. Harrison and the hunting party were not far away, which, right now, she wasn't sure if it was a good thing or not.

'I've never liked having someone's second helpings,' Cai murmured, still fixated on her neck. 'But it does smell so sweet.' He leaned closer, bending over her wound, and she felt his teeth clamp down.

She lashed out through the pain, striking him in the side, which he deflected with frightening ease. She had no dezmian with her, no ring of yew this time and so she hit again and again, trying to find a way through his defence. Cai chuckled at her attempts as they became weaker, finally catching her arms and holding them above her head, pinning her once more to the wall. She was panting now, the exertion of trying to defend herself using up all the energy she had regained that day.

'What will you do now, Robin?' Cai asked tauntingly, 'How are you going to strike down the fearsome Nightwalker without a weapon?' He leaned in towards her and she caught a glimpse of his face through the shadows. His eyes were darker than usual, burning with a frenzy she had never seen before. She barely recognised him. Yet his words triggered a memory, inspiring her to try a different approach.

'Oh Cai,' she whispered, 'what has happened to you, *liebeshem*?' And then she pushed through the darkness to press her lips to his. He went rigid as she kissed him tenderly, tears sliding down her cheeks and ignoring his stillness, try-ing to move as close to him as her position allowed. He shivered, a tremor shaking through his whole body and then his hands released her wrists to hold her waist, pulling her closer.

'Tash?' He shook his head, confused, the shadows lifting to reveal his eyes had returned to normal. She gave an incoherent moan and clung to him, unable to speak for a moment.

'What's going on?' he asked, looking around the room, before noticing her injuries. 'Tash, what happened to you?' He reached out, hands lingering over her neck, and the aching pain began to lessen. From downstairs she heard the door being unbolted, loud furious voices and the sound of heavy feet climbing the staircase.

Tash didn't answer him, too focussed was she on the hunting party's approach. 'Cai, you need to go. You need to run, now.'

'What are you talking about?' he asked, 'You're hurt. I can't—'

'You have to *go*,' she pulled him up, wincing despite her best efforts.

'Tasha? Tasha?' Harrison's voice shouted from the hallway, banging on the door. 'We're coming in, hold on.' Cai turned in the direction of his voice, snarling and Tash pulled on his arm, trying to drag him to the window.

'Cai, you must leave. They'll kill you.'

'Who was that?' he demanded.

'We don't have time for this,' Tash snapped desperately, still pushing him away but he didn't budge. The door crashed open, splinters of wood flying into the room and Tash cried out, covering her face with her arms. Cai moved quickly, twisting her behind him as the group of hunters plunged in, Mellie on their tail. Harrison raced forwards, striking Cai over the shoulder with a blow from his club, and yanked

Tash out and away. Cai growled and lashed out as the other hunters pressed in with their weapons. He retreated, trying to move back to the window whilst evading their blows.

'Stop,' Tash screamed, 'please, don't hurt him.' She fought against Harrison's grip, 'Make them stop, Harrison, *please.*'

'Shut your woman up, Harrison,' Vallus grunted, as Cai wrestled out of his grip, striking upwards with his claws, leaving a jagged cut along Vallus' arm. Harrison obeyed, covering her mouth with his hand, silencing her. Cai glanced around and saw, snarled and tried to change direction again, moving towards Tash and Harrison instead. However, as he tried to reach her, they circled him, using their combined brute force to beat him savagely until he lay in a crumpled heap, unmoving. Tash's eyes were wet with tears and she pulled against Harrison's grip, her screams muffled as she watched Cai fall in a bloody mess.

'Take it away,' Vallus barked, and two of the town's militia stepped forward to drag Cai out of the room.

'You can put it in the cellar,' Mellie spoke up from the doorway, 'I keep it locked tight. We don't want to run the risk of it waking up and escaping.'

'Or hurting anyone else,' Harrison said curtly, glaring at Cai's limp body.

'What do you mean?' Tash asked as Mellie began to lead the men to the cellar, finally breaking away from Harrison. The other villagers left, casting Tash dirty, distrustful looks, and Vallus refused to meet her gaze as he stalked out after them. She twisted her hands, unable to look at the traces of blood on the floor. 'He didn't hurt me, Harrison.' Not when he had been in his right mind, at least, she added privately.

'*It* attacked Klara,' Harrison's face darkened. 'We found her on the edge of the Heath, spread out like a trophy. It was there, Tasha. I know what I saw.' He turned to the remnants of her door and flipped his dezmian, reforming it so that it was as good as new.

She shook her head mutely, unable to accept what he was saying. 'He's not an *it*. He's innocent, Harrison. He's not the one responsible for the murders.'

'You'll have a hard time proving that after what happened tonight,' Harrison snapped angrily. 'When it leapt at your window, Klem got hit by the arrow aimed at that monster. I think you should be thanking me, Tasha. We saved you from the Nightwalker. You should be grateful.'

'You're not *listening*,' she pleaded desperately, gripping him by the shirt. 'Cai is not normally like he was tonight. Let me talk to him, find out what went wrong. He wouldn't hurt people, Harrison. He's not like that.'

His gaze became icy and she paused, confused. 'I was hoping that my suspicions were wrong, Tasha, but it seems that they weren't.' He reached into his pocket and withdrew the faded journal that had been under Tash's pillow. 'I don't know how the Nightwalker has bewitched you, Tasha, but I'm not going to let you make a mistake that you'll regret.'

'Harrison,' she interjected, eyes fixed on the journal, 'what are you doing with that? Give it back. You don't understand what's going on.'

'I understand perfectly,' he retorted, 'but it seems that you no longer remember who you should be loyal to, Tasha. The Order is committed to banishing evil spirits and Dæmons, to protecting the helpless and restoring justice in the worlds. It seems to me that this monster has bewitched you. You're not yourself and until you come to your senses, I must keep you safe.'

'Harrison,' she said with mounting panic as he moved to the door, collecting her dezmian from her bedside table on the way, 'what are you doing? Give back my dezmian!'

'I'm protecting you,' he said simply. 'When the creature's dead, the spell will lift and you will thank me, Tasha.'

'No,' she cried, rushing forwards but he had already shut the door in her face and locked it from the other side. She hammered on the wood, calling out, pleading, desperate for someone to let her out but no one answered. By the time the sun had risen, Tash was sprawled on the ground, shaking with uncontrollable sobs, unaware of what was happening in the cellar of the inn or how much longer Cai would have left.

***

She had been locked in her room for three days. Tash had fumed and railed at her jailers, most often Mellie and Harrison, who were firmly of the opinion that she had been bewitched and was in no fit state to go anywhere. She had no idea what was happening to Cai, although from Mellie's pinched expression and Harrison's perpetual scowl, she figured that he was still alive. Mellie finally relented enough on the third day to say that Vallus and Harrison were interrogating him, trying to find out about where the other Nightwalkers were and why they had been targeting Nordhaven. According to Mellie, Cai had not been particularly forthcoming with information so far.

Tash was sitting by the window, watching the procession moving down the street, the sheets from her bed spread at her feet, hands working methodically. The mourners didn't look up at her, refusing to acknowledge her presence as they passed, the coffin balanced on the shoulders of Vallus, Harrison, Jervois and Florrick. Ines followed, supporting Pyrrus, her sobs cutting through the late afternoon. Pyrrus' grief seemed to be internalised, he held himself straight, slowly placing one foot in front of the other. Tash felt a pang of grief at Klara's loss, at the injustice of her death and not having been able to prevent it. She gripped the windowpane, wondering how Klara had been lured to the Heath and attacked, and why Cai was responsible. She had seen a different side of him that night, one that was akin to the monster she had impaled with the stake, which proved all the warnings she had read about Nightwalkers right. Tash saw the mourners continue on, heading towards the temple and distant graveyard, until they faded from sight.

For the first time in three days, she was completely alone, the inn empty and silent, as all members of the community were going to Klara's funeral. There was no one in the street, and she was going to take the opportunity to escape.

'I promise to find out how this happened to you, Klara,' Tash whispered, bowing her head in a momentary prayer, 'may your soul find peace and rest.'

There was a faint breeze from the open window, the cool caress of the afternoon chill and then it was gone. Tash stood, tied the end of the sheets to the bed post and tossed the rest out the window. She fastened her cloak and, without giving herself time to overthink, sat on the windowsill, gripping the sheets, and began to lower herself down. The material stretched with her weight and she didn't waste any time, descending the wall as quickly as possible, feet gripping to the stonework. There was a ripping sound from above her and she glanced upwards, praying that the sheets would hold until she reached the ground.

When she was close enough to jump down, she let go, landing hard on the cobblestones with a wince. The sheets swayed from the momentum as Tash opened the door to the inn, slipping inside and sliding the bolt across behind her. She had had plenty of time to think over the past days, to probe Mellie and Harrison for information about where Cai was being kept. Now she just had to find the cellar and get him out before the funeral and the wake were over.

First, though, she wanted to get her dezmian back and climbed the stairs two at a time, racing to Harrison's room. She twisted the handle and tried to push the door open but it stood firm, locked tight. Tash bit out a curse and returned downstairs, noting with disappointment that there was no door under the staircase. She would have to try and find the cellar through process of elimination, then.

The dining room was empty; the bar gleamed with polish and clean glasses filled the shelves, glistening in the light. Tash moved fast, lifting the rugs up and shifting furniture, checking under them for a trap door but finding nothing. She ran her hands over the blank stretches of wall, lifting the paintings down to see if there was anything– a button or lever– behind them. Again, nothing.

She strode behind the bar, noting the even floorboards and entered the kitchen. Just like the dining room, the kitchen was spotless, pots and pans neatly stacked away, and the fire blazed in the grate. She peered around, all too aware that half an hour had already passed. The funeral would be nearing its end soon, and then the mourners would return to Pyrrus' windmill for the wake. After that she had no idea how long it would be before someone returned to the village and saw the sheets from her window, indicating her escape.

'Cai!' she called desperately, 'Cai, where are you?'

There was no response to her cries, although a part of her had expected as much. She began to search the room, moving the wide table to pull out the rug from underneath it. As she dragged, a faint sound reached her ears and she paused, listening intently. Then she heard it once more, a distant scratching noise from underneath her. Tash heaved on the rug with renewed determination, revealing the trapdoor with a thick, metal ring.

'Hold on, Cai,' she muttered, lifting the ring in her hands and pulling with all her might. The trapdoor creaked and trembled, gradually rising several inches. It was heavier than she had expected, yet Tash kept going, slowly but surely revealing a ladder that descended into a brightly lit room. She dropped the trapdoor onto the ground and began to climb down, almost slipping in her haste.

'Cai?' She turned and saw him, gagged and bound in heavy chains along one of the walls. His eyes were half open and glazed, but on seeing her approach they focussed, widening slightly. His body was covered in varying injuries, burns, cuts and dark bruises, with some bones twisted into new shapes. Despite this, there were places where she could see that he had already begun to heal, his Nightwalker blood slowly trying to repair the damage inflicted on him.

The room was bathed in bright, white light, from lanterns that hovered in the air, banishing any shadows. Tash recognised it, sensing the divine magic that had been used to create them so that they would never go out. It was similar to the magic she had created the night of the new moon, and she remembered how that had impeded Cai's Nightwalker abilities. Cai made a motion, scratching against the chains to get her attention and she moved closer, reaching out to cup his cheek.

'I was scared that I wouldn't find you,' she whispered, casting a glance over the chains that were fastened with thick padlocks as she removed the gag from his mouth. 'I got away as soon as I could.'

'Tash,' he mumbled, voice raspy and dry. 'You're here.'

'Of course I am,' she said absently, lifting the padlocks and examining them closely. 'Do you know where the key is?'

'They took it with them,' he managed to say as he pulled against the chains, trying and failing to break them. 'But that was left by the other Robin.' He jerked his head at a small stone, lying discarded in the far corner of the cellar. Tash's heart leapt and she picked it up, feeling a sense of power returning for the first time in days.

'Hold still,' she instructed, tossing the dezmian into the air and focussing intently on the chains. There was a soft clicking sound as the padlocks opened, before the chains clattered to the ground and Cai staggered, unsteady on his feet. Tash rushed to his side, supporting him over to the ladder. 'You need to get somewhere safe,' she said, gasping as she struggled to hold him steady.

'The lights,' he muttered, 'turn off the lights.'

She threw her dezmian again and the ethereal lanterns were extinguished, casting them into darkness, save for the light shining through the exit above the ladder. There was a low hiss and a cracking sound from next to her and she felt Cai move away, sinking into the shadows.

'Cai?' She reached out for him but felt nothing. 'We need to get out of here.'

'It's alright,' he whispered, 'I just need a minute to recover.' She followed the sound of his voice, locating him in the corner of the room where it was darkest, and took his arm.

'You can't stay in here,' she pressed. 'When they find out that I've escaped, I don't know what will happen.'

As if her thought had summoned them, she heard distant voices from upstairs, shouts and the shattering of glass. Someone had seen her bedsheets then. Their time had run out.

'Trust me,' Cai breathed as the footsteps drew closer, one hand reaching around her waist to hold her tightly. She returned the pressure, sending out a silent prayer as Vallus' furious voice reached them.

'I told you to set a guard– look what's happened, the monster's gotten loose.'

'I thought that the chains would keep it contained,' Harrison's voice replied.

'That girl was trouble from the beginning,' Klem's voice added hotly, 'I warned you, didn't I? She's a witch, working with that monster.'

'She's not a witch,' Harrison retorted, 'it's cast a spell on her. She would never willingly work with a Dæmon.'

Tash could barely breathe, as she saw a foot step down onto the first rung.

'Hang on,' Cai breathed, as they tumbled backwards into nothingness, leaving the room an instant before it was illuminated with the lanterns once more. Tash held on tight, as they slipped through the darkness, plummeting downwards, her face pressed into Cai's shoulder, the dezmian held firmly in her free hand.

They landed with a splash, submerged in freezing water, sinking down into the depths before their heads broke the surface, coughing. As usual, Tash saw nothing around her, relying on her other senses instead. She tasted salt and felt

Cai's hand grip hers, guiding her towards the shore. Shivering, she clambered out of the water, stamping her feet to warm up, rubbing her arms furiously. She sensed Cai beside her, gasping for breath.

'I didn't realise that you could enter the Shadow Realm from the cellar,' she managed to get through her chattering teeth. 'How did you know?'

'I had a feeling it might be there,' he said, starting to lead her away. She followed automatically, listening for anything that might be prowling nearby.

'I thought they would catch us,' she muttered. 'They'll be hunting us both now.'

'They won't find us here,' he replied abruptly, increasing his pace. 'My cave isn't far.'

Tash tried to keep up, but her own injuries made it difficult. She stumbled, ankle twisting and let out a sharp cry. Without warning, Cai surprised her, lifted her up and carried her over the invisible terrain.

'Cai, put me down,' she urged, 'I can walk. You're hurt, this will only make it worse.'

'It's fine,' he said gruffly. 'The worst of the wounds have already started to heal. Besides, the darkness helps with the pain.'

She didn't think that sounded reassuring, and was about to reply when he jumped, leaping into the void and her voice was lost in the wind. They landed with a jolt, which Tash felt shudder through her bones, before he continued running, following a familiar path.

'You could've given me some warning there,' she grumbled, bouncing unceremoniously in his arms and wincing as pain shot through her.

'It wouldn't have made a difference,' he muttered, as he

slid down a steep slope and then came to a halt. 'Hold still.' She was deposited on the ground, and held herself, shivering again at the cold. There was a rush of light as Cai summoned a fire that filled the cave with a rosy glow, and Tash leaned closer to it, reaching out for the warmth. The dezmian dropped from her fingers and rolled away, bouncing off Cai's foot. He picked it up and turned it over, moving to join her by the fireside.

Tash's eyes widened slightly as he knelt down, registering the change in him already. The physical signs of the attack and his imprisonment had faded, the broken bones mended as though it had never happened. He met her gaze and smiled wryly.

'It's easier to heal when I'm in my natural habitat.' His eyes travelled to her neck, to the other wounds that hadn't healed, and the ankle that she was stretching out, trying to keep her breathing even. 'Here, let me.' He reached over her, scarlet eyes narrowing with concentration and she felt the magic begin to work.

'Thanks,' she said, rubbing her neck and feeling only smooth skin under her fingers. She wiggled her ankle experimentally, felt nothing out of the ordinary and sighed with relief.

'What happened to you, Tash?' he asked. 'How did you get these injuries?' He was watching her intently, concerned, but she avoided his gaze and leaned closer to the fire, shivering again.

'I could ask you something similar,' she said. 'After we went into Trencher's Pit you disappeared. I thought you had died. I called for you and even joined one of the hunting parties on the Heath to look for you.'

He frowned. 'You were on the Heath? But—'

'The monster found us,' Tash continued, unable to stop now she had begun. 'It separated us and attacked me. It said that you were dead, that it watched as you were killed. I stabbed it but the next day Harrison said that its body hadn't been found. They thought it was you.'

'You killed it?' His voice was tight, but she still refused to look at him.

'I thought I did,' she whispered, 'but it was gone. And then a few nights later you were in Nordhaven, they were chasing you in the streets. They said you killed Klara.'

'Klara?'

'The miller's daughter,' Tash clarified. 'She was found on the Heath. Harrison said that you were there too.' He shifted beside her, rising and starting to pace the cave.

'I don't remember,' he said, 'I don't remember anything after telling you to leave Trencher's Pit.'

'I called to you,' Tash said, the memory returning vividly. 'You weren't yourself, Cai. There was something wrong. You weren't in control of what happened.'

He halted in his pacing. 'Did I hurt you, Tash?'

She didn't reply, remembering the crushing pressure on her neck, the tearing as he bit into her wound, draining her blood away.

'Tash?' He was kneeling beside her again, forcing her to meet his gaze and then he recoiled, seeing the answer in her eyes.

'You weren't yourself,' she repeated, but he shook his head, face blanching with horror.

'I hurt you,' he whispered, 'and I don't remember it. I *am* a monster.'

She reached out, catching his cheeks in her hands and said, '*You* didn't hurt me, Cai. Whatever it was, it *wasn't* you.

I know that you wouldn't hurt me.'

'How did you stop me?' he asked, his voice shaking. Tash smiled softly and twined her fingers in his hair, pulling him closer.

'Like this, *liebeshem*,' she murmured, and then she pressed her lips against his, pouring all the things she hadn't been able to say into the kiss. She revealed her grief on thinking he was gone, her joy when she found out he was alive and the agony when she realised that he might be lost forever. She was aware of little else save the rapid beating of her heart as she leaned into his arms and the temptation to allow her hands to explore him, to appease the aching emptiness she had felt for days. Time seemed to pause, as she lost herself in the feel of him, the pressure of his lips against hers, their clothes still wet and dripping onto the ground.

Tash smiled as they broke apart, the sweetness of the kiss still lingering, fuelling the desire that it had ignited. He was speechless for a moment and then finally managed to say,

'I don't understand.'

'Perhaps,' Tash laid a hand on his chest, 'you can figure it out later.' His eyes blazed as she pulled on his tattered shirt, tossing its remnants on the cave floor, pushing him down after it. 'But right now, I need you to not worry about that for a while. I've missed you.' She pinned him underneath her as she straddled his waist, bending down to kiss him again. He groaned and gripped her tightly, locking her in place as he kissed her back, moving down to her neck.

The memory was overwhelming her before she could stop it and she froze, sudden terror infusing her blood. She struck out blindly, a cry ripping from her throat as she felt again the pain from the last two occasions a Dæmon had approached her neck. The change was immediate and caught him off-guard so he was slower to react, getting hit several times before he held her wrists steady as her arms flailed.

'Tash,' he said, concerned, 'Tash, it's alright.'

Slowly, she quietened, taking a while to recognise that she was safe again. She was shaking uncontrollably and Cai was watching her, his expression shuttered as it was wont to do when he was hurt. Darkness flickered across his face, distorting his features and she felt a trickle of fear.

'I'm sorry,' she whispered, 'I didn't mean… I'm sorry.'

'Why are you apologising?' His voice was brittle, enough to make her heart bleed. 'You don't have to apologise for being afraid.'

'I…' She struggled to find the right words, wanting him to understand. 'It wasn't your fault, I just—'

'You keep saying that what happened to you wasn't my fault,' Cai retorted sharply, 'but I'm the one who hurt you. And you're scared of me. Admit it, Tash.'

'No,' she denied, 'I just… I remember that creature and I can't get it out of my mind. I'm sorry.' She moved away, holding her knees to her chest, ashamed of the outburst, angry that it had ruined the moment they shared and terrified that the memory would not leave her. She blinked back hot tears, wiping them away with the palm of her hand, embarrassed. Cai remained silent and she could almost hear his own recriminations, his certainty that he was the reason for her reaction, that he was the monster everyone claimed him to be.

Eventually, she grew anxious in the silence and said, 'Please, Cai. Just hold me. Help me to forget it.' She turned luminous eyes towards him, begging him to come closer and make her feel safe again. His expression twitched and he obeyed her plea, drawing her back and resting his head on hers.

'I'm sorry too,' he whispered into her hair, 'I'm sorry you had to go through that.'

'Promise you won't leave again,' she said quietly, 'stay with me.'

'As long as you want me to,' he replied softly, kissing her head as she closed her eyes, the trembling finally stopping, allowing her to relax into him. Before she knew it, sleep had overtaken her and Cai was left alone with his thoughts, wondering how he could protect the woman in his arms from himself.

Chapter Nineteen

Mistress wants blood. She wants them to feel pain. Weak, pitiful creatures, with no use for anything except to be food. She says I'm everything she needs, everything she wants. She promises things that we will do together, but I have to please her first.

~ A torn-out extract from a hidden journal in the Shadow Realm

Tash's dreams were strange and nightmarish. She saw Cai running down the alleyway, the sound of bells ringing in her ears, before she was caught and dragged away from him. She called out, turning to see that Harrison was the one leading her, telling her that she needed to see The Robin, that her report was overdue. She was joined by Mellie, who explained that she really should be going now, that Nordhaven was safe again and the Nightwalker was dead. Vallus was laughing at her from the inn's doorway, pointing at something hanging above her. She looked up and saw the familiar face, the lifeless body swinging in the winter wind and screamed.

'Tash?' Someone was shaking her awake and it took a while for her to realise that the scene she had seen wasn't real. She clung onto a worried Cai as her heartbeat slowed, forcing herself to recognise that he was alive.

'It's alright now,' Cai murmured, stroking her hair soothingly. 'It was just a dream.'

Tash nodded, glancing around the cave to make sure that they really were safe, that they hadn't been discovered. Cai noticed her looking and said, 'I've put a protective spell on the cave entrance. Even with the fire in here, the other monsters will not be able to come in. Unless they are extended an invitation, the entrance is closed to them.'

She nodded again, still unsettled and asked, 'How long was I asleep?'

'A few hours,' he replied, shrugging.

'And did you sleep?' she asked, 'Did I wake you?'

'It doesn't matter,' he said gently.

'I saw terrible things,' she murmured into his chest. 'It was like the dreams from before but in this one you were dead.'

'I'm not dead,' he reminded her and then his gaze sharpened as he processed her words. 'What do you mean "like the dreams from before"?'

She looked up at him, biting her lip, unsure how to answer without it sounding strange. 'Do you remember the night of the new moon?'

'It was quite hard to forget,' he said, squeezing her lightly.

'I said that I had met you before,' her voice was so quiet that he nearly missed it. 'In your human form, I mean.'

'I remember,' he said gently.

'The truth is that I'd dreamed of you for weeks,' she admitted, blushing furiously, 'I never knew who you were, and you never spoke your name.' He was looking at her with an impenetrable expression and she became impatient. 'Say something, Cai. Please.'

'Would it surprise you if I said that I had dreamed about you as well?' Her eyes widened and she stared at him. 'Although my dreams,' he smiled briefly, 'had been going on for years. I thought that I would never find you until that night at the Temple. I thought you must be a figment of my imagination, and then you were there.' He laid a hand to her cheek tenderly. 'For so long I hated you for not being real, for tempting me whenever I slept. But then there you were, arguing with me, refusing to show any sign of weakness.'

'I remember,' she murmured, entranced by his words, the look in his eyes mesmerising her. 'You scared me, but there was no chance I'd let you see it.'

'And then I just had to wait,' he said softly. 'Until we met again and I could finally get to know you.'

Tash smiled, liquid gold sliding through her veins, filling her with a sense of warmth. 'I'm glad that you did.'

'I was hoping that you would feel that,' he said. 'Your Robin friend seemed to think that you would regret it. They called you his.' Tash frowned, shaking her head.

'I don't know what Harrison said to you,' she said firmly, 'but I am not *his* anything. I thought we were friends, of a sort, until recently. I've never felt for him that way.' Cai's grip tightened and she returned the pressure, wanting to calm his concerns but not knowing how. So she raised her mouth to his, kissing him before he could speak again and instead showing him what she felt. He responded immediately, the fiery desire from earlier rekindling with barely any effort although this time he made sure to avoid her neck.

Her clothes were gone before she could register it, his hands grazing over her skin, making it quiver with anticipation as he went lower. She stifled a moan, head rocking back and hitting the ground.

'You don't have to worry about being quiet here, Tash,' he whispered, continuing his torturous perusal of her body. She gasped and mumbled incoherent words, too lost in the sensation to register him removing the rest of his clothes. He chuckled, pushing her to the brink of madness, before he entered her, making her cry out and grip him tighter, begging him to never stop. He complied, driving her to the moment when everything shattered and she screamed, nails biting into him as he joined in her release. She collapsed against him as he pulled out, the words that she wanted to say on her tongue but something held her back from uttering them aloud. Instead, she held him in the aftermath, wondering why she was such a coward, unable to admit to him that he had become dear to her like no other. How he made her heart sing when he was close by and it was now almost second nature for her to think about his needs before her own. Yet still, she remained silent, a small part of her terrified of uttering words that, if they weren't reciprocated, would lead to more heartache than she was willing to bear.

Tash sat up, reaching for her clothes and pulled them on, avoiding Cai's eyes. She wasn't prepared to face her emotions, and so thrust them down to a place where she could avoid them. Her body ached from their exertions, reminding her all too well of what she was trying to pass off as a mutual attraction and nothing more.

'Tash?' She glanced around, getting caught in his gaze like a fly in a web.

'Mm?'

'Is everything alright?' he asked, frowning slightly as she nodded, seeing through her pretence with ease. She opened her mouth to reply, and then paused, listening intently. There was the sound of scrabbling from the cave mouth, which was gradually drawing closer.

She stared at Cai, who rapidly pulled his breeches back on, moving to her side. 'I thought that you said we were safe in here,' she whispered as the sound became louder, turning into footsteps. Her heart was in her throat, wondering who or what was making its way towards them. She ducked down to get her dezmian, clutching it in one hand and Cai with the other.

'The barrier protects us from my kind,' he murmured, tail swiping back and forth as he watched the edge of the darkness intently. Tash swallowed uncomfortably, as a cold voice filled the cave.

'I never expected this from you, Tasha.' She blinked and Harrison appeared from the shadows, his face set and hard, glaring at her with something akin to betrayal. 'You've thrown everything we learned away, for this monster.' He spat the last word, shooting Cai a venomous look.

'Harrison,' she began, stepping forwards placatingly. 'I need you to listen to me. Cai isn't a monster.'

Harrison's dezmian spun and a blade flashed through the air, only missing Cai's neck because he dodged to the side, grabbing Tash and pulling her out of harm's way.

'What are you *doing?*' she cried as Harrison summoned another blade, 'You could've killed me.'

'I wasn't aiming for you, Tasha,' he retorted, 'but if you get in my way you'll get hurt.'

'No, Cai,' she felt the Nightwalker tense, ready to pounce and clutched his arm, 'let me talk to him.'

'Talk quickly, Tash,' he muttered, 'this friend of yours doesn't seem to want to listen to reason.'

'You'll thank me eventually, Tasha,' Harrison said. 'You'll see that everything I've done has been to make it easier for you.'

'You're being obtuse,' she retorted angrily. 'You're not even *listening* to me, Harrison.'

'Tash,' Cai growled, 'perhaps try not to antagonise him.'

She ignored him, stepping closer. 'Unless you stop acting like an ass, Harrison, I won't ever be thanking you. You're mistaken about Cai and me.'

He let out a strangled laugh, 'I don't think I am, Tasha. To think that you've stooped this low. And *you*,' he pointed the blade at Cai, eyes flashing, '*you* think that you have a claim on her? She deserves much better than a monster.'

Cai snarled and Tash snapped, 'If there's one thing I've learned since leaving the Temple, Harrison, it's that there are many types of monsters and right now, you'd fit in that category.'

It was as though she had slapped him. Harrison's gaze turned back to hers and in it she saw the pain and irrational fury churning just under the surface. 'You don't mean that, Tasha,' he muttered. 'It's bewitched you. You're not yourself.'

'Stop telling me what I mean and what I should feel,' she cried, 'you have no right.'

'I have every right,' he retorted, 'Romulus *told* me to come after you. He said that you would change your mind, that you'd realise—'

'Romulus did *what?*' She blanched, whether from shock or embarrassment she wasn't sure.

'He's been able to see what's between us for years, Tasha,' Harrison snapped, losing his patience. 'So has everyone else in the Temple. Except, it would seem, *you*.'

'I don't love you, Harrison,' Tash replied, her voice rising with anger. 'And I never will.'

'Well, this is awkward,' Cai remarked sardonically, breaking the uncomfortable silence that stretched out after Tash's words had rung out, echoing through the cave.

'Shut up, monster,' Harrison struck out again, dodging around Tash, blade sweeping in a wide arc as Cai ducked and spun, evading it with ease. This only inflamed Harrison's anger more, and he pressed harder, trying to catch Cai off-guard and bring him down. Cai laughed, retaliating with speedy efficiency, until Harrison's blood speckled the ground and his dezmian rolled away into the corner.

'Stop it, both of you,' Tash yelled, flipping her dezmian and the ground opened, swallowing both men to their ankles, effectively pinning them in place. She tottered briefly, regained her balance and strode in between them, glaring at them. 'Violence isn't going to get us anywhere.' Both men shot her dirty looks, and she continued doggedly, 'What are you doing here, Harrison? How did you find us?'

'Yes, I'd like to know that as well,' Cai said roughly. 'It's important to know how a Robin entered the Shadow Realm and found his way to our hideout without a guide.'

Harrison began to laugh and Tash felt a momentary shiver of dread. 'Who said that I was alone?'

'What do you mean, Harrison?' Tash asked, 'Speak plainly.'

'I had an interesting trip to find you in Nordhaven, Tasha,' he said softly, 'I heard a few tales on my way about you. Stories about your mind being enchanted by a Nightwalker, who murdered an innocent family while they slept. Horrible tales, if I'm honest. But she said you could be saved. I just needed to bring *him*,' he lifted his blade to point at Cai, 'back to her.'

'Gods, Harrison,' Tash spoke through numb lips, 'what have you done?' Cai's face had drained of all colour as Harrison spoke, until it was like a death mask.

'I've done my best, Tasha,' Harrison said, 'she just needs him and she'll let us go free. The murders will stop and he'll be gone forever.'

'You're delusional,' she whispered, 'if you're talking about who I think you are, then you've been tricked, Harrison.'

He shook his head, laughing again. 'There's no escape for him this time, Tasha. She's outside. In fact,' he thought for a moment, 'perhaps she should join us.'

'No,' Tash cried but it was too late.

'Come in my dear,' Harrison called into the darkness, 'you have my permission to enter.'

There was a momentary hush, and then there was a faint jingle of bells and the thump of hoofbeats. The sound grew louder and louder until Tash could make out the figure in the shadowy cave entrance. It gradually became clearer and she saw a horse step forwards, its coat dull and its eyes glowing white. Its rider wore a long, hooded cloak and caressed the horse's neck as it came to a halt, the bells on its halter and saddle glinting in the light.

'Harrison, my boy,' the rider's voice was melodious and rich, unlike anything Tash had heard before. 'You've done so well. But Natachatet, now you have *really* exceeded my expectations. It's you I should be thanking, I think. If it wasn't for you, my Nightwalker wouldn't have started to reach his true potential.'

The figure pulled back the hood and dismounted. She was tall and curvaceous, her long red hair flowing down her back and green eyes glistening with malice.

'Melisande,' Cai snarled, trying to pull himself out of the earth but Tash's spell held him firm. 'You witch.'

'Who are you?' Tash demanded, not recognising the woman, and distrusting her immediately, her dezmian humming in her hand, desperate to unleash its magic.

'I'm hurt, Natachatet,' Melisande said, with false sincerity. 'Perhaps you need a bit of a reminder.'

She moved so fast that Tash wasn't prepared, toppling her to the ground and pinning her down. Melisande was now no longer a stunning redhead but a smaller creature with black eyes, its red hair blood stained and bedraggled with sharp teeth that were bared in a smile. 'I had hoped that I made an impression on you,' she crooned, as Tash struggled and wheezed, winded from her fall. 'Or perhaps, you would feel more comfortable with a familiar face,' Melisande snickered. Her flesh melted and reformed, contorting into a new shape and Tash shrieked, kicking her away and struggling backwards.

'Tash, let us out,' Cai snapped furiously but she was too preoccupied to listen.

'I warned you, Tash,' Melisande said, her form solidifying into one that had become someone Tash knew well. She pushed her stringy hair back and grinned, brushing the dust off her skirts.

'Mellie?' Tash whispered, shaken. 'You've been Mellie the whole time?'

'I've been following you the whole way, Tash,' Melisande hissed. 'Ever since it became apparent what Cai would risk to help you.' She moved away from Tash, losing interest in her and approached Cai, reaching out a hand towards him. He went rigid, unable to swipe her away as she touched him.

'You've got what you wanted,' Harrison interjected, 'let Tasha and I go home. The monster's yours, as promised.'

'You are impatient, Robin,' Melisande murmured silkily, her gaze not leaving Cai's. 'My Nightwalker still requires incentive to become mine.' She turned back to Tash, shadows seemingly spreading out from her as she moved closer, the sound of distant screams lingering in Tash's ears.

'Stop it, Melisande,' Cai snarled, the moment her hand was removed he was able to move again, trying to get out of the ground. 'Let us *go*, Tash.'

'I hoped that you would die in Trencher's Pit,' Melisande whispered, the sound making Tash's skin crawl. 'But even though you escaped, my minions brought Cai back to me. There, in the shadows, he was reborn; stronger, faster, and far more vicious than I could have dreamed.' She smiled, 'I finally had the servant I required, especially after you killed two of my faithful minions.'

'Two?' Harrison interrupted, confused and Melisande cackled.

'Your friend should learn to trust you, Tash. If I hadn't been there to make my minion's body vanish on the Heath, he might not have blamed Cai for the murders. But when Cai was brought back from the shadows, he became the pariah Nordhaven had claimed he was, and your Robin friend was determined to hunt him down.'

Tash retreated, until she hit the cave wall, trying to escape from the dangerous glint in Melisande's eyes. 'It must have irritated you when Cai came back to himself, then,' she bit out.

Melisande's smile hardened. 'A small setback,' she said coldly, 'once you are out of the way, there will be nothing to stop him from being mine.'

'You promised to let us go,' Harrison yelled, now he was struggling too. 'Keep your word.'

'Mortals are so easy to manipulate,' Melisande said thoughtfully, pulling a silver blade from her belt and fingering its edge, watching as a pinprick of blood trickled down. 'Once you know what their weaknesses are, Tash, it is really all too simple. And yours are particularly interesting, aren't they?' Tash was silent, watching the blade flash in the light as it drew ever nearer. 'How would your friends react, I wonder,' Melisande continued softly, 'if they knew that *you*, the star pupil of the Order of Song, had succumbed to a Nightwalker? If they knew that you demeaned yourself and the values of your Order, choosing a monster over the people who you swore to protect. Your friend here thinks that you're under a spell, but I think that there was always darkness in your heart. I know your fears, girl, the desires and wishes that you kept hidden throughout the years.'

'Shut up,' Tash whispered, 'you know nothing.'

'I know the truth about how your village was destroyed,' Melisande's voice was gloating now. 'I know certain beasts are drawn towards anger and resentment. A little girl's hurt, perhaps, when she is cast aside and ignored, pawned off to a passing stranger as though she was nothing. Some creatures respond to that unbridled emotion and let it control them.'

'You're lying,' Tash gasped, unable to suppress her dread and fear that Melisande was in fact speaking the truth.

'Oh, am I?' Melisande murmured silkily, leaning in close to Tash's ear. 'I'm not the one who's barely able to control their emotions. It's no surprise to me that the people you love get hurt.'

Tash's dezmian spun, releasing Cai and Harrison as she felt the knife press into her side and she crumpled.

'Pathetic,' Melisande hissed, stepping away from her body and crossing to where her horse stood silently, white eyes still glowing. She waved a hand and Cai and Harrison were sent flying, slamming into the cave walls.

'Tash,' Cai was crawling to her, and clutched her to him. 'It's alright, it'll be alright.' He lifted his hand over her wound, allowing the flow of magic to seep into her.

'Naughty boy,' Melisande chastised, clicking her fingers and he froze, a silver collar forming around his neck, with a chain connecting it to Melisande's hand. 'Come, we have places to be.' She yanked on the chain and Cai choked, stumbling backwards. 'Don't try to follow us, Natachatet, *dear*. He won't remember you if you do, and,' she glanced at her horse, 'I don't think Glaive will be content to let you leave here alive. You should have taken my advice when I gave it, girl. I told you to pick that one,' she waved a hand at Harrison's unconscious body, 'but you refused to listen. And now, you will never see your precious Nightwalker or Temple again.'

'Cai!' Tash cried, trying to stand and failing, the wound in her side still throbbing with pain. 'I'll find you, I promise.' There was another snap of Melisande's fingers and he stopped fighting, eyes going blank, before turning and followed her meekly, like a puppet.

'*No!*' Her chest was burning, the desire to cry rising like a flood, yet she pushed it down, focussing on the need to follow them, to stop Melisande and get Cai back. She gripped her dezmian and stood, holding onto the wall for support as she eyed the horse that was watching her intently. It let out a strange high-pitched shriek and bent over, much like its mistress, its body twisted and stretched, growing until it was twice the size of the horse it had been. The saddle and halter broke, the bells jingling as they bounced away along the ground. The monster before her now had the same glowing, white eyes, but spikes covered its body, its barbed tail sweeping back and forth. Its narrow legs ended in sharp talons, and it had a long maw filled with several rows of teeth.

'Oh Gods,' Tash muttered, swearing under her breath, 'you're a Dragutash.'

Chapter Twenty

There was once a queen who had everything. Looks, power and a handsome man who she loved more than all else. He was the only one who could calm her rages and tease her into laughter. When the queen discovered that she was with child, the couple were overjoyed and their kingdom celebrated for weeks. Yet their happiness was not to last.

A stranger entered their hall one day, a traveller from the Mortal world, who sought shelter. He took one look at the queen and became filled with a fierce passion, determined to make her his own. Despite his best efforts, the queen rejected him, banishing him from her hall and thinking that it was settled. She was soon to find that she was wrong, for the next day when she awoke it was not her husband sleeping beside her but the Mortal. Incensed at his impudence, she called for her guards to take him to the dungeon until she found her husband.

The king's body was in the heart of their court, laid out for all to see. The queen's fury was boundless, casting the kingdom into shadow and she transformed the Mortal into a monster, cursing him to feel the same pain she did until the end of time. As she grieved, the queen's anger and resentment grew, channelling inwards and corrupting her power. Without her husband to calm her, the queen changed, so that by the time her child was born, it was no longer a creature of light but one of darkness.

~ An extract from 'A Robin's Collection of Inter-world Lore'

'You can call me Glaive,' the Dragutash whispered, its voice akin to the scratching of nails on slate. 'I've been looking forward to meeting you, Robin.' Its eyes blinked as it examined her, turning its head to the side and inhaling. 'I can smell your fear, girl.'

'Tasha?' Harrison was starting to come to on the other side of the cave and the sound of his voice had Glaive turning to face him, eyes narrowing hungrily.

'No!' Tash's dezmian flipped as she called out, the whip of light flashing across the cave and striking Glaive across the face with a crack. She moved between them, pulling the whip back and preparing to attack again. In a low voice she began to sing, the sounds blending together as Glaive snarled and leapt forwards, swiping out with a talon. Tash dodged and snapped her wrist, the whip lashing out at the Dragutash again, this time slicing across its hide, catching on the spikes on its back. When the whip returned to her side, there was a trail of blood staining the ground.

'Nice try, Robin,' Glaive growled, 'but a whip isn't going to hold me back for long.'

There was a flick of his tail and barbed spikes rained down on her, catching her unawares. She ducked, raising an arm to protect herself, feeling it get impaled by multiple barbs that dug into the flesh. Tash's song halted as she cried out in pain, Glaive's sickening laugh reverberating off the cave walls.

'Leave her alone, monster,' Harrison was back on his feet, bringing his sword down into the Dragutash's side. The blade pierced the creature and Glaive shrieked, twisting, catching Harrison on the spikes on his back. Time seemed to pause as Harrison's eyes widened in shock as he looked down at the spike in his chest and the dark flower of blood that was starting to bloom on his shirt, and then he was sent flying through the air, although this time he didn't get up again. Tash was too numb to scream. There was a thud as Harrison's body hit the ground and Glaive's white eyes turned back to her greedily.

'I thought Robins would be stronger,' he hissed, 'but I find myself disappointed.' He struck out with one of his talons, catching the shoulder of her injured arm and toppling her. The whip vanished as she dropped her dezmian, gasping in pain. Glaive kicked the stone away, moving closer to lean over her, saliva dripping onto her face from his mouth. His breath was hot and rancid, and she gagged, struggling to move away. A talon held her skirt down, pinning her in place.

'Pathetic Robin,' the Dragutash leaned over her, as she lay paralysed by agony and terror, certain that this would be the end. There was a loud, harsh cry and something large and black swooped down, striking Glaive with hooves in quick succession. The Dragutash turned, snarling, and swiped upwards but the Willowing flew higher, just out of reach.

'Lir,' Tash cried, 'be careful *liebeshem*.' Her Willowing dived again, kicking out at Glaive's face but this time the Dragutash was prepared, and his tail swung out, catching on one of Lir's wings. The Willowing let out a piercing shriek and tumbled out of the air, trying desperately to dislodge himself from the barbed tail. Tash took her opportunity while Glaive was distracted, reaching out with her good arm and gripping the sword that had fallen out of the Dragutash's side.

'Oi, Glaive,' she shouted, 'I'm the one you want to kill. Come and get me.' She turned the blade, holding tight to the handle and thrust upwards as Glaive's head shot around towards her, teeth bared in a growl. The sword pierced the underside of his neck and she pushed harder, feeling it slide upwards towards the Dragutash's skull. Glaive thrashed backwards, let out an agonised roar and then collapsed with a resounding crash. His white eyes stared unseeing at Tash as she tremulously got to her feet, slowly removing the barbs from her injured arm in between short, sharp gasps. Lir stepped towards her, whickering in pain, his wing dragging behind him.

'You saved me, *liebeshem*,' Tash whispered shakily, pressing her forehead against his neck. 'How did you find me?' Lir snuffled into her hair and nuzzled her neck, clearly relieved that the Dragutash was gone. Tash gently disengaged from her Willowing and hurried to collect her dezmian, before moving to crouch beside Harrison.

'Harrison?' She lifted her hand to his neck, feeling for a pulse. His skin was pallid, the gaping wound in his chest oozing blood. She thought that she felt a flicker and began to pray, tossing her dezmian as she extended her fingers over him, begging the Gods of the old faith to help her heal him. She felt faint from her own injuries, her right arm was numb, her shoulder aching, yet she persevered, concentrating on repairing the damage that Glaive had inflicted. Tash watched as the skin slowly knitted back together, and felt the pain from her own injuries lessening. It was becoming easier to focus on Harrison, to control the magic she was channelling and to direct it to obey her more effectively. When he lay in front of her, healed but still unresponsive, Lir butted her and she turned to mend his wing, now getting the grasp of the healing magic. The Willowing snorted happily, stretching his wings experimentally as she drew away, stowing the dezmian in her pocket.

'We need to get back to Nordhaven, Lir,' Tash said gently. 'It's not safe for us to remain in the Shadow Realm without Cai.' Lir ducked his head, flicking his mane in acknowledgement of her words and knelt down so that Tash could slide Harrison across his back. It took almost all of her energy to do it, but eventually she was able to sit up behind him, keeping him secure between her arms. 'Fly, *liebeshem*,' she said softly, 'take us back to Nordhaven quickly.'

Lir whinnied and plunged into the darkness, skimming through it like water, wings beating rhythmically as the cave was left behind them. Tash didn't look back, knowing that she would never want to return there again and fixed her thoughts instead on what she should do next.

***

They landed in front of the inn as the sun was rising. Several residents of Nordhaven had already woken up, shutters were opening and when they saw Tash, Lir and Harrison clatter to the cobbles, they shouted, calling for their friends and neighbours. Before Tash knew it, she was encircled by a group of armed men with roughened, distrustful faces, including Jervois and Vallus. She dismounted, held up her hands placatingly and said,

'I'm not here to cause any trouble, I swear. I can explain everything that's happened.'

Jervois bit his lip, 'I'd like to believe you, Tash, I really would. But the last we heard you had been enchanted by the Nightwalker. Has that changed? Has it been killed?'

'I was never put under a spell, Jervois,' Tash said firmly. 'The Nightwalker was not the one responsible for the murders, except for Klara's death.'

'Lies,' Vallus barked, the vein in his temple pulsing.

'No, it's not,' Tash snapped back, 'there were at least two other types of Dæmon who were terrorising your town and they were responsible for both the blight and the murders. Atticus can support what I say,' she gestured to him and he shifted uncomfortably. 'He was tricked by a Dæmon while trying to help his father's farm.'

'Is she speaking the truth, Atticus?' Jervois asked and the young man nodded miserably, bowing his head in shame.

'But what about the Nightwalker?' Vallus demanded hotly, 'We know that you helped it to escape. Klara's murder needs to be avenged with its death. You cast your lot in with a beast.'

Tash took a steadying breath, forcing herself to remain calm. 'Your town has been terrified of Nightwalkers for decades. Didn't you ever stop to wonder why they might keep coming back here?'

'No one can understand the minds of these monsters,' Vallus snapped. 'They only care about causing death and destruction.'

'That's not entirely true,' Tash argued, stepping closer to him. 'Cai was the main reason why The Robin sent me here. He wanted to protect your town from the Dæmons, not to destroy it.'

'Why would a Nightwalker do that?' Jervois asked but Vallus cut him off with a snort.

'I don't see any proof, Tash. We appreciate your help in getting rid of the blight, but you've chosen your side. The people of Nordhaven will not support someone who is affiliated with Dæmons.'

'Have you heard from Mellie recently?' Tash retorted, losing control of her temper at last. 'She's been tricking you this *whole* time. She's a witch who, I believe, was responsible for the murders here.'

'Do you know how far-fetched that sounds?' Vallus was disbelieving now. 'Mellie's in her inn, probably still abed.'

'Send someone to get her then,' Tash said simply. 'See if she's there. But know that *I* saw her in her true form. She was the real cause of your problems all along.'

'Atticus,' Jervois interjected before Vallus could reply, 'do as she says.' He was watching Tash intently and she felt momentarily grateful that he was at least prepared to trust her word this far.

'Jervois—' Vallus said but the mayor stopped him, raising a hand.

'Tash is a Robin, Vallus,' he said firmly. 'You cannot forget that. She healed the blight and went onto the Heath with your hunting party. She deserves to be heard, at the very least.'

There was silence as the group waited for Atticus to return. Vallus tapped his foot impatiently, while the others watched Tash closely, weapons at the ready. Finally, Atticus appeared in the doorway, looking shaken and distressed. He glanced from Tash to Vallus to Jervois nervously until Jervois snapped,

'Tell us what you found, Atticus. Is Mellie home?'

'No,' the young man replied, 'all her things are gone. Her room's empty like she was never there.'

'She must have gone to one of the farms,' Vallus said, but his voice wavered slightly with uncertainty. 'Or to see her sister in the next town.'

'When has Mellie ever travelled anywhere?' one of the men piped up, 'Since her husband passed, she's refused to leave the inn. Why would she suddenly change now?'

'Does she even *have* a sister?' Jervois frowned, 'I don't think that she does.'

'And she wouldn't leave without saying goodbye,' another man said adamantly, lowering his pitchfork. 'There's something off about this.'

'Of *course* there is,' Tash said, her voice loud and clear, 'because she is *gone*. The Mellie who has been here for the past weeks is not the one you all knew. She was a witch called Melisande.'

'I believe her,' Atticus was looking around the group, eyes blazing, 'she saved my life. If Tash says that Mellie is gone, then she's gone.' His words made Vallus turn to him sharply, disconcerted by the force in the young man's voice.

'By the Gods,' Jervois lifted a shaking hand to his eyes, 'what have we done to deserve this?'

Tash patted his shoulder as the villagers lowered their weapons. 'I promise you that I will find out, Jervois,' she said quietly, 'Melisande has taken Cai away. If she controls him, he won't be able to suppress his darker side.' Her eyes met Vallus'. 'That was how Klara was killed. Melisande was controlling him.' Vallus' face whitened and his jaw set.

'What happened to Harrison?' Jervois interrupted, 'What's wrong with him?'

'Melisande set a Dragutash on us,' Tash replied, moving over to Harrison's side as several of the men lifted him off Lir's back. 'He got injured in the fight. I tried to heal him but he's not woken up.'

'Take him into the inn,' Jervois ordered. 'Even though the innkeeper is gone, it's as good a place as any for you to recuperate after what's happened.'

'I should go after Melisande,' Tash said quickly but she was overruled by Jervois' hand on her arm.

'You need to stay here, Tash,' he said with surprising gentleness, 'Harrison will need you when he wakes up and you must rest as well.'

She opened her mouth to argue but Vallus said brusquely, 'You can't go after Klara's killer without preparing yourself.' With that, he turned and strode away towards his house, leaving her feeling baffled.

'Come on, Tash,' Jervois said, as he guided her into the inn, Atticus leading Lir to the stables. 'I'd like to hear a full explanation for what's been happening in our town.'

And so, Tash found herself seated at one of the tables, telling Jervois almost everything that she had discovered. He remained silent throughout her explanation, which surprised her. She was also startled when other members of the town entered the inn, but one direct look from Jervois had them keeping quiet, as they listened in. By the time she had finished, the dining room was full of people and Tash was feeling both tired and hungry, the exertions of the past twenty-four hours finally catching up with her.

'I should go and check on Harrison,' she said, rising from the table. 'Excuse me.'

'Thank you, Tash,' Jervois said as she began to climb the stairs, 'the people in this town misjudged you.'

She nodded an acknowledgement of his words and left, not wanting to remain any longer in the middle of the group, reliving her interactions with different monsters. The stairs creaked under her feet as she climbed, the sound reminding her vividly of rushing up to her room, Cai's hand in hers. A feeling was niggling away at her and had been since she started to tell her story, some things didn't add up.

'Why,' she murmured, 'didn't she just capture Cai when he was in his human form? Or when he would visit me here at night? If she was so desperate to control him, it doesn't make sense that she wouldn't have acted sooner.'

She pushed open Harrison's door and perched on the edge of the bed. He lay on top of the covers, still unconscious, but his chest moved slightly, which made her sigh in relief. She didn't want to consider what she would have felt if he had died. Gently, she took his hand in hers, squeezing it.

'You had me worried for a time there, you idiot,' she said softly. 'You should never have come here, looking for me. I know you meant well,' she pressed his hand again, 'but now things have only gotten more complicated. You've got to wake up and return to the Temple, without me. I wish Romulus had never gotten such foolish ideas in your head, Harrison. Deep down, I think you know that we would drive each other crazy if we'd ever been stupid enough to date. It would never have worked out.' There was no response to her words, and she sighed in disappointment, as she rose again. 'I've got to rest. I'll check in on you later, Harrison.'

Her room was just as it had been when she'd run away, although her bed had been remade, the sheets removed from the window. She sank onto the mattress, wishing that she didn't need to rest, that she could just take Lir and start searching for Melisande and Cai.

But you don't even know where they've gone, the irritatingly practical voice said in her mind. *You're going to look pretty foolish galivanting off with no plan or idea of where to find them.*

Tash sighed, covering her eyes, the tightness in her chest threatening to rend her apart as the tears bordering the edge of her vision refused to fall. She kept seeing Cai being dragged away, a metal ring around his neck as the chain pulled, twisting his head backwards. And then how he had changed as Melisande began to exert her control, breaking down his resistance in mere seconds. How would she be able to fight against a witch with such an innate grasp of magic? What chance did she have when each time she had faced Melisande, she had faltered or run away? She rolled over into the pillow, trying to block the thoughts out, and fell into a light doze.

It seemed as though she had only blinked and then she was awake, still feeling the same churning anxiety. She left her room and headed to the kitchen in search of something to eat. To her surprise she wasn't alone when she entered it, finding Pyrrus sitting by the fireplace, his wrinkled hands gripping a cup of tea. The pot sat on the table and, on hearing her approach, he glanced up, almost as though he had been expecting her.

Tash wasn't sure what to say, all too aware that she hadn't spoken to Pyrrus since before Klara's death, although she had seen him from afar. Up close, he looked frailer, with the emptiness of unimaginable grief lingering as heavy shadows under his eyes.

'I was hoping that you would come,' he said softly, indicating for her to join him in the other chair. She collected a cup from the shelf and some bread and cheese from the pantry before she did as instructed, somewhat awkwardly.

'I'm so sorry about Klara,' she said.

'She was a good girl,' he said gruffly. 'The mill's not the same without her. I can't… it's too painful to be there alone.'

Tash nodded, understanding. She was starting to feel the same way about her room in the inn, Cai's presence lingered there, reminding her of everything they had done together. She looked down and saw the trapdoor, now closed, to the cellar. Her eyes narrowed, the memory assaulting her again;

Cai chained and gagged, his broken body struggling to heal in the bright light. The townsmen beating him in her bedroom, their faces alight with malice and hate as his blood speckled the floor.

'Tash?' Pyrrus' voice broke through her thoughts, recalling her to the present where he was watching her expectantly.

'Yes?' She was startled, had he asked her a question?

'I asked if the Nightwalker is still alive.' He looked gaunt now, yet his hollowed eyes blazed.

Tash paused and then nodded slowly. Pyrrus let out a hiss, hands clenched on the tabletop and said, 'I tried to warn her, Tash. I told her we were being punished. No one believed me– and now it's too late. I couldn't save her from his vengeance.'

'I don't understand,' Tash frowned, confused. 'What do you mean, Pyrrus?'

She remembered vaguely that he had mentioned something about the town being punished when she had visited the mill, but Klara had laughed it off as a fantasy. Pyrrus seemed to know what she was thinking, for his forehead creased in frustration and he smacked a book down on the table, making the teacups tremble with the force of it.

'I heard it from my grandfather,' he said stubbornly, 'when I was just a boy. He'd been the town mayor for many years and remembered the incident well. It haunted him until he passed on.'

Tash was still confused. 'Pyrrus—'

'It's all in here,' he pushed the book across to her. 'I think you'll find more use for it than I will. I just wish that we could have made amends before Klara... before she...' He broke off with a sob and Tash reached out, patting his arm comfortingly. 'I knew the Nightwalker would want vengeance,' he said in between sobs, 'but not by killing my girl. Not my Klara.'

'I'm so sorry,' Tash murmured, still at a loss about what he meant as she continued to soothe him. It took a while until Pyrrus had regained command of his emotions and he shuffled up from his chair, with a mumbled farewell. His energy seemed to fade as it had all those days before, his mind descending back into forgetfulness and obscurity.

'Let me help you home,' Tash made to follow him but he waved her off, a spark of his former self returning.

'I'll manage, Tash,' he said gruffly, 'I've walked that way many times before.'

She held back, unsure whether she should insist on accompanying him or allow him to leave alone. In the time she was debating with herself, he tottered out, shutting the inn door with a soft thud. Tash drained her teacup, stuffed the remaining bread and cheese into her mouth and left the kitchen, book under her arm. She returned to her chair by Harrison's bedside, lit the lamp and settled back with the book open in her lap, determined to pass the time reading while she waited for him to awaken.

The book was as old as Cai's journal had been; its pages yellowed with age with some crumbling away in places. The inside cover described it as the property of one Derrick Alterton, a name which rang a bell in Tash's memory. The first entries were short and emotionless, summarising crop yields, petty issues that had been resolved and Derrick's aims for what he would accomplish as mayor.

The lantern burned steadily as the world outside Harrison's room turned dark, yet Tash continued to read. There must have been a reason why Pyrrus gave her this journal, a reason why he seemed insistent on the fact that the attacks had been the town's punishment. She turned to the next page and began to read.

The first day of winter has arrived. Our stores are full and ready for the oncoming months, and I have had Elena encourage the women of the town to knit extra blankets for the needy. So far, she has done well so we should be able to keep everyone warm. I helped Reggie cut up lumber for fires– we were joined by several of the boys, including my own Leon and Cai, who insisted on taking his share back to that hovel.

Those two have been inseparable recently and I'm not sure if it's a good thing– true, the boy's spending more time here instead of roaming the Heath but he seems adamant to remain there. Perhaps in time he will see that moving into town will be the better choice– his mother needs to be looked after by someone who truly cares for her and he needs a job, preferably one far away. Will it even be possible to make the boy civilised though?

Tash finished the entry and felt a ripple of anger at Derrick Alterton's assessment of Cai. This was the first time he had mentioned the boy, and as she scanned the next page, she saw that Derrick's entries were lengthening, focussing more on his personal thoughts and musings than the town's problems. Perhaps he had become complacent in his duties as mayor, she wondered, or he had simply stopped caring about who might read through his notebook.

The winter snows have melted at last and it warmed my heart when Leon asked me to find him an apprenticeship. He wants to try carpentry, although I think he has the ability to follow in my own footsteps, given time. But then he asked for me to find an apprenticeship for Cai as well, claiming that they wanted to work together. He said that since Cai has no father, I should be the one to help the boy as the mayor. He didn't know how those words affected me.

It's hard enough to look at the boy as he grows, to see the proof that Ryla chose another man over the one who had cared for her since she was a child. He's not a normal boy, although one should give him credit for wanting to do the right thing. At times I feel a crushing anger, like I did when Ryla told me she was pregnant and moving out to the Heath, leaving me to marry Elena instead. It makes me want a drink, to feel nothing but oblivion. Then I remember that Ryla was abandoned by the bastard and I feel slightly better.

Leon and Elena never knew, although I think at times Elena suspected. It doesn't matter. She was a means to an end, a way to ensure that my line didn't die with me. Besides, she makes reasonable meals and has never refused my advances. She doesn't know that I think of Ryla still.

Tash's eyes widened and she turned the page, intrigued to learn what happened next.

Ryla's condition is deteriorating. Cai saw me today to explain how she's taken to wandering the Heath. I blame his father— Ryla was perfectly normal before she met the bastard. I suggested to him— again— the possibility of him moving her into town. I would have Elena take care of her in a heartbeat. The only problem would be the boy— he'd need to leave, get a job in a distant town. I could arrange that if he would just let me. And he had the arrogance to reject my offer— he said that he would take care of his mother.

He mentioned seeing people on the Heath. I should send out some hunting parties just in case— the last thing I'd want is Ryla to fall into the hands of strangers who would possibly hurt her. There's finally a chance for her to return to the village and I'll be damned if anyone else ruins my plans. Hells, I'll lead the hunting party myself.

Tash's eyes were getting heavy now, the words starting to blur together on the page, and her head lowered, the book slipping into her lap as sleep overtook her.

Chapter Twenty-One

The pain is immeasurable. Melisande laughs at me, taunting me with word and blade, trying to make my heart bleed. She says that I have been forgotten, that the months spent denying her have been for nothing. She reminds me that Tash is dead, that if she had loved me, she would have come looking. I don't know what to believe anymore. The blackouts are coming on more often so when I am back to myself I write down what I can. I can't afford to forget her, even if she is dead.

Melisande says that Mortals' promises cannot be trusted, that they only seek to use and hurt us. Could she be right? Was I always just a means to an end? I'm getting so tired of fighting.

~ A hastily scrawled note hidden in a cell in Melisande's
Court

Harrison had not awoken and Tash was rapidly growing concerned. Something must have gone wrong with her healing magic and she feared that keeping him in Nordhaven would only make it worse.

'I need to take him back to the Temple,' she told Jervois over lunch the next day, having gone to join him at his office. 'He will have better care there than I can provide him here.'

'And the Nightwalker?' Jervois asked, 'Melisande? Do you think that she will leave us be?'

Tash thought for a while. 'I think that the murders were only a means to an end. Now that Melisande has Cai under her control, I don't believe that she will send him back here. It would run the risk of bringing back too many memories. If I'm wrong, send word to the Temple and I'll return as soon as I am able.'

'I hope that you're right,' Jervois said tightly and then he handed her a large pouch, heavy with coin. 'Take this, as compensation for your services though. Thanks to you the blight is gone and the creature that was responsible for the killings is dead. I'm just sorry that we were so quick to mis-judge you, Tash.' He gave a formal bow and she shook his hand, stowing the pouch in her belt. She'd return it to The Robin along with her report when she got back to the Tem-ple. He would be pleased.

'Goodbye Jervois,' she said simply. 'I wish you and the people of Nordhaven well.' She made her way to the door, paused and added over her shoulder, 'Just make sure to not be so quick to judge others in the future. Part of the issue was your town's fixation on blaming Cai for your problems and refusing to move on from that prejudice.'

She didn't wait to hear Jervois' reaction and departed for the stables, not taking too long to prepare Lir and Harrison's Willowing for the journey. The saddlebags were packed with enough supplies for several days. Tash was eager to be gone, all too aware of the need to get Harrison proper help. As she led the Willowings out into the main street, she halted on seeing Atticus outside the inn.

'I heard that you were leaving town,' he said. 'Thought that you might want a hand getting Harrison downstairs.'

'Thanks,' she replied gratefully, not having considered how difficult it would be to carry him from his room. Atticus nodded and disappeared into the inn, reappearing not long afterwards with Harrison slung over his shoulders. He heaved Harrison's body onto the back of his Willowing and assisted Tash with securing him to the saddle so that he wouldn't fall off.

'I'll never forget what you did for me,' he took her hand and shook it firmly. 'You helped to save me from myself. I wish there was something I could do to repay you for it.'

'You already did,' Tash affirmed, smiling. 'You stood up for me when Vallus wasn't listening to reason.'

Atticus shrugged. 'Vallus is still pretty cut up about Klara's death. He was sweet on her.'

Tash had suspected as much, remembering all too well the looks exchanged between the two of them, the way Klara had supported Vallus instinctively, how his eyes had softened whenever he spoke of her. It was a shame that something so fleeting had never had a proper chance to flower into something lasting. She felt a moment's regret for the couple, before she mounted Lir and clicked her tongue for Harrison's Willowing to follow. It stood to attention, dark eyes watching her and Lir as they turned, preparing to depart.

'I hope that things will settle back to normal,' Tash said. 'Now that the Dæmons are gone, it gives everyone here a chance to start anew. Good luck, Atticus.'

'Goodbye Tash,' he lifted his hand in a wave as Lir took off, Harrison's Willowing close on his tail, circling over Nordhaven for Tash to get her bearings. She squinted at the horizon, saw a faint shimmering over the Heath and urged Lir towards it, relieved that the Barrier was relatively close. The wind rushed through her hair, caressing her cheek with its icy chill as they flew, soaring high above the blackened hills and furrows of the Heath that she had wandered through. They passed Cai's old shack with the caved-in roof and the place where the hunting party had been separated by the Dæmon that terrifying foggy night. The heather that spread out beneath them was burnt from the fire Harrison had conjured. She wondered how long it would be before the flowers on the Heath grew back in their vibrant glory. Gradually, the Barrier drew closer until they had reached it, a shimmering wall of haziness in the sky, promising Tash the chance to return home.

She breathed in deeply and sang, the melody a strange cadence that could have brought a tear to even Vallus' eye. It was haunting in its beauty, capturing the essence of the soul of the woman who hovered in midair, urging the Doorway to open and allow them passage. She sang of the trials faced, the pain of her loss and the need for retribution, to reclaim the one who was taken from her. The Barrier flickered and the Doorway appeared, providing Tash and Harrison a way to leave Kinet.

Tash didn't hesitate, clicking her tongue for Harrison's Willowing to remain close, and Lir sped through, the Doorway closing soon after them with a faint pop. They found themselves above a palace beside a glacier that met the waters of a grey lake far below. There was a shout from the ramparts and some guards lifted their bows, preparing to fight. She saw another glimmer down over the ice and they dove, snow catching against her cheeks and eyelashes, making it difficult to see. Regardless, Tash began to sing, trusting in her instincts and sure enough, the Doorway appeared, allowing them through moments before they hit the ice.

Lir lifted his wings, rising upwards to avoid hitting the ground, Harrison's Willowing following suit. Tash glanced around, marshland spreading as far as she could see. Humidity filled the air, putrid gas rising from the pools of bubbling mud below. She saw spindly creatures moving through the muck, scaly skin glittering in the light. Some peered upwards as the Willowings' shadows blocked out the sun, clicking their pincers menacingly. Tash nudged Lir on, not wanting to land anywhere near the creatures. Spiky grass rose around the pools, swaying in the breeze, and the spindly creatures returned to their business, searching the mud for food.

The sun began to descend across the sky and by the time night fell, they had reached a point on the edge of the marshes where Tash deemed acceptable to spend the night. Lir descended, landing on the ground with a thump and immediately began to graze, swishing his tail in satisfaction. Harrison's Willowing copied him, although it deigned to kneel so that it was easier for Tash to drag Harrison off its back. Once he was lying on the ground, his steed moved away, too focussed on the feast of grass to care about its owner. Tash withdrew her dezmian and flipped it, conjuring the campsite and bedrolls, the familiar sharp twist of her stomach winding her for an instant.

She pulled Harrison onto a bedroll and tried to get him to swallow some water from her flask. Most of the liquid ended up trickling down the side of his face, although some went down his throat. There had been no change in his demeanour, no flicker of life, no sign of waking, even when they had flown at breakneck speed. Tash knelt beside him and lost herself in a quick prayer, asking the Gods to watch over him until they got back to the Temple, to let her get him back there in time before he was lost.

When she had finished, she took care of her own needs, making chai and helping herself to some bread, apples and cheese in her saddlebag. As she ate, she withdrew Derrick's journal and opened it to the next entry.

I was approached by a red-haired woman today on the Heath. She said that she wanted to help me, that she could take the boy away from Nordhaven if I could separate him from his mother. I didn't trust her at first, but she knew things about me, secrets no one else knew, and showed me what the future will be like when he is gone. She said that Cai will be showing his true nature soon and that once he does, I will need to act fast. Her words filled me with eagerness, so that even now as I write I am desperate for that future to become a reality. Ryla will be mine again and Cai will be nothing more than a memory.

Foreboding filled Tash as she turned to the following page, guessing who the red-haired woman might be.

I didn't expect things to work out so easily. The boy's a monster— a gruesome beast and finally the town can see what I have always suspected. I knew he wasn't normal, and now I know why. He's a Nightwalker and the only good Nightwalker is a dead one. Ryla was terrified when I took her from the shack, crying and wailing, spouting idiotic nonsense. I didn't care, I just wanted to get her away from his burning red eyes, the claws and fangs that no one should have to look upon. If that red-haired woman doesn't come to collect him, I'll send out hunting parties for his head myself.

She put the book down, hands shaking and feeling sick. The words hovered before her eyes, full of bitter hatred for a boy who had done nothing wrong, except to be born. Her heart ached as she remembered Cai's own journal entries, his assumption that Derrick had been a mentor, a friend, while deep down the man had harboured a corrosive loathing towards him.

Tash glanced across the campfire to where Harrison lay, and then looked out over the marshes, the shadows stretching out over the water. Insects buzzed in the air, some trying to bite her and she swatted them away. It was still, the silence only broken by the sound of frogs croaking, the flames crackling and the insects waiting for the opportunity to catch her unawares.

A part of her ached as she looked at the darkness, wishing that Cai would appear as he had done so often before, emerging from the shadows and crouching by the fireside, a wry smile on his lips. She missed him with a fierceness that scared her, which only fuelled her desperation to get him back.

'Perhaps The Robin will know where Melisande has gone,' Tash wondered aloud, and Lir whickered in response, nudging her shoulder as if to encourage her to rest. She patted him absentmindedly, thinking that The Robin might in fact be her best chance. Not only was he the leader of the Order with multiple resources at his disposal, but he knew about Cai, had worked with him for years, and perhaps he had had run-ins with Melisande as well. As she settled down to sleep, Tash hoped that her assumptions were right and that The Robin would know more.

***

Tash dreamed of crows. A murder of them, swooping her, their taloned feet extended, wings beating as she covered her face, shrieking. Black feathers fell to her feet as they pecked, and she fell down, crying out for them to stop. Someone was laughing at her terror, a rich, female voice that she recognised. Tash struck out, scrabbling to find purchase for her hands as she struggled to avoid the crows' onslaught.

'Melisande,' she shouted through the haze of wings, 'stop hiding. Show yourself. What have you done with Cai?'

'You can fight all you want, Natachatet,' Melisande's voice whispered in her ear, 'but you will not be able to find him. And even if you did, whatever makes you think he would want to return with you? He has a new purpose now.'

'I will find you,' Tash cried, fury giving her new strength to fight back the crows. 'If it takes me years, I will find you. You cannot hide from me forever.'

Melisande's laugh rung in her mind. 'I'd like to see you try, Natachatet. I'd like to see you try.'

The dream faded and Tash awoke, sweating, the words on her lips dying away as she registered where she was. The fire had burned low, Harrison lay motionless and the Willowings rested, snuffling gently in their sleep. The remnants of her dream still haunted her, and she got up, vanishing the campsite with a flick of her dezmian. The Willowings awoke, disgruntled at needing to leave before the sun had risen, but Tash ignored their snorts as she rolled Harrison into his saddle. She set about securing him and then mounted Lir, checking the stars which still glimmered faintly in the sky. She knew the constellations from star charts and the observatory at the Temple and felt a wave of relief. These were Venetican heavens, and that meant that they were leaving the Western Marshes. With any luck, they might reach the Temple in the next day or two. She glanced at Harrison's unresponsive form, hoping that they would reach it sooner rather than later. It was hard to tell how much longer Harrison would last when it was almost impossible to give him food or water.

'Fly, *liebeshem*,' she commanded and the two Willowings swept away, following her directions as they headed for the Temple.

By the late afternoon, Tash recognised the mountains and forest in the distance, and let out a whoop of joy. Lir strained underneath her, pushing himself to fly faster, sensing that home was close. Tash gripped onto his neck, murmuring words of encouragement in his ear, and soon the Temple was in sight, its tower and sprawling buildings on the mountain top all too familiar. Lir dipped his wings, bringing them towards the stable yard, clattering down as the sun was setting in the sky.

Tash dismounted, their arrival encouraging some apprentices to come pouring out of the dining hall where they had been studying, excited by the newcomer. On seeing Tash, they cried out in welcome, rushing forwards to hug her, bombarding her with questions.

'I need some help,' she interrupted, lifting a hand to stifle their exclamations, 'Harrison needs to go to the infirmary at once. He's been hurt.' A few apprentices helped lift Harrison down, carrying him away towards the infirmary, eyeing him curiously. 'Blythe, would you and your friends mind settling Lir and Harrison's Willowing in the stable?' Tash asked, turning to the girl in question who nodded shyly. 'I need to see The Robin at once.'

'He's not here, Natachatet.' She turned and saw Romulus making his way across the courtyard. 'Welcome home, my child.'

She moved to hug him and he gripped her tightly as she asked, 'Do you know when he will be back? It's vital that I speak to him as soon as possible.'

'You will need to be patient, my dear,' Romulus answered calmly. 'He left a week ago, but I expect he will return soon. He didn't take supplies for a long visit.'

Tash bit back her annoyance and forced herself to nod. Romulus chuckled at her impatience and led her towards the dining hall. 'Why don't you come and tell me about what has happened instead? Where's Harrison? I thought that you would be together.'

She shot him a glare, 'I'll be having a chat with you later about your meddling, Romulus. You caused quite a few problems sending Harrison after me. He ended up getting hurt by a Dragutash, badly. I tried to heal him but he hasn't woken up since. I've had him taken to the infirmary. I hope that Chris can take care of him.'

Chris was the healer at the Temple. He had tended to many burns, cuts and bruises over the years, not to mention the odd broken bone or two from Robin apprentices falling off their Willowings mid-flight.

Romulus didn't react except to grip her arm momentarily, his expression remained calm and unreadable, although she could tell that deep down he was shaken by her words. 'That is dreadful news,' he said gravely, 'come and tell me everything that happened in Kinet, Natachatet. I wasn't aware that Dragutash had entered that world.'

She nodded and allowed him to lead her into the dining hall, where the evening meal was spread out on the tables. Her stomach rumbled after the long hours of fasting, and Romulus smiled, indicating for them to sit in their usual place and to serve herself as much as she needed.

Tash didn't wait on formalities, ladling food onto her plate and digging in ravenously. After a few minutes, she slowed down, took a long draught of ale and then began to speak, telling Romulus in a low voice the summary of what had happened in Kinet. She spoke quietly so that they would not be overheard, and Romulus leaned closer to her, listening intently. Tash talked for a long time, until the other apprentices had been sent to their dormitories to study and she and Romulus were the only ones left.

'You had no right to send Harrison after me, Romulus,' she said now, allowing the hint of anger to graze her words, so he would know how she really felt. 'I told you before I left that I didn't care for Harrison in a romantic sense, and yet you chose to meddle. I honestly wish you hadn't. It raised his hopes and now look at him– I don't know if he'll wake up.'

'Chris will help him,' Romulus said gently. 'And I'm sorry, Natachatet. I wanted so badly for you to have help on this trip– Nightwalkers and a poisonous blight and murder were too much for me. I thought you'd struggle on your own.'

'So you didn't think I was capable?' Tash asked tightly, hurt.

'No,' Romulus countered calmly, 'you're one of the most capable Robins I know. But I couldn't bear the thought of anything happening to you. I wanted someone who knew you to be there in case things went wrong. I admit it, I meddled where I had no right to. I wanted you and Harrison to find happiness together, and believed that you just needed to see him in a new light, a new environment where he could show you the man he has become instead of the boy he was.'

'I would be grateful if you do not interfere in my love life anymore, Romulus,' Tash said tightly. 'I did receive help while I was in Nordhaven but it wasn't from Harrison.'

Romulus sighed deeply, looking pained. 'The Nightwalker.'

'*Cai.*'

'Cai,' he repeated heavily, 'I feared as much.'

She glared at him now, 'I've got to get him back, Romulus. He needs me now more than ever. I think I'm the only one who can help him.'

'Are you prepared for what that might mean, Natachatet?' Romulus asked quietly. 'You'd be putting aside your vows, your allegiance to the Temple and the Order if you chose to pursue the Dæmon. We do not support evil creatures in our midst.'

She stared at him, momentarily speechless with shock. When she managed to speak, her voice trembled with suppressed fury. 'He is *not* evil, Romulus. He was cursed to be a Nightwalker. I would've hoped that after hearing what he did for me, you'd understand.' She got to her feet shakily, 'I'm going to bed. It's been a long day.'

She left the dining hall before she said something she might regret, leaving Romulus sitting there pensively, reflecting on her words. Tash headed for the female dormitory, wanting to scream at the anger she felt. How could Romulus be so blind? How could he think such a thing? She'd worked so hard for so long to be a Robin, but now she was wondering if it was worth the cost. If it meant giving up on Cai, she wasn't so sure.

She grabbed a towel and went to the bathing pool, studiously avoiding the curious glances of the apprentices, who glanced up at her over their work. She'd spent enough time explaining herself tonight, the last thing she wanted was to relive the past weeks again for a bigger audience. The bathing pool was thankfully empty and she stripped off, plunging into the hot water and swimming back and forth for a few laps. She dived under the surface and let out a silent scream, beating her arms and legs until she was exhausted. When her head resurfaced, she felt better, although now she was tired as well. Reluctantly, she swam back to the edge of the pool, hauled herself out and wrapped the towel around her body. Silently, she padded back to her room and rolled under the covers, staring across at Laura's empty bed in the moonlight. There was no sign that her friend had ever slept there, the personal effects were now different, indicating that another apprentice had moved in. Tash felt a wave of loss, wishing desperately that her friend was there, to hear about what had happened. Tash was sure that Laura would hear her out and, most of all, understand. After all, Laura and Tim had realised their feelings for each other when they left on a quest all those months ago. Surely Laura would know how Tash felt, and she longed to have her there, needing her friend's support now more than ever.

Laura would have known what to say, how to make Tash feel like what she wanted was possible. She wouldn't have judged Cai immediately like Romulus had done, not when she realised the depth of Tash's feelings for him. Tash was certain of it.

Chapter Twenty-Two

They say that the faerie queen went mad when she discovered her child was not pure but tainted, a reminder of the Mortal who had ruined her life. She killed it in a mad frenzy, and with each strike she was cast further into darkness. By the time she came to herself, her hands were stained with blood and she had changed into a monster far worse than the Mortal she had cursed. When she saw what she had done, the queen cried out in pain, unable to accept it. The queen had always wanted to be a mother, and so began her new obsession— to find a new mate to give her the perfect child she sought.

> ~ An extract from 'A Robin's Collection of Inter-world Lore'

Tash put down the faded copy of 'A Robin's Collection of Inter-world Lore' with a sigh. She'd just finished reading the tale of the faerie queen, and theories swirled through her mind. Ideas about who Melisande really was, questions about what her intentions were with Cai and, yet again, the repeated question of where her Court was. It had been a week since she returned to the Temple, and The Robin was still not back. She had finished her report the day after she had returned, so that it would be ready to give him when he arrived. The only positive news she had had was that Harrison had awoken, at last, from his comatose state. According to Chris, there had been a poison deep in the wound which had lingered, delaying his recovery. Now though, Harrison was back to his usual, irritating self, and had been trying to catch her alone for the past day. She had avoided him, still blaming him for being responsible for Cai's abduction and his stubborn pig-headedness during their time in Kinet. At least Cai had listened to her when she raised concerns, whereas Harrison had discounted her opinions as the ravings of a madwoman, bewitched by a monster.

Deep down, Tash was relieved that Harrison was alright. She didn't want to think about how she would have felt if he had died, but she was still angry. No amount of apologies was going to quickly change that. However, the one place she couldn't avoid him was the dining hall, and it was there that he eventually cornered her.

'Tasha,' he slipped next to her and began to pile his plate with food, 'you've been avoiding me.'

That's stating the obvious, she thought curtly, but instead said, 'I thought you would take a hint, Harrison. I don't want to talk to you.'

'I need to explain,' he pressed, reaching out to hold her down as she made to leave. Tash glared at him coldly.

'Let go of me.'

'Not until you hear me out.' His jaw jutted forward stubbornly and she sighed, irritated.

'You have until I finish my food.' As soon as his hand released her arm, she began to eat, stuffing the remaining food into her mouth, not caring how petty she appeared.

'I'm sorry for coming after you,' he said quickly, 'for interfering. I thought you wanted me there, that I could help. And, admit it, we did stop the murders from happening.' He paused at her withering glare and then continued, 'We're safe and back at the Temple. You got everything you wanted, Ta-sha. The town of Nordhaven's safe and the blight was cured. You're the Robin you always wanted to be.'

'Cai is gone because of what you did,' Tash snarled, barely recognising her voice through the pulsing hurt. 'You invited Melisande into the cave. You broke the protection spell. He's gone because of *you*.'

Harrison went red, whether with anger or shame Tash didn't care. She rose from the table, pushing her empty plate aside.

'I have things to do,' she said, tone short and cutting, 'goodnight.'

Now she was closeted in the library, amongst the books she knew so well and loved so much, searching for an answer. Searching for anything really. All she could think of was finding something– anything– which would help her locate Cai. She had gone through all the books she could find about Nightwalkers and witches, noting many similarities across the tales of the faerie queen who had descended into darkness. The more that she read, the more she was certain that Melisande and the faerie queen were one and the same. A normal witch would have similar powers to a Robin, and not be able to shapeshift, command Dæmons, a Dragutash or subdue a Nightwalker with such ease. No, Melisande was no ordinary witch, Tash was certain of it.

What she couldn't understand was why Melisande had been desperate to capture Cai. It made no sense to her that the faerie queen would want to have anything to do with the descendent of the man who had ruined her happiness.

'What is she up to?' Tash muttered to herself, knowing deep down that whatever it was Melisande planned could not be good. She stretched, yawning. It must be very late.

Tash got to her feet, replacing the books on their shelves, feeling slightly disgruntled that her searching had yielded next to no information. With each day that passed, she felt the possibility of Cai slipping away increase. When would The Robin return? What was taking him so long?

She clenched her fists and sighed, trying to curb her impatience, leaving the library and heading for the stables. Lir would help to calm her down, and she hadn't spent much time with him since they returned, so focussed had she been on searching for a lead. Her shoes rang on the cobbles as she crossed to the stable, the soft rustling of the Willowings in their stalls meeting her ears. Lir was half asleep already, but on seeing Tash approach he rose to his feet and whickered in greeting.

'Have you been resting well, my *liebeshem?*' Tash murmured, pulling an apple from a nearby bag and offering it to him. 'The flight back here really tired you out.' He flicked his tail and began to munch on the apple, finishing it quickly and then sniffing her hand for more. 'If we're lucky, The Robin will be back soon, Lir.' Tash continued softly, 'Once he's back I'll ask for his help. He cannot sit idly by and allow Melisande to harm Cai. We'll need to be ready to leave as soon as he gives us the information we need.'

Lir's eyes gazed into hers approvingly. Tash smiled and ran her hand over his neck, 'You want to get him back too, don't you *liebeshem?* It seems that the Nightwalker had more of an impact on you than I thought.'

Her Willowing snorted and tossed his mane, stretching his wings eagerly. Tash laughed, 'We can't leave yet, Lir. Perhaps I'm not the only one impatient to be gone.'

Her attention was suddenly caught by a distant sound from outside, footsteps crunching through the dead leaves and half-frozen earth in the forest, moving gradually closer to the Temple walls. Tash reacted automatically, a mad hope filling her and she raced out of the stable and through the gate towards the sound.

'Cai?' she called desperately, 'Cai, is that you?'

She was on the edge of the tree line when she saw the figure approaching and halted, the disappointment crashing through her. This man didn't have Cai's build or glowing eyes, and although he was a similar height, she knew instantly that he was not the man she had hoped to see.

'Natachatet,' the voice sounded surprised by her outburst, 'I hope I didn't startle you.'

She froze, recognising finally who the figure was. 'Sir,' she ducked her head, embarrassed. 'Forgive me, I didn't realise it was you.'

'It's no trouble,' The Robin said coolly as he reached her, adjusting the bag over his shoulder. 'But I am curious as to why you thought I might be a certain Nightwalker.'

Tash hoped he couldn't see her blush in the darkness. 'I have my report for you, sir. If you would give me a moment to retrieve it, I have—'

He held up a hand. 'Deliver it to me in the morning, Natachatet. I am tired from my travels. See me after breakfast.'

'But—'

'Tomorrow.' His voice was firm now and brooked no argument. Reluctantly she stepped back and nodded.

'Yes, sir.' She watched resentfully as he walked to his tower, shutting the door behind him and leaving her alone. Tash let out another breath, irritation rising again. She'd been waiting for a week, and now that The Robin was back, she needed to wait even longer. Who knew what Cai had already been put through in the past days?

Disgruntled, she headed back to her dormitory, ignoring her new roommate and sliding into bed, staring at the ceiling with a frown etched on her forehead. When she finally fell asleep, it was to be haunted by dreams of Cai and Melisande, with Tash caught and bound, unable to intervene. She awoke with Cai's name on her lips, sitting up abruptly. Her roommate mumbled something and rolled over, unaware of Tash as she got up, dressed and collected her report and bag. It was still too early for breakfast, but she padded outside all the same, settling under one of the trees on the edge of the forest and allowing herself to lean back against the rough bark.

Hard frost covered the ground, sending tiny chills through her but she didn't mind. From her bag she withdrew Derrick's journal, there were still a few entries left and she wanted to distract herself while she waited for breakfast to be ready.

The boy won't leave the town alone. He's banging on doors, shouting for Ryla and Leon. It's taking everything I have to keep them contained, to subdue Ryla and to convince Leon to remain inside. He doesn't understand how his best friend is a monster, but I have reminded him of how the Gods reveal one's true nature over time. In Cai's case, they have warned us of his real identity before he became too ingrained as a member of our community. I told him to think about how lucky we were that he hadn't moved into the town as we had been urging him to. Leon eventually fell silent, hopefully recognising that this was for the best. Personally, I was thrilled.

I met the red-haired woman again tonight. She told me that I had done well, that Cai would soon be gone and Ryla would be mine again. She said that he needed to be broken, that I would know what to do when the time was right.

Tash turned to the next page, scanning the words keenly.

Elena tried to speak to me again tonight. She doesn't understand that everything I'm doing is for the town, to protect our people from that monster. She argued with me, said that Ryla wanted to see her son and that we should accept her wishes. I lost my temper and hit her. I felt a sense of power I've not felt in a long time and reminded her that she was my wife and she should obey me. Her shock and sniffling didn't faze me but then she had the audacity to repeat her demand for Ryla to be let go. I don't remember much afterwards, except that by the end of the night, Elena now knows better than to contradict me and my wishes.

Tash bit her lip, feeling sorry for the woman who had tried to stand up to her overbearing husband. The next entry seemed to have been written hastily.

Elena let her out. The bitch. I'll deal with her later. Now I need to get Ryla back where she belongs before she finds that monster of hers.

The familiar foreboding rippled through Tash as she turned to the next page. In the distance she could hear voices of apprentices moving into the dining hall but she was too enthralled by the journal to care.

What have I done? Gods, I don't know if I'll be forgiven. My hands are still shaking, I can still feel her blood on them, staining my sleeves. I found her on the edge of the Heath, calling out for Cai. She heard me and turned, furious that I had kept her safe, that I had kept them separated for her own good. She was raving, like the madwoman I'm sure she had become. I told her that if the monster disappeared, she would return to normal, that she could live with me as we had always dreamed of when we were children. Her eyes narrowed and she pushed me away, shouting that she would rather choose to be with her son over a monster.

I began to laugh, Ryla really had gone mad if she got her son and I confused. I've only ever loved her, and wanted to keep her safe. She pushed me again and I snapped. I don't know how it happened but we were there, struggling on the edge of the Heath. One moment she was screaming at me, and the next I had knocked her down and she lay still. Her words echoed in my mind and I lost control, using the knife in my belt to strike her again and again until I felt the haze lift and saw what I'd done.

I fled, cleaned myself up and raised the alarm in town, that Ryla had escaped, already putting together a plan. The red-haired woman wanted Cai to be broken and I could do that. It worked even better than I had hoped. Our hunting party found him, hunched over his mother's body, her blood on his hands, wailing like a banshee. I was pleased that Leon was in our party so he could see what his friend was capable of firsthand. It was a relief to send the men after him, to see him run away from their torches and pitchforks, and most of all to know that no one would ever find out my involvement in Ryla's death. After all, the Nordhaven Monster was responsible for it— and I am not a monster.

Tash shut the journal with a snap, anger pulsing through her as she thought of Derrick Alterton and how he had gotten away with murder. Melisande had been right. Believing that he killed his mother in one of his blackouts had sent Cai over the edge, pushing him to flee Kinet and remain in the Shadow Realm, until he understood how to control his powers better. She headed to the dining hall, ignoring the chatter of the other apprentices and settled down to eat alone, lost in her thoughts.

She wondered what had happened to Elena and Leon after the last entry, whether Elena had suffered a similar fate to Ryla or if she had been spared, forced instead to live alongside a man capable of murder. As for Leon, how had he moved on once he thought he saw his best friend commit matricide? Tash was so preoccupied, that she barely noticed that the plate before her was empty and had been for a while. When she did realise, she got to her feet, remembering all too late, that she would be going to visit The Robin this morning. Her report was in her bag and she hurried towards his tower, halting in the doorway when a voice called out to her.

'Tash.' She turned slightly unwillingly to see Chris, the Temple's healer approaching her. She had allowed him to do a temporary check up on her when she returned, letting him take some of her blood to ensure that the darkness was no longer contaminating her. She hadn't seen him since, but now he approached, a strange, closed expression on his face.

'Chris,' she held the door to the tower open with one hand, 'I have a meeting with The Robin. He's expecting me.'

'I won't take long,' he said, 'although I would rather share this with you in private.'

'I really need to go, Chris,' Tash said, glancing pointedly at the open door. 'Can you just tell me if I'm alright?'

'Yes, you are,' he said slowly, 'but—'

'Excellent,' she beamed and turned to leave. Chris caught her arm and handed her a folded piece of parchment.

'I wrote everything down in detail in case you were in a rush,' he admitted, 'just be careful, Tash.'

'Thanks.' She put the parchment in her bag, not looking at it and wondering why he was watching her with concern. 'I really have to go now though, if I have any questions, I'll see you in the infirmary later, alright?'

'Of course,' he said, stepping back and watched as she left, climbing the stairs two at a time in her eagerness.

The Robin had been expecting her. After she knocked twice on his door, it opened to reveal him standing by the window, looking out over the forest. As she entered, he held out a hand.

'Your report, Natachatet?'

Silently, she moved closer and handed it over, watching as he began to read through it intently. She waited, forcing herself to refrain from tapping her fingers against her thighs impatiently. Time spread out painfully as he turned the pages of the report, keeping her in suspense. Finally, he closed it and nodded, satisfied.

'You've done well, Natachatet,' he said. 'Very well. You may go.' He moved over to his desk and placed the report down, sitting in the chair and withdrawing a quill. She waited a moment and then the words spilled out before she could hold them back.

'That's it?'

'I beg your pardon?' He sounded surprised, bordering on offended. She didn't care, but said,

'That's all you can say after reading my report? Give me a pat on the head, a well done and a dismissal? Did you *read* it all?'

'I did, Natachatet.' His voice was cool now, which in earlier times would have scared her into silence, but that was before she had gone to Nordhaven and lost Cai.

'I need to know what you can tell me about Melisande,' she said forcefully. 'I have to help Cai. He's in danger.'

The Robin raised his hands to his head, his expression hidden by the darkness around his face. 'You ask a great deal, Natachatet. A Nightwalker should not elicit such a reaction from a Robin, and Melisande is not someone to be crossed. There are some creatures in the worlds who I prefer to avoid and she is one of them. Cai has been able to take care of himself for more years than we have both been alive– I wouldn't worry about him.'

'I shouldn't *worry?*' Her voice began to rise as the anger she had kept hidden for days finally resurfaced. 'You have known him for years and used him to locate specific information. He's not just *a* Nightwalker, he's been a friend to you. Is this how you will repay him, after everything Cai has done for you– and the Order– by refusing to go to his aid when he's in need of it?'

'You are not aware what you're asking of me, Natachatet,' The Robin said tightly.

'I'm not scared of her,' Tash shouted, throwing caution to the wind and slamming her fist down on his desk. 'I'm not giving up on Cai and I will get him back. Melisande can rot in the hells for all I care, but she is *not* keeping Cai. Robins are supposed to help those in need, to protect and ensure justice is served. You can help me or not, but I'm leaving either way.' She was shaking, her fury uncontrollable as it rolled off her in waves.

'Natachatet, you do not have the permission from the Order to do such a thing,' The Robin said coldly, standing as well. 'You do not understand what such an undertaking would entail. Melisande is a being that is far more malevolent and powerful than you could face alone. It would be tantamount to suicide. I will not permit it, not when you have worked so hard to be an exemplary Robin. If you try to go after him, you will be leaving the Order.'

Her breath was catching in her chest now, the ripping sensation piercing through her as she was forced to make a choice. 'Then I will do it without your permission, *sir.*'

She turned and stormed out, pushing past a surprised Laura who was just outside the door.

'Tash, what—'

She didn't pause to answer her friend, but descended the stairs just as quickly as she had climbed them, the anger spurring her on. She went to the stable and saddled Lir, leading him after her into the forest. There was a place she needed to go to before she left, somewhere peaceful where she could recover her emotions before she left the only true home she'd ever known in disgrace.

Tears streaked her cheeks as she cut through the trees, burning with the injustice of it. The Robin *knew* Cai, knew that he was in danger and still refused to do anything about it. He claimed it was too dangerous but what did he know? She cursed out loud, startling some birds from where they perched in the branches and they flew away. Lir nudged her shoulder comfortingly but she drew back, her fury now turning inward at herself for losing control of her temper.

'I shouldn't have yelled at him, Lir,' she groaned, 'I should have been calm and collected, told him about how it would be beneficial for the Order if Cai was released. I could have gotten him to tell me what he knew about Melisande and where her Court is. I'm such an idiot.'

It didn't take long to reach her destination. She'd been unsure if she would remember the route, but it seemed that years of muscle memory kicked in and soon she was back where– for her at least– it had all begun.

The clearing in the forest was tranquil and still, not as mysterious as it usually had been in the moonlight, which was the only time Laura and Tash had been there. She preferred it like this, without the lengthening shadows stretching across the ground, hiding some of the dangers that Romulus had said lived in the forest. And yet, as she sat down beside the pool, her fingers trailing in the icy water, she still glanced at the spot where, all those months ago, Cai had emerged from the darkness. A part of her longed for him to reappear, to saunter out from the trees and smile at her mockingly.

'Oh Cai,' she whispered, 'I will find you. I promise.' She opened her bag, realising belatedly that she hadn't given The Robin the coin purse Jervois had gifted her. She also didn't have any supplies, which meant she would need to visit Boolwra before she began to look for Melisande and Cai. The piece of parchment Chris had given to her brushed against her fingers and she picked it up absentmindedly, opening and scanning it.

The words on the page shifted beneath her gaze, forcing her to read them again, slowly taking in their meaning and feeling a new type of fear clench in her stomach.

'By the Gods, Lir,' she whispered, 'what am I going to do?'

Chapter Twenty-Three

The faerie court followed their queen down the path of darkness. All except for her sister, who watched as the queen descended into madness. She tried on many occasions to reason with the queen, to remind her of what the late king would have wanted. Instead of bringing the queen back to herself, the sister's intervention merely spurred the queen on. One night, in despair from having failed, the sister fled from the court, disguising herself in the form of her familiar to avoid being tracked. The faerie queen was outraged that her sister had escaped, that she had rejected the new regime of blood and slaughter. She sent Dæmons to find her sister and bring her back, alive or dead. To her annoyance, the sister had magic of her own, and used it to protect and hide herself from the queen's minions. She faded into obscurity, and eventually the queen moved on, finding newer victims for her wrath.

~ An extract from 'A Robin's Guide to Inter-world Lore'

Tash was in a state of shock, the words on the parchment spinning before her eyes.

Accelerated development. Risk of contamination from darkness. Rest and prayer recommended. Chances of survival reasonable, but not certain. Diet should consist of cooked meats, fresh fruit and vegetables.

She was so distracted that she didn't hear the footsteps behind her.

'You know,' a light, familiar voice said, 'this is bringing back memories. I haven't been here since we met that Dæmon.'

'His name's Cai,' Tash said tautly, still taking in the words on the parchment.

'What've you got there?' Laura moved closer and Tash held it out for her, knowing that she wouldn't be able to keep this particular secret. Laura swiped it from her fingers and began to read, her eyes widening and then she squealed in excitement.

'By the Gods, Tash, you're *pregnant!*'

'Shout it for the whole forest to know, why don't you,' Tash muttered to herself.

'I can't believe it!'

'Forget the forest,' Tash continued, 'maybe everyone at the Temple will hear you if you shout loud enough.'

'Oh stop it,' Laura admonished, 'it's so exciting! But how?' She blushed when she caught Tash's raised eyebrow and sardonic gaze. 'I mean– is it– Fred's?'

'Fred's?' Tash repeated dumbly, and then she blushed profusely as she realised how it must look. 'No. No. *No.*'

'Then whose is it?' Laura asked pointedly. 'Is it Cai's?'

Tash was momentarily dumbstruck but finally managed to nod. Laura took a breath and released it slowly. 'I think I need to hear what happened in Nordhaven. And don't leave anything out. If Cai is important enough for you to consider giving up the Order, then I want to be told everything.'

'You overheard what I said?' Tash asked softly and Laura nodded.

'My father was really shaken up. I've not seen him like that for ages. You really knew how to get to him.'

Tash looked at her friend, surprised. 'He seemed so cool and collected; I really don't think I—'

'Forget that,' Laura said dismissively, 'I know him better than you do. Now, tell me everything and we can discuss my father later.'

She sat beside Tash, settling down and watching her, hazel eyes expectant. Tash smiled and gave a faint laugh, before complying, and laying out the whole story. She went into more detail than she had in her report and in her debrief with Romulus, knowing that Laura would understand from her own experiences of her quest.

She spoke for close to an hour, until she finished with, 'And now, The Robin won't support me to find Melisande. He said I'd be cast out of the Order if I left. I thought there was that possibility but still—'

'He shouldn't have done that,' Laura muttered angrily. 'You want to protect those in need and restore justice. From everything you've told me, Cai has been Melisande's victim for a long, long time.'

'Exactly,' Tash replied hotly. 'But he refused. He wouldn't tell me anything.'

'Luckily,' Laura said, smiling wickedly, 'I'm not my father. Come on, I've got to get back to Boolwra before Tim gets worried and you need to buy supplies for your journey.' She stood and clicked her tongue, her Willowing Elaret emerging from the trees. 'I'll explain everything I know to you on the way, Tash. It's not much, but it might help.' Tash gazed at her, hope burning in her chest again, and jumped into Lir's saddle, following Elaret and Laura as they lifted off, heading towards Boolwra.

***

On the flight, Laura told Tash about her own experience with Melisande. It was like something out of a fairy tale, Tash thought to herself, the way Laura had needed to prove her love for Tim for him to be released from being Melisande's puppet.

'It was in Renderfell,' Laura was saying now, as Boolwra came into sight, 'in a forest. It was a strange place, Tash, but there didn't seem to be any traces of the Shadow Realm.'

'I'm starting to realise that sometimes things that seem to be safe and secure turn out to in fact be more dangerous than what hides in the shadows,' Tash said softly. Laura glanced over at her, and said,

'You'll still need to be on your guard, Tash. When I met her, Melisande already seemed powerful and malevolent, but from what you've said, she's even more fearsome than I had thought. Do you want help? Tim and I can come with you.'

Tash faltered for a moment, strongly tempted to say yes. She would love for Laura and Tim to accompany her, yet if anything happened to them she couldn't bear it.

'No,' she finally replied as they landed near the Boolwra stables, 'I can't ask you to do that, Laura. The Robin would hunt me down himself if anything happened to you. I'm technically disobeying his command and leaving the Order by doing this. I won't ask you to do the same thing.'

Laura's lips tightened and she nodded. 'I understand, Tash. But at least let me help you buy supplies.'

Tash smiled and allowed Laura to lead her towards the shops, purchasing all the items she thought would be necessary for her journey.

'You have to find the city of Roshterdam first,' Laura said as she stuffed a bag of rice and a pouch of Tash's favourite chai tea into Lir's saddlebags. 'Be on your guard there, though. It wasn't the most pleasant city to visit.' Her eyes darkened for a moment with a memory but Tash didn't pry. She understood all too well how one's memories could come back to haunt them. 'I can't quite remember the route from Roshterdam to Renderfell unfortunately,' Laura continued, 'so much has happened since then and my memory was never that good with directions.'

Tash laughed and hugged her friend. 'You've given me more than I could have hoped for, Laura. Thanks to you I have a lead so it'll be much easier to find Melisande. She can't hide from me forever.'

'Be safe, Tash,' Laura whispered. 'Remember that if anything happens, Tim and I will come if you call. You're not alone. Besides,' she held Tash's gaze meaningfully, 'you've got more than just yourself to think about now.'

Tash released Laura and smiled again, although this time it was slightly more pained. 'I know, Laura. But I can't give up on Cai. I won't.'

'Good luck then,' Laura said. 'I've got to get back home before Tim starts to worry. Do you mind if I tell him about where you've gone?'

Tash shook her head. 'He'll hear about it from Harrison or another Robin soon enough. It won't be kept quiet that I have chosen to leave the ranks of the Order and disobey The Robin himself. I'll see you when I get back.' She tried to keep her tone light, to hide the tremor of fear that flitted through her, and from her expression, Laura was not fooled. She gave Tash a smile, turned and walked away, leaving her to face the final stop she needed to make before she could leave for Roshterdam.

'Come, Lir,' she murmured and led the Willowing out of the stable and down the main street, towards the shop that had haunted her nightmares for months. The bell over the door tinkled as she entered, the smell of sulphur, herbs and incense assaulting her nostrils. There was a shuffling movement from above her and, even though she knew what she would see, Tash's gaze lifted to see the black crows, sitting on the rafters and eyeing her intently. Sweat beaded her forehead and she took a calming breath, fighting back the memories of the nightmares.

The words she had heard over and over rang through her ears again, reminding her of the last time she had entered the shop. The prophecy had seemed at the time to be a silly trick, a gimmick for some extra coin. Yet now, she realised how it had come true in different parts.

Hearts wild,
Lovers flawed.
Contamination tamed,
Hope is wrought.
Help too far,
Leaving too soon.
He who awaits,
Each turning of moon.
Beware the night,
Be cautious of day.
When all strays,
You will stay.

'Are you going to stand there all day, Natachatet, or do you have something particular that you came for?' Leonora's voice was curt, piercing through Tash's reverie and drawing her back to the present. She surveyed Tash keenly from behind the counter, one eye a dark brown, the other a bright blue, the scars disfiguring her face grotesque in the light. Her plaited hair still brushed the back of her knees and her apron was dirty and smeared. She was pounding a variety of ingredients together in a mortar with a pestle.

'Did you know I'd come?' Tash asked boldly, stepping up to the counter and refusing to back away from Leonora's gaze.

'I suspected you might,' Leonora said simply. 'I might be just a humble alchemist—'

'I doubt that,' Tash interrupted firmly. 'No mere alchemist would have the magical ability to see the future or deliver prophecies. No *humble* alchemist would know people's names before they have even met. Just who– or what– are you, Leonora?'

Leonora smiled, revealing cracked teeth. 'You're a smart one, Natachatet. I always had high hopes for you and it seems you will not disappoint.'

'What do you mean?' Tash asked warily. 'You've only met me twice including today.'

'I have been watching over you for much longer, child,' Leonora said, lifting a hand and a crow fluttered down onto it, turning to stare at Tash. 'But you're not here to go over the past, are you?' Tash was disconcerted by her words, yet managed to shake her head. 'I thought as much,' Leonora continued, placing down the pestle and moving around the counter to look Tash up and down assessingly. 'You will need something to protect the babe you carry, first of all,' she murmured, 'and something to make it easier for you to pass unseen through the worlds, she will be on the lookout for you.'

'Do you mean Melisande?' Tash asked through her shock.

Leonora nodded. 'She's very powerful, my child, but I can help you to find the way to her realm.'

'It's in Renderfell,' Tash said, 'isn't it?'

'That is one of the easiest ways to enter it,' Leonora said simply. 'Other ways might take too long or be too dangerous for both you and the child. The longer you spend in the shadows, the higher the risk of contamination.' She lifted a hand to press against Tash's abdomen. 'There are already traces of it. I will give you something to help remedy the effects.'

'How do you know all of this?' Tash breathed, watching as Leonora clapped her hands and the crows flew around the room, retrieving ingredients and depositing them on the counter. Leonora smiled and didn't reply, focussing on preparing the ingredients together in a pot that hung over the fire. She tossed in the powder from the mortar and began to crush new items together, leaving Tash to watch, confused.

'What are you, Leonora?' Tash repeated, 'And why are you helping me?'

'I thought that you might figure out who I am for yourself.' Leonora said smoothly, measuring out a dark powder and tossing it into the pot. Tash frowned, straining her memory for a fragment of information that could help. Eventually, a segment of one of the tales she had read came to mind, and she mused,

'You know about Melisande and her realm, which suggests that you know both well. Are you a witch?'

Leonora laughed, 'Guess again.'

Tash gazed at the crows as they continued to circle the room, retrieving ingredients and assisting Leonora with her potion. She remembered the crow in Nordhaven, the night she had been locked out of the inn, leading her down the alleyway and disappearing into the shadows. Had that been a coincidence?

'In one of the tales I read,' she began, 'it told of the faerie queen's descent into madness. How she killed her child and lost herself in the process.'

'An act that further twisted her magic inwards to contaminate her soul,' Leonora said softly.

'The tale spoke of a sister,' Tash continued, eyes not leaving Leonora's face. 'A sister who tried and failed to bring the queen back to the way of light. She ended up fleeing the court, to live a life of obscurity so that the queen would never find her.'

'Is that what the books say?' Leonora asked, a brief flicker of pain crossing her expression.

'Was it you?' Tash asked, finding it hard to believe that a member of faerie royalty was now an alchemist in a small town.

'Once,' Leonora admitted sadly, 'many years ago. My sister took my wings when I tried to stop her. She had already lost her own when she became the creature she is now. The rest of the court followed suit, losing part of their identity in the process. I barely escaped with my life, but I had to remain hidden as Melisande's anger at my betrayal did not fade with time. Over the years I have found peace in my new life, finding ways to fight back against her in small ways.'

'Is that why you're helping me?' Tash asked, 'For revenge?'

Leonora turned away from her and bent over the pot, stirring continuously. 'Melisande was not always evil, Natachatet. When she and her husband ruled together, the Court was a vibrant, happy place. Once her love had died, it became withered and rotten, a bleak memory of what could have been. I have seen what damage can be done when one loses a loved one. You and Cai deserve a chance at happiness.'

Tash blushed hotly. 'I don't– I mean– *love* isn't—'

Leonora stopped her with a knowing look. 'You cannot lie to me, child,' she said quietly, 'and you cannot continue to lie to yourself. Only knowing the truth in your heart and acknowledging it openly will assist you in my sister's realm.'

'Why did she take Cai?' Tash asked, trying to ignore the anxiety Leonora's words had caused her. 'What does she want with him? Why did she wait so long before capturing him in Nordhaven?'

'I can only guess,' Leonora said, returning to her work. 'I'd assume that when you appeared, she was curious by the interest he showed in you. She was observing you both from afar, identifying how she could use your bond to her advantage. I believe she realised that, if something happened to you, it would push him over the edge, much like when he lost his mother.' Tash bit her lip, furious that Melisande had used their feelings, used *her*, to entrap Cai. Leonora continued, 'As to why she wants him, he is a highly skilled hunter. Melisande has always admired monsters who are strong, primarily ones who have given in to the evil whispers of the Shadow Realm and lost any trace of humanity. She is obsessed with having children– perhaps she still hopes to bear the perfect child after her firstborn was contaminated by the darkness.'

'But if she's become corrupted by the same forces, surely that is impossible?'

'It should be,' Leonora said, 'although if she finds a man of pure heart, one similar to how her husband was, perhaps she has deluded herself that it *is* possible.'

'She's mad,' Tash whispered.

'Or, perhaps she wants to create a child of pure darkness,' Leonora continued, 'in which case she would require a powerful mate, one who had succumbed to their evil side.'

Tash paused, concerned as a thought occurred to her. 'Someone like Cai?'

'If he stopped resisting his urges and gave up hope, then yes,' Leonora said calmly. 'Nightwalkers are some of the strongest types of Dæmons in the Shadow Realm. They are useful allies and formidable enemies, but there are not too many of them left.'

'Wouldn't Melisande reject that, though?' Tash asked, 'Cai is the descendent of the man who killed her husband, after all, I thought she hated him.'

'I cannot say,' Leonora said simply, 'only that over the years darkness contaminates and twists the mind. It could be that now she sees a Nightwalker as the perfect mate– a creature as dark and unshackled in its desires as she is.'

'That's sick,' Tash muttered, feeling suddenly queasy. 'Cai would never agree to that.'

'I hope for both of your sakes that you are correct,' Leonora said, filling a bottle with the potion over the fire. 'Although I should warn you, time in Melisande's kingdom is not like it is here.'

'What do you mean?' Tash felt fear grip her stomach, icy tendrils reaching up through her veins.

Leonora shrugged, handing her the bottle. 'If he has faith in you, time will not matter. Now you will need to have a sip from this each day. It will keep your trace hidden from Melisande and her minions until you reach her realm. They will be on the lookout for you, since her Dragutash was killed. Once you're in Renderfell, it will be less effective, as that is where her power is strongest.'

'How do you—'

'And this,' Leonora pushed a pouch of crushed herbs into her other hand, 'will need to be steeped with your tea. It will help protect the baby.'

'But I—'

'You should get going, Natachatet,' Leonora said briefly. 'Remember what I said. You will need to be honest with yourself if you are going to succeed. Good luck, child.'

Tash was speechless, wanting to ask more questions, but one look at Leonora's face told her that she would get no answers. So instead, she bowed humbly and said, 'Thank you, Leonora. I will do my best.'

She turned and left; the door tinkling shut behind her. Leonora watched as Tash mounted Lir, took a swig of the potion and placed it along with the pouch of herbs in her saddlebags, and then lifted off into the sky. She turned to the crow on her shoulder, 'Go and keep watch over her, Diarmid. Keep her and the babe safe.' The crow let out a harsh caw and flew up the chimney, disappearing into the shadows.

Chapter Twenty-Four

I can't recall her face anymore. Her name is a faint whisper in my memory, lost before I can grasp it, like a leaf in the wind. Melisande says Mortals cannot be trusted. She says that if the woman I knew truly felt the same way she would've come searching. I don't know how long it's been now. Weeks? Months? Years? All I know is that I have waited and I am still alone.

> ~ A short entry on a discarded piece of paper in a cell in Melisande's Court

Tash camped out under the stars that night, a good distance from Boolwra with Lir kneeling on the other side of the fire. She was sipping her cup of chai tea, the herbs Leonora had given her making the taste slightly bitter. The fire crackled and sparks shot upwards, lighting up the dark night and banishing the winter chill. Tash glanced down at her abdomen, noting that it didn't seem to have changed much, perhaps it was a touch more tender than usual but there was no sign yet of the life growing within it.

'I'll do my best to get your father back, little one,' she whispered, 'I promise.'

She thought for a moment that she felt something, but then dismissed it as mere imagining. There was a loud caw and she was distracted as a large crow landed at her feet, shuffling its wings in a disgruntled fashion. It eyed her beadily and cawed again, the noise startling Lir out of his doze. Tash began to hum a familiar lullaby and Lir settled down, although he still watched the crow distrustfully. She recognised it as the one that had perched on Leonora's shoulder in her shop, and wondered if it was merely a coincidence that it was there, but doubted it.

'You don't need to follow me,' she said testily. 'I just need to find a Barrier to Roshterdam and I'll be able to find Renderfell.'

The crow clicked its beak and fluttered its wings, lifting into the air and swooping back and forth over the fire. Lir got to his feet, Tash's soothing melody no longer working at keeping him calm.

'What is it?' Tash asked the crow, as it hovered in mid-air, squawking loudly. The bird moved to the edge of the firelight and back, waiting for her to follow. Tash sighed, finishing the mug of tea and flipping her dezmian, the campsite vanishing in moments and plunging them into darkness.

'I'd better not regret this,' she muttered to herself as she mounted Lir and the crow let out a caw of satisfaction. 'See where it wants us to go, *liebeshem*,' she murmured in Lir's ear and he whickered in acknowledgement, following the crow into the depths of the shadows.

Time and space seemed to pause as they plunged after the bird, Tash blind to the environment around her changing and reforming, as they entered the Realm in-between worlds. Lir swept after their feathered guide, navigating the shadows with ease, the distant sounds of screams and roars didn't faze him anymore, as he focussed on keeping the crow in sight. Tash still didn't quite understand how Lir could see through the darkness, but clung on tightly to his neck, trusting in him to lead them to safety. The crow she wasn't as sure about, although she knew that if it had been sent by Leonora, then she had nothing to fear. It wouldn't be like the crows in her nightmares– she hoped.

There was a caw from up ahead and they twisted, plummeting down a deep ravine, the wind slicing against her cheek. Tash felt her stomach rise to her throat, the momentary sensation of weightlessness as they fell making her queasy again. Lir's wings widened and they swooped upwards. Tash was grateful, fearing that if there were many more sudden drops, she would empty the contents of her stomach into the abyss.

They weren't flying for too long before the crow turned again, Lir close behind, and then they were pushing through thick underbrush, heavy vines that caught and clung to her clothing. Tash fought against them, breaking them away from her hair and cloak, as Lir came to a halt and she could stop and see where they were.

There was a waterfall not far away, the sound of water hitting a lake a clear beacon in the night. Tash turned Lir in its direction, thinking that if there was water there would be a chance to replenish her flask. The crow flew ahead of them, darting from tree to tree, infrequently illuminated by the moonlight. When they reached it, Tash felt a sense of calmness descend, taking in the small lake and waterfall. She dismounted and flipped her dezmian, conjuring the campsite and then doubled over as a searing pain spread through her stomach. She clutched her abdomen, moaning in pain as she staggered to the ground, blinking back tears. The crow let out a loud shriek and took refuge on one of the tree branches while Lir snorted and pawed the earth, flicking his tail in distress.

Tash felt dizzy as the pain began to subside, and slowly sat up woozily. There was a figure on the other side of the campfire, dusting ashes from his clothing, and her mouth dropped open in surprise. How had he gotten there so quickly? Without any warning?

'I had hoped to catch up to you before you reached Renderfell,' The Robin said conversationally, turning to face her. 'It wasn't easy.'

Tash was speechless, still half nauseated from the sudden pain she had felt and half shocked that The Robin was there.

'I cannot stay for long, Natachatet,' he said. 'It is not wise for me to linger in this place. Melisande will sense me and that will lead her to you.'

'You sent me away,' Tash said dumbly, 'you said you wouldn't help– that I was rejecting everything the Order stood for.'

'I did,' he said coolly. 'But you raised some important points. I owe Cai more than you can possibly imagine, and I cannot allow my old fears to keep me from helping him.'

'Old fears?' Tash asked, confused. The Robin didn't elaborate further, instead withdrawing a vial and handing it to her.

'This is a concoction of powdered dragon's claw and silver from the Yarishnak Mines,' he said. 'It should be enough to temporarily subdue any lesser Dæmon that Melisande sends after you. It'll give you a chance to escape if you need to. Her Court is in that direction,' he indicated to the west of the clearing, 'you'll need to approach on foot.'

'Thank you,' Tash took it and stowed it in her bag.

'I must go,' he said, turning to head into the trees.

'Wait,' Tash said quickly and The Robin paused on the edge of the firelight. 'What made you change your mind?

How did you get here? How do you know Melisande and where her Court is?'

The Robin glanced back at her. 'Laura,' he said simply. 'She reminded me of our values and explained that if you left the Order, she would as well.' Tash sucked in a breath, as he continued, 'I know Melisande from many years ago. Cai is not the only one who has been cursed by her.' He gestured to the shadows that clung around his face, forever shrouding it from view. 'When I first ventured into the Shadow Realm, I was led astray by her and my actions resulted in the loss of many lives. Cai saved me.'

'But how did you find me?' Tash persisted, recognising that he was on the verge of disappearing into the trees. The Robin laughed, a harsh sound that rippled through the forest.

'You are not the only one who can navigate their way through the Shadow Realm when required, Natachatet. We have both been touched by the darkness, and over time you might learn to see the pathways there too. After my last venture into that place, I swore never to return— but it seems, for Cai, I had to. Don't let him down, Natachatet. If you succeed, I want a full report.'

'Yes sir,' Tash replied automatically, as The Robin vanished into the night, the vial in her bag the only proof that he had not been a mirage. She knelt by the flames, pondering his abrupt arrival and departure, and the brief amount of information she had been able to glean from him. She sent a silent prayer of thanks out to Laura, for taking a risk and it paying off.

'I think this means that I may not be an outcast any longer, Lir,' she murmured as she lay down, one arm under her head, gazing up at the stars, the other resting on her abdomen. The pain from earlier had faded away, a strange feeling of satisfaction stretching through her. For the first time all day, she felt at peace, and not nearly as scared or uncertain as she had been earlier. There had been far too many revelations today, from her conversations with Leonora and The Robin, to finding out about the new life growing inside her. She hadn't expected that and a part of her wondered how Cai would react when he found out. With that in mind, she closed her eyes, the sound of the waterfall soothing her and sending her into the world of dreams.

***

A loud cawing brought Tash back to the world of the living, pulling her rudely out of a dream where she lay safe in Cai's arms. She opened her eyes grumpily, glaring at the crow perched on the nearby branch, watching her with its jet-black gaze.

'You didn't have to wake me at the crack of dawn,' she grumbled, sitting up and stretching out the kinks in her back. 'Especially after making us travel through the Shadow Realm for half the night.'

The crow clicked its beak disapprovingly, as if to say that it saw no reason for her to complain. She rolled her eyes and filled the kettle from the lake, adding more wood onto the fire and waiting for the water to boil. Her dress was tighter around her waist than it had been the previous day, and it cut into her as she reached into her bag and pulled out some seeded bread and an apple. It wasn't much but it would have to do to ease the aching hunger in her stomach.

Once she had eaten several mouthfuls of the scant fare, she remembered the potion and took a quick draught of it. It tasted like watery cabbage, with a hint of spice– something like cinnamon. Tash wrinkled her nose, grimacing as the liquid went down her throat, forcing herself to swallow it and not spit it out. Gods, she hoped that it wouldn't take long to reach Melisande's Court and get Cai out. She didn't know how much longer she could drink that potion. Already her stomach churned from the sip she had taken, and now she needed to drink her tea with the special herbs as well.

This had better work, she thought grimly, as she drank the scalding tea, ignoring the bitterness. When she had drained the cup, she vanished the campsite and then paused again, the same pain from the night before tearing through her stomach. It was enough to make her hands tremble and legs shake uncontrollably. Lir approached her, steadying her against him, nuzzling her worriedly.

'I'm fine, *liebeshem*,' she whispered, but she decided to splash her face with water from the lake to wash away the sheen of sweat on her brow. As soon as the water hit her skin, she felt the pain fade, the strange contentment once more filling her. She stowed her dezmian safely in her pocket and moved to mount Lir, but the crow swooped her, cawing repeatedly.

'What?' she cried, raising her hands to protect herself from the sharp talons and beating wings. Lir shifted uneasily, following the crow with a murderous gaze. Tash released Lir's saddle and moved away, noting that the crow stopped swooping her as she stepped back, heading instead towards the forest. She remembered what The Robin had said and sighed, indicating for Lir to follow.

'On foot it is, then,' she muttered, and the crow clicked its beak in approval as she hefted her bag over her shoulder. She trudged after its fluttering feathers, trying to figure out why casting a simple spell had had such an effect on her. Was it something in the potion or herbs she had to drink that was making it more draining for her to use her magic?

The forest around her was quiet, save for the crunch of Tash's footsteps and Lir's hooves on the dead, frosty leaves, there was no birdsong and even the sound of the waterfall soon faded away. It wasn't natural, in Tash's opinion, who had been in many forests over the years. This one seemed to be filled with a sort of tension, a hush of expectation, as though something unseen was watching her progress, waiting to see what would happen next.

The crow flew from branch to branch, never quite stopping long enough for Tash to catch up, yet not moving too far for her to lose sight of it. She followed, hoping that trusting blindly would steer her in the right direction. If everything Leonora had said had been a ruse, a trick, then there was a possibility that she was walking into a trap. Tash shook herself, mentally chastising the thought from even crossing her mind. She couldn't afford to mistrust the people who had helped her, not when Melisande's Court was close. If this forest was in Renderfell, as The Robin had implied, she couldn't have too far to go.

'Will we get there soon?' she asked the crow, who cawed once and then swept on. 'I'll take that as a yes,' Tash muttered to herself, stepping over a fallen tree limb and slipping on the icy ground. She fell against the log and winced, rubbing her tailbone which ached painfully. Lir halted behind her, nose raised to sniff the air and he snorted anxiously. Tash looked around, scanning the trees but seeing nothing out of the ordinary. The crow had paused too, swivelling its head from side to side cautiously. There was a snarl and something leapt out from the trees, swiping at the crow which let out a squawk of fear and flew off. Lir followed suit, not waiting for the creature to turn on him, fleeing in the opposite direction, back towards the lake and waterfall. Tash reached for her dezmian, eyeing the creature warily as it turned to look at her, its white eyes dull in the light. It had a small, pointed snout and its lips were pulled back in a growl, its claws long and glistening with something dark and wet. It sat back on its haunches, scratching behind a torn ear with one foot, almost like a dog. It leaned closer to Tash, sniffing intently. She wondered whether she ought to pull out the vial of powder, but decided against it. The creature didn't seem poised to attack her– not yet, anyway.

'*Mortal.*' Its voice was ragged and sounded unused, as though it rarely had the opportunity to speak. '*Mistress wants Mortal to come.*'

Tash felt herself shiver, then steeled herself, reigning her emotions back in. So what if Melisande knew she was there, Tash was ready to face her. As she followed the creature, she began to consider her plan, how best to approach their confrontation. Absentmindedly, she held onto her stomach protectively with one hand, the other in her pocket, gripping her dezmian.

The creature led her to a spot where two dead trees met, having long since fallen together to form a triangular archway. As Tash stepped through it, the world melted away and she was surrounded by a scent of burning and decay. She felt ill as she glanced around, realising that she stood in what once might have been a great hall, decorated with high columns and windows overlooking a magnificent vista. Now though, the windows were either broken or caked in grime, the columns were stained and had vines growing up them and the view showed a damaged land, blackened and burned. Before her was a large group of people, tall, ethereal beings who appeared to be more beautiful than any Mortal could be. In their centre sat Melisande, seated on a throne of twisted obsidian, that rose up from the ground like a jagged dagger.

'Our esteemed guest has finally arrived,' Melisande announced, clapping her hands with glee, her eyes sparkling with excitement. 'As soon as I sensed the use of magic in my forest, I suspected it might be you, Natachatet. It was quite sneaky of you, trying to hide from me with that little spell of yours, but nothing can stop me from finding my prey.'

Tash remained silent as the courtiers laughed, snickering behind their hands at her. She lifted her chin and said, 'I am not hiding from you, Melisande. I'm here for Cai.'

Her words caused another wave of laughter to ripple through the crowd and Melisande smiled cruelly, her eyes glinting lazily.

'Cai doesn't want to see a Robin like you,' she said dismissively. 'He has forgotten you even existed, pathetic girl. Whyever did you come all this way? It was a fool's errand.' Her words rang out across the hall, sparking more cackles from the audience.

'I don't believe you,' Tash said firmly, refusing to be goaded into anger by Melisande's words. The faerie queen's smile flickered for an instant and her cheek twitched once, but that was the only evidence she gave away of losing her temper.

'There was no reason for you to come here, Natachatet,' she purred. 'As I said, Cai doesn't want to see you.'

'Then bring him out here so he can tell me himself,' Tash retorted, her voice echoing off the walls. 'If it is as you say, then surely there is no issue with him rejecting me in front of your whole Court. That is,' she glanced down at her hands, 'unless you have doubts about what he will choose. If you do, let me see him alone.'

The courtiers fell silent, their collected eyes darting from Tash to Melisande and back again, desperate for their queen to relent and have the Nightwalker shame the impudent Robin for their entertainment.

Melisande's lips tightened a fraction and her gaze narrowed infinitesimally before she announced, 'Very well. Mavelock,' she waved at a tall man with long, brown hair and a hawkish nose. 'Bring him in. Let him know that we have a *visitor.*'

Mavelock bowed low and swept out of the hall, his long robes dragging on the dirty floor, sending up small clouds of dust. Tash wrinkled her nose, looking back around and noting the spiderwebs and crumbling stonework in the corners of the room. On the floor there were carcasses, some animal, some human, long since dead but still in a state of decomposition. Her stomach rolled, a wave of nausea rising up unbidden and she took a deep breath, trying to settle it. The last thing she needed was to be sick.

'When Cai rejects you, Natachatet,' Melisande said conversationally, 'I'll make sure that the last thing you see is him killing you. Because of you, my Glaive is gone. He was beautiful, glorious, not a weak-willed creature like those Willowings. You killed him, so it is only fitting that Cai will show you the same mercy.' Tash clenched her jaw, refusing to give way to the threats. Melisande watched her closely and continued, 'I must say, I think I will prefer it that way. I want to see the light fade from your eyes as you realise that no one will be here to save you.'

'I don't need to be saved,' Tash withdrew her dezmian from her pocket, sliding it between her fingers, drawing on its familiar weight for comfort. 'I'm not running away from you this time, Melisande.'

Melisande laughed. 'Such arrogance. So much wasted potential. I can see why the Order would toss you out, Natachatet. Even here, my spies heard the news of your exile, the scandal of a Robin refusing to uphold her mandates and vows.' She turned to the court, 'Imagine the disgrace her family and friends must feel. Oh but,' she peered back at Tash with a wicked smile, 'I almost forgot, you were responsible for your parents' deaths, weren't you Natachatet? Your emotions led the Dragutash right to your town. We seem to have a serial murderer in our midst.' Her courtiers cackled again, their voices rising in cruel laughter.

'Perhaps your defection from the Temple will push your mentor into an early grave as well,' Melisande cooed. 'My informants told me that he was taken ill when he found out. I fear he will not last long after this betrayal.'

Tash's ears were ringing, a haze hovering around the edges of her vision, unbridled anger and fear pulsing through her in a strong current. She could barely think, let alone speak, as Melisande's poisonous words wormed their way into her mind, creating horrific images, just as she had intended them to. Tash focussed on her breathing, forcing the anger down and keeping her gaze fixed on Melisande's. The faerie queen's eyes widened slightly and her smile deepened as she realised that Tash was not going to lose control. She wouldn't allow Melisande to paralyse her with her words again, tapping into her fears and secrets with such ease.

'You do not know of what you speak,' Tash spoke through gritted teeth, and although quiet, her voice was clearly heard by all in the room. 'You do not understand the tenets of my Order, not since you descended down this path into darkness. Your sister claimed that this place was once vibrant and welcoming,' she glanced around at the rundown hall, 'it would shame her to see it now, I think.'

'Be silent, Mortal.' Melisande was on her feet, her eyes flashing and a dark cloud hovering around her, spreading out like a fog in inky tendrils. The members of the Court began to back away, casting fearful looks at their queen as she stepped down from her obsidian throne.

'You have met my sister? Where? *Tell me.*' Her voice was cutting and direct, with the sound of one who was used to giving orders and having them obeyed.

'I don't bow to you,' Tash smiled. 'All I know is that she would be disappointed in how you have lost yourself. You are no better than the Dæmons you created.'

Melisande let out a shrill cry, lifting her hand and a gash appeared across Tash's cheek, her head struck to the side.

'I thought I told you to be *silent*, Mortal.'

'I have a name,' Tash retorted, her neck aching from the magical assault. Pain spread through her stomach, as she gasped out, 'I am not your servant, Melisande.'

'You will learn *respect*.' Melisande snarled, and Tash's face snapped to the other side, as though an invisible hand had hit her hard. She felt a trickle of blood and realised that she had been cut on that cheek as well. The pain in her stomach was becoming excruciating and she inhaled sharply through her nose, trying to focus.

'Respect is *earned* not given,' Tash goaded. 'You have done *nothing* to warrant anyone's respect. You prey on the weak and the innocent. You are nothing more than a monster in the old tales, a faerie queen who murdered her own child. If your husband was still alive, Melisande, what would he say to see you now? A faerie with no wings, a creature who feasts on human blood and takes pleasure in causing others harm? Would he still love you, knowing what you have become? I think not.'

Melisande made another slashing gesture and Tash fell to her knees, a long cut appearing across her chest, right over her heart.

'You dare to say such things, Mortal,' Melisande's voice was icy in its fury. 'I should finish you myself.'

Tash's vision blurred as she bent over the ground, coughing and spluttering, blood staining her clothes. Her stomach twisted and she cried out, gripping it in agony, before heat filled her, spreading from her toes to the tips of her ears, and the pain faded away. She looked up, getting slowly back to her feet, feeling the wounds on her chest and face vanish as though they had never been.

'Impossible,' Melisande sounded shocked. Her expression gave little away, except for the glint of surprise in her eyes. She was watching Tash intently, clearly trying to discern how she had recovered so quickly. Tash was perplexed herself, uncertain how it was that she was not coughing up blood anymore.

'Mistress.' There were two sets of footsteps from behind her. Mavelock had returned. 'I have brought you the Nightwalker as you requested.' He bowed and slipped back into the crowd, waiting expectantly for the show to begin.

'Excellent.' Melisande's expression smoothed over, her smile widening. 'Approach, Cai.' Her tone was commanding, much as it had been when she tried to order Tash into submission, but this time her request was obeyed. Cai stepped forward, not casting Tash so much as a glance, and on seeing him her heart plummeted.

He was thinner than he had been, the bones visible through his skin. It looked like he hadn't slept in days, perhaps weeks, and he was dirty and bloody, whether it was his own or another creature's, she couldn't tell. His clothes were even more tattered than before, barely providing any protection from Melisande's wandering gaze. Tash felt a stab of angry possessiveness, the urge to find Cai proper clothing rising with a vengeance. He wasn't a creature to be used and ogled by any passer-by, especially not someone like Melisande.

'Cai,' the woman in question was saying now, her voice a seductive purr. 'This visitor has something that she wishes to say to us. You remember how we treat our visitors, don't you, my love?'

'Yes, my queen.' His reply was wooden and unfeeling, and the eyes that met Tash's were equally so. There was no glint of recognition, no surprise or relief at seeing her there. Melisande's term of endearment cut Tash deeper than she thought possible but she didn't visibly react, knowing that all eyes in the room were on her.

She had to be strong, calm and collected, on the outside at least. Deep inside, her heart was pounding, her ears ringing from Melisande's words and a cold chill was spreading through her veins, terrified at the prospect that he had gone beyond the point of saving.

'Cai,' she mustered the strength to say, stepping towards him cautiously. 'I'm here. I've come to bring you home.'

Melisande laughed, her head tilting back in mirth. 'He *is* home, girl. He had no home before.'

'Perhaps not,' Tash said softly, 'but he will have one when he leaves this place. With me.'

Melisande snorted, but Tash didn't care. She was focussing on Cai, holding her free hand out to him. 'I'm sorry I couldn't come immediately, Cai. I had to return to the Temple, to get Harrison proper medical attention after we were attacked by the Dragutash.'

'Glaive,' Cai said suddenly, turning to check with Melisande. 'This is the one who killed Glaive?'

Tash's concern mounted. She didn't like that he was clarifying information he should have already known, or at least guessed when he saw that she was alive and right there in front of him.

'That is the Mortal who murdered my Glaive, yes,' Melisande said, a false tear dripping from one eye. Cai turned back to Tash, his expression now hard and resolute.

'You have made my queen weep,' he said bluntly. 'For that you will pay with your life.'

'Cai,' Tash began, 'you must listen—'

But he was already striking out, ducking under her outstretched hand and kicking her in the side of the leg, toppling her to the ground again. Tash grunted, twisted sideways and narrowly evaded his next blow. She couldn't avoid the tail which slashed through the air, gripping and spinning her across the room until she crumpled in a heap, one hand clutching her stomach protectively. Tash spat the hair out of her mouth and rose, facing him and flipping her dezmian, summoning her whip into her hands. It glowed with ethereal light as she snapped her wrist, watching as it spun and caught him, wrapping around him tightly.

'I didn't want to have to do this, Cai,' she said, adjusting her grip on the handle to hold him firm as he struggled, 'but you've given me little choice.' She ignored the ache in her belly as she exerted her magic, and continued, 'Cai, it's Tash. You have to remember.'

'Witch,' Cai spat as he tried to wrestle himself free of the whip. 'I know no one of that name.'

Tash's hope faltered, as she realised that he had given up, just as she had feared he might.

'How long has he been here?' she asked Melisande, refusing to look away from Cai's face, contorted with fury.

'Let's see,' Melisande sounded exultant, 'we've had a nice sojourn in my realm for, goodness, it must be at least a year and a half now. It might even be longer.'

Tash paled. 'Your sister was not wrong when she said that time moved differently in your realm.' Melisande sniffed disdainfully.

'Time is immaterial,' she said. 'Ask what you came to, Natachatet. I am growing bored.'

'Cai,' Tash said, 'you must understand that it's not been a month since I saw you last. I was delayed in finding you, but I didn't forget. I didn't abandon you.'

Melisande yawned pointedly.

'Cai,' Tash was struggling to keep her balance now, to hold him steady, 'come back to me. Remember, *liebeshem*.'

As he broke free of her whip and leapt at her, Tash ducked away, moving onto the defensive to avoid being caught by his claws. Blow after blow she dodged, and as she evaded him, Tash began to sing. The Ancient Tongue swirled through the hall, transforming her whip into glimmering lights in the candle brackets, casting the shadows away to the edges of the room and Melisande's courtiers gasped, fleeing to the remaining vestiges of darkness.

'No,' Melisande screeched, 'stop her.' Several figures tried to approach, but the lights shone brighter, forming a barrier between Tash and Cai and Melisande and her subjects.

Tash ignored them, just channelled all her energy into singing a tale of two imperfect souls who had become lovers. She told of how one of the lovers was dedicated to restoring balance, far and wide, never remaining in one place for long. Her song described how a plague was cured, the lovers reunited, albeit briefly before they were torn apart again after the new moon. Tash sang of the dangers of night and day, and how she waited, her heart remaining constant as she stayed loyal to the counterpart of her soul and her faith that they would find their way back to each other.

As Tash sang, the lights grew stronger, blinding Cai until he paused in his assault, one hand lifted to block it out. He began to shake, much as he had the night of the new moon when he transformed back into a Nightwalker. Tash continued her song, moving closer towards him, the magic spilling out of her, encasing them in an ethereal glow. She sang of the things she had been too scared to say, the way he made her heart soar, that their times together had created a new life, a new hope for their future. She stopped when she was kneeling in front of Cai, her arms came around him and he stilled, as her cheek pressed to his.

'Don't leave me alone, *liebeshem*,' she whispered, 'don't leave us. Not when we need you here. Not when I've found you again.' As her lips met his, the lights faded as the energy from exerting the magic finally sapped out of her. Hands pulled her roughly away, dragging her by the hair across the floor towards Melisande's throne. Tash cried out, the pain from the roots of her hair and her stomach incapacitating her.

'That was a very pretty lightshow, my dear,' Melisande said curtly, sharp nails digging into Tash's scalp before she was tossed away. 'But my patience is used up. If my Nightwalker cannot best you, then I will have to intervene myself.' She flicked her hand and Tash was lifted into the air by invisible bonds, her throat slowly constricting.

'For too long you have escaped me, Natachatet,' Melisande said coldly. 'You have become a problem and there's only one effective way to deal with those.'

Her hand tightened, the bonds around Tash's neck following her command, and Tash struggled weakly, gasping for breath. Melisande laughed, moving closer to look Tash up and down. 'You should have given up, Natachatet. I tried to warn you. You could've just let Cai remain with me, and lived your life peacefully once you returned to the Temple. I had no need to come after you, I already had everything I wanted.'

'You… lie.' Tash managed, and Melisande smiled cruelly.

'Whatever made you think he would welcome you back, Natachatet? He is happy here, he will be immortal in my Court, never fearing another or lacking power. With you he would be hunted, ostracised, and you would be ashamed. Here he is appreciated, he is loved, he is *home*.'

'You know nothing about any of those things,' Tash spat out, and she was dropped abruptly, landing back on the ground with a crash. Her ankle cracked and a new agony pierced her leg. She cried out blindly, momentarily lost in the sensation, one hand reaching for the throbbing ankle, the other curving around her stomach. When her eyes opened, she was trembling, blinking up at Melisande who stood over her furiously.

'What did you say, *worm?*' Melisande hissed. Her eyes travelled over Tash and then widened when they fixed on her abdomen, a mocking laugh filling the room. 'Did you honestly think that you would win him back by bearing his bastard child? He has no need of you now, girl. He has a queen and the spawn we have will instil fear in each and every world. Nowhere will be beyond our reach, our control. Everyone will fear us and our power. No one will stand in our way, not you, your precious Order or my godforsaken sister.'

Tash felt sickened. 'You will never love him, Melisande, nor will you love your children. Your heart has forgotten how.'

'Cai, to me.' Melisande commanded, and Tash heard his footsteps approach. He stood beside her, gazing at Tash stonily, mouth pulled back in a snarl of disgust.

'Yes, my queen?'

Melisande caressed his face with the back of her hand, 'You know that I love you, don't you, my pet?'

'Yes, my queen.'

'And you will do anything I require?'

'I live to serve you, my queen.'

Melisande's cruel eyes turned to Tash, glinting with malevolence. 'Then rip the babe from her womb. I want her to see it before she dies.'

Chapter Twenty-Five

Liebeshem, I miss you. Each night I imagine you are there, emerging from the shadows to keep the nightmares at bay, but when I wake, I am alone. You told me once that we would be whatever I desired, that I just had to decide what I wanted our future to look like. Back then I wasn't sure, I was scared of what I felt and of what people would say. I've been cast out of my Order, although in my heart I know I will remain faithful to our rules. Even if I'm no longer a Robin, I will find ways to stop the injustice in the worlds. I hope that you will be by my side.

The news Chris gave me today has brought new fears, that I will not be enough for our child, that you will never see them grow. It makes me wonder if this was how your mother felt when she discovered that she was pregnant with you. Like her, I won't give up on you. I'll keep trying, no matter the cost. Even if it's only for a moment, I want to see you again, just so that I can finally tell you what is in my heart.

~ A private letter, carefully written and folded, hidden in Lir's saddlebags

Tash couldn't breathe. She pulled herself back across the floor, still too weakened after using her magic to draw on it again. Her gaze flicked from Melisande's gloating expression to Cai's shuttered one. The throbbing from her ankle was fading away as the adrenaline took over. She could feel her pulse beating out a fast, staccato beat, shards of dread mingling with the blood in her veins.

'You will have to choose, Natachatet,' Melisande said sweetly, 'will you protect the child or save the father? Either way, you will die.'

Tash struggled backwards, reaching for her bag which had slipped to the ground earlier. She kept an eye on Cai as he slowly advanced, a hunter stalking his prey. The marks around his chest from where the whip had held him firm had faded already, leaving no indication that she had ever bested him.

'Don't force me to do this, Cai,' she whispered, her hand reaching into the bag for the vial of silver powder, carefully taking out the stopper. A new sense of power was rising in her now, the need to protect, to wound any who tried to harm her unborn child. It wasn't something she recognised, the force of it overwhelming all other pain and fatigue and it only increased as he drew closer.

'Do it, Cai,' Melisande ordered. 'Prove your love for me and I will give you more power than you could possibly dream of.'

Something flickered in Cai's scarlet gaze, a hint of hesitation, of uncertainty. Tash saw it and took the chance, pouring part of the powder into her hand and throwing it into his face. Cai recoiled, grunting in pain as he was temporarily blinded.

'Forgive me, *liebeshem*,' Tash whispered, 'but I won't let you harm our child. When you come back to yourself, you will thank me.'

'Kill her!' Melisande shrieked, and the rest of her Court obeyed, striking out at Tash with a frenzy that she could barely withstand. They crowded her, cutting her away from

Cai, their beautiful faces changing into horrifying visages akin to some of the Dæmons Tash had seen from the Shadow Realm. She fled backwards, tossing the silver powder at them, using the momentary distraction to duck out from their flailing arms and limp towards the exit. Something hot flew over her head and she skidded to a halt as a wall of flame blocked her escape.

'Useless minions,' Melisande spat, drawing the same blade she had used on Tash in the Shadow Realm, as she advanced. 'I'll do this myself.'

Tash reached into her pocket for her dezmian, flipping it and calling the whip back into her hands and then focussing on her damaged ankle. There was a searing heat around her injury as it healed and she could put her weight back on it. She felt shaky, the urge to flee strong, but the flames pushed her back into the fray, towards Melisande and her dark court. She paused when Cai fell at her feet, knocked over by Melisande's minions, his hands still covering his eyes in agony.

'*Liebeshem.*' Unthinking, she reached down and gripped his hand, pulling him to his feet beside her. His hand froze in hers, and she stilled, wondering if he would strike out and finish her. When she looked into his eyes, she saw that they were inflamed, the silver dust and powdered dragon's claw concoction making it hard for him to focus on her.

'You're not real,' he muttered, his spare hand rising to touch her cheek. 'You're not her.'

'I'm here, Cai,' she whispered, praying that this time it would make a difference, 'it's me, Tash.'

He shook his head, confused and unsteady. 'She's dead. You're another illusion. Another witch's trick.'

'You can feel me, *liebeshem*,' Tash replied, squeezing his hand with hers and leaning into his touch. 'It's not a dream or an illusion. I'm real.'

'End her, Cai,' Melisande snapped. 'I want her to bleed.'

Tash's gaze narrowed and she struck out, the whip cracking across the space between herself and Melisande, making the faerie queen pause in her approach, a thin trickle of blood staining her cheek. She lifted a hand to her face, incredulity quickly being replaced by fury and she snarled. Cai didn't react to Melisande's words, but continued to stare at Tash as she stepped away from him, although her free hand lingered in his.

'I'm not going to run, Melisande,' Tash said, the whip striking out again and catching the other cheek. 'And even if I do not leave here alive, I'll at least be content in the knowledge that I made *you* bleed too, with the Gods as my witnesses.' The energy that flowed through her returned with a vengeance as the whip cracked, glowing with the same white light from before. Melisande faltered as it coiled around her, burning her with holy fire. Tash felt the wordless song rise up, spilling forth as it had before, although this time she was no longer trying to protect but to exact justice, to rid the world of the darkness that Melisande had brought into it.

'Cai,' Melisande screeched as another fireball shot towards Tash, 'rip out her throat. Prove yourself.'

Tash heard the words and then she was being pulled to the side, losing her grasp on the whip handle, her song cutting out as she hit the ground and rolled, held firm in a pair of strong arms. The fireball flew overhead, right where Tash had just been standing. She felt Cai shaking beside her, his hold on her tightening until it was almost painful.

'*Liebeshem*,' she murmured. 'Let me go.'

'You're real,' he muttered, leaning back to check her for injuries, 'you came for me.'

'Of course I did,' she retorted, struggling to her feet, and then dodging to the side as a blade slashed out of nowhere. Melisande pushed on the attack, her knife cutting fast and deadly through the air, while Tash tried to hold her at bay, her whip retaliating against each blow, cracking as she maintained a gap between them. Cai growled as several members of the court joined in Melisande's assault, the powder now wearing off. He struck out at them, drawing them away from Tash and Melisande's circling figures. The two women had begun a new type of dance, the dagger and whip darting back and forth as they tested each other, neither prepared to back down. Tash spun, her arm rising up and around, the coil of light striking the dagger away, catching Melisande on the hand. The woman hissed as blood dripped from the wound.

'You cannot best me, Natachatet. Even with help from your Gods you will fail. I have known many like you over the centuries, and none of them have succeeded. Whatever makes you think that you will?'

There was a cry from behind her and Tash spun to see Cai surrounded, the corrupted faerie court using their sheer numbers to overpower him. Although bodies littered the floor, gazing sightlessly up at the darkened ceiling, more still came to answer their mistress' call to arms, swarming through the broken windows like a plague. She began to run towards him, her whip moving automatically, circling up and over her head, and coming down in a blaze of light. She flicked it back and around herself, before it struck out again, knocking one of Cai's attackers down. A loud caw distracted her momentarily and she glanced upward as she drew the whip back, to see a mass of black feathers dive at Melisande, deflecting the blade that had been intended for Tash.

'Leonora's little friend has come to play as well,' Melisande laughed maniacally. 'What a shame he won't last long enough to lead me back to her.' Using her temporary distraction to her advantage, Tash continued to help Cai, cutting back his attackers until her arm and shoulder ached. As the last creature crumpled, there was a piercing cry and Tash turned to see the crow fall to the ground, the dagger protruding from its chest. Melisande chuckled and drew the blade out, eyes locking on Tash and she lifted her free hand, once more holding Tash in invisible bonds. The whip fell to the ground with a clatter as Melisande moved with uncanny speed, her blade sinking into Tash's breast as she let out a celebratory cry.

Tash felt the cold spread through her as she sank down, gasping as she pulled the dagger from her chest, the metal clanging on the ground. Cai roared and lunged at Melisande, trying and failing to strike her down. The faerie queen laughed, glorying in her success, deflecting his blows with ease.

'You cannot hurt me, Cai,' she gloated, 'I made you what you are. You cannot harm your creator.'

'I'll do my best,' he grunted, trying and failing to reach her through an invisible barrier that seemed to protect her skin. He reached back and thrust his hands forward, knocking her backwards with a blast of magic. Melisande gave a little shriek as she was thrown across the room, hitting her throne with a thump.

'*Liebeshem*,' Tash was pushing on the wound, her strength fading. On hearing her voice, Cai paused in his assault and knelt at her side, his hand hovering over her injury, trying to heal it.

'Why is it not working?' he muttered roughly, trying again only to see the wound continue to bleed steadily.

'In my bag,' Tash whispered, 'I wrote… letter for you. Something important… to tell you.'

'You can't help her, Cai,' Melisande taunted from the other end of the hall. 'I wasn't going to let anything get in my way this time. That blade has been enchanted, so that none who have been loyal to me can cure who it attacks.'

Cai made to leap at her, but Tash gripped him, her breathing becoming more laboured as the cold intensified.

'Don't forget, Cai,' she forced the words out through the pain, 'no matter what she does to you, I love you.' Something twinged in her stomach and she gasped, 'We both do.'

As she spoke the words, the cold began to evaporate, rapidly being replaced by a searing heat that made her cry out. There was a loud scream, as Cai fell back, dropping her hand and writhing on the ground, while Melisande shrieked out her displeasure. Tash blinked and the world began to come back into focus, the heat lessened in its intensity and she glanced down. As she had suspected, the wound was healing, looking now like it was several days old. Slowly, she reached down to grip the dagger, a sense of resolute calm filling her as she rose to her feet.

The faerie queen had moved to Cai's side as he screamed again, thrashing out in agony.

'What have you *done?*' she demanded, raising her gaze towards Tash. 'You have ruined *everything*.'

Melisande didn't wait for Tash to reply, but lunged at her, mindless in her fury. There was a moment when she realised, too late, what she had done, yet already the blood had started to flow, spreading out like a crimson rose from where her own dagger protruded from her heart. It was a wound similar to Tash's, although this one would not heal.

A hush fell over the hall, as sunlight pierced the gloom, burning away the shadows. Melisande staggered backwards, eyes wide and uncomprehending, her form shifting and blurring as her lifeblood drained away. She opened her mouth in shock, and her gaze found Tash's, so that she could see the momentary glimpse of the woman Melisande had been before the darkness consumed her.

'Thank you,' Melisande breathed, slumping to the ground as the light faded from her eyes. Tash withdrew the blade and wiped it on Melisande's skirts, stowing it in her belt for safekeeping. She took the position beside Cai, watching over him as his cries lessened, unable to help or intervene, recognising deep down that this was a battle he had to fight alone. So, instead, she bent her head in prayer, whispering under her breath as the sun began to rise.

***

She looked up when Cai had gone silent. The sounds he had made when his bones broke and reformed or his horns had retracted into his skull still ringing in her ears. Her cheeks were stained with tears, for his cries had cut her deep, and she had been powerless to alleviate his suffering.

Yet now, he lay in front of her, cobalt eyes blinking open in the sunlight, searching her out and fixing on her.

'Cai,' she barely got his name out before he had pulled her into his arms, cradling her against him.

'You saved me,' he spoke wonderingly. 'You broke the curse.'

'How?' Tash asked, gripping him tightly. 'I don't understand— it all happened so fast.'

He chuckled, 'Nightwalkers were cursed to never know love again. Once you declared your love for me, it broke Melisande's spell.'

'Did you know that would break it?' Tash sat up curiously, her hand resting in his as she gazed at him, the fact that he was human again still taking a while to absorb. He shrugged and nodded. 'Then why didn't you say anything?' she demanded hotly and he laughed again.

'I wasn't able to go into any detail about the curse, Tash. It was forbidden. Besides,' he eyed her teasingly, 'if I had been able to mention it, you would have run in the other direction. Don't deny it.'

She couldn't. It had been hard enough to acknowledge her feelings, and if she had found out earlier there was a strong possibility that she would have run as he said. His gaze sharpened on her and he added, 'Are you feeling alright, Tash? I was sure that I would lose you.'

She smiled and nodded, looking down at the still damp patch of blood on her chest, at the wound that was half-healed under the torn fabric. 'I don't quite understand how that happened either.'

'I can explain that, though, my dear.' A new voice spoke from the edge of the hall and Tash and Cai turned, startled. Cai moved forwards automatically, blocking Tash from the newcomer. However, Tash recognised the voice and stepped around him, gazing in surprise at the woman approaching them, her long skirts brushing the dirty ground, white hair sweeping the back of her knees.

'Leonora,' Tash said, 'what are you doing here?'

'I was summoned, Natachatet,' she said simply. 'Diarmid sent me a message before he sacrificed himself, and once I felt my sister's life slip away, I knew it was safe to return here.' She lifted her hands in a sweeping motion, magically removing the traces of the battle and years of neglect. She moved to where the crow had fallen, lifting its body into her hands and cradling it, not caring as it stained her dress red.

'Are you the reason Tash survived?' Cai asked, one arm encircling Tash's waist, anchoring her safely next to him.

'My potion aided her slightly,' Leonora admitted, 'although I cannot take all the credit. Your child's connection to magic is strong, it draws on that power to grow and survive. In the case of that dagger,' she eyed the blade in Tash's belt, 'it accelerated your ability to heal, as it did with your connection to the holy magic Robins often tap into. It is your child who saved her life. The herbs I gave you to drink clearly helped to awaken its power.'

She was in front of them now, and she paused, gazing down at Tash's abdomen where new life stirred. 'The babe will have stronger powers than most, for its parents were not mere Mortals. As its father was touched by darkness, this child will have a susceptibility to it. They will share a monster's ability to travel at ease through the Barriers, but you will need to guide them to follow a path of light.' Leonora's eyes met Cai's and Tash felt him shiver. 'A former Nightwalker, you may be, Cai, but you will find that certain vestiges of that period of your life remain. You will never be completely human again, for you have spent too long in the darkness. I cannot save you from that, I'm afraid.'

Cai ducked his head. 'As long as I can be at Tash's side, I will be content.'

'An admirable sentiment,' Leonora said, a smile playing on her lips. 'I ask that you watch over my chosen and your child, I foresee that they will not make life simple for you.'

Cai chuckled, 'I think a simple life would get boring pretty quickly.'

'What will you do, Leonora?' Tash asked, sensing that it was nearing the time for them to depart. Her mind was racing from what Leonora had just said about her child, and she rested a hand on her abdomen protectively. No matter what would happen, she would do her best to keep her child from the evil of the Shadow Realm.

'I must rebuild what has been lost,' Leonora said. 'This hall was once a happy place. Perhaps, in time, it may be so again.'

Tash bowed, 'I hope it will be. Thank you, again, for helping me.'

'You will need a guide to take you back to Venetica,' Leonora lifted her hand and the sound of hooves filled the hall. 'Fly safe and remember to trust in each other. One day, I am sure, we will meet again.'

A snort drew Tash's attention from Leonora and she cried out, rushing towards the Willowing who was standing by the exit. His liquid eyes gazed at her lovingly as she flung her arms around his neck and he whickered softly.

'Lir, you came back, you coward,' she smiled into his mane, 'I was worried that you had been caught by some of those Dæmons.' Lir snuffled and pawed the ground, recoiling slightly when Cai approached, momentarily not recognising him.

'Hush, *liebeshem*,' Tash murmured, 'it's Cai.' Lir sniffed Cai's outstretched hand and then butted him in the shoulder, knocking him off balance. Tash bit back a giggle as Cai staggered and righted himself, readjusting her bag on his shoulder from where he had collected it.

'Let's go,' he said, lifting Tash into the saddle and jumping up behind her. Lir snorted in amusement, as if to say that he wouldn't take orders from this stranger.

Tash grinned, leaned down to his ear and murmured, 'Take us home, *liebeshem*.' Her smile widened as Cai's arms gripped her waist, holding her securely against him as Lir spread his wings and soared away from Leonora's Hall.

Chapter Twenty-Six

Each morning I wake and look at her beside me. In sleep, one cannot see the shadows from what has happened over the past months, yet now I feel content knowing that those memories are fading away, just like my own are. She is so beautiful; I thank the Gods that she was sent to me. It's hard at times to believe that it's real, that it isn't an illusion or dream. I never expected that she would break the curse, not after giving up on it so many years ago.

~ An extract from a new journal, carefully placed in Cai's saddlebags

Tash awoke lazily to the sound of a pen scratching on parchment. She stretched, still feeling the afterglow from their lovemaking in the early hours of that morning. It had surprised her how eager she had been the past two weeks, craving Cai's touch to the point of obsession. She hadn't known that she would desire him at any hour of the day, although he seemed to need her just as much. Their progress back to the Temple had been slow, perhaps due to the numerous stops they made to catch up on lost time in each other's arms, or perhaps due to the difficulty in finding Barriers between worlds.

Tash had been relieved when Cai managed to cross the first Barrier intact with her, although the transition between worlds seemed to sap his energy more. She had been worried when he became human again that he would no longer have that ability, which Robins and magical creatures possessed. Yet it seemed her worries had been for nothing. Traces of his years as a Nightwalker still lingered, as Leonora had said, but if that meant he would be able to travel with her, she would consider it a blessing. Now though, she was happy, for the first time in a long time and grateful for no longer being alone. She didn't mind their rather meandering way back to the Temple, finding joy in those times in towns when Cai's face alit with excitement at markets or fairs, or their long nights in the wilderness, entwined in each other's arms by the campfire. Her mouth crinkled in a smile at the thought as she wondered what new adventure the day would bring. A roughened hand brushed her cheek and her eyes opened, meeting the cobalt gaze smiling down at her.

'You slept in,' Cai said softly. 'It's nearly noon.' Tash blinked, surprised for a moment, and sat up, adjusting her skirts around her growing belly. It hadn't even been two months, but as Leonora and Chris had said, the babe was developing at an accelerated rate. The use of magic, particularly going through Barriers or summoning campsites, only increased the speed of its growth. While Cai's own magical ability had diminished, it seemed that their child was thriving, so that after a week Tash's pregnancy was clearly visible. She didn't mind too much, although it had required going into town to purchase new clothing that was looser around the waistline.

'Tash?' Cai was looking at her expectantly and she tilted her head, coming back to the present.

'Sorry, what?'

'Did you want me to make lunch before we head off?' he repeated, eyes glinting humorously. 'Or do you want to get going sooner? We could reach Boolwra by this afternoon.' His voice trailed off, and Tash understood his hesitation. Once they reached Boolwra, they would be close to the Temple and Tash would find out if The Robin would formally acknowledge her back into the Order. She would have to introduce Cai properly to her friends and Romulus, which caused her more anxiety than she had voiced aloud. She knew that Cai was nervous about it as well, that he, like her, had been enjoying their time travelling together, caught up in their own bubble, not meeting anyone they knew and not worrying about what would happen next.

'We should probably move on,' Tash said regretfully, getting to her feet and withdrawing her dezmian as Cai saddled Lir. With a flick of the wrist, the dezmian spun, and the campsite vanished. Cai helped Tash into the saddle and leapt up behind her as she slumped, the exertion of using her magic already draining her. Lir whickered and soared upwards, brushing the tips of the trees with his hooves as he flew.

'It should only take a couple of hours to reach Boolwra,' Tash said over her shoulder. 'We can stay in one of the inns for the night and head to the Temple tomorrow.'

'That sounds like a good idea,' Cai replied, sounding relieved. Tash smiled, hoping that Laura and Tim might still be in Boolwra, although she knew that there was no guarantee that they would be. She squeezed his hand reassuringly and he returned the pressure, as she relaxed into his arms and allowed herself to doze off.

It seemed as though she was asleep for only a few minutes, yet when her eyes opened it was to see the roofs of

Boolwra beneath them. Cai was navigating Lir down to the stable, and the Willowing landed with a jolt on the cobbles. Tash was eager to dismount and stretch out the aches in her back, before locating the nearest inn and having a late lunch. Cai led Lir into one of the free stalls and slung the saddlebags over his shoulder, catching Tash's hand in his as they made their way down the main street.

The inn they stopped at was bustling with customers, but they were served bowls of hot soup quickly. Tash began to eat immediately and Cai joined her, until both bowls were empty in very little time.

'I've arranged for us to have one of the free rooms,' Cai said, leading her away from the dining hall and upstairs to deposit their bags. 'I thought we could—'

His words were interrupted by a loud cry and then someone had grabbed Tash from behind in a tight hug. 'You're back! I was so worried!'

'Laura,' Tash grunted as she pulled away to turn around and return the hug, 'you scared me.'

'Sorry,' her friend didn't sound repentant at all, she was too busy beaming at them. 'Have you just arrived? You seem well, is this…?' She trailed off, looking from Tash to Cai expectantly.

'Cai, this is Laura,' Tash smiled, 'and that's Tim.'

'A pleasure,' Cai nodded at Laura and at Tim, who was hovering behind Laura, looking faintly exasperated with her.

'You could have given them a chance to settle in before pouncing on them, Laura,' he admonished gently. 'It looks like you scared Tash half to death.'

'I'm fine, Tim,' Tash grinned. 'Have you both been staying here long?'

'We're going to be moving on pretty soon,' Tim said, 'Laura wants to visit Earth again.'

'But I couldn't leave until I heard from you,' Laura said, gripping Tash's hands and dragging her back downstairs. 'Walk with me and tell me everything that happened.' Tash cast Cai a quick, apologetic look as she was led away, leaving the two men to stand awkwardly in the hallway.

'Want to dump your bags and join me for a pint?' Tim asked, 'There's no telling how long it'll be until they're back.' Cai nodded, watching Tash disappear, partially on edge that she was leaving unprotected. As if he could read his thoughts, Tim said, 'Laura will take care of her. Don't worry.' Reluctantly, Cai glanced away, left the bags in their room and joined Tim as they made their way to the bar.

***

Laura was determined to hear the entire retelling of Tash's trip to Melisande's Court. She and Tash meandered down the main street, peering into shops as Tash told the whole story, sparing no details. Laura gasped at all the right moments, clutched her friend's arm at others and then her face split into a beam as Tash finished, recounting how Cai had returned to his Mortal form.

'I can't believe it,' she said excitedly, 'and he's able to cross the Barriers without issue?'

Tash nodded. 'So far, at least. Leonora did say that he wouldn't be completely human– he spent too long in the Shadow Realm to completely be free of the darkness.'

'That's lucky,' Laura said and then quickly added when she saw Tash's raised eyebrow, 'I mean, this way he can stay with you when you go in-between worlds. You don't have to give up on your dream.'

Tash nodded, unconsciously lifting a hand to support the extra weight around her middle, pausing to catch her breath. It surprised her still how quickly she seemed to get tired these days.

'That's if The Robin welcomes me back into the Order. I thought he would, but—'

'Don't be silly,' Laura interrupted, 'of course he will.'

Tash wished that she had her friend's confidence, yet there still remained a shred of anxiety about the upcoming meeting.

'Have you seen Romulus at all since I left?' she asked, remembering all too easily the cruel jibes Melisande had taunted her with in the faerie court.

'He will be better once he sees you,' Laura said gently. 'He didn't take your leaving well. He's been in his rooms mostly, from what I understand.'

Tash sighed, guilt at having taken so long to return rising with a vengeance. 'Perhaps we should continue on to the Temple tonight, then,' she muttered but Laura shook her head.

'No, Tash,' she said bluntly, 'you need to rest. Let's head back to the inn– I can tell that you're about ready to drop. The Temple and Romulus will be able to wait until tomorrow.'

Tash smiled faintly and allowed Laura to lead her back up the main street, opening the inn door and pausing as she saw Tim and Cai in deep discussion at one of the tables. Both men had several empty tankards in front of them, but seemed to be getting along well, laughing and joking, Tim's laid back charisma clearly had put Cai at ease in the bustling inn.

'Let's join them,' Laura said mischievously, 'I'm thirsty now too.' She tugged Tash's arm and they moved to sit with their partners, the two men halting in their conversation and glancing up at them as they approached. Cai smiled at Tash, standing to pull a chair out for her, one hand lightly grasping hers as she sat.

'Tim,' Laura's eyes glinted with affection as she looked at her fiancée, 'can you get us some drinks as well?'

'Ale?' Tim asked easily, as he too got to his feet.

'Just water for me, please,' Tash said quickly. She hadn't drunk any ale since she saw the note from Chris, finding that water or tea was better for settling her stomach. Cai squeezed her hand and she smiled at him, suddenly struck anew with how happy she was when he was nearby. She was sure that at some point he would start to irritate her again and drive her crazy, but until then she would enjoy the glow that seemed to surround them for the past weeks.

She leaned back in her chair and appreciated the fact that Laura and Tim were there, accepting Cai and helping to make him feel welcome. Her gaze flickered over their faces, noting Cai begin to contribute more readily to the conversation as his confidence grew and she felt a warm sense of rightness fill her. By the time they retired to their respective rooms, they had eaten a hearty meal and the dark sky outside was glittering with stars.

Tash closed the shutters before unfastening her dress and lifting it over her head as Cai locked the door behind him. He watched her as she washed up, slowly discarding his own clothing and following suit, taking the cloth and soap from her hands. She pulled her nightgown on, shivering at the cool air and crawled under the covers in an attempt to get warm. Her back ached as she lay down, and she winced slightly in discomfort. Cai noticed the brief shadow of pain cross her face and moved instinctively to her side, pulling her against the curve of his body as he rubbed her back, easing some of the tension that had built up throughout the day.

'How did you find tonight?' Tash finally broke the silence, a part of her glad that he couldn't see the flicker of anxiety in her eyes as she asked it. She wanted so desperately for him to get along with her friends, to feel like he could fit into her world and begin the transition back into society.

'It was nice,' Cai replied softly, and she realised that he perhaps understood all too well her concerns. 'I like Tim— we managed to find a few things to talk about while you were out. Laura has changed since I saw her last— she seems more confident in herself than she was in Calcitya, and they suit each other well.' He fell silent, and Tash smiled, relief easing the knot of anxiety that had begun to form in her stomach.

'I'm glad,' she said simply. He chuckled and his hands began to wander, brushing over her skin and leaving a trail of sensation behind, awakening her body to his touch in mere seconds.

'What I don't understand,' he murmured in her ear as he pressed a kiss just underneath it, 'is why we're talking about Laura and Tim when there are so many other things that we could do.'

Tash grinned as she bit back a low moan. 'What do you suggest?'

Cai's hands became more insistent, tracing new teasing paths to all of his favourite places and finding ways to make her gasp and whisper incoherent words as he demonstrated effectively what he meant.

***

Their lovemaking that night had banished all of Tash's fears and anxieties about what would happen once they reached the Temple, until the moment before their arrival. Her stomach was a roiling mess, churning at the thought of how Romulus and The Robin would react. Cai held her close against his chest, yet that only meant that she could feel the pounding of his own heartbeat, and recognised that he was just as nervous as she was. When Lir landed in the courtyard it was mid-morning and the majority of the apprentices were in lessons. Tash had chosen this time specifically to arrive, wanting to avoid the open stares or mutters which would no doubt have been cast their way if the apprentices were in-between classes.

Cai helped her to dismount and she felt a tremor as she hit the cobbles, the sensation jarring through her legs to her back, and she winced. Together, they led Lir into one of the stable stalls and as Cai lifted the saddle down, Tash fed Lir one of the rosy apples from a nearby bucket.

'Are you ready?' he asked gently, as she watched the Willowing devour the fruit, delaying the inevitable moment when they would need to leave the stable by another minute. She lifted her gaze to meet Cai's, and reluctantly nodded, taking his outstretched hand and allowing him to lead her back outside. The overcast sky made the day feel oppressive and did little to alleviate Tash's mood as she took charge and headed towards The Robin's tower.

She was about to open the door to the tower when she paused mid-step, suddenly changed direction and led Cai towards the main building. Her worries needed to be eased first, and that meant that The Robin would have to wait.

'Where are we going?' Cai asked, slightly disoriented by her abrupt change of pace. Before she had been dragging her heels, whereas now she sped forwards, driven by a desperate urge to see Romulus. His acceptance of Cai was more important to her than The Robin's, not to mention that she had to ensure that he was alright. Laura's and Melisande's words lingered in her mind still.

'I need to introduce you to Romulus,' she replied, crossing the hallway and climbing the steps to her mentor's rooms. The door was shut and there was no sound from the other side, but Tash knocked anyway, the sound echoing in the silence. She tried to open the door but it was locked firm. Her forehead crinkled in concern and she began to knock again, more insistently this time.

'Go away,' a tired voice grumbled from inside, 'I've already said that I don't want visitors.'

'Romulus, it's me,' Tash called, 'let me in. Please.'

'Natachatet?' He sounded uncertain, yet nevertheless there was the sound of footsteps and a key turning in the lock. Slowly the door opened to reveal her mentor, the sight of him warming Tash's heart in an instant. She rushed forwards and hugged him, catching him off balance as he registered that she was really there. He had lost weight in the time that she had been gone, his cheeks were hollowed, eyes sunken and his beard had grown long and scraggly from lack of care. In spite of all this, Tash felt tears fall down her cheeks as she gripped him tighter, relieved that he was not dead, like Melisande had implied.

'You're home my child,' he murmured, his hands almost frail as they clasped her against his chest. 'You came back.'

'Of course I did,' Tash smiled, blinking away more tears. 'And I'm not alone.' She drew back slightly, motioning for Cai to step out of the shadows on the landing. 'This is Cai, Romulus. I found him after all.'

Cai moved into the light and held out a hand which Romulus shook, his own shaking. 'You're not a Nightwalker anymore,' he finally managed. 'How is it possible?'

'Tash freed me,' Cai replied, casting Tash a look that conveyed far more than the words could summarise. Romulus noted it, his sharp eyes taking in the glow that flushed his ward's cheeks as she met Cai's gaze.

'We're going to have a child, Romulus,' Tash said softly, her free hand rising to her abdomen, to the growing evidence of the new life that was there.

'A child?' he repeated, momentarily shocked. Then he smiled widely, a vibrant energy suffusing his features as he embraced both of them. 'That is joyous news indeed, I am so pleased for you both.'

'Thank you, Romulus,' Tash said, grateful that he had accepted the news so readily. Her mentor ushered them inside, leading them to his balcony where he urged them to sit. As she settled in the chair, she was reminded of that moment, all those months ago, the night before her initiation when she had been given the two missives from Kinet, detailing her mission. The balcony looked the same, from where they sat, they could see over the walls to the forest, the trees rustling in the cool morning breeze.

'I've been wanting to apologise to you, Natachatet,' Romulus said as he settled beside her, 'to both of you.' He gave Cai a slightly ashamed dip of the head, holding himself taut as a spring, as though he had been practising this speech for a while and was wanting to get it right. 'I was so fixated on how I wanted your life to be, who I wanted you to be with, that I was unwilling to accept that you might want different things. I'm sorry for pushing Harrison to pursue you, even after you told me to leave it alone.' He looked from Tash to Cai, 'I'm sorry for encouraging her to leave you behind. I did

368

not believe that a Nightwalker would be a suitable companion for my ward. I couldn't bear the thought of her being ostracised or cast out of our Order because of a Dæmon.'

Cai acknowledged Romulus' apology with a nod, his expression inscrutable. Tash watched her mentor closely, taking in the deepened lines on his face, the clear signs of sleepless nights and troubled thoughts over the past weeks. She remembered how angry with him she had been, how hurt at their parting, whereas now, she only felt relief that he was alright and sorry for what had been said and done.

'I am not guiltless, either, Romulus,' she admitted softly, taking his wrinkled hand in hers. His skin felt like roughened paper, like it would break if one held it too tightly. 'I was angry when I left and I did not say goodbye. I'm sorry that my leaving caused you such worry.'

'You needed me to support your choices, my child,' Romulus said, 'I regret that I did not do so.'

Tash squeezed his hand, conveying silently how his words eased the emptiness that their parting had caused. Now he accepted Cai, although a small part of her wondered if he would have done so if Cai had remained a Nightwalker. She pushed the thought away, not wanting to linger on what ifs, especially ones that might have unpleasant answers. Instead she focussed on the temporary moment of relief, grateful that Romulus' response to them had been enough for her to understand that he blessed their relationship.

'Is Harrison…?' she began, half afraid of the response he would give, half concerned about how Harrison would react to Cai's presence.

'Harrison has left on another mission,' her mentor said. 'He wanted you to know that he wished you the best. I don't think he will come back for a while.'

Tash privately thought that that was a good thing. There was still a lot of resentment and anger between them, although now Cai was by her side and safe, she didn't want to run the risk of them meeting again anytime soon. She was sure that Cai would struggle to maintain his composure, and she didn't think she would put up much of a fight to stop him. Romulus coughed, his eyes had gone watery and he rubbed them gruffly with his free hand. When he had regained control over his emotions, he eyed Cai and Tash beadily, his expression becoming curious.

'Tell me about Melisande's Court, Natachatet,' he said, 'how exactly did Cai return to his human form? How did you manage to get away?'

'Yes, that is a story I would like to hear as well,' a dry voice spoke from behind them. 'I had hoped that Natachatet would remember to give me her report in person, but it seems that I need to be the one to seek her out to receive it.'

It was hard to tell from The Robin's tone whether he was angry or not, but Cai got to his feet and clasped his arm.

'It is good to see you, Corvis,' he said, grinning. 'It's been too long.'

'And you, Cai,' The Robin replied. 'You're looking well. No more bloodthirst, I take it?'

Cai chuckled. 'Thankfully not. Although I have a partiality for rare steak.'

Tash was barely taking in their words, she was too surprised by the change in The Robin. No shadows lingered over his face, shrouding his features from view as had been the case for so many years. For the first time Tash could see the leader of the Order and she was struck by how similar he looked to his daughter. The Robin's hair was short and the colour of burnished copper, although sections of it were now grey, his eyes were hazel and they flickered with a humorous glint.

'Melisande's death lifted your own curse?' she whispered, and at the sound of her voice The Robin and Cai paused, glancing back at her.

'I knew that you had succeeded when I came back to myself,' The Robin said calmly, 'I hadn't thought it would be possible.'

'Does this mean that you will reinstate Tash in the Order?' Cai pressed, folding his arms resolutely, 'She's done more for the Robins than they probably know. With Melisande gone, the fae will need to find a new leader, one who is hopefully more benevolent.'

Tash thought of Leonora, and hoped that what Cai said was true, and that Leonora would be the one to lead the fae back into the way of the light.

'Natachatet will always have a place in the Temple and in the Order,' The Robin said gravely. 'However, I still need to hear her report in full and I am not known for having much patience.'

Cai grinned and then sank back down into his chair, crossed his hands behind his head and leaned back, watching Tash with lazy ease. The Robin flipped his dezmian and another chair appeared, and he sat on Romulus' other side.

'It is good to see you again after so long, old friend,' Romulus murmured. 'I have missed you.'

'You had me worried that you had taken ill,' The Robin replied. 'Next time you have a personal crisis, let me know so that I'm not sending people to check on you and then dealing with their snivelling when you order them away.' He gave Romulus a rather pointed look and the older man smiled faintly.

'I'll do my best,' Romulus said, before he squeezed Tash's hand and indicated for her to speak. His gesture made relief spread through her, all the fears she had had vanishing in an instant, as Laura had assured her they would. The Robin and Romulus were watching her expectantly as she straightened her shoulders, faced them and began her report.

Epilogue

I didn't think that I would be ready to be a father. Yet from the first moment I held my daughter in my arms, something changed. She is perfect. We named her after my mother, Ryla. After Tash gave me Derrick's journal, I could finally understand the answers to many questions that had haunted me.

I see my mother at times in my mind, her long, dark hair and pale face. Her eyes large and wide, gazing off into the distance at a fey land beyond the mist. While some questions were answered, there are still some that I will never know. When I hold Ryla in my arms though, at times I can almost sense my mother's presence, the boundless love and pride that she would have felt for us, almost overwhelming me to tears.

-An extract from a new journal, placed in Cai's saddlebags

Ryla was finally asleep. They had navigated through the Shadow Realm with caution, trusting in Lir to lead them safely home. For Tash, the darkness remained impenetrable, however for her husband and daughter, their eyes could penetrate the shadows, glowing with a faint light. The Robin had asked them to traverse the Shadow Realm after receiving a summons from Leonora. The former alchemist had relayed to him a message that she had a gift for them, and urged Tash and Cai to come without further delay. Despite this, Tash hadn't been keen to go, not wanting to brave the dangers of

the Shadow Realm with her newborn daughter. Nevertheless, she had obeyed, allowing Cai to assuage her fears and
spending the flight cradling her child close. Ryla had cried
for some of the trip, although Lir had sped through the darkness, evading the monsters that heard the disturbance and
came to investigate. With Cai's bow and ability to see their
pursuers, those creatures were soon lying dead behind them
and Tash was able to breathe a sigh of relief.

Leonora had joined them in the cave that had once been
Cai's, a place that Tash had been sure she would never see
again. It brought back too many painful memories, and the
bones of Glaive the Dragutash remained, ghostly white in
conjured firelight. Leonora had not spoken much, beyond
giving them a blessing of good fortune and a smile. In her
hands she had held out a small cage with a creature inside.

'This is Griphon,' she had said, her mismatched eyes
watching both Tash and Cai intently. 'He will be a guardian
for your little one.'

'Thank you,' Cai had replied, bowing and accepting the
gift courteously. Tash had gripped Ryla tighter as she murmured her own thanks, ducking in an awkward curtsey.

'The Shadow Realm is a dangerous place for your daughter, as you know,' Leonora had said as she turned to leave.
'Griphon will help to protect her from the darkness.'

Her words sent a shiver of foreboding through Tash, but
she refrained from asking any questions, knowing that Leonora would probably not answer them. And then, as quickly
as she had appeared, the faerie queen had departed again for
her Court, leaving Cai and Tash gazing at each other, and
then down at the creature in the cage.

Now, they were not far from the Temple, in a small cot-
tage that Romulus had gifted them when they married. Tash

eyed the ring of yew around her finger, although this one had been carved by the man who was preparing a pot of chai tea, his dark hair glinting in the firelight. Their daughter lay in her crib, Griphon curled up beside her. Her hands were clasped in his tufty fur, ignoring his small wings and long whiskers, holding him close to her. Griphon's ears flicked back and forth, and his eyes opened, two faint gold orbs blinking up at Tash slowly before he settled back into sleep beside Ryla, purring contentedly. His fur was honey-coloured and speckled with brown, and his wings were a soft tawny gold. Tash was sure that it wouldn't be long until he was too large to fit in Ryla's crib, but until that time, the two of them were perfectly contented being close to each other. It had only taken one look for the two to bond and she wondered how it would develop over time.

'Tash,' Cai said gently, 'come and rest. It's been a long day.'

He was holding out a steaming cup of chai, a half-smile playing across his lips, and as she looked at him her heart flipped and her breath caught in her throat. She stepped closer and took the cup, sinking down beside the fire in the circle of his arm and drank.

Cai took a sip of his own tea and finally broke the silence by saying, 'I think I'd like to go back to Nordhaven. Make sure that everyone there is alright and thank Pyrrus for giving you that journal. It's time for them to realise that the Monster of the Heath won't be stalking them any longer.'

'If you're sure,' Tash said softly. 'You know that they're going to be distrustful at first. Although I think it would be a good idea to go back. Even if it's only for a short while.'

'I would like that,' he replied. 'Time may not heal all wounds, but it might allow the chance for forgiveness.'

Tash nodded, leaning against him, and allowed her eyes to close momentarily. Cai watched her, noting the firelight cast shadows across her face. Slowly, he put down his empty cup and stroked her cheek, marvelling at the silkiness of her skin. She made a sound at the back of her throat and opened her eyes, looking up at him invitingly. He chuckled and bridged the distance between them, capturing her mouth with his. When they broke apart, it was only to check that Ryla still slept peacefully, undisturbed with Griphon in her crib. Then Tash and Cai allowed themselves to love each other, slowly and languorously late into the night. And when the lights had been extinguished and Tash lay in her husband's arms, listening to his steady breathing as he slept, she felt complete.

The End

Acknowledgements

'Nightwalker' was a story that I had long wanted to get onto paper, originally because I felt that Tash's prophecy needed to be answered and that she deserved her own book. Writing it has been a whirlwind of research and enjoyment, but it wouldn't have been possible without the help from several key people.

Firstly, thank you to Ian, Brittany and Anja as well as the Book Reality Experience team. I am so grateful for your support, advice and experience in this journey. Also I'm glad you were keen to support another project– this time a slightly darker one!

Secondly, to my *liebeshem* Jordan. Thank you for your support and talking through ideas, including listening to my half hour convoluted explanation of the plot when I was struggling to write a certain scene. I am lucky to have you demanding to read the manuscript the minute it is done, even if you want to claim half the writing credit. Also to my boys, Romeo and Gnocchi, who somehow found their way into this book as they were consistently keeping me company during the writing process. Although I am glad that Romeo didn't succeed in deleting the entire manuscript– otherwise 'Nightwalker' might have had a very different ending!

To my family and friends– thank you for getting excited by the premise of the book and all the support you provide. Let's not forget the times I would stay home to write instead of attending different family events– unfortunately that will continue to happen. All the same, I appreciate your support and advice, especially those who were particularly keen for Tash's story to be written.

Finally, to my readers, thank you for voyaging back into the world of Venetica with me and discovering Kinet and the Shadow Realm in 'Nightwalker'. I hope that you enjoy this continuation of the series and are ready to return to Venetica in the future. There are still more tales to tell, questions to be answered and magical worlds to be explored.

About the Author

A booklover from an early age, Rose began writing stories from the age of seven and this passion continued into a life-long dream of becoming a writer.

When she is not reading a new book, jotting down ideas in a notebook or pottering around in her veggie garden under her cats' supervision, she can be found either on the stage in her other passion – amateur theatre – or teaching English and French to high school students.